L.A
WOMI

ALSO BY ELLA BERMAN

THE COMEBACK

BEFORE WE WERE INNOCENT

L.A. WOMEN

ELLA BERMAN

BERKLEY | NEW YORK

BERKLEY
An imprint of Penguin Random House LLC
1745 Broadway, New York, NY 10019
penguinrandomhouse.com

Book design by George Towne
Cover design by Jordan Jacob
Cover images, top to bottom: *British Railways poster advertising Weymouth*, c. 1960.
Fish, Laurence © Christie's Images / Bridgeman Images; *Pattern Design SB 510*. Bownas,
Sheila Catherine © Leeds Museums and Galleries, UK / Bridgeman Images; *British Railways
poster advertising Exmouth*, 1958. Fish, Laurence © Christie's Images / Bridgeman Images;
(watercolor banana leaves) Nongnuch L. / Getty Images

Export edition ISBN: 9780593956755

Library of Congress Cataloging-in-Publication Data

Names: Berman, Ella, author.
Title: L.A. women / Ella Berman.
Description: New York: Berkley, 2025.
Identifiers: LCCN 2024043341 (print) | LCCN 2024043342 (ebook) |
ISBN 9780593639153 (hardcover) | ISBN 9780593639160 (ebook)
Subjects: LCGFT: Novels.
Classification: LCC PR6102.E753 L3 2025 (print) |
LCC PR6102.E753 (ebook) | DDC 823/.92—dc23/eng/20240920
LC record available at https://lccn.loc.gov/2024043341
LC ebook record available at https://lccn.loc.gov/2024043342

Printed in the United States of America
1st Printing

The authorized representative in the EU for product safety and compliance is Penguin
Random House Ireland, Morrison Chambers, 32 Nassau Street, Dublin D02 YH68, Ireland,
https://eu-contact.penguin.ie.

To my parents—for giving us the world and more.

L.A.
WOMEN

ONE

NOW

SUMMER 1975

Put yourself in the (finest caviar leather) shoes of Lane Warren. Here, inside the glittering compound in the foothills
of Laurel Canyon, she is the person everyone wants to
meet—her house is filled with dear friends and shiny young
things, and they'd all gut her in an instant if it would make them
famous. Because isn't that why they all gather here every Sunday?
To prove that they are also people to know? That they too have
something to offer the world?

Sometimes, Lane tries to remember when the hunger started
in her, but, as always, memories of her early life are hazy, untrust-
worthy.

Over there, by the towering yucca plant, sits the jaded almost
rock star—a local celebrity who never made it past the L.A. city
limits. Watch him pretend his hands aren't twitching for the last
two quaaludes in his pocket as he recounts the time he almost
filled in for David Crosby when the Byrds played the Whisky. And
there—just feet away, a French poet regales a crowd with the

story of the night he asked Simone de Beauvoir to marry him, a story Lane has heard thirty times in the past decade, a story that has changed ever so slightly with each retelling to the point it is no longer recognizable. And, up the grand staircase, Lane's husband, Scotty, putting the twins to bed, taking his time so that he can later impress some young ingenue (someone new to L.A. who doesn't know anything yet) with his humble insistence on how equality starts at home. And in the middle of it all—Charlie, holding court as always, seamlessly directing any latecomers to the trays of champagne, the lines of coke, the fascinating people they'll later go home with.

For the past ten years, Laurel Canyon (and the winding roads off it) has been the center of everything. A hidden neighborhood in the Hollywood Hills filled with restless young souls who just want to create and fuck—some of whom have gone on to become unfathomably famous, others who will remain the same age forever—and through it all, Charlie has been working his magic behind the scenes. As Lane watches him tonight, he raises an eyebrow and she nods, smiling back at him. It's only because of Charlie that Lane doesn't have to *be* Charlie.

Lane sinks against the bookcase, already thinking about bed, when she catches sight of an acquaintance of Scotty's, Dimitri (a ballet dancer with a lithe body and a mind like the stock exchange), pressing a young blond woman into the corner of the deck. The night is dark, the moon thin as Lane edges outside, her loose cream silk suit lifting in the June breeze. She slips into the shadows, unnoticed by either Dim or the young woman.

"It's not what I expected," the girl, shivering in a gold Lurex jumpsuit, says as she dips her head to do a thick line of coke off the wooden handrail. The sycamore trees rustle above, and, when she looks back up, she seems momentarily bewildered.

"What, did you think it would still be orgies and LSD?" Dim says, his voice unpleasant as ever. "Nothing stays the same. Not even here."

"I don't know," she says, either missing or ignoring the scorn in his voice, the way it invites her to embarrass herself further. "It all feels . . . maybe a little sad. Like when you stay too long at a carnival, and you see everyone packing up. It's a little like that."

Lane feels a dull sting of recognition. Dim takes a drag of his cigarette, about to say something else, when she clears her throat to avoid any further humiliation.

"Lane," he says, his voice suddenly warm and expansive, stretching her name until it gains an extra syllable. "My dear Lane. Please do illuminate yourself—I'd like for you to meet my terribly ill-mannered, unforgivably young friend."

Lane swallows her distaste and steps toward them, accepting the lighter Dim holds up for the cigarette in her mouth. The girl studies Lane and there is something about her, some blank openness, that makes Lane want to tell her to run far from here.

"Nancy Dennis, all the way from Terlingua, Texas, meet the fabulous Lane Warren," he says with a flourish, and Nancy smiles sheepishly.

"Fuck off, Dimitri," Lane says, waving her hand at Dim, shooing him inside. After a pause, he obliges, stepping away with a pointed look in the girl's direction that riles Lane up all over again.

"Nancy," Lane says, and Nancy nods, her fingertips wrapped around the wooden railing.

"Nancy," she says again, tapping her cigarette so that the fine ash falls to the ground. "Nancy Dennis."

Nancy widens her heavily lined eyes.

"Why exactly are you here?" Lane asks, not unkindly.

Nancy frowns, her mouth moving silently for a few moments while she works out whether the older woman is laying a trap for her. *I'm asking if you're an explorer or an observer*, Lane thinks as she takes another drag of her cigarette. *I'm asking because one lasts a lot longer here than the other.*

"I'm here because everyone I admire has been to one of your parties," Nancy says finally. "And I've been hearing about them for as long as I can remember. I guess I didn't want to . . . miss my chance."

Lane pauses, unsure now of what she can say to this person, who can't be a day over seventeen—twenty-one years Lane's junior. Perhaps Lane should explain that the reason Nancy is disappointed by this evening, perhaps by Los Angeles in general, is that everyone's already done anything worth doing here, and back then they did it out of a frenzied wonder, so consuming it felt like their soul was on fire, or because they were so fucking high they didn't know what they were doing, but *never* just because someone had done it before them.

Lane glances inside the house, the golden glow of the church candles lining the bookshelves, the cigarette smoke spiraling away from a crowd that gets both ever younger and ever more knowing as the years pass, at her valiant husband, who is slowly coming down the stairs now, scanning the room for god knows what, and she thinks that, actually, this is the only reason any of them are here. They are here because their world was once so vivid, so *beautiful*, that they are all somehow willing to settle for a ghost version of it. And that's the problem with living in a place that shines so brightly—it has to fade sometime.

Nancy is still rigid, unblinking, bracing herself for what Lane is going to say next. Instead, Lane reaches out and touches her lightly on the bare arm. Nancy's skin is cool and covered in a layer of fine goose bumps.

"Don't think you owe Dimitri anything," Lane says. "Come find me if he suggests otherwise."

SCOTTY PUTS HIS hand on Lane's waist and brushes his lips against her cheek. Lane can feel every pair of eyes in the room on them, the golden couple nobody understands, and she smiles at him in a secret way they both know is only for show.

"Lane! Scotty!" someone calls from the kitchen. Scotty takes Lane's hand and guides her into the room where a naked Jim Morrison once swung from the exposed ceiling beams like a sloth, but that is now filled with photos of their children and dead friends.

The guests in the kitchen are young and dressed wrong, far too much glitter, as if they're on their way to a club in Manhattan instead of in a Craftsman at the foot of Laurel Canyon. Their conversation grinds to a halt as Lane and Scotty approach, and Lane understands that something has happened, and they will expect her to fix it. Because somewhere along the way, without even noticing, she and Scotty have become the adults in the room, and that means they will throw parties with the expensive tequila, yes, but also that they have a duty of care to destroy anything that threatens the illusion of this party, this house, this perfect, cloudless life.

For a moment, Lane imagines walking past them all and straight out into the cool night until she reaches a place where nobody cares what she has to say. She knows she wouldn't have to go far, just south of Wilshire would do, but instead she allows herself to be pulled into the fold once more, bracing herself for the news of a friend OD'ing in her bathroom, the paramedics already racing up Hollywood Boulevard to get here, or perhaps a drunk straggler who saw fit to set fire to the piles of research papers in her office. It wouldn't be the first time for anything.

"It's Gala," someone says then. A man with black eyes and a square jaw—Oliver something. A fashion designer dressed head to toe in brown leather. Lane feels a pit form in her stomach at his words and the way his gaze lingers on her for too long. Scotty reaches for her hand, but it isn't his reassurance she needs, and then—there he is, across the room, watching her closely. Charlie. Lane meets his eye, searching for something, and he nods. She feels a flicker of calm at his solidness.

"What happened?" Scotty asks, still squeezing Lane's hand.

"Well, you know she hasn't exactly been *around* recently," Oliver says, his words rolling luxuriously off his tongue as he savors his moment in the spotlight. "And we all thought she was just having one of her 'dips,' but apparently *nobody's* heard from her in months. Not even her parents. So someone must have raised the alarm or something, and her landlord went into her apartment to check on her and those cats. Did you know that she has cats now? Maybe five of them. Purebred, of course. Vile creatures, but she babies them like you wouldn't believe. Anyway, her landlord went in there, and she wasn't there. Her cats had nearly eaten through the front door."

The relief comes now as Lane parses the data, noting the lack of meat on Oliver's story. *All bubbles, no body,* as Charlie would say, usually in reference to cheap Californian "champagne."

"It's Gala," Lane says calmly. "She's probably gone to Mexico or something."

"Or rehab," Scotty says.

"Or maybe she finally joined the Synanon Foundation," a

woman with silver hair calls from across the kitchen. "Can't you just picture Gala holed up by the beach, humiliating other addicts for sport?"

The others laugh a little, but Lane can tell they're still suspended—waiting for her lead on how they're all meant to feel. Whether they can still laugh about her.

"The big deal is how much she loved those damned cats," Oliver says, irritated. "There wasn't so much as a bowl of *food* left out. She just . . . left them to die."

There is a silence as this information is absorbed.

"You know, we actually have the same drug dealer—Rod, on Formosa?" Scotty's friend Aimee, a British socialite partial to downers, says slowly. "And he said he hasn't heard from her in over six months. Gala's pickups used to be as regular as the moon cycle."

"Has anyone tried the Chateau? Maybe she was so out of it she forgot she had the cats."

"Gala hasn't been able to afford the Chateau in years."

"Gala's never been able to afford the Chateau. And that's saying something."

"Didn't she always say she was going to die before she turned thirty-six?"

"Is that her 'stage thirty-six' or the real one?"

The voices, the gibes, start to echo in Lane's ears, and she drops Scotty's hand, stumbling backward, just as Charlie glides toward them. He puts his arm around Lane's waist, steadying her as he assesses the scene.

"Whatever you're talking about, stop it," he says in the old-fashioned way he has that makes people feel instantly chastised. "I'm all for idle gossip, but you're either boring or depressing Lane, and *that* is a capital offense in my eyes."

Lane rests her head on his shoulder and breathes in his familiar scent of Moroccan spiced cedarwood. He kisses the top of her head.

"Don't worry, darling," he says softly. "Gala is the queen of the underworld. She always emerges from the darkness."

It's not the first time Charlie has likened Gala Margolis to Persephone, and it's always struck Lane as a careless comparison. Because if Gala is Persephone, beautiful goddess turned queen of the underworld, then Lane wonders who it was exactly that ruined her.

TWO

NOW

SUMMER 1975

Lane wakes up late not with a hangover exactly, but with an irritating tightness in her chest that reminds her something is wrong. Scotty snores beside her as she climbs out of bed gingerly so as not to wake him, a habit left over from when they used to fuck every morning, his tanned arm reaching out and pulling her back under the covers without his even needing to open an eye. Now she creeps out of bed like a jaguar so as not to remind him of what they've lost. She slips on a kimono and heads downstairs.

On any other morning, Lane would make herself a cup of coffee before setting herself up for the day in her writing room with the view of the hills, but today it doesn't feel entirely appropriate. Something is wrong, and, as usual, that something is Gala.

LANE HAD NEVER exactly intended to write a book about Gala, but what had begun as a series of observations, sketches really, had somehow joined up to create something altogether more significant, like a flower unfurling so slowly it was imperceptible to the human eye. It wasn't a biography, but it wasn't exactly a novel either—it landed somewhere in the formless space between the two, and it meant Lane could amplify certain aspects of Gala and contract other parts, like she was composing not a book so much as a symphony about her old friend.

At the start, she figured Gala wouldn't mind, not really. She'd never exactly shied away from attention before, and she should be grateful that anyone wanted to immortalize her, let alone a writer as thoughtful and incisive as Lane. And then the work had taken on a life of its own, and who was Lane to fight against the gods of creativity? Lane is one of the most respected chroniclers of her generation, and it isn't as if the book is some trashy exposé—she herself features heavily as the authorial voice, so she isn't hiding from anything. Rather, she finds it comforting to think that, while their friendship may not have lasted, the novel would exist long after either of them were no longer here.

Of course Gala's disappearance can't have anything to do with the book. There are a thousand reasons why Gala might have left L.A., none of which involve Lane. She hasn't seen her old friend in half a year, anyway, Lane reminds herself as she reaches the step with the gnarly creak (the one Scotty promised to fix when they moved in six years ago), but the tight feeling in her chest only intensifies.

Something is wrong, and, as usual, that something is Gala.

THE TWINS ARE already at the kitchen table with their nanny, Rose, an English aristocrat who left her family to chase her dreams of being an actress in L.A., but who somehow ended up in Lane's guesthouse instead. Lane watches for a moment through the open doorway as the girls pick at something leafy and green, some macrobiotic lunch that another nanny will have told Rose about at the gates of their private school, and she knows they'll be hungry again within hours. Instead of slowing down, they seem to become more *everything* when they're hungry—more argumentative, more hyper. More demanding.

Audrey is telling Rose about an animal, a type of bear perhaps, her friend at school claims to have seen, while Dahlia is transfixed by the colorful book she holds open behind her bowl. They both stop what they're doing when Lane walks into the room, their eyes suddenly tracking her closely. She bends down and kisses each of them on the head, trying not to breathe in their individual scents because it's easier to think of them as a unit—a dual-minded creature who will never know what it's like to feel so lonely you can barely remember your own name.

"What are you reading?" she asks, and Dahlia instantly snaps the book shut like she's been reprimanded, even though Lane hadn't meant to frighten her.

"I said she could read over lunch as it's the first day of summer," Rose says, her pale cheeks flushing, and once again, Lane finds herself at a loss for what to say. Audrey is still watching, so Lane tries to smile, even though she's now thinking of her own mother, of what her hardness could have been hiding.

"Of course she can," Lane says brusquely to Rose. "I didn't mean . . . She can read whenever she wants."

There is a silence, and the twins look at her expectantly. Are they waiting for her to say something else? She racks her brain for something benign, something motherly, anything that can't be misconstrued, until she realizes that they're probably just waiting for her to leave. She feels a familiar clawing in the back of her throat as she forces a smile.

"I have some errands to run," she says. "I'll be back before bedtime."

Three heads nod in polite unison as she walks out of the room. Lane doesn't know who of them is more relieved.

LANE WALKS DOWN the canyon, past the houses of friends present and past, some grand and glittering in the sun, others shaded by overgrown foliage—glorified shacks at the foot of the Hollywood Hills, inhabited by artists and weirdos who would be outcasts anywhere else. Today, nobody calls out her name as she passes, and she's grateful for it.

When she reaches Hollywood Boulevard she turns left, and she's almost on autopilot now, even though she hasn't done this particular journey for a while. A man with hair down to his waist stands barefoot at the intersection, holding a sign that reads FREEDOM IS A LIE. As Lane walks on, she realizes she recognizes him from a couple of movies from the 1950s.

Gala lives in an apartment block on Laurel Avenue, right between Hollywood and Sunset Boulevards, a fourteen-minute walk from where Ciro's Le Disc once existed, and less than an eight-minute walk from the Liquor Locker beneath Chateau Marmont. Lane knows all this because her husband, Scotty, once lived in this block too.

Hacienda Heights is split into eight units surrounding a courtyard. The exterior, a peachy cream stucco with brown shutters, looks worn down, as if even the building knows its best days are mostly in the past. The gardens, presumably rich and verdant when they were conceived in the 1920s, are now overgrown, with curious strands of lichen hanging from the trees and blankets of pipe vine creeping up the sides of cracked plant pots, a general aura of neglect dampening any remnants of glamour.

Lane crosses the courtyard to Gala's unit—number 4. From the outside, there is nothing to suggest anything is wrong—no mail overflowing on the doorstep, no visible sinkhole Gala might have slipped into—and Lane rings the doorbell before peering through the window. The place is shadowy and still, and, from here, Lane can almost convince herself that nothing's changed.

"It's a mess," a voice from behind her says, and Lane swivels around like she's been caught. A man with wiry amber sideburns is sitting on a camping chair in the courtyard, holding a copy of Carl Jung's *Dreams*. He's wearing jeans and an open knit waistcoat in the crackling heat, and is clearly pleased at having spooked her. Lane dislikes him instantly.

"Are you the new landlord?" she asks.

"My grandfather built this place. We've taken the management 'in-house,' as they say."

"Right," she says, trying to soften her tone. She figures that a man like this, overstyled and entitled, will be only too happy to talk if she lets him.

"It's beautiful," she says. "I know Gala's never wanted to leave."

He shrugs. "It's a hassle."

Lane smiles as if she too knows what it is to be handed anything in life. She glances back at the window, the stillness on the other side.

"Did she say where she was going?"

The man shakes his head. "I barely saw her by the end."

Lane feels like she's been winded. The end of what?

"I'm out here most days," he continues. "So I figure whatever happened to her must have happened in the night. It's almost always someone you know in these situations. And Gala obviously knew a few people."

Lane swallows, trying to stem the panic climbing through her veins like vines.

"Have the police been over?" she asks, and he nods.

"They came around three weeks ago. I don't think they found anything. I don't know if they were even really looking."

"Could I take a look around?"

He assesses her. "You're asking me to let you into someone's home without their permission?"

"How do you know I don't have her permission?"

He narrows his eyes. "Because you're asking *me* where she is."

Lane glances longingly at the brass door handle, both wishing she could just reach out and twist it to find it unlocked, and terrified of what she might find inside.

"Someone came by to pick up the cats last week," he says then. "It was starting to reek in there."

Lane frowns at him. "Who came for the cats?"

"A good-looking guy, I don't know. He'd been feeding them for months anyway."

"And yet you let him, a stranger, into her home without her permission."

"I had a cat problem." He shrugged. "This guy offered to fix it."

Lane wonders whether, if she'd come last week, she'd be walking out of here with five cats or if it's her lack of a penis that hinders her. She tucks her hair behind her ears and recalibrates, attempting a new approach.

"I can imagine Gala can be an . . . entertaining tenant," she says, forcing a conspiratorial smile, like Gala is their shared problem.

"Maybe at the beginning," he says. "You know, I never saw her work so much as a day the entire time she was here. No job, no husband, just a hell of a lot of partying. When I took this place over, I figured she was one of those Beverly Hills kids pretending to slum it before she married someone just like her daddy. If I had to guess? A money man. A banker or something. But lately I started thinking I got that wrong."

"In what way?"

"She started to look . . ." he starts. Then just: "There were less . . . friends visiting. Fewer men around. And the ones that were around weren't the type to stay more than a couple hours. I know women like that, where their only power is their looks, and when that fades? There's not much left to draw people. No job, no husband, no nothing. Their luck dries up."

Lane swallows a surprising swell of rage that makes it difficult for her to speak for a moment.

"That's not exactly how it was with Gala," she says tightly.

"Well, I've been here three years, and I don't think I've ever seen you before," the landlord says smugly.

Lane turns back toward Gala's front door so that he doesn't get to see the impact of his words on her face.

"Can I take a look around or not?"

He pauses, looks her up and down one final time.

"I'm sorry, but I can't let you in there without permission from my tenant, or her next of kin," he says, suddenly Mr. Professional, his voice straining with the weight of it.

"Her next of kin?"

"Her parents," he says. "If they're still around."

Lane peers inside one last time, pressing her forehead against the cloudy glass. Inside, she can make out a bowl of something on the coffee table, and sheets of paper strewn all over the sofa. On Gala's rattan armchair she can identify a pile of books, including a copy of Lane's second novel, *The Unraveling*. The sight of it makes her feel sick, like her fingerprints have been found at a crime scene. She turns back around, and the landlord has opened his book and is lazily flicking through the first few pages. She wonders how long he's been pretending to read it.

"Well," she says finally. "Thanks for your discretion."

Lane makes a move to leave, but finds herself turning back at the last moment.

"Gala was a *writer*, by the way," she says. "That was her job."

THREE

THEN

SEPTEMBER 1965

Gala surveyed the room before launching her empty glass at the sandy-haired man in the corner. He ducked, and it hit the cabinet behind him, shattering loudly. Everyone turned to look at him, and, a few seconds too late, Gala realized her mistake. Someone had asked her to tell the story of the first time she saw the actor Ray Donaldson's cock, which (as legend goes) broke records in at least five states, and, as she started telling them the same tale of how she approached it (much like one would a feral animal), the sandy-haired man had heckled her.

She didn't even know what he'd said, but the outburst had stolen the focus from her. She wouldn't have minded if he'd been a worthy opponent, but this loser was straight off the Greyhound from *Kentucky* for fuck's sake, trying to make it in a band because he'd seen how well some of his peers were doing, how much of a *scene* Laurel Canyon was becoming. So he may or may not have deserved the glass thrown at his head, but he definitely didn't deserve the ensuing attention, attention that she'd hustled and awed and put in the *hours* for, but she'd already fucked up and now people (*friends* of hers!) were on their hands and knees, picking the glass out of his clothes, and he was pretending not to love it as she stepped down off the table and slunk over to the kitchen to pour herself a drink.

LANE WARREN WATCHED her go, her face inscrutable. She had never met anyone like this woman, at least six feet tall with swaths of glossy black hair and charmingly crooked teeth, had never even seen anyone like her on TV. Lane was new to L.A. then but, over the next ten years, she would still never meet anyone quite like this statuesque twenty-five-year-old: the twentieth-century Hollywood incarnation of Dante Gabriel Rossetti's Mnemosyne standing in a pink and orange dress with an unlit cigarette hanging out of her mouth and visibly regretting throwing a glass at a stranger's head, but only because she'd inadvertently given him the most precious thing of all—a story he could tell for years to come.

Lane was at the party because a New York friend of hers had a cousin whose old bandmate, a drummer who went by the name of Beck, lived locally, and he'd invited Lane so that she could get to know a few cool people in her new neighborhood. He'd turned out to be kind of a letch, with putrid breath and lingering hands, and she'd been actively avoiding him since they arrived, but she was still grateful for the introduction.

As a journalist, Lane had infiltrated the Hells Angels in San Bernardino, interviewed the founder of the Minutemen militia in Missouri, and had kept up with Andy Warhol and his consort for three consecutive *days*, but somehow none of that had prepared her for the chaos at the top of Wonderland Avenue that night—

the bodies clamped together, the twin offerings of industry intro-ductions and hallucinogens, the near-hysterical pursuit of pleasure. Since walking through the door an hour ago, Lane had already seen more bare flesh than she'd seen in nearly four years in New York, and definitely more than in her previous twenty-five years growing up in Phoenix, Arizona. At one point, she'd wan-dered into what she thought was a bathroom to find two beautiful young men draped naked around a woman she would later recog-nize as the star of a wholesome '50s sitcom, before she'd hurried back out. She knew that kitchens were generally the safest place to blend into a party, but, while quiet, Lane never wanted to be too far from the action. It's what made her the best at what she did.

LATER, GALA SAT in the hot tub in her underwear (unmatching, of course; she wasn't a suburban housewife), surrounded by bod-ies in various states of undress. *Human soup*, she thought, or maybe she said it out loud. It was hard to tell as the mushrooms she'd taken were wearing off, and she was finally starting to feel the effects of the quaaludes someone had pressed into her palm an hour earlier—the slow sinking, the horniness, the way she could feel words gurgle and form at the back of her throat, and the expanse of time that seemed to unfurl before she needed to decide whether to speak them or let them melt away.

Next to her was the bratty son of a legendary film producer, his perfect teeth shining in the light of the hot tub as he extolled the virtues of Godard. On the other side was a cute music jour-nalist she'd slept with a couple of times a few years back but who was now hitting on a young girl from just over the hill. Gala never begrudged any of these young women, teenagers practically, who were flooding to the canyon, mostly because she knew they didn't pose any real threat to her. Men had been drawn to Gala for as long as she could remember, and she figured it was for her wildness, her candor, her quick wit, and these girls wouldn't know a punch line if it hit them over the head. Gala tilted her head up and scanned the sky quickly. She'd seen so many stars over the years, she'd never bothered to learn their names.

Gala grew up in the heart of Hollywood in the 1950s. She had parents who still adored each other and (almost as an afterthought) her, and the type of unorthodox home life that meant she had little to rebel against. Her father, Stan, had left Germany for New York before the Nazis took hold, and, determined not to waste his freedom, had worked for a few months as a carpenter before joining a traveling circus as a magician. He specialized in something called Metamorphosis—an illusion made famous by Houdini that involved Stan being bagged, bound, and chained in a wooden trunk before reappearing on top of it in the place of his female assistant. He traveled the country for five years before he met Gala's mother, Penny, a (soon-to-be-lapsed) Catholic waitress, in a bowling alley in Highland Park.

When Penny became pregnant, they moved to a house just off Franklin Avenue, opposite the private estate that would later, fortuitously, become the Magic Castle. By then they had already set up a business in their garage making specialty props for illusionists, prestidigitators, and showmen, and some other traveling outcasts they didn't question too closely. Gala grew up sawing her schoolmates in half in magic wooden boxes and *transposing* herself to the other end of her parents' workroom until, not too much later, she graduated to transposing herself from her classes at Hollywood High into the bars on the Sunset Strip. She went to school when she could be bothered, and she prided herself on never, not even once, having entertained the idea of becoming an actress. Not one headshot photographer or casting director had ever had the opportunity to give her the once-over and decide she was too tall, too fleshy, too much. Instead, Gala watched as her friends either slept with the type of unsavory industry type who swore they could make or break your career only to forget they'd ever met you, or fell pregnant with their high school boyfriends, understanding that she wanted something else entirely. And what Gala wanted was sublime, unforgettable, *bone-crushing* fun.

After a moment, Gala became aware of a presence above her in the hot tub. She opened one eye to find Beck Andersson, current creep of Wonderland Avenue she'd mistakenly slept with once, four years ago, standing over her with a woman she didn't recognize. Gala looked down at her hands, which had turned soft and mealy in the water, and she wondered how long she'd been in the hot tub. It couldn't have been as long as it felt because the birds weren't singing yet.

"Gala," Beck said, his voice already a discordant strike on her mellow. "This is Lane. She's just moved here from New York. Lane, this is Gala. She'll tell you she's the only person you need to know in L.A., and maybe she's right. But don't trust her for a second."

While he spoke, Lane was studying Gala in a way that felt consumptive, greedy, so Gala stared right back at her. She took in Lane's sensible dark blond hair cut bluntly a few inches above her shoulders, her fine knit top over a flat chest tucked into high-waisted wide-leg pants. She was too thin and almost gratuitously pale with eyes the color of the dreary Hudson in February, and she looked exactly like the type of woman who believed herself to be too good for Los Angeles.

"Fuck off, Beck," Gala said lazily, before turning her attention back to Lane. "What do you want, honey, LSD?"

"God no," Lane said, which was the wrong thing to say, and Gala shrugged, turning her attention instead to the young artist who had slipped himself in beside her, reaching out to touch the exquisite turquoise feather hanging from his ear. He turned and kissed her neck, and she felt herself start to melt away again.

IT WAS THE wrong end of the party, and Lane had no idea how she was going to traverse the three steep, curb-less miles down to her rental on Holloway Drive. The sky was already a brisk blue, and the same record had been skipping for two hours, but somehow the backyard was still half-full with bodies, legs wrapped around bare waists in the pool.

Lane was sifting through the coats hanging in the cloakroom, looking for her jacket, when Beck, having spent most of the night chasing unsuccessfully after various teenagers, opened the door. His unfocused eyes landed on her the way they might on the sole, wilted-looking bunch of flowers left at a gas station on Valentine's Day, with a sort of determined resignation. He leaned against the doorframe, effectively blocking her exit, and Lane could sense rather than see just how out of it he was.

"Excuse me," Lane said crisply as she tried to duck under Beck's outstretched arm, but his hand was instantly around her waist, like a damp sea creature's tentacle, as he used his free arm to close the door.

"Are you going to thank me for bringing you here?" he said, his hot breath tickling her ear and making the hairs on her arms stand on end.

"I'm just looking for my coat," she said, her tone measured.

He laughed a little.

"You think you're smarter than me," he said, and it was something she'd heard so many different times from so many different men, not always in situations like this, but still the intent was the same—not only to undermine her achievements, but to diminish her as a human. And so she wasn't surprised when Beck leaned forward and angrily mashed his face into hers, and he tasted like nachos or maybe just some type of cheese she couldn't quite put her finger on. She froze as his hands slipped down the waistband of her pants, his finger reaching down into her underwear until the door to the cloakroom flew open. Gala stood in the doorway with her hands on her hips, eyes flashing as she assessed the scene.

"Didn't I tell you to fuck off already," she said, and then she was elbowing Beck away from Lane like he was nothing more than a bothersome gnat. It made Lane feel both grateful and humiliated that she hadn't been able to do the same herself. After a moment, Beck shrugged and walked out of the room so that it was just Lane and Gala left, sizing each other up all over again. Lane wiped roughly at her mouth to get rid of the taste of cheese. *Asiago*, she thought finally.

Gala pulled two cigarettes out of a vintage-looking gold cigarette case and handed one to Lane.

"Someone should have told you," she said finally. "But I can't do everything."

Lane nodded as she lit her own cigarette and then Gala's, embarrassed to find that her hand was shaking slightly.

"That's nice," she said, looking at the gold cigarette case still in Gala's hand. Gala held it up and squinted at it as if she were seeing it for the first time too.

"I guess so," she said. "I bought it off a homeless guy with a gecko in Venice. He stole it from Marilyn Monroe when he stayed with her in Paris."

Lane frowned as she exhaled a plume of smoke into a row of coats. She was feeling slightly more herself now. "I don't think Marilyn Monroe ever lived in Paris."

"Oh, you sweet fool," Gala said, almost gleefully. "You don't know?"

Lane felt a rush of embarrassment. "What?"

"She faked her own death. *Obviously* she ran out of options in Hollywood and the government couldn't have her humiliating our beloved dead president anymore," Gala said, twirling one hand as she spoke. "But Marilyn is alive and thriving in Paris—probably cycling around Montmartre as we speak."

"Do you really believe that?" Lane asked, and to her surprise Gala seemed to consider the question before shrugging.

"Does it matter?"

"I guess not," Lane said, even though she knew it did. Because what was the point of telling a story if it wasn't at least partly true?

FOUR

THEN

NEW YEAR'S EVE 1965/66

The second time Lane met Gala was four months later, on New Year's Eve. Lane had spent the latter part of the year settling into her new existence in Los Angeles. She found a coffee shop she could walk to in the morning for a dark roast (no milk), and a neighborhood Italian restaurant, Villa Mia, in which she occasionally felt comfortable enough to sit alone with a single scoop of pistachio ice cream. Dinner at home consisted of a hastily made sandwich or soup that she'd eat as she wrote at the kitchen table, but otherwise she existed mostly on cans of her favorite club soda and the occasional fruit salad she'd pick up from the street vendor on the corner of Fountain and Havenhurst.

Lane wasn't yet sure if her modest fame in New York would translate over here, but, for the first time in her adult life, she found she didn't mind. While she knew she was objectively isolated, she was somehow less alone than she had been in Manhattan, where she saw thousands of people every day but hadn't felt connected to any of them. She liked the predictability of her new quiet life, and the novelty didn't seem to be wearing off, perhaps because she knew the insularity would inevitably end once she finished writing her novel and returned to journalism, where you literally couldn't afford to cut yourself off from the outside world. Soon she would build a life for herself in Los Angeles, she told herself. She just needed a little more time.

LANE HAD BEEN living back in her empty family home after college when she became something of an overnight sensation. A *LIFE* magazine editor, a mentor of Lane's from Barnard, had finally sent some work her way, and Lane had spent three days in her hometown of Phoenix following around a young, mostly unknown actress, Angelica, who was set to star in one of the most anticipated movies of the following year. The resulting profile, "Angelica Threw a Fishbowl at Me," was a skewering both of the misogyny of the film industry's treatment of young starlets, and of this particular young starlet who, as Lane saw it, was doing little to justify her impending success. Angelica was five two, bubble-gum cute, and prone to violent outbursts, as experienced by Lane firsthand when she took against Lane's questions about rumored vocal dubbing for the film's musical numbers.

The *LIFE* issue in which the initially low-stakes piece was printed (split inauspiciously between the eighteenth and seventy-third pages of the magazine) happened to hit the stands less than a week before Angelica shot and killed her model boyfriend before turning the gun on herself, and the issue sold out within hours of the news breaking. It would be the first and last time Lane brought herself into her journalism, and she always felt uncomfortable that her own career ascension was mostly coincidental and, if she was being honest, at the expense of two human (and three goldfish) lives.

In the three years she'd been back in Arizona, Lane had written for smaller publications on subjects as far-ranging as the diminishing business of taxidermy to the Pill's impact on campus sexual assault figures, but nobody ever wanted to talk about any of those pieces. Still, the Angelica piece was enough to ensure Lane was booked up for the foreseeable future and meant she could finally afford to sell her family home and move back to New York, leaving the ghosts of her childhood behind her.

Lane liked the cachet of working in Manhattan and traveling the country for story assignments, and she certainly liked the money that trickled in from sales of her debut essay collection, *Paradise Found*, but she had always harbored dreams of writing a novel. While most of her childhood memories were shadowy and gnarled, the worlds laid out within the pages of the books Lane loved as a kid were still as powerful as the day she'd discovered they could form the tissue that connected her to the rest of the world. It was through reading that Lane discovered that her shyness wasn't a fatal affliction, or that friendship didn't come naturally to everyone, or that not all marriages were built to a laugh track like Lucy and Desi's—some were as miserable as her own parents' union. Soon, Dickens and Hawthorne and Faulkner would make her feel like her own emotionally stark existence wasn't quite as extraordinary as it felt when she saw other families lining up for ice cream on the street, or siblings squabbling gloriously in the back of a stalled car.

On her twenty-eighth birthday (four years after arriving in New York), Lane signed a two-book deal with a good publisher, and then she flew to Los Angeles (a city she felt lent itself well to the

level of single-mindedness required to finish a novel, with its lack
of cultural distractions). Within days she had found a small apartment on Holloway Drive to sublet, and she'd started writing the
book that she already knew would change her life.

Her debut novel was about a depressed young woman coming
of age in New York in 1960, and while the main character had
shades of her own history, she avoided touching on the messier
side of things. Most days the words would flow out of her to the
point where she felt almost nauseated at the end of a long writing
session, as if she'd been in a trance. It meant that she often felt a
sense of disconnect too when she read back her words—she knew
what she'd written was good, but she felt a little ashamed, as if
she'd had little to do with it in the end. Still, Lane didn't know it
at the time, but this would be the most fulfilled she would ever
feel, in this bleak rental in Hollywood, often going full days without seeing another person.

IN LATE DECEMBER, the sole L.A.-based employee at her publishing house, a diminutive art director named Stavros, invited
her to a secret New Year's Eve party in the back lot of Paramount
Pictures. Lane's instinct had been to turn him down, but her curiosity got the better of her.

The party took place in the dusty streets of the back lot's fading Western Town, complete with a working saloon, a general
store, and a strangely realistic mountain backdrop made from
plaster and chicken wire. It was unclear whether those in charge
at the studio were aware of the party, and it had a delightfully
lawless appeal—bottles of booze produced from underneath saloon tables, a Motown group singing in front of the blue-sky back-

drop, and frequent interruptions whenever someone tripped over the amp lead. It was also filled with more celebrities than Lane had ever seen in one place.

She was holding a cup of warm white wine in the line for the bathroom (a porta-toilet that emanated a sickly sweet smell), listening to two women loudly discussing the ending of *In Cold Blood* (and getting everything wrong), when she spotted Gala walking out of the general store. Since their meeting that fall, Lane had asked a few people about Gala, and while everyone seemed to know her, Lane never quite got to the bottom of why.

Gala, wearing a white shaggy fur coat over a black lace-trimmed teddy, was fiddling with the same gold cigarette case. Lane left her place in the line and pushed her way through the crowd, approaching just as Gala lit her cigarette.

"Hey, isn't that Marilyn Monroe's?" Lane said, smiling.

"Huh?" Gala exhaled as she turned her wary gaze onto Lane.

"The case," Lane said. "You told me the story when we met."

Gala's eyes, already slightly unfocused, showed no signs of recognition.

"At the party on Wonderland?" Lane said, less embarrassed than she was annoyed. "I was with Beck Andersson."

"How unfortunate for you," Gala said, and it seemed like she was about to say something else, but then someone called her name and her attention was pulled away. Lane felt another flash of irritation.

"So what's your story, Gala?" she asked, her voice now sharp. "Are you a dealer or just a groupie?"

As soon as the words were out of her mouth, Lane slightly regretted them, but there was already a hint of a smile on Gala's face as she finally turned her full, blinding attention onto Lane.

"What's your name?" she asked.

"Lane Warren," Lane said. "But we've already been introduced."

"Oh yeah, I know you," Gala said. "You're the journalist who hates women."

"I don't hate women," Lane said.

Gala shrugged. "Okay. But you write like a man."

Lane felt an annoying flush of pride at this. It was true that she wrote in the type of short, stark sentences with few adjectives and even less emotion that were typically attributed to male writers—the humor and pathos depending more on juxtaposition than anything overt—but she really didn't see why she had to adjust anything about herself solely to become more palatable to women like Gala.

"You didn't answer my question," Lane said. "What do *you* do?"

"Why do I have to do anything?" Gala replied. "Why can't I just be?"

Lane stared at her and Gala sighed.

"Fine," she said. "Maybe I'm a storyteller too."

"You write?"

"No, honey," Gala said, almost sympathetically. "I live."

Lane was thinking of a clever retort when a man wearing a lavender slip dress wedged himself between them. He threaded his arm around Gala's waist and nuzzled her neck before picking her up and carrying her away. Lane watched them go, aware she'd been insulted but unsure exactly how.

GALA LOOKED AROUND the dusty make-believe land where all the most beautiful people in L.A. had come together to see in the second half of the greatest decade yet under the glittering stars and thought how she had lived her entire life in this city and it could still surprise her. She was on her third margarita—you had to know the right guy to get hold of any ice—when she spotted Lane again, now lurking incongruously by a hay bale. She was standing between two men who were gesturing animatedly as they spoke, but Gala could tell Lane wasn't exactly in the conversation. Rather, she happened to be there while the two men conversed, most likely fresh from doing a bump of speed, or even coke, that crystallized just how fascinating they found themselves. Lane seemed to be listening closely, and Gala figured she may as well get out her ratty little notepad to take notes, she was so obviously just a spectator here.

There was something sad about this woman, despite her obvious success and middling attractiveness. She didn't seem like she could ever get past herself to have fun, and for that Gala pitied her. For a few seconds Gala considered taking Lane under her wing, maybe slipping her a few quaaludes to loosen her up, but the thought of having this person following her around even for a night filled her instantly with doom. No, it was better to introduce her to someone else who might actually want to know her.

Gala had always had girlfriends, some she'd been friends with since they were just kids, but they all knew better than to depend on her for anything. Having grown up in a twinkling playground with all the freedom she wanted, the threat of obligation (and its ugly companion, guilt) was entirely repellent to Gala. When embarking on either a new friendship or fling, she made it clear from the start that she wouldn't be someone they could expect to unload on. It wasn't that she was selfish or unfeeling (she'd often turn up with a bottle of tequila after hearing of a friend's heartbreak and had even been known to key several cars belonging to overly handsy bosses), but any acts of kindness needed to be entirely of her own free will and not out of some imposed sense of duty. It was a self-selecting process, and Gala found that she was left mainly with friends and lovers like herself—dreamers who felt the harsh gales of the world as little more than a gentle breeze, a light directional suggestion rather than a path set in stone.

After another sip, Gala begrudgingly waved Lane over and watched as the other woman politely excused herself from a conversation she was never actually in. Gala sighed and drained the remainder of her margarita.

"YOU DON'T HAVE any friends here, do you?" Gala said once Lane was close enough to hear. As she talked, Gala reached out and untucked Lane's hair from behind her ear, and Lane felt a stab of annoyance.

"I know Stavros, who invited me here," Lane said, even though she hadn't seen him yet. "And Benny and Sam over there, they've written for *Harper's* and *LIFE* before."

"Those are colleagues," Gala said. "Not friends."

"You hardly have a harem of people around you either," Lane said haughtily. "You're always either alone or surrounded by men who probably just want to fuck you."

"I'm not trying to hurt your feelings," Gala said. "I'm just figuring out what I can do for you."

Lane stared at her. This woman with the transparent nightwear and smeared eye makeup didn't seem like the type to help out a stranger for nothing.

"Is this because of what happened with Beck?" Lane asked.

"If I'm being honest with you, Lane, it's because you make me feel sad," Gala said. "And I don't like to feel sad. So if you're going to keep showing up at parties I'm at, I would rather figure out a way to make you at least *look* like you're having fun so I can continue on with my night, and my life, without thinking about you again."

Lane felt a sickening surge of embarrassment as Gala spoke. The problem was, she believed Gala. Lane knew she wasn't trying to be unkind, and that made it infinitely worse. After a few breaths, Lane fixed a withering stare onto Gala, zoning in until she could see the pores of her skin, the small crumb of sleep still in the outside corner of her left eye, the discoloration of the one pointy tooth that sat slightly behind the others. And what exactly had this woman achieved in her life? In New York nobody would have even bothered to learn her name.

"I don't need your help," Lane said coolly. "In fact, I've still yet to understand what you contribute to the world besides being at one hundred percent of the parties I've gone to since I moved here, and presumably having slept with the same percentage of men in L.A."

There was a pause, and then Gala let out a howl of laughter. After a moment, Lane found herself smiling back, and Gala looked like she was about to say something, when she spotted someone over Lane's shoulder.

"*Charlie!*" she yelled, so loudly that Lane flinched. Lane turned around as the man in question raised his hand warily in response, while Gala beckoned him over. He said something to the woman beside him that made her laugh not entirely kindly, before making his way toward them.

"I know you want to come across all smart and superior, but I can tell you're more than that," Gala said quietly to Lane, just before he reached them. "You're scrappy too."

The man looked Lane up and down before kissing Gala on

each cheek. He was classically handsome but seemed more conservative than the other men at the party, in a clean cream turtleneck with pressed chinos and slicked-back hair, not an inch of velvet or paisley in sight. When Lane looked closely, she could see that he had a fine white scar that intersected his top lip, and somehow it only made him more perfect.

"Who's your friend?" Charlie asked Gala after a moment, his tone flat and disinterested. "Let me guess . . . Vassar class of '60. Class president. Valedictorian. *Both?*"

"I'm Lane Warren," Lane finally snapped, her cheeks flushing. "And you must be the two least interesting people at this entire fucking party."

Lane turned and walked away from them just as Gala and Charlie burst into fits of uncontrollable laughter.

LATER, CHARLIE WOULD tell people how he met Lane, and nobody would believe him. That Lane Warren, who always said the right thing at the right time if she said anything at all, had not only called Charlie McCloud uninteresting but also had cursed at him was almost inconceivable. No, it was presumably just another story cooked up by Lane and Charlie to make their friendship all the more mythical.

FIVE

THEN

JANUARY 1966

A few weeks into the New Year, Lane received a handwritten note from Charlie McCloud, asking whether she would meet him for dinner at Dan Tana's. In the beautifully written note, on monochromatic stationery embossed with a distinctive CMC monogram, Charlie said he'd be waiting for her in his favorite booth at the back of the restaurant from 7:00 p.m. on Tuesday, January 25. Lane didn't respond to the note, resolving instead to make a last-minute decision on whether she felt like meeting him. She figured someone, Gala perhaps, had told Charlie who she was, and that he wasn't the type of person who collected enemies he didn't need, particularly not those with as many barbed opinions and bylines as Lane.

The day of the proposed dinner, Lane found it increasingly difficult to concentrate. She wasn't lonely, exactly (or rather, she had *always* been lonely, so barely noticed anymore), but having sent over copy for an article about a trio of gruesome murders in Tujunga the week earlier, she'd been finding it hard to get back into writing her novel, and she couldn't help but feel like something was missing. It turned out that the only thing worse than feeling like you were being possessed with a story trying to fight its way out of you was the opposite—staring at a broken page and waiting for the demons of self-doubt to come for you. Lane had known she was a writer before she knew almost anything else about the world, but for the first time in her life, she felt the true weight of this obligation. For Lane, failure wasn't an option.

At 6:15 p.m. on Tuesday, January 25, Lane got up from the kitchen table, opened a fresh can of club soda with a twist, and decided to take an entirely noncommittal shower. As she massaged her drugstore conditioner into her hair, she told herself she could back out at any moment and Charlie wouldn't know any different, and she told herself the same thing again as she slipped into a brown shirt and cream knit skirt with tan leather boots, and again when she sprayed herself with her classic Rochas Femme perfume and locked the front door behind her, even the porch light flickering in surprise.

THE BLOODRED BAR at Tana's was packed with shimmering ingenues draped over stools, and each table in the restaurant was confined within its own rising halo of cigarette smoke. Lane spotted Charlie instantly, but she flicked her eyes away so that he could watch her for a moment. She shook her hair out and picked an imaginary piece of lint from her skirt, and then feigned vague recognition when she looked over at him again. He waved to her, standing up as she approached. He was wearing a simple white shirt with pleated brown trousers, and seemed again born of an era different from the frothing, careless crowd.

"Lane Warren," he said, kissing her on each cheek when she reached the booth. "The most interesting woman in any room."

She rolled her eyes and slid into the booth opposite him. She already smelled like his cologne—something spicy and woody.

"Charlie," she said evenly.

"Have you been here before?" he asked.

"No," she said.

"Initial thoughts?"

She glanced around the room. There was a table of men tucked in the corner who looked straight out of a mob movie, and a woman leaning so far over the bar you could see her complete lack of underwear. Lane turned her attention back to Charlie.

"It's very red."

Charlie burst out laughing, and she had to admit that he looked beautiful when he laughed.

"Fine," she said. "That couple next to us are on their first date, but he hasn't told her he's married."

"How do you know that?" Charlie snuck a glance at the couple to his right.

"The ring indentation on his left hand."

Charlie squinted at the man's hand, which rested on the table-cloth, obscured from his date by the bread basket.

"He could be divorced, or separated."

"Maybe," she said. "But the way he's doing everything with his right hand would suggest otherwise. He hasn't lifted the other one once."

"It sounds like you know what you're talking about," he said, and she felt her cheeks flush.

"It's my job to know what I'm talking about," she said tersely.

"People's habits, their instincts, their motivations—the things even *they* don't know about themselves. That's why I'm the best at what I do."

Charlie flashed a smile at her, and she found herself adjusting her shirt to expose her clavicle a little more.

"Lane, you look great," he said slowly, in that sardonic way he had. "If not *entirely* to my own taste."

Lane felt her cheeks heat up at having been insulted all over again, and she thought about getting up and walking right out of the restaurant, until she caught the expression on Charlie's face. Her only friend at Barnard (*not* Vassar) had been gay, and Lane had seen in her the same swiftness to broach the subject after a lifetime of either hiding her true self or being rejected for it, and the same rawness in her expression as she waited to find out which it would be this time. For a moment, it was as if everything, all Charlie's airs and witty commentary and slickness, had been stripped back and he was like anyone else, asking someone he'd only just met if he was lovable.

"Oh," Lane said now. "I see."

"I hope you're not too disappointed," Charlie said, smiling slightly. "Try as I might, I'm somehow irresistible to every woman in Los Angeles."

"You know, I think I'll survive," Lane said, and she opened up her menu. "Now . . . what's good here?"

Charlie smiled and reached across the table for her hand.

OVER A BEAUTIFUL, golden dinner and after two and a half martinis, Lane found herself captivated by Charlie's humor and warmth. She hazily noted the seamless way he steered the subject away from anything uncomfortable and how *good* he made her feel by sharing just enough of his insecurities so as to make her feel chosen. The fact that she knew that this was all happening didn't diminish its power; if anything, it just impressed her more—like watching a master conductor at work. Lane felt protected by Charlie's emotional proficiency, and she wondered what she could learn from him.

While barely sharing any of her own history, Lane learned that Charlie had grown up in the affluent but rigid Beverly Hills, in a family that was as accepting as possible of him, considering his father was the attorney general of California. Charlie himself was the head of publicity at a record label, National, where he had both launched and salvaged the careers of some of the biggest artists of the last few years. He liked what he did, but he said that he'd never met one person who was improved by fame, and Lane could tell he meant it.

At a certain point in the evening, with the second martini swimming in her stomach, Lane asked Charlie about his friendship with Gala.

"Oh, Gala's good value for an hour or two," he said, waving his hand in the air as if to dismiss her presence even in conversation. "But she's not like me and you, Lane. She's never been hungry for anything."

Lane took another sip of her drink and wondered what exactly it was that he'd seen in her.

THEY WERE FINISHING up their shared main courses of linguine with clams and veal scaloppine, and Charlie had just told her the story of how he got the scar on his lip when he was a baby (a deranged cousin from West Virginia and a blunt pocketknife), when he checked his watch.

"I have to catch a show around the corner in an hour or so," he said. "Some British band I'm seeing as a favor to a friend."

"Oh?" Lane said, disappointed at the thought of stepping outside of Charlie's glimmering orbit so soon. She wondered if she'd bored him. "I guess I should get back to work too."

"Why don't you come with me? I've already distracted you for three hours," Charlie said, laughing kindly at her in a way he would do countless times over the next decade. "What's a couple more?"

Lane pretended to think about it. "That *is* true . . ."

IT WAS LANE'S first time at the Troubadour, and the burly man working the door let Charlie in as soon as they walked up, despite the line creeping around the corner of Doheny. A few people waiting shouted Charlie's name, and he waved at them good-naturedly.

"You're famous," Lane said in his ear as they walked into the dark, smoky venue.

"I'm no Lane Warren," Charlie said, squeezing her arm.

Once inside, Lane spotted Gala sitting on a barstool, surrounded by adoring men. Lane realized she felt slightly more charitable toward Gala after she'd cared enough to introduce her to Charlie. Maybe Gala was one of those women who only came across as a bitch because she too hated the notion of some ideological *sisterhood*—the uncomfortable concept that women were so generally unexceptional they could be clumped together as a homogenous entity.

Charlie ordered two martinis while Lane stood a few feet behind, and she watched as Gala clocked Charlie first, and then Lane. Gala looked surprised for just a moment before she lifted her glass up. Lane smiled back at her.

GALA HAD STEPPED out of the club to use the restroom, but also to escape the awful British band onstage; the singer was so clearly high on something he was barely able to make it to the end of a single line let alone *song*. In the bathroom, she was shrugging off her white fur coat to assess her rainbow jumpsuit, the left pocket of which wouldn't lie flat and was therefore ruining the entire look, when Lane walked in and stopped beside her. Once again, she was dressed inappropriately for the occasion, her cream skirt already stained with strangers' drinks. Gala wondered if she looked this uptight on purpose—who wore *cashmere* to the Troubadour?

"Hideous, isn't it," Gala said, still fiddling with her pocket.

"What?"

"The noise," Gala said. "The fucking *cacophony* out there."

Lane smiled as Gala now tried to rip the pocket out with her hands. Lane watched her for a moment before digging into her purse and pulling out a small pair of nail scissors.

"Why . . ." Gala started, then shrugged and took them from Lane. "Thanks."

She started hacking at the pocket.

"Don't cut too high up or there'll be a hole," Lane said, just as Gala snipped right across the top of the fabric. She froze and they both stared at the hole now at her hip bone, exposing her bare skin. After a pause, Gala shrugged and cut the other side so at least her hips would match.

"I don't mind the music," Lane said. "But people are physically moving me out of the way to get closer to Charlie."

"So you guys are getting on . . ." Gala said.

"Charlie's great," Lane said. "Thanks for almost introducing me to him."

"You ran away before I had the chance," Gala said, rolling her eyes. "Look, Charlie is Charlie, and that will work for you until it doesn't."

It seemed like a warning, but not one that Lane entirely understood. Gala handed the scissors back to her and appraised them both in the mirror—Gala smoky-eyed and glittering, Lane watchful and birdlike.

"He can be callous," Gala said.

Lane paused, then nodded her understanding.

"I'll wait for you if you need to go," Gala said then, pointing toward the empty stalls.

Lane nodded again before walking into one and closing the door behind her. There was a short silence, and then—"Gala? Can you turn on the tap?"

Gala shook her head in disbelief.

LANE AND GALA emerged to no sign of Charlie, and some kind of a commotion onstage. The singer of the band had finally passed out and was in the process of being carried off by the guitarist and bassist. The drummer had climbed out from behind his drum kit and was now standing under the lights in the center of the stage, his dirty blond hair brushing the shoulders of his jacket, cheekbones hollow under the purple top light. Both Gala and Lane stood along with the rest of the crowd, watching as he picked up the mic and murmured an apology into it.

The crowd was amped up now and started chanting "*Sing a song. Sing a bloody song*" in fake British accents over his apology. When the guitarist and bassist returned to the stage, the drummer conferred with them for a moment before the opening chords of the guitar rang out, and the crowd erupted into applause. The drummer shed his suit jacket and stood at the front of the stage in a billowy white shirt and too-tight trousers. Over the next few minutes, he performed a near a cappella rendition of Mel Carter's "Hold Me, Thrill Me, Kiss Me," his voice all the more haunting for its many flaws. A gritty sexuality radiated off his skinny frame as he moved up and down the stage, sweat pouring off him.

"He's sexy," Gala said in Lane's ear as the crowd broke into applause.

"I don't know," Lane said, her eyes still locked on him once the applause dried up and the band had another onstage conference. "He reminds me of someone I used to know."

"Wow," Gala said, impressed. "Remind me to ask for an introduction to *that* friend."

"My ex," Lane said tightly, and Gala raised an eyebrow.

"That still works fine for me."

"I need to find Charlie."

Gala felt Lane close off beside her, but she didn't care to inquire any further either. She'd met enough men like this drummer and enough women like Lane to know how that story went. Instead, she closed her eyes and swayed a little as a new original song started, the only passable one of the set in her opinion. She decided to find the band afterward to tell them as much—her *second* charitable deed of the night.

"Okay, Lane," she said to herself as she danced away. "You keep your sad secrets."

AFTER THE SHOW, the elite of Hollywood's music scene gathered in the bar. Nobody quite knew what to say about the performance they'd just witnessed—it was undoubtedly a mess, but there had been something thrilling about it.

When the band, whose name Lane couldn't recall even if

someone tried to torture it out of her, joined the masses, all eyes were on the drummer turned singer, Gabriel. His hair was dripping with sweat, and up close he looked young and almost wholesome despite his acute cheekbones. After grabbing a beer from a fawning barmaid, he made a beeline for Charlie, who was standing with Lane in a far corner of the room.

"Charlie McCloud, the wizard of spin," he said, his voice a northern English drawl. "I'm Gabriel Ford. And I know I should probably pretend to be too fucking cool to care who you are, but I wanted to come over to tell you I'm a huge fan of what you're doing at National."

Charlie smiled at him, but it was a wry smile, as if this was an everyday occurrence for him and not anything to be disarmed by.

"Thank you—Gabriel, was it? That's very kind of you to say. This is my dear friend, Lane Warren."

Gabriel turned his cool violet eyes onto Lane, and she was surprised to feel that he was really looking at her, not skipping over her like most men would if they too were trying to bag a record deal in a bar.

"Pleasure to meet you, Lane," Gabriel said. "That's an unusual name."

It felt like each word had a hidden meaning when Gabriel spoke them, and when he smiled at Lane, she felt a tightening in her stomach. She reminded herself that men like Gabriel were trained to make women like Lane feel like this, so she offered him only a small smile just as Charlie reached out and took one of Gabriel's hands as if to tie up the exchange.

"You have an undeniable charm, but you're green," Charlie said, and his tone was almost gentle now. "You want to be someone you're not, or at least not yet. My advice to you would be to live a little, Gabriel. Let Los Angeles warp you."

As Charlie took her arm to guide her away, Lane thought how unfazed Gabriel seemed by the entire experience, even after Charlie's strange advice. She found herself turning back to him.

"Did you always want to be the lead singer?" Lane asked, and they locked eyes.

"Not really," he said, after a short pause. "I only joined the band a few weeks ago because their old drummer got married."

"Wow, how very . . . fortuitous." Lane put her head to one side and assessed him, then asked, "Do things often just fall into your lap like this? Opportunities, puppies, naked women . . . ?"

Gabriel grinned widely before recovering his humility, but by this point Lane had seen enough to know there was a reassuring level of self-awareness underneath his good nature. As she felt the warmth of his presence wrap around her, Lane changed her mind about her initial impression—this person was nothing like her ex, an almost-famous film director who may have had the same cheekbones and magnetism, but who was also both earnest and self-important, and who hadn't had the first clue how to laugh at himself.

"If you call our front man falling asleep onstage at the start of the biggest show of our lives lucky, then I guess I must be," Gabriel said, with a slight laugh.

"Well, a voice like yours is too unique to hide for long," Charlie said smoothly, again trying to wrap up the conversation, as Gabriel and Lane ignored him.

"And what about you, Lane?" Gabriel asked. "You've seen me humiliate myself onstage in a suit that was made for someone else. What's your story?"

Finally understanding he was no longer required, Charlie stepped back slightly, raising an eyebrow at Lane as if to check her consent for him to leave the conversation. She flashed him a quick smile in response. It wasn't exactly her usual style to sleep with a wannabe rock star who looked to be around ten years her junior—nineteen or twenty at most—but maybe that was where she'd been going wrong. Plus, he'd most likely be leaving town in a few days, so it could be the perfect situation. No opportunity to get too attached to his Cupid's bow lips.

"My story?" she asked.

"You know, your hopes and dreams, your childhood wounds?"

Lane felt a glint of discomfort. She had been willing to be fucked by this beautiful creature in a hotel room, not psychologically appraised. Perfectly on cue, an image of her mother's face flashed into her mind, and Lane dug a sharp nail into the inside of her wrist to distract herself. She'd told only one living person— the director—about her memories of Phoenix, and that had resulted in a broken heart and three weeks in a private mental institution where she drank only dandelion tea and had nearly been indoctrinated into a cult. So, no, she probably wasn't going to pour her heart out to this baby heartthrob just because he had a British accent and violet eyes.

"You'll have to buy me a drink first," she said lightly.

Gabriel grinned back at her and was about to ask her something, when the energy of the room shifted, and a whirl of dark hair and rainbow sequins blew past Lane like a tornado destined to land directly on Gabriel. When Lane blinked, she opened her eyes to see Gala's hands planted on either side of Gabriel's chest and her body pressed against his. Somehow, Gala's white fur coat had ended up in Lane's arms.

"Gabriel," Gala said, her voice urgent and breathy like she was Scarlett O'Hara reincarnated. "I couldn't wait a moment longer!"

Gabriel smiled bemusedly, first at Lane, then at Gala. "For what?"

Gala let out a husky laugh before she tilted her face up to his, her heavily lined amber eyes half-closed as she stared into his open face, noses almost touching. Her expression was one of rapturous awe, and Lane watched it all unfold with a macabre interest, even as she took a step back from them. Gabriel and Gala were already undoubtedly entwined—bound together by the golden thread Gala had spun around them both while Lane had been standing just inches away.

"For you of course," Gala said.

Then, with barely a glance in Lane's direction, she pulled Gabriel away into a dark corner, glittering like a beacon in front of him.

SIX

NOW

SUMMER 1975

Lane has forgotten about the book event until Charlie flings open the bathroom door. He stares down at her, and she shifts in the bathtub, long since having given up any attempts at modesty when it comes to him.

"What on earth are you doing?" he asks as he sits on the marble edge of the tub.

"Reading."

"Yes," he says with forced patience as if she's senile. "But why are you reading that?"

Lane puts down the copy of *Inhalation*, Gala's collection of short stories.

"Where do you think she is?" she asks him, and she thinks he's about to answer with some quip or other, but instead he stops himself, softens slightly. He reaches out and tucks a loose strand of wet hair behind her ear.

"Oh, Laney, this really doesn't have anything to do with you," he says. "Gala's always made her own choices."

She hands him the book and ducks underwater, rubbing her head vigorously to get rid of the conditioning treatment. When she reemerges, Charlie is watching her with some concern.

"She thanks me in it," she says as she stands up, the soapy water cascading down her body and back into the tub. "In the acknowledgments. I never read it, so I didn't know."

Charlie nods. "As far as I remember, you were a little preoccupied when it came out."

Lane thinks of the sticky hospital mattress, the churning in her stomach, the feeling of utter helplessness as she left the hospital with two new humans who needed her in a way that she knew could only break their hearts.

"This has nothing to do with you, Laney," Charlie says. "Whatever mess Gala is in, she did it to herself. She never knew when the party was over."

His tone is soaked in disgust, and Lane remembers that Charlie dislikes anything that either depresses him or reminds him of his own mortality, but particularly when he thinks these things could have been avoided with either better planning or self-control.

"Charlie . . ." Lane says, and for just a moment, she wonders what he would say if she told him everything. "I think . . ."

He looks at her, a yellow towel suspended in his arms, waiting.

"Where do you think she is?" she repeats instead as Charlie wraps the towel around her. They meet each other's eyes in the mirror above the sink, and Lane is the first to look away. There are some things she'll never admit to another living human. Not even Charlie.

Lane knows better than most that love is always conditional.

THE EVENT IS being held at a bookstore on Sunset Boulevard to celebrate the twelve-year anniversary of Lane's acclaimed collection of essays—*Paradise Found*. The shop, Book Soup, is located in-auspiciously between a head shop and a gritty strip club, but Lane's publicist promises her it's the future of the Los Angeles literary scene, and who is she to argue with such a claim. It's been a while since anyone has thrown her a party, anyway.

She arrives with Charlie and Scotty, wearing the artichoke-green silk suit made for her by a Parisian friend a few years ago. On the inside of the jacket, there is a secret pocket with her initials embroidered on it in a tasteful silver. Inside the pocket is a piece of paper filled with notes in case she freezes onstage and needs to pretend to be herself.

The reading goes well, and, as is always the case, Lane finds that what starts off as a chore ends up becoming almost enjoy-able. The essay she's chosen is one in which she recasts sexual assault in Hollywood as less of an unsightly blip in its history than the very foundation it was built on, but none of the fame-hungry feminists ever want to remember this one when they're accusing her of exceptionalism at best, isolationism at worst.

Next up is the Q&A session, which Lane figures will be easy enough because the journalists have all been approved in advance by her publicity team. She answers questions about her favorite essays and the usual invasive question about juggling work with her home life. She answers the latter with her standard proclama-tion of appreciation to Scotty and the nanny for holding down the fort when she's locked away working, even though she knows it will annoy Scotty, as he wants to be the supportive husband but only on his terms.

Toward the end of the hour, Lane's publicist points to a man with his hand raised in the second row.

"We hear you're still working on that third novel . . . Can you give us any details?"

Lane feels a clamping sensation in her chest even as she smiles self-deprecatingly at the reporter.

"Oh, you know," she says. "I'm taking my time with this one. None of you exactly thanked me for the last one, if you remember . . ."

The crowd laughs, and Lane glances over at her publicist to get her to wrap things up, but she appears to be showing off her gold Egyptian earrings to the woman next to her.

"Hey, Lane," someone else calls from the back of the room, where a group of people, mostly Lane's friends, stand. "Is it true the new book's about Gala?"

Lane freezes, her eyes flicking across the crowd. She scans face after face, most curious, some hungrier than that, until she finds the one that matches the voice. It's Ruby Roblex—Gala's friend from Hollywood High. She is almost unrecognizable now—her once signature cotton candy–pink hair reduced to a natural taupe as if she's afraid of standing out too much. Lane swallows and tries to keep her face neutral as she chooses her words carefully.

"I understand the temptation to simplify things," Lane says, and her voice is luxurious in its forced smugness even to her own ears. "And like any writer, any *human*, I'm naturally influenced by the people I come across, but I would never write a novel *about* someone, no. Nothing against Gala Margolis, but I've been lucky enough to spend substantial time with the most brilliant minds in the world, and they're *still* not fascinating enough to sustain an entire novel."

Pleasure ripples through the crowd, but Lane knows her answer hasn't endeared her to Gala's childhood best friend. Lane's eyes flick over to Scotty, who is staring at her, a strange expression on his face.

"Do you know where she is?" Ruby asks then, and her tone is so sharp, the question so blunt, that a few people turn to stare at her. Lane feels a flash of irritation now—why isn't her publicist stepping in?

"I haven't spoken to Gala in a long time," Lane says, forcing a rueful smile. "But I'm sure wherever she is, she's raising hell."

The more knowing members of the crowd laugh, and then the publicist finally announces the end of the Q&A part of the evening, and the start of the real drinking. Guests snatch flutes of champagne as they make their way over to congratulate Lane, while she finds herself looking over their shoulders for Ruby. She finally spots her outside the front of the store, when Scotty grabs her arm.

"What's she doing here?" he asks, nodding toward Ruby's back.

"No idea. Last I heard she was living with a drug dealer in Vallejo," Lane says, then frowns. "Does this event feel low-rent to you, Scotty? Didn't they used to pay for canapés? And catering staff?"

"But is it true?" Scotty asks. "About your book."

Lane meets his eyes firmly. A steady pacific blue beneath dark blond lashes, his skin tennis gold and always on the dry side (*attention-seeking skin*, he'd told her once, back at the start, when they were still selling themselves to one another).

"Of course not," she says. He kisses the top of her head, and, for just a moment, it feels like old times.

RUBY LEANS AGAINST the glass window, exhaling a stream of fruity-smelling pot. When Lane appears, Ruby raises one thin eyebrow but doesn't seem surprised.

"I haven't seen you in a long time," Lane says, standing beside her and looking out at the lights of Sunset Boulevard.

"I left the scene for a while," Ruby replies levelly. "Too much . . . everything."

"It happens," Lane says, and the other woman fixes her eyes on her.

"Not to you."

"No," Lane agrees. "Not to me."

A car speeds past, and they both flinch at the shrill sound of screeching tires as it brakes for a light at the last possible moment.

"I was always planning on showing it to her," Lane says quietly, but she's aware of how useless a point this is even before Ruby's mouth twists into a smirk.

"How fucking thoughtful."

Lane glances inside the window, at the packed room of golden people waiting for her to rejoin them. Charlie is standing in the window, frowning at her, and she can feel the pull of the life she's created. She should be inside with the people who still think she is worthy and brilliant and better than them, not out on the street with yet another soul lost to L.A.

"Everyone used Gala," Ruby says then. "Her whole life, people just pecking away, stealing tiny pieces of what came so naturally to her, until she woke up one morning to find she was threadbare. And then, suddenly, all the people who had pretended to love her wanted nothing more to do with her."

Lane thinks about Gala prancing down the Sunset Strip, her glittery platform shoes in one hand and a cigarette in the other, and for just a moment she feels so real that Lane could reach out and touch her.

"She'll be somewhere," Lane says, as much to herself as Ruby.

Ruby drops her joint, and the roach simmers on the ground.

"Even her parents haven't heard from her in months," she says as she stamps on it. "And someone paid her rent for a year up front, but Gala wouldn't tell me who. Don't you think that's fucking strange? The girl who could never keep a secret in her life, suddenly refusing to give up her benefactor."

Lane swallows hard. "I don't know what I can do for you, Ruby. Gala will be found when she wants to be found."

Ruby leans in close then, her hand gripping Lane's slim wrist, her breath hot and fruity from the pot.

"She always defended you, Lane. Anyone who said you were a narcissist or a woman hater, she'd make sure to tell a few stories about the things you've done for her over the years. I've always had my doubts, and I think we both know she did too by the end. But I thought you might still *pretend* to care at least."

Ruby drops her grip, but she still looks disgusted.

"What can I do?" Lane asks, struggling to keep her voice level.

"Take everything you have that Gala doesn't—your clout, your money, your reputation—and don't waste it," Ruby says. "Use it to find her. You know L.A. is her home and she wouldn't just leave unless she was in trouble."

Lane stands numbly as Ruby turns away, sticking close to the shadows like someone trying to disappear.

"Ruby?"

Ruby turns around and waits, an eyebrow raised.

"Gala will be okay," Lane says. "She's like a cat. She has at least nine lives."

"Maybe," Ruby says. "But we both know she's used up a few already."

Lane thinks about what happened to Gala after Gabriel, and she knows Ruby is right. But what is Lane, of all people, supposed to do about it?

SEVEN

THEN

JUNE 1966

Gala had been fucking the British drummer for six months now. She was a little ashamed of it, since it was the longest exclusive *situation* she'd been in (she was loath to call even this a relationship), and people were starting to ask questions.

Gabriel Ford was a poet at heart but not one of the dull ones who wanted to talk about feelings all the time. He'd seemed barely coherent onstage that first night, but when Gala found him at the bar afterward it had turned out to be just nerves (and a little too much whiskey), and he was somehow both perfectly grounded and reassuringly weird. He had a sexy accent and a way of leaning in so close when he talked that the hairs on the back of her neck stood up, and he also wore a near-constant expression of bemusement, which she saw as a type of grace, as if he was just waiting to be entertained by the world. They spent the rest of that first night at the Troubadour together, and she'd fluttered around the bar as he looked on, unafraid to show how impressed he was by her. There weren't many men who could keep up with her, but Gabriel gave it a go that evening and then later that night in his dirty room at the Chateau.

The next morning, she instructed Gabriel to tell his publicist they would no longer be playing the Troubadour that evening, before calling a meeting to discuss a restructuring of the band. Gala sat on the floor of the hotel room as she laid out the new plan: Danny, the incapacitated front man, was out, and Gabriel was to take over lead vocal duties. She strongly advised they scrap the first half of their set and focus on covers until they had a better roster of original songs. She also told them to ditch the folk shtick and move over to electric, like Dylan had the previous summer. And, in the cramped hotel room, she created an origin story for them, one with local villains and broken homes—four scoundrels from the roughest council estate in Manchester who had come to America in pursuit of freedom—classic lore in which to wrap themselves.

After the meeting, she escorted the somewhat dazed four remaining members to her friend's studio in Chinatown to commission custom-made leather pants and silk shirts to replace the done-to-death Beatles collarless suited aesthetic they'd been chasing. The rest of the band, all barely out of their teens and almost blindingly naive at times, seemed relieved to be guided by someone in this unforgiving city, and when they expressed some concern over time constraints and their contract with the Troubadour, Gala called in every favor she knew to make things happen smoothly.

This wasn't the first time Gala had worked her magic in this way, and she knew it wouldn't be the last. There was the plot hole she'd solved for the novelist who went on to sell 160,000 copies, the artist she'd taken on a spiritual journey in Joshua Tree who painted his best work on his return to L.A., and countless musicians she'd proved to be endless lyrical fodder for when they stopped over in Hollywood. And each time she watched someone set the world alight from an ember she'd stoked, she felt a strange beat of something close to envy, until she remembered that she wanted to be brilliant and charming because she *felt* like it, not because she had signed some deal that said she had to be. If you wanted to be frank about it, Gala was a muse, and she told herself that this—helping brilliant artists (brilliant men)—was her destiny. Her own glorious contribution that made the world a little more glittering for everyone else. And who gave a damn if she barely ever got any credit for it? She knew what happened to women who needed it.

On Thursday night, after a humiliating amount of groveling to the owner of the Troubadour, Mr. Weston, the newly rebranded Belle Vue (named after both an amusement park near Gabriel's Manchester hometown and the notorious New York hospital) appeared again at the club. Gabriel was so nervous he drank a bottle of whiskey in the dressing room, so he was audibly slurring onstage, and the guitarist, Aiden, forgot the chords to half the songs, but there was a certain raw charm to the performance that drew the attention of some people whose opinions mattered.

After the show, Gabriel and Gala fucked in the humid dressing room, with his leather trousers around his ankles and her miniskirt pulled up around her waist. Afterward, they froze for a moment, noses touching and eyes locked on each other.

"What are you thinking?" he asked her then, as he had frequently over the past forty-eight hours. It was a question that would have infuriated her had anyone else asked it, but when it was Gabriel, with his slow northern accent and even slower smile, she didn't mind all that much.

"What are *you* thinking?" she asked back.

"I asked you first," he said, then shrugged. "I'll count to three, then we'll both say it."

After a pause, Gala wiped the sweat off her upper lip with the back of her hand and nodded.

"One . . . two . . . three . . ." Gabriel said, then—"I think I'm in love with you," at the exact moment Gala said, "I hate that third song."

They both started laughing, and then Gala pulled out a joint she'd rolled earlier, and she put it in her mouth before lighting it. When she handed it over to Gabriel, he seemed to deliberate for a moment, watching as it simmered in his hand.

"It's not going to kill you," she said, smiling at him. He smiled back and took a tentative drag, his eyes closed as he exhaled the fragrant smoke.

When Belle Vue was offered a record deal three weeks later, Gabriel sweetly asked Gala to join the band as a backing singer or even a percussionist, and she laughed so hard she choked on her coffee. Still, she couldn't deny that she had once again enjoyed molding something from practically nothing, even if she'd never get any recognition for it.

LANE REACHED THE end of the first draft of her novel at the start of June. Despite her misgivings, she had somehow found a tentative rhythm again, and soon she was working from 6:00 a.m. to 6:00 p.m. each day before meeting Charlie at some hip new restaurant, or drinking martinis on his impossibly vast white leather sofa.

On the afternoon she finally typed the words THE END (which

had felt like a bad idea, superstitiously, at the time), she joined Charlie by his pool up on Appian Way, a winding street at the very top of the hills that meant he could look down on everyone he cared about or judged or, at the very least, employed. From his position on a white float, golden skin glistening with baby oil, Charlie told Lane he'd already started planning a party for her to celebrate finishing her novel, since he knew she'd never get around to doing it herself.

"But I haven't even sent it off yet," she said. "Esther could hate it."

"Darling, we both know that's not going to happen," he said, assessing her over his sunglasses.

"It still feels premature," she said. "Like we might jinx something."

"We don't believe in jinxing," Charlie said firmly. "That's for people who believe in *luck*. And it's already half-planned, so you can't back out."

Charlie said the word *luck* like it was a jinx in itself, and Lane had to admit that little Charlie did seemed left up to chance—if he wanted something, he made sure he got it. There was no alternative outcome. It was something Lane admired about him, and, even as she felt a flutter of anxiety, she couldn't deny that she was touched that Charlie had cared enough to go behind her back to plan a party for her.

"It's never too early to formally announce your arrival on the L.A. literary landscape, if you'll excuse the oxymoron, and besides, you don't have to do anything except turn up and be your radiant self."

Lane smiled at him. Nobody had ever called her radiant before, but with Charlie, she occasionally felt it.

"Of course we'll need to drop in at Fred Segal to find something for you to wear, and then I'll set you up with the only hair girl I trust in L.A.," he said, with a sheepish smile.

Lane paused. She was clearly "radiant" with caveats.

"Is any of this negotiable?" she asked dryly.

"Unfortunately not," Charlie said winningly. "What you can do, though, is let me know if you have any thoughts on the guest list. I've already covered the music set, plus a few fun movie people who know how to have a good time and won't spend the entire party trying to pitch you something."

"Have you invited Gala?" Lane asked as she rubbed another layer of Coppertone into her freckled shoulders.

"You don't have to *invite* Gala anywhere, she tends to just appear," Charlie said. "Like a mirage. Or a poltergeist."

Lane had noticed that Charlie didn't seem to like Gala much. He was polite to her when he saw her, but Lane thought he looked down on Gala, particularly for her tendencies toward excess. He was always making snarky comments to Lane about Gala's weight, her bad skin, her notorious lack of funds, her excessive drinking—her general sloppiness. It made Lane uncomfortable even though she tried to see it as the other side of the coin that meant he liked her so much—Lane had eaten the exact same breakfast and lunch since she turned eighteen in 1954, and she'd pretty much stayed the same weight too. She rarely drank to excess, and her only true addiction was to club soda with a twist of lemon. Lane knew she had the blood of an addict (if not the disposition), and had consequently created a life filled with enough discipline, rituals, and boundaries that she felt in control, but the thought that she too could fall out of Charlie's graces one day over something so arbitrary as her genetic makeup made her feel vaguely sick.

"What do you think of Gabriel?" Lane asked then. She'd

thought of him a few times since the night at the Troubadour, and she always felt a small sting of humiliation at the way Gala had maneuvered her way into his sights, as if Lane wasn't even worth a second thought. And, as it turned out, she hadn't been.

"She's going to eat him alive," Charlie said gleefully. "You should have fucked him when you had the chance."

Lane threw a bottle of sun lotion at him that landed with a splash in the water beside him. Charlie's skin was turning a beautiful bronze in the early June sun, and she felt a flutter of excitement then at the thought of her own party, yes, but also at this new season of their burgeoning friendship. Who needed Gabriel or Gala anyway.

EIGHT

THEN

JULY 1966

True to Charlie's word, on the day of her party, all Lane had to do was turn up at 9:00 p.m. at the address he wrote down for her, once the party was already in full swing. In the late afternoon, she'd stopped in to Charlie's friend's salon, where a frighteningly chic stylist had convinced her to chop inches off her hair until it grazed her jawline instead of her shoulders, and then she drove home to put on the outfit she and Charlie had picked out together with Fred Segal himself—a sheer bronze shirt paired with flowing bronze brocade trousers—and she tried not to feel like a fraud, celebrating something that barely existed yet, in clothes that didn't feel like her own. She hadn't worked up the courage to send the manuscript to her editor yet (despite Esther calling every Friday morning to chase her), and it was sitting on top of her bedside table, the fateful words THE END somehow still taunting her from underneath 270 pages.

———

THE PARTY WAS at Charlie's aunt's house in Bel-Air. The house
was a mammoth Spanish colonial–style mansion that took up the
equivalent of a New York block, but the real draw (and the reason
Charlie had schlepped everyone out ten miles farther west than
they liked to go) was the five acres of land it sat on, manicured
to within an inch of its life to re-create a Moroccan paradise.
Fragrant herbs, palms, banana plants, and birds-of-paradise
bloomed as guests mingled under glowing lanterns around the
centerpiece—a mosaicked pink and turquoise fountain set in a
lake of crystal-clear water. It was by far the most absurd house
Lane had ever been in, and Charlie had leaned into the theme
with his trademark enthusiasm. He deemed traditional butlers
too stuffy and old guard, so instead there were octogenarians in
gold sequined dresses mixing and handing out drinks like it was
a Palm Springs retirement home, with real flamingos weaving in
between the guests. The rented lighting was low and pink, and it
was somehow tacky enough that it made its way back to tasteful,
or at least it did once you knew it came from the mind of Charlie
McCloud.

For Lane, the best thing about a party being held in her honor
was that she didn't have to say anything witty or brilliant for people to be impressed with her. Throughout the night, Charlie
would direct her toward groups of people he thought she should
meet, and he would talk her up as if she was the only person in
the world they needed to know. All she had to do was humbly
object to his praise and they became the most charming double
act. It was a relief to yield to Charlie's natural charisma, and she
felt the other guests' warmth and respect for him radiate onto
her too.

For a long time, Lane had felt as if her day-to-day persona didn't match that of the woman who wrote the award-winning essays and articles, and that she was something of a disappointment in the flesh—too diminutive, too tightly coiled. Until this novel, she had never doubted her ability to write, but it was almost as if her brain was wired to do only that one thing well, and, unless she was furious, she found it nearly impossible to be as verbally articulate as she wanted to be. It was the thing that had impressed her about Gala, that she seemed to be able to access her wit at the exact moment she needed it, unlike Lane, for whom the perfect line would only materialize months later, once it had snuck its way into her writing. It was also the thing that drew Lane to Charlie—charming and quick-minded as he was, the fact that he could see past her flaws and find someone worth loving and celebrating made her feel worthy for possibly the first time in her life.

IT WAS MIDNIGHT, and Charlie was high on something, Lane didn't know what, and he had put on some peach sunglasses in an attempt to disguise it, but he was also now nuzzling her neck in a way that felt both nice and troublingly out of character.

All night, a younger man with masses of dark curls and a permanently unlit cigarette hanging out of his lips had been shadowing Charlie, and even though they hadn't uttered a word to each other, Lane could tell something was wrong from the way Charlie was both refusing to look at him and drinking faster than she'd ever seen him drink. When Charlie's sentences eventually stopped making sense, she led him to a quiet corner of the party and sat him down on a tiled bench. He drank the bottle of sparkling water she gave him, and she waited awhile for the buzz to wear off.

When his leg stopped jittering and he'd taken off the sunglasses, she looked up at him.

"Hey, Charlie," she said softly. "Who's the guy?"

"Oh," Charlie said, slurring less now as he tried to sound dismissive. "Just someone I used to know."

"He's been following you around all night."

"I know," Charlie said, turning away from her slightly.

"You seem sad," Lane said.

Charlie shrugged.

"Are you lonely?" she asked.

"Are you?"

Lane shrugged. "I don't know how not to be."

There was a pause of gentle understanding as Charlie met her eye.

"I liked him," he said quietly. "But he's not worth losing everything over."

Lane wondered if there was anything she could say to make him feel better but knew any words would just be empty platitudes. Nobody was worth risking this perfectly starry slice of the world he'd built for himself, however tempting. Lane realized then that perhaps she'd been asking herself the wrong question about Charlie since their first dinner at Dan Tana's—perhaps it wasn't so much what he had seen in her that formed the foundation of their friendship, but rather what he hadn't seen. Some shared deficiency that drove them both to each other. Instead of saying anything, she reached out and squeezed his hand as their party continued without them.

THE MAN'S NAME was Elijah Jones, and he was one of the junior studio engineers at Sunset Sound. Charlie had crashed into him in the lobby of the National offices, and had been instantly struck by the younger man's good humor and charm, as well as his perfectly sculpted calf muscles as he bent down to pick up the briefcase Charlie had dropped. In a move that was unprecedented for him, Charlie had hunted Elijah down through his place of work, pretending he had a personal item, a wallet, to return. When they eventually met at a coffee place on Wilshire, Elijah arriving in a pair of tight-fitting jeans that made Charlie's heart stop in his chest, the younger man had seemed quietly bemused by Charlie's efforts, and didn't seem to believe him when he said that he'd never done anything like it before. What Charlie didn't mention that day was that he generally met his sexual partners only at night, and that they would almost always part before the sun rose. It felt cleaner that way, since nothing genuine could progress while Charlie had the job he held—while his was an industry in which his sexuality could be something of an open secret, nobody would want an *outed* head of publicity working for them. It would prove that Charlie couldn't even handle his own secrets, let alone anyone else's.

Elijah lived farther east than Charlie usually ventured (nearly in Chinatown), and he frequented the bars in Silver Lake that were aimed toward people less refined than the men Charlie usually met: working-class homosexuals, if Charlie was to be frank about it. But Elijah was razor-sharp, and engaged in the gay scene in a way that none of Charlie's other friends were, or maybe they just didn't bother mentioning it to Charlie. He felt like a bourgeois troglodyte whenever Elijah brought up the significance of the upcoming gubernatorial election (Charlie never quite got around to mentioning that his parents were significant Reagan donors), or his friend who was writing a play about civil rights activist Harry

Hay that would (inexplicably to Charlie) be shown in a secret stage under a grocery store in Koreatown.

The last time they'd seen each other, Charlie had tried to explain to Elijah that he simply didn't have as much to prove as Elijah—his own parents had been aware of his sexuality since he was in his late teens and, while it was never discussed, it was implicitly accepted as an unassailable fact, whereas Elijah's mother had paid for his bus ticket out of Virginia to avoid tarnishing the family reputation after she caught him pining after his football teammate. Elijah had listened carefully, his hand gently stroking Charlie's bare thigh as they lay in his colossal bed, gazing out the window at the glittering houses below. The stroking was both arousing and patronizing, and Charlie tried not to get too wound up either way.

"But, Charles," Elijah said softly. "There's no freedom in secrecy. Whatever they say, your parents are still putting caveats on what your life can look like. How would they act if you brought me home for Christmas?"

"This is our third fuck," Charlie said dryly. "Frankly, it feels a little soon."

Elijah smiled but said nothing. Charlie sighed and squeezed his eyes shut.

"It's not that I couldn't," he said. "It's that I wouldn't. Out of respect."

Elijah's hand stopped moving, but he didn't lift it from Charlie's leg.

"Respect for what?" he asked quietly.

"Respect for Eleanor Roosevelt, Elijah, I don't know," Charlie snapped. "What does it matter? My father is attorney general of California, and your mother won't even look at you, so how's your freedom working out for you?"

Elijah slowly lifted his hand from Charlie's thigh. After a moment, he turned over, pulling the duvet to his chest. In the darkness, Charlie willed himself to say something to fix the situation (he already knew from experience that Elijah forgave easily) but he was too wound up. *Respect for what?* he wondered, even as he prayed this wouldn't be the last time he woke up to Elijah next to him.

LANE WAS ABOUT to leave the party when she heard someone shout Gala's name from the other side of the courtyard. She hadn't seen Gala all night, but now there she was, at the top of the steps leading down to the garden. She was wearing a burnt-orange minidress with an embellished collar and appeared to be wobbling precariously in her silver platform boots. A few steps below her, Lane recognized the furiously tight leather pants of Belle Vue drummer turned national sex symbol, Gabriel Ford, as he tried (and failed) to reach out to Gala. A small crowd had formed at the bottom of the stairs to watch the action unfold.

"Don't insult my intelligence," Gala roared, her entire body radiating fury. "And don't you *dare* touch me."

"Gala," Gabriel said, his voice cracking slightly. "Let's just go home."

"I know where *my* home is," Gala said slowly. "But why don't you ask Jessie or April where yours might be tonight?"

"Gala," Gabriel pleaded again. "*Please.*"

Gala let out a furious shriek that made Gabriel move two steps farther down. Lane had a better view of him now, and she could see the film of sweat that coated his pale skin and the telltale unnatural claw of his right hand that indicated overconsumption of uppers. He looked a lifetime away from the clear-eyed kid she'd met at the Troubadour only seven months ago, and any lingering regret Lane may have been feeling about their aborted connection fizzled away into sweet relief.

"Gala?" Lane called. "Is everything okay?"

Gala's eyes landed on Lane.

"You," she said. "Of course."

Then the crowd watched as Gala turned and bolted inside the house.

It took Lane twenty minutes to find Gala, who was in the en suite of a first-floor guest room, overlooking the front of the house. The room was papered in a dizzying toucan print that also adorned the carpet and curtains of the bedroom, and Gala was sitting on the floor, her head resting on top of the closed toilet. When Lane cleared her throat, Gala opened an eye and then let out a small groan.

"Perfect," she muttered. "Come on in."

Lane closed the door gently behind her and approached Gala tentatively. There was a heavy stench of vomit in the air, and Gala's skin looked damp and green, her dark eye makeup pooling underneath her eyes like bruises.

"How . . . unusual," Lane said when she noticed the gold toilet handle shaped like a cherub.

"It's hideous," Gala said. "You can just say it's hideous."

Lane smiled, but then Gala started retching. She opened the lid of the toilet and spat in it a couple of times. Lane tried not to grimace. She wasn't sure if Gala was drunk or high, but she figured Gala was better off with whatever she'd taken flushed out of her system.

"Where's Gabriel?"

"Who cares," Gala growled.

"He cheated on you?"

"It's never been like that with us," Gala said, but she sounded like even she may not have believed that anymore.

"Did he hurt you?" Lane asked, pointing at the red marks on Gala's forearm.

"Oh, honey," Gala said. "Gabriel wouldn't know how to hurt me."

Lane paused before clearing her throat.

"I'm not . . . bitter about you taking him," she said. "Just so you know."

"I don't know what you're talking about," Gala said.

Lane didn't know how to respond, and eventually Gala exhaled wearily.

"Gabriel discovered the dual delights of drugs and teenage girls on tour," she said flatly. "Which should have come as no surprise to anyone, but especially not me."

"Were you exclusive?"

Gala raised a withering eyebrow.

"You think that would have changed anything? Look, I've fucked enough rock stars to know how this story goes, but . . ." Gala broke off before shrugging. "I just didn't know he was a rock star when I met him."

"Charlie says fame never improves anyone," Lane said.

"Charlie has no heart," Gala said, but it was without her usual fervor. After another pause, she sighed. "I actually think I'd be an excellent famous person. If only I'd been born rich."

"Not all famous people are wealthy," Lane said.

"Yeah, but the ones who are famous for doing nothing are," Gala said. "And if they're poor and well-known, they're usually infamous. Which is a very different thing."

Lane was thinking about this when Gala threw up again, the sound of vomit hitting the basin loud and violent.

"You know if you flush as you vomit, it's a little more manageable," Lane said.

Gala lifted her sweaty head and glared at her.

"What's wrong with you?" Lane asked, trying not to flinch as Gala wiped her mouth.

"I ate some bad shrimp," Gala said after a long pause, her voice hoarse.

"Bad shrimp," Lane repeated so slowly that Gala glanced up again, her expression now challenging. Now that Lane thought about it, Gala didn't seem inebriated at all. And from the little she knew of Gala, it seemed pretty out of character for her to have exploded at Gabriel like she did, and in front of everyone; she was far too cool for any of that, or at least she pretended to be. No, Lane had a feeling she knew what was up with Gala, and a strange compulsion to comfort this prickly woman whom she barely knew came over Lane.

"You know, I had some bad shrimp once," she said quietly.

Gala lifted her head long enough to squint at Lane.

"What?"

"I had some bad shrimp, but I found someone to help me handle it."

Gala still just gawped at her in response and Lane tried once more.

"There are doctors who are . . . willing to point you in the right direction," she said, more firmly now.

"Just so we're clear here—*you* had an abortion?" Gala asked.

"Sorry, did you assume I was a virgin?" Lane asked dryly, even as she felt the familiar tangle of emotions at hearing the word *abortion*. The tangle that never started with shame but often ended up there anyway. The tangle that almost always started with gratitude, not that she'd ever tell anyone that part.

"Not a virgin," Gala said, too surprised to play along. "But I never would have thought you'd have done something so interesting."

Lane frowned. She wasn't sure what she'd expected from the first person she'd ever told, but it probably wasn't this.

"It didn't feel interesting at the time," she said. "It felt like the most uninteresting thing in the world."

Gala opened her mouth to speak, but Lane cut her off. "Look, I don't want to talk about it but I'm just saying, there are ways you can deal with this. Gabriel doesn't even have to know."

Gala stared at her.

"Lane, I really appreciate you opening up to me, but honestly? I just ate some rotten fucking shrimp."

Lane felt her cheeks go hot until Gala grinned at her, and soon they were both laughing, and somehow, for Lane, the laughter made more sense than anything had in a long while. On the surface, Gala was everything Lane wasn't—flippant, silly, frivolous, seemingly motivated by only the basest of desires, and yet there was something about her that intrigued Lane. She suspected that underneath the shimmering swaths of sequins lay someone infinitely more complex.

When Gala was well enough to stand, Lane helped her out of the bathroom, careful not to grip her too tightly.

NINE

THEN

JULY 1966

The next morning was unrelentingly hot, and so dry Lane felt as if the skin on her face could crack as she walked along the uneven pavement, periodically checking the address written on the piece of paper in her hand as if it were about to change. She had predicted the walk to be around fifteen minutes but it was already closer to thirty, and she was somehow still traipsing north up Laurel Avenue. It was something that always surprised her about her new home, how despite its clean grid system from the sky, it was mostly hellish to navigate on foot.

The apartment buildings Lane passed were architecturally diverse, some stucco blocks with prison-style windows, others (like Gala's) with Spanish accents and birds-of-paradise blooming outside. As Lane approached Gala's block, a tall man with wavy chestnut hair was leaving, and Lane ran a few steps to make it through the gate he held open for her. As she smiled her thanks, she noticed the book tucked under his arm: *Herzog* by Saul Bellow.

"At this time he had no messages for anyone. Nothing. Not a single word," she said, and he stopped, looking mildly amused.

"Excuse me?"

"It's the final line in the book," she said.

He put his head to one side, his brown eyes gently teasing. When he smiled, Lane could see almost every perfect tooth in his head.

"Well, I guess you just saved me a few hours," he said. "Lunch?"

After a moment, Lane smiled uncertainly back at him.

"I'm Lane," she said, sticking out her hand for him to shake.

"Oh, I know," he said, not in the least embarrassed. "I'm a fan of yours. Lane Warren—skewerer of powerful miscreants turned ruiner of *New York Times* bestsellers."

"I really didn't ruin it," she said. "I didn't even tell you about Herzog's homicidal tendencies that led to this epiphany."

The man threw his head back and laughed loudly, and there was something comforting about his confidence. It was almost like how Lane felt around Charlie, although this stranger's charm felt less otherworldly and more steady. He was good-looking too, in a wholesome RFK way.

"Are you here to see Gala?" he asked curiously.

"I am," she said.

"You're about four hours too early," he said, checking his watch. "I've rarely seen her emerge before two p.m."

Lane wondered then if Gala had slept with this person, and found she didn't feel jealous so much as intrigued.

"I'll try my luck," Lane said, glancing down at the bag in her hand. "I brought Canters chicken soup."

"A shrewd move," he said. "You must want something from her, although I can't think what."

The man's tone was almost dismissive here, and Lane noted

that the men of Hollywood were just as quick to put Gala down as they were to sleep with her. She glanced back down at the piece of paper in her hand. She was looking for unit 4.

"Well, it was good to meet you . . ." she said politely.

"Scott," the man said, smiling more ruefully now. "Scotty Ryan."

Lane nodded at him and then scanned the units in front of her.

"Far left," Scotty said as he turned away. "And tell Gala I said *Guten Morgen*."

Lane nodded, and just before she was about to leave, he reached out and touched her arm gently.

"Lane," he said, his eyes looking into hers with a calm intensity she felt deep in her stomach. "Let me know if you change your mind on that lunch."

TO LANE'S RELIEF, Gala was fully clothed and notably less green around the gills when she opened the door, her feet bare and her wet hair leaving damp patches on the shoulders of her white T-shirt.

"I didn't think you'd actually come," she said grumpily, despite being the one who gave Lane her address.

"Chicken soup. All the way from Canters."

Gala peered inside the bag suspiciously and, when she saw that Lane wasn't lying, stepped aside to let her inside.

The first thing Lane noticed about Gala's apartment was the glorious squalor. The salmon-pink walls were cracked and peeling but covered in colorful doodles, and the interior was a clumsy mishmash of eras, giving the overall impression of a particularly indiscriminate thrift store. The second thing Lane noticed was the books. Floor-to-ceiling shelves lined two of the four walls in the living room, and almost every other surface was topped with precariously balanced piles of books, most with multiple book-marks or pages folded down, some disfigured from having been dropped in the bath or—more likely in L.A.—pool. Books cover-ing a range of genres and subjects, fiction and nonfiction, all of them seemingly well-handled if not read. From where Lane stood, she could reach out and touch a copy of both *The Group* and *The Rise and Fall of the Third Reich*.

"Huh," Lane said. "You can read."

Gala laughed and walked into the kitchenette. Lane followed her, stopping only to glance at the open book on the sofa. They both had the same issue of *We Have Always Lived in the Castle* by Shirley Jackson. It was one of Lane's favorites.

"I met your neighbor," Lane said, unsure why she felt the need to bring him up so soon.

"Vikrim?" Gala asked, looking puzzled.

"Scotty," Lane said, trying to ascertain if she felt anything when she said his name out loud.

"Oh. I call him the overlord because he knocked two units into one," Gala said. "He's the only non-renter here."

"What's his story?" Lane asked, wincing as the words left her mouth because they were so conspicuous, so plainly an attempt to play it cool.

"His story?" Gala repeated. "His story is that he's as emotion-ally repressed as every other man in town and he built himself a *gallery* that either looks like a giant penis or a prison, depending on where you're standing."

Lane raised an eyebrow and gave up on asking any more about Scotty Ryan.

"How are you feeling?" Lane asked, and Gala waved her hand.

"A little better," she said.

"And Gabriel?" Lane prompted. "Where is he?"

"Fuck knows," Gala said, her voice level as she took two bowls from the drainboard next to the sink.

"I've already eaten," Lane said as Gala sloshed half the container's contents into each bowl.

"I'm not eating alone," Gala said, and she carried the bowls over to a white plastic table that reminded Lane of the ones at the farmers' market.

"I'm actually not much of a host," Gala said wryly as she handed Lane a spoon and plonked a roll of toilet paper down on the table between them. "I don't know if that surprises you."

Lane smiled and tore off some toilet paper as nonjudgmentally as she could, which was hard when it was already a little damp. Her bowl had a chip the size of a nickel, which she pretended not to notice.

"I prefer going to parties than hosting them," Lane said. Then, when Gala didn't respond, she added, "At home you're too close to all the things you do when you're alone, only ever an inch away from an embarrassing reminder of your own *ordinariness*, but at a party? You can pretend to be whoever you want."

Gala frowned as she took a loud slurp of her soup.

"I've never thought of myself as ordinary," Gala said eventually, more curiously than unkindly, as she wiped at a trail of soup dribbling down her chin.

"Of course you haven't," Lane said, and she took a sip of her own soup, painfully aware of how careful she was in contrast to Gala, dabbing her mouth discreetly with the toilet paper after each controlled sip. When she looked up, Gala was watching her.

"I can't get pregnant," Gala said simply. "A birth defect. Not that I'd want to. Anyway, a fortune teller told me I was going to die before I'm thirty-six, so it's for the best. But I still appreciate what you thought you were doing last night."

Lane frowned, but found that she didn't feel shame, or regret, or any of the things she might have expected. She didn't even feel sorry for Gala, because she didn't think the other woman was open to it. She wondered what it would feel like to like yourself so much that you never questioned a thing that happened to make you that way.

"You're welcome," Lane said.

The two women ate their soup in silence for a while.

"You're going to die before you're thirty-six?" Lane asked eventually.

"Oh, I've made my peace with it," Gala said, almost gleefully. "There's something sort of chic about dying young, isn't there?"

Lane didn't think there was anything chic about dying young at all.

The women went back to their soup.

"Was it in New York?" Gala asked eventually, and Lane knew what she was asking about. She wiped her mouth and nodded.

"Was he married?"

After a moment, Lane nodded again. "How did you know?"

Gala shrugged. "You're not the only one who's good at reading people."

Lane felt a rush of discomfort even as she asked, "And what's your read on me?"

Gala assessed Lane, then shrugged and leaned back in her chair.

"You come across as uptight and controlled, but I think you're hiding most of yourself," she said. "You don't want to reveal too much, because you've scared yourself in the past and anytime you've let your guard down, you've been hurt. So you diet and dress like a Midwestern mom with a mild eating disorder, and you spend most of your time hiding away working, and you go to parties and impress just enough so that people remember you, but you never leave much of a mark. But not because you don't know how, only because you don't want to risk being marked yourself."

Gala sat back on her chair, her face filled with a smug self-satisfaction that Lane knew she could despise if she wanted to. But, for reasons she couldn't entirely explain, she didn't want to. There was something surprising about this woman, which was why she found herself doing what she did next, which was to lay down her spoon on the table and clear her throat.

"Are you working at the moment?" Lane asked.

Gala squinted. "Working?"

Lane nodded.

"I do odd jobs," Gala said slowly. "I make dog bandannas and crystal key rings for friends. I also painted a mural outside this new surf shop in—"

Lane had stopped listening after dog bandannas.

"Gala," she said, interrupting. "If I drop my manuscript over later, will you read it?"

Gala stopped. "You want me to read your book?"

Lane nodded. "If you don't mind."

Gala frowned.

"Why me?" she asked curiously.

"People underestimate you," Lane said. "But you're a writer, aren't you?"

Gala laughed. "I famously got a worse grade in English than the French exchange student," she drawled, but Lane's gaze just got even more intense. There were a few things Lane would joke about, but writing wasn't one of them.

"You need to take yourself seriously, or no one else ever will," Lane said.

"Taken seriously by whom, exactly?" Gala asked slowly. "Old establishment men with zero sense of humor? Believe it or not, I'm not actually trying to impress anyone, not even you."

"The first time we met, you were telling a story to a crowd of drunk people," Lane said, leaning forward, "And it was all there— the setup and the payoff, the humor and absurdity. You already have the instincts of a writer, even if you don't know it yet. And you clearly have the desire to be seen, however much you want to deny it."

Gala looked away for a moment, watching as the sun streamed through the window. And then a small smile formed on her lips.

"Okay," Gala said.

"Great," Lane said.

The two women went back to eating their soup, both lost in their own thoughts. Then Lane looked up again.

"Sorry—*what's* your problem with the way I dress?"

TEN

THEN

AUGUST 1966

Johnny Carson was riffing loudly on Gala's TV set, but for once she wasn't listening. Since finishing Lane's book a week earlier, she had been experiencing unfamiliar waves of uncertainty over what to say to Lane. It was rare for Gala to encounter a quandary like this—usually she had to ask herself no more than two questions before she had her answer. (She often joked that these were *Do I want to?* closely followed by *Will it kill me?*) This, however, felt infinitely more complex. Lane had already come by twice in the past two weeks, and Gala had pretended to be out.

Gala had initially been thrilled when Lane asked her to read her manuscript. She was well aware of her own creative value even if, up until this point, it had been only men who believed Gala could make them brilliant. However, the novelty had quickly worn off, and the gesture had begun to feel more like a curse than anything else when she understood exactly what it entailed: Gala simultaneously knew that she herself would never create anything half as good as Lane's novel, and exactly what Lane needed to do to make it truly brilliant.

Lane's novel was about a young woman (a thinly disguised Lane, Gala assumed) working as a writer in New York, and who, throughout the course of one summer, came to terms with the loneliness of her singular brilliance. The problem was that Lane seemed to want the crux of the book to be the woman's affair (and abortion) with a tortured, married (*and rather dull-sounding*) film director, when it was really a wry meditation on the loneliness of being a "brilliant" woman. The book had beautiful passages philosophizing about monogamy and how domesticity could become appealing only once it was all but unobtainable, and Lane's writing was already excellent when showcasing the character's intellectual and cultural coming of age, but Gala felt it was missing something. She didn't doubt that Lane had the ability to fix it, she just knew it would involve Lane excavating something of herself in the process, something she was clearly hell-bent on avoiding.

In the end, when Lane stopped by again, with even more soup (at this point Gala didn't have the heart to tell Lane that, despite being Jewish, she didn't like chicken soup), Gala reluctantly let her in and paced up and down the living room while Lane sat on the sofa like a schoolchild awaiting her fate.

"You're avoiding something," Gala blurted. "And the reader can feel it."

Lane frowned and crossed and uncrossed her legs.

"It's *my* invention," she said eventually. "How is that possible?"

"You write about this woman's relationship with the director, but you never explain why it means so much to her," Gala started slowly. "You mention that she craves instability, but you never say where she learned it. In starting your character's story at the moment she arrives in New York, you're making it impossible for anyone to ever know her. Or maybe the problem is that you don't want them to. You haven't even given her a *name*, Lane, come on."

Lane pushed her hair behind her ears as she listened, a growing irritation visible on her face.

"The novel is a snapshot of a moment," she said in an imperious tone. "It's meant to feel disorientating and sudden, like a New York summer."

"Look, I can hardly bear to be in New York for longer than thirty-six hours, but isn't the winter what gives the summer context?" Gala shot back. "Otherwise just set it in L.A."

Lane rolled her eyes in a way that pissed Gala off. Maybe she should have trusted her instincts about Lane—how entitled to not have even *thanked* Gala for taking the time to read her 270-page book, not to mention for having worried about it for two weeks straight before giving her a note that would transform the entire fucking thing, taking it from head to heart in a way it badly needed. And obviously Lane knew it wasn't good enough—why else would she have given it to Gala to read before sending it to her editor? No, the more she thought about it, the more annoyed Gala felt. This person had practically *stalked* her way into Gala's life, spilling her depressing secrets and stealing her friends, and what was Gala getting in return? Cold chicken soup she didn't want?

"Listen . . . I have a date I need to get ready for . . ."

"Sorry," Lane said, still frowning and making no move to leave. "But, just to be clear—what you're saying is you want me to spell out this character's backstory so you can make a direct link from her past to her present, her trauma to her perversions?"

"No," Gala said, exhaling. "But I'd like to know what's at stake.

And if you don't want to write about where she's from, that's okay, but it needs to be a deliberate choice you've made for the benefit of the story, not because you're scared to find out yourself."

"And what if her past has nothing to do with this story?"

"Then maybe you need a new protagonist," Gala said.

Lane's cheeks were flushed, and she leveled her withering gaze onto Gala.

"You think that's the only way readers will want me? What does that say about your opinion of women? That we're built for consumption? Sontag has certainly never had to do that shit."

"Sontag's never written a novel about a woman," Gala shot back. "And you can argue all you want that there shouldn't be a difference, but I'm telling you that this book is missing something, and it's a sense of where this woman came from. It's the first time her mom took her for a Shirley Temple, the first time she drove around listening to her favorite song. Her first crush, the first band she saw live. It's a *childhood*, Lane."

"And what if she never had any of those things?" Lane asked. "What if it wasn't the moments that shaped her, but all the ones she missed? What happens then?"

"Then that needs to go in too," Gala said softly.

For a moment, Gala worried that Lane was about to burst into tears. Instead, she watched as Lane closed her eyes and sunk the nail of her right index finger into her left wrist like a brand. Gala looked away.

"You skim over this woman's abortion without ever actually writing about it," Gala said, her voice even softer now. "Again, it's this giant ellipsis. This thing that happens that completely changes the course of this woman's summer, and her life, and yet you refuse to engage with it in any real way. Lane . . . if you're as unwilling to separate yourself from this story as you seem to be, you need to at least commit to it. Everyone has a past, even if they wish it were someone else's."

Lane opened her mouth as if to argue again, but Gala pushed the manuscript across the coffee table toward her. "You asked for my opinion, and I'm giving it. It doesn't mean you have to take it." She shrugged. "But I'm going to take a wild guess that you're willing to sell out anyone in your life for your work except yourself."

For a few seconds, Lane looked like she wanted to throw something at Gala. Then she took a few deep breaths before glancing at the manuscript between them and forcing a small, gracious smile.

"I assumed you'd tell me it needed either more drugs or more fucking."

Gala laughed. "Oh, honey, *obviously* it could do with more of both, but it's also you all over—uptight, a little moralistic. But funny. We'll save the juicy stuff for my future book."

Lane offered Gala another smile as she gathered up the manuscript and stood. She walked toward the door and Gala followed her.

"Thank you," Lane said, and Gala waved her hand.

"It was nothing," she said. "Or this part was hell, but I liked reading it."

Lane smiled and opened the door.

"Maybe you should do it, you know," she said graciously. "Gala Margolis's opus on the pleasure principle."

"Wow," Gala said, widening her eyes. "It turns out you really can make anything boring."

LANE STOPPED BY Villa Mia on her way home. As she pushed her pistachio ice cream around the bowl, she felt the weight of her manuscript in the bag on her lap and only just resisted depositing it into the trash can on the other side of the bar. She felt almost recklessly unspooled by her conversation with Gala.

She wanted to believe that Gala was wrong, that Lane and her protagonist weren't like everyone else, that some women *could* create a new, sublime life out of thin air, free from the limitations of their past and people they'd loved who had only ever hurt them. Back in Gala's apartment, it had been easier to tell herself that Gala would never understand, because she would never be brilliant, and that Lane had made a mistake sharing her pages with someone who didn't even take herself seriously. Someone with soup dribbling down her chin and feet with dirty soles, and who had slept with half of L.A., and who used toilet paper instead of napkins when guests were over *for god's sake*. Only, now that she had left, Lane had a dizzying feeling that Gala was right. For once, Lane hadn't been as clever as she thought she'd been.

ON THE RARE occasions she allowed herself to think about her childhood, Lane remembered mostly the silence. Her family home, a vast Queen Anne Victorian in Phoenix, had its own sounds, of course—the sharp creak of the floorboard directly outside her bedroom, the hiss of the kitchen stove catching fire—but the TV set was rarely on, and there was never any conversation filtering down the hallway, let alone music. In fact, most days, nobody was home at all except for Lane, who would make herself a tuna salad sandwich before spending her evenings inventing elaborate stories about orphans and runaways in notepads she'd stolen from school.

Lane's father, Frank, was a successful man—the owner of a beloved independent department store in Phoenix. Handsome in a beady, avian way, he was prone to emotional outbursts and the occasional cruel revelation, which he would try desperately to take back only once it was too late. Lane thought that, in different circumstances, he might have been a kind man, a good father. But like her, he was mostly a bystander in his own life—it was Lane's mother, Alys, who dictated the weather pattern in their home.

Lane's mother was A Difficult Woman. This was a phrase Lane heard repeated often, mainly from friends of her father or other parents at school. It was always said with an air of knowing, as if everyone except Lane understood exactly what this was shorthand for. All Lane really knew was that sometimes her mom took her to church every day for a week, and other times she stumbled home with strange men, and that she'd never once let on that she liked Lane, let alone loved her. When she was very young, Alys had tried to do the things a mother was supposed to do, but even then Lane had known she was pretending—a cigarette in hand and cool gray eyes remote as Lane played cautiously in a sandbox, pretending to be like the other kids even as she tracked her mother's every move. Later, she'd think that her mother had always had one eye on the exit, planning her escape.

When Lane was eight, her father let slip that Alys had her first nervous breakdown shortly after giving birth to Lane. From that moment on, Lane had understood that her mother was trapped in the purple house like a rat in a cage. Trapped in her marriage. Trapped in her part-time job at the store. But most of all, trapped by Lane. That night, after a particularly searing fight with Frank, Alys had torn through the liquor cabinet before lying on the carpet next to Lane's bed, black hair fanning out beneath her and limbs slack. Lane had listened closely, heart beating hard in her chest as Alys told her how, at nineteen, she'd planned to move to

New York City to become an illustrator, even had a letter of encouragement from *Vogue*'s favorite artist, Carl Erickson, to prove her talent, but that she'd gotten pregnant before she ever made it. The word *pregnant* was uttered with both awe and fury, confirming what Lane had always known—without Lane, Alys could have done anything she wanted. Lane memorized her mother's lost dreams like a prayer.

As Phoenix exploded after the end of the war, bigger and better department stores opened up in the city, causing the family business to sell its final handbag on Lane's ninth birthday. Soon, Lane couldn't remember a time when her dad hadn't been drinking in the morning, or her mom wasn't slurring through Lane's parent-teacher conference because of whatever new medication she was taking to help her tolerate being alive. She took a blend of downers she'd stashed over the years, and she'd mix them with alcohol until she became someone Lane barely recognized as her mother. Occasionally, when it was raining, Alys would cup Lane's chin in her hands and tell her she would try to be better, but they both knew by then that she was incapable of it. Even on her best days, she would flinch when Lane reached out for her.

So, no—there were no Shirley Temples to speak of, no first cars or first dances, no first crushes, no best friends, and no first concerts. There were no family portraits, no pets, no favorite TV shows or trips to the movie theater. No school plays or ballet classes, no conversations that weren't engineered solely to catch someone in a lie, no surprise picnics on the living room floor, no visiting friends and family to break up the endless summers, no flowers in the vase on the kitchen table. No kisses on the head before bed, no birthdays that didn't descend into vitriol or violence.

There was only Lane coming home from school to a house

that had been left unlocked all day, and the two adults who rarely remembered she was there. There was only her mother's back in her favorite crepe de chine blue dress, the hem as mottled as a moth's wings, and her father's face, crumpled in grief for the life he once thought he'd have.

Until, suddenly, it was only Lane left anyway.

FOR THE NEXT three weeks, Lane cut herself off from everyone in her orbit, even Charlie. She edited from sunrise to midnight, eating and drinking only when she remembered to, and she would break the writing spell only to call Gala. The truth was that Lane felt entirely weightless in these days, surrounded by the ghosts of her past as if she were tethered to the real world by only the lightest gossamer thread. And she came to rely on Gala's voice to bring her back to earth.

ELEVEN

THEN

JANUARY 1967

Gala pulled the radio plug out of the wall socket, and only just resisted throwing the entire thing across her living room. As hard as she tried, six months on from their breakup, it was impossible for her to escape Gabriel.

Belle Vue's dumb second single, "Talk Nothing to Me," was on every radio station in L.A., occasionally played twice in the same hour to satisfy "listener demand," and their debut record had been at the top of the *Billboard* album charts for the past five weeks. Gabriel had made the national news twice—once when he was arrested for indecent exposure at a county fair in North Carolina (he'd ridden a champion horse naked), and then again after accidentally setting himself alight onstage. Gala avoided actively seeking out information about her ex or the band she'd helped shape, but she often caught snippets about both from either a drunk acquaintance or a stranger in the Barney's Beanery restroom. And the news that Gabriel was driving a brand-new Lamborghini through the heart of the country while she was hopelessly behind on her rent made everything sting all the more.

Gala was lighting a cigarette when Lane rang, and she held the phone in between her shoulder and ear as she nudged the front door open with her foot so that she could blow the smoke outside. Lane still didn't know much about Gala's history with Gabriel, and Gala made sure her tone was light as cotton candy when she asked Lane how she had been, as if Gala hadn't just heard the jaunty lyrics to a song she once thought was written about her.

"I did it," Lane said, her voice uncharacteristically loose. "I mailed the book to Esther."

"About time," Gala said, smiling even though Lane couldn't see her. "How long until you hear back?"

"It depends," Lane said. "Soon if Esther likes it."

Gala nodded and exhaled a stream of smoke.

"How are you going to celebrate? Two cans of club soda instead of one? A whole carrot?"

"Thanks, Gala," Lane said witheringly. Then: "I was actually thinking we could go for dinner. If you don't have plans."

Gala considered this. She and Lane had spoken often over the past six months, and Lane had dropped pages off for Gala to read every Monday morning (Gala rarely offered feedback on the writing but knew this handover was an integral part of Lane's process), but they didn't socialize outside of this. Gala presumed that Lane saw her as some sort of book medium (although Lane would never have used that word), but Gala was learning from Lane too. From observing Lane churn out word after word, Gala learned how someone could coax even their worst fears out into the light, day after day. And even Gala had to admit there was a certain beauty to Lane's single-minded ability to drag herself through hell for the thing she wanted most in the world.

From reading Lane's new pages, Gala also understood why Lane had been reluctant to probe that wound. It seemed that, even before the deaths of her parents, Lane's childhood had been almost Dickensian in its emotional scarcity. Gala's own family home in Hollywood had been filled with the crackling static of an old 78 and rigorous debates about art and magic and music. There was never enough money, but there were visits from eccentric aunts who smelled like lavender, and parties with guests like Billy Wilder and Olivia de Havilland and her father's favorite me-chanic, Frankie. The protagonist in Lane's book (now named P, which was better than nothing, although still not a name exactly), lived in a creepy purple house that seemed to be filled only with crushing silence and resentment. No wonder Lane seemed so at-tached to her identity as a writer—if her life was anything like P's, she had no safety net of unconditional love, no existing foun-dation at all to return to when she was alone.

Still, Gala knew that Lane wouldn't want to be pitied, and Gala didn't exactly. Perhaps she just understood her a little more. Which was why they rarely spoke about Lane's new pages during their phone calls. Instead, Lane would call at eight every other evening, her voice shaking only slightly, and Gala would stop whatever it was she was doing and she'd fill Lane in on all the gossip—who had stolen whose drugs, who had gotten a little too political and was being edged out by the group, who secretly came from oil money—and she would hear Lane's voice gradually re-turn to normal as she reacted to the stories with her perfectly Lane-*esque* incisive remarks. Lane never explicitly thanked Gala for the phone calls, in the same way that Gala never told Lane that they had become a welcome distraction for her too, from any thoughts of Gabriel.

"Dinner," Gala repeated. "Are you paying?"

Lane laughed. "Sure."

"Musso and Frank then," Gala said cheerfully. "I'm craving a bloody steak."

GALA WAS WRAPPED in a black bath towel and was brushing her wet hair in the mirror when she heard a knock at the door. Briefly, she wondered if it could be her neighbor Scotty. She'd bumped into him earlier on her way out for lunch, and Gala had flashed him a big smile, running her tongue across her teeth as he held open the gate for her, but perfect Scotty had still just offered her his usual robotic greeting. She would have assumed he was gay, if she hadn't met his ex-girlfriend a few years back—a beautiful war photographer with the longest legs Gala had ever seen. Still, Gala thought now, as she made her way to the front door, maybe that tongue flick had done the job and Scotty had finally seen the light.

Gala opened the door and felt her heart flip in her chest. Behind a brilliant bunch of purple roses (her favorites) stood not Scotty, but Gabriel. His cheeks were hollow, his violet eyes agitated and wild. He thrust the flowers at Gala almost apologetically, and then he ran his hand through his dirty blond hair as he opened his mouth and closed it again. Gala gripped the stems and held the flowers between them, as if she might shield herself from his magnitude.

"Gala," he said, and his voice was hoarse with something that could have been longing, but that Gala interpreted as tour flu

(also known as snorting absurd amounts of cocaine). The last
time they'd seen each other, on the steps of Charlie McCloud's
aunt's mansion, Gabriel had told her he would never so much as
look at another woman if that's what she wanted. By then it was
too late though. Despite what he (and everyone else) thought, it
wasn't the fact that he'd been sleeping with other women that
concerned her so much as her own visceral response to finding
out about it. In that moment, she'd felt as if Gabriel had reached
inside her and gripped her heart in his hand, and the idea that
someone could have so much power over her made her feel unforgivably exposed.

As if he could read her mind, Gabriel reached out a hand to
her now, and Gala felt her heart leap in her chest, like it had been
asleep for the longest time. Gala swallowed, and then dropped the
flowers just as Gabriel scooped her into his arms.

LANE SAT AT the booth in Musso and Frank, her fingers resting
on the base of her empty martini glass. She had now finished her
second drink (which was really her fourth, because Musso and
Frank served martinis in a carafe that meant you were getting two
drinks in one), and Gala still wasn't here. Lane checked her
watch. It was 9:00 p.m., which made Gala an hour late. Lane
briefly considered whether she should worry about what happened to Gala, but she figured it would be a waste of her energy.
It could have been anything from a bad hair day to coming across
an injured cat on her way. People like Gala didn't care whom they
kept waiting.

Lane raised a hand to call over the waiter and was about to ask
for the check, when she changed her mind. She'd just finished the
most grueling writing exercise of her career, and while it may have

gutted her a thousand times over, she knew that what she'd sent to Esther was good. Maybe even brilliant. And she wouldn't let Gala's selfish behavior stop her from celebrating, even if it was alone.

"Filet mignon, please," she said to the waiter. "The bloodier the better."

WHEN GALA PHONED Lane the following morning to apologize for standing her up, Lane breezily told her not to worry about it.

"I lost track of time," Gala said, her voice as sheepish as it ever got.

"So you've mentioned," Lane said, refusing to ask why.

"I should have called the restaurant," Gala said.

There was a long silence, and Lane could hear Gala light a cigarette. She could picture that dumb gold cigarette case Gala probably spent a fortune on without ever thinking to check its provenance. Or maybe she got it for free, if free meant sleeping with its previous owner.

"I should get going," Lane said, her voice clipped. "Charlie's invited me to some Grammys brunch with him."

"Oh, how wonderful," Gala said, sounding relieved. "Have a glass of champagne or six for me."

Lane nodded and was about to hang up, when Gala spoke again.

"Lane? Congratulations. I'm proud of you."

There was another long silence.

"I couldn't have done it without you," Lane said eventually. And they both knew it was true.

TWELVE

NOW

SUMMER 1975

There is a knock at the bedroom door, and, when Lane doesn't move, Scotty growls and climbs out of bed. He treads across the whitewashed floorboards, and, while his back is to her, Lane allows herself to take in his naked form. Scotty is sinewy and fleshy in all the right places, and she's never stopped finding him attractive. That has never been their problem.

Scotty pulls on his bathrobe before opening the door. Dahlia is standing there holding a tray, and even though his back is to her, Lane can tell that her husband is trying not to laugh.

"Come in, girls," Lane says, sitting up in bed, and when Audrey rushes ahead of Dahlia, Scotty scoops her up and rests her on his hip. With a little bit of coaxing from her sister, Dahlia approaches with the tray, her cheeks already turning pink. Lane forces herself to look right at her daughter instead of glancing away to spare her shyness, because she knows all too well that allowing Dahlia to retreat into herself will only come back to bite her later on.

Dahlia places the tray at Lane's feet, and she understands why Scotty was trying not to laugh. On the tray is a piece of whole wheat toast, no butter; three halved strawberries; and a can of club soda. Next to the plate is a clump of daisies freshly picked from the garden, mud still attached. Lane looks up at her perfect daughters and her handsome husband and tries to feel what she knows she's supposed to feel in this moment—gratitude that they have built this together. That this sweet life is *hers*. Instead, she feels only a dull sense of panic.

This has never been what she wanted, and there is only one other person in the world who knew it. And she's nowhere to be found.

AN HOUR LATER, Lane sits down in her home office to write, like she has done every morning for the past few years. And, just like all those other L.A. days, her window is open, the humming-birds are thrumming, and the scent of eucalyptus is light in the air. Her desk is perfectly organized, with her prized vintage Royal Quiet Deluxe typewriter (Hemingway's preferred model) and a selection of notepads and pens to suit every whim, and every member of her family knows not to so much as touch the door while she's inside. Only today, Lane finds she can't construct even a single sentence that means anything.

AROUND LUNCHTIME, WHEN Lane is tracing the pattern of her old oak desk for the seven hundredth time, Scotty knocks at the door.

"Yes?" Lane says impatiently. He knows better than to inter-rupt her when she is working and, to his credit, rarely does it.

Despite lacking so much as a single creative cell in his body, Scotty is the one who gave her the idea to write about her friendship with Gala in the first place. Or rather, it was Scotty who suggested she stop trying so hard to write something with universal meaning, and instead look closer to her own life. After the failure of her second novel four years earlier (a novel Lane could admit to herself now hadn't been written under the best circumstances), Lane had returned to journalism, needing the short-term validation it provided. In private, she had toyed with a few ideas for a third novel—writing openings that would never close, or outlines that lost momentum halfway through—but nothing ever stuck. At first, Lane had wondered if Scotty was giving her implicit permission to write about their marriage, and she didn't have the heart to tell him that there was hardly enough meat on its bones to sustain an entire novel. Still, his advice was solid, and as she'd begun to put words onto the page, it felt strangely comforting to think that he might have known her better than she gave him credit for.

"How's it going?" Scotty asks now, still in the doorway. His expression is sheepish as he holds out a glass of freshly squeezed orange juice.

"Fine," Lane says curtly. Then she sighs. "Not great, actually."

Scotty seems to take this as an invitation to enter. As he hands her the glass, his eyes land briefly on the page in her typewriter, and, for the first time that day, Lane is grateful she hasn't managed to write so much as a single word. He turns back to Lane, and she can tell that he's assessing her emotional state, ready to adapt to whichever version of her he finds, in the way Lane used to do with her mother. She takes a sip of juice and attempts to smile at him calmly.

"What is it, Scotty?" she asks, trying to soften the edges of her voice.

"I wanted to see how you were doing," he says, leaning against the bookcase, a stream of golden sunlight illuminating him like a Renaissance god. "The other night, at the bookstore, when people were asking me about the book, I realized I had no idea what to tell them. I don't know anything about it."

"Tell them it's about a man who falls desperately in love with a hermit crab," Lane says.

"Lane." Scotty frowns at her.

"Scotty, you know I can't tell you," she says.

"Can't or won't?"

Scotty flashes his wholesome white teeth at her, and Lane fights a wave of irritation and pretends she finds his attention charming.

"I don't talk to anyone about my work. It's a superstitious writer thing. Or maybe a neurotic writer thing. Describing the story drains the life out of it."

Scotty looks as if he's trying to relate, and then he just shrugs.

"I could never understand," Scotty says, after a pause. "As a suit."

"Suits never understand," Lane says. "Otherwise they wouldn't be suits. They'd be some weird hybrid creature without a name and nobody to love them."

"Like Esther," Scotty says, referring to Lane's editor, a woman who makes Nixon seem like a Labrador, and who flat out refuses to acknowledge the time difference between L.A. and New York. Lane lets out a laugh despite herself.

"Like Esther," she agrees.

"She telephoned for you," Scotty says. "But I thought you wouldn't want me to interrupt you."

"You figured you'd save that for now," Lane says, and Scotty absorbs it, shrugging.

"I just wanted to know if you needed anything," he says, stretching in a way that exposes a couple of inches of his toned stomach. "Although god knows what I could ever offer you. My beautiful, secretive wife."

Lane smiles warily at him.

"If Esther calls again, tell her I have a migraine," she says. "Nobody can argue with a migraine."

Once he's gone, Lane stares at the blank page, willing the words to come back to her.

THE BOOK WOULD be marketed as a novel, but, up to this point, there was nothing fictional about it. Instead, each chapter chronicles a different story that reveals something significant about Gala and, more often than not, the illusory nature of Los Angeles. Lane had pitched it as a classic Hollywood story, filled with dreams and bloodiness and the pitfalls of building a personal brand on something as insubstantial as desire, and sometimes she let herself believe it might live up to it.

The problem is, when Gala was still a couple of miles down the road, she felt like fair game, but now everything feels infinitely more complicated. All of the questions Lane explores in the book, all of the conflicting facets of Gala's personality as well as her own, will be deemed cruel and unethical, as if Lane is once again being mercenary in her treatment of another woman. After people were gone, you were no longer expected to understand them, only to exonerate them. Lane had assumed that Gala would be around forever, as much a part of the Hollywood infrastructure as the iconic letters in the hills or Grauman's Chinese Theatre, but now that she is gone, everything feels murkier somehow.

Perhaps Lane could invent an ending, and this version of Gala would end up like so many L.A. women before her—violet and vomit-streaked in a stranger's bed at the Chateau, or maybe she would buy a baby grand piano and move to the coast to start over, bright-eyed and sober with a new sense of wonder for the world. Either of these options might be satisfying if Lane could just find the words. It was never meant to be a *biography*, so what does it matter if she's liberal with the truth? Only every time Lane tries to write her way to the end, nothing seems to work. Gala's voice is suddenly too syrupy, too knowing, the jokes contrived and corny, and Lane can no longer capture Gala's inimitable mix of warmth and savagery at all. The sentences are stiff. Unusable.

After five hours of no writing, Gala's mocking face appears in the remaining pulp of Lane's orange juice. Lane knocks the glass over and watches the orange liquid spill down her desk as she finally lets the thought hanging in the back of her mind crystallize: There is no ending without Gala.

THIRTEEN

THEN

FEBRUARY 1967

Elijah was the one who told Charlie about the protest. He hadn't actually been at the Black Cat the night the police raided it, but he'd been down the road at New Faces, and had seen the aftermath—the bloodied men dragged off in hand-cuffs, the pain that moved like a bayonet through the community. He explained to Charlie the events of the night, the injustice of the undercover LAPD officers who waited until midnight to strike, causing instant panic among patrons who didn't know they were cops, and who would have been even more terrified had they known. Charlie listened and made all the right noises in the right places, all the while knowing he wouldn't be going to the protest on the eleventh, and certainly wouldn't be making the requested calls to ten friends to notify them of its existence.

The irony was that Charlie actually *had* been at the Black Cat on New Year's Eve. He'd started the night at his parents' annual party, a decadent affair filled with politicians and white-collar criminals and enough foie gras to feed an entire continent, and, in the middle of yet another conversation with someone with food caught in their fake teeth who promised to set him up with their daughter/cousin/client, Charlie had found himself walking straight out of the house and into the cool December night.

He'd been looking for Elijah, of course, who had been avoiding his calls and letters since their last tryst in the rainy days of October. That time, they hadn't argued over Charlie's family explicitly but, as always, it was the specter hanging over the conversation. Elijah had invited Charlie to the opening of the Black Cat, a new gay-friendly bar opening in Silver Lake, and Charlie had demurred, saying proletariat fags weren't exactly his thing, which had wound Elijah up. Not his use of the word *fag*, or his snobbishness, but the chronic insecurity the slur failed to cover, since Elijah thought that Charlie wouldn't be able to experience joy until he fully stepped into his brilliant gay self. Charlie shot back that Elijah had clearly never felt the joy of receiving a juicy end-of-year bonus after keeping a band of reprobates out of jail, and this hadn't gone down particularly well. Still, the exchange hadn't felt significant enough to signal the end of whatever their existing situation was (the first real situation of Charlie's life), but somehow it had done exactly that—Elijah's slow, sinking realization that Charlie would never tear it up with him at a drag queen show in West Hollywood or take him out for dinner anywhere that wasn't either glaringly unfashionable or dark as a Joshua Tree night.

So, on New Year's Eve, Charlie had, like a sad dog without an owner, left his family's party and trailed around the gay bars of L.A., looking for Elijah. He hadn't known what he would say when he found him, but he was the wizard of spin and was sure something poetic would come out of his mouth at exactly the right moment. He figured this fixation on his family was a product of his living in the same city as them. Maybe if he suggested bi-monthly romantic weekend trips, Elijah would feel like they had more of a future together. Maybe he could even buy a place in Northern California and Elijah could live there full-time, looking after their pool and pets (would there be pets? A retriever? Too slobbery. A pug? Too noisy . . .) while he waited for Charlie to fly up every Friday after work. That was real commitment, wasn't it?

It was nearly midnight when Charlie arrived at the Black Cat. The lights were low and the Christmas trees were still up, twinkling over the mass of bodies getting ready to celebrate the promise of a new year. As Charlie watched, a glass of cheap whiskey in his hand, he tried not to feel superior to the drunk men and women gathered around him, people who had chosen this surface-level revelry over building anything stable and significant, like a career at the helm of the most prolific record label in the world. He was, after all, the one who was alone, searching for someone who would no longer answer his calls, let alone fuck him.

The countdown began, and then it was midnight, and even Charlie got caught up in an embrace with an overzealous man with glitter in his beard, and everything felt light and shimmering for a moment, but then something changed and people were shouting, and why were those men being dragged across the room? And who was screaming like that, and why was someone hissing at him to run, and who was this man-child with the meanest eyes he'd ever seen, eyes like a fox, grabbing his arm and shouting that he was under arrest for lewd conduct, and who was the stranger who wedged themselves between him and the fox-child so that Charlie could free his arm and move with everyone else to the exit, ducking low and spilling outside before zigzagging through the streets until he lost his bearings, shaking silently for three hours alone in the dark, Elijah's words repeating over and

over in his brain—*respect for what?*—even when he begged for it
to stop.

THE PROTEST WAS against the lawlessness of the LAPD in their
pursuit of the gay community. That particular night, they had arrested fourteen people, most of whom had pleaded guilty to lesser
charges to avoid the punishment of having to register on the sex
offenders registry, leaving two men who would go to trial for "lewd
conduct" and who would become the first men to argue for the
same rights as heterosexual people. It was the first time anyone
had dared to stand up in court and argue not that they hadn't
kissed, but that they had a right to, and the jury still chose to deny
them this right. Charlie watched all of this with a heavy heart but
also a certain grim satisfaction, because it wasn't as if they'd
needed any more proof that *this* was what happened when you
dared to think you could beat the system. *This* was why he played
it instead. *This* was why he wouldn't bring Elijah, or anyone, home
for Christmas. Not this year, or ever.

"Soo, what do you think?" Elijah said, once he'd finished describing the logistics of an event Charlie already knew he wouldn't
go near. "Are you in?"

His voice had a hint of a challenge in it, and Charlie knew that
Elijah was undoubtedly expecting him to mention the very real
possibility of Charlie being photographed and outed and fired
from his job and shunned by his family, or, even worse, being arrested or sectioned, his attorney general father having no choice
but to approve as every human right was stripped away from his
son because of how he was born. For just a moment, Charlie considered telling Elijah the truth instead—that he had been there
that night looking for him. That he still had a dark bruise on his

hip to prove it, and nightmares about the cop with eyes like a fox who had looked him in the eye and wanted to destroy him. That he'd even shaved off his precious hair in early January to make himself less recognizable if they ever crossed paths again, because he had felt the hatred in the other man's heart and it had left him petrified. Charlie felt his chest start to cave in as he thought about all the things he could say while he had Elijah on the phone, waiting. He cleared his throat. And then—

"Sorry, E," Charlie said, and he could hear it was his work voice, low and slick but with a drop of humor in it so you couldn't quite hold anything tangible against him without seeming churlish. "Not really my thing."

AT DINNER THE next night, Lane asked him if something was wrong, and Charlie found himself breaking down in the middle of the Formosa Cafe. It had been years since Charlie cried, and he found himself apologizing over and over. Lane left some cash on the table and helped Charlie up, his body racking with grief, before she led him outside.

"Hey," she said as she wiped gently underneath his eyes. When she lifted her hand away, her thumb was covered in his glossy tears, and they both just stared at it, both unsure of what to do next.

"Hey," she said again, and this time she wrapped her arms around his waist and hugged him tightly before pulling back again.

"I'm so fucking sad," Charlie said through his heavy sobs, and he watched as her face crumpled.

Much later, Charlie would think back on everything he'd done for Lane, and he was always led back to this moment. It would have been different if she'd told him what anyone else he knew would have told him—that everything was going to be okay, that he wouldn't always feel this way. If she'd lied to him. Instead, Lane pulled back and met his eyes, her own filling with tears.

"I know," she said softly. "I believe you."

Sometimes he figured they were just two clumsy children playing at being adults, neither one of them fully understanding the depth of their own pain but desperately wanting to fix it in each other.

FOURTEEN

THEN

NOVEMBER 1967

The day after Lane's debut novel, *The Ringtail* (named after Arizona's state mammal—a carnivorous and solitary animal closely related to a racoon), became an instant bestseller, making it to number four on *The New York Times* bestseller list before it would climb to the top spot and linger for an unprecedented number of weeks, Lane arrived at a hotel in New York to start her four-week publicity tour. Her publisher had arranged the tour before they realized the power of this book—that Lane could have done only her two TV spots and two national newspaper profiles the week of release, and it still would have made its way into the hearts of thousands of Americans. And not just the coastal ones either, no, *The Ringtail* was a truly sprawling novel, garnering universal praise usually reserved for older male writers, critics zeroing in on the clinical yet unyielding descriptions of the protagonist's lonely childhood as a metaphor for the disconnect between the two generations, and the unemotional way she handled the more complex (read abortion-y) plotlines.

And yet, despite its instant success, Lane had still chosen to honor her commitments in New York, then DC, then on to Virginia, before traveling through the bulk of the country to Nevada (stopping anywhere but her home state of Arizona), over the four weeks between Thanksgiving and Christmas, because, if she were being honest, she didn't have much else to do. Charlie (who didn't like mixing friends with family, despite his repeated assurances of how *wonderful* his parents were), hadn't invited her to Beverly Hills for either holiday, and she had barely spoken to Gala since the beginning of the year when (it transpired) she had reunited with Gabriel.

Lane had expected to feel different when the book came out, particularly as the first reviews started to come in and were almost embarrassingly glowing, but of course she still felt like exactly the same person, with exactly the same problems. Only now the entire country knew about them too. She sometimes wondered what would have happened if she hadn't taken Gala's advice, if she'd left her protagonist nameless and rudderless instead, drifting through her first New York summer without a past to weigh her down. Lane thought that while it would have made for an objectively lesser book, she might not feel quite so exposed every time anyone asked her a question about it.

THE FIRST EVENT of the tour was at a small bookstore in Greenwich Village, where the clientele was younger than Lane had expected, and much more bohemian. She knew that it was considered somewhat revolutionary to write about things like abortion and sex so matter-of-factly but, compared to most people in L.A., the reality of Lane's own day-to-day existence felt practically saintly.

Her editor, Esther, was there, along with her new publicist and the person they'd chosen for Lane to be in conversation with—a well-known women's magazine editor called Mamie Dawson. Mamie was small and loud, with magenta lipstick and a cropped hairstyle, and, if Lane was being polite, she'd describe her as "enthusiastic." Sitting at the table next to her, looking out at the crowd of fifty or so twenty-year-olds, Lane felt a pang of dread.

The event started, and Lane answered Mamie's questions about her career transition from profiles to novels, or, as Mamie put it, from *other* to *self* ("Well, I'm not entirely sure how to answer that, Mamie, as this *is* a work of fiction . . ."), and if she'd ever met Gabriel Ford ("Met him? I watched Belle Vue's first ever performance. It was *dire*, but I'm pleased for everything he's achieved"). Soon, Mamie moved into thornier territory, asking Lane how she felt about the Vietnam War (a sober "unimaginable," and a swift change of subject to avoid a loaded conversation about something entirely unrelated to her book), then about Lane's view on the state of reproductive rights (wasn't the graphic inclusion of an abortion enough of an answer?), and, finally, what Lane thought of Betty Friedan and her cohort. It annoyed Lane that everyone needed her to take a stance on these things, as if *she* were personally at fault for these outdated policies instead of the thousands of men who had fine-tuned them over the centuries.

In her answer, Lane was careful to seem approving of the existence of *any* movement challenging the status quo, without personally aligning herself with any of them, and she watched as Mamie's cheeks grew pink and her eyes dug into Lane disapprovingly. The thing was, however much Lane may have agreed with the principles of this type of feminism, she knew that she would never shake the label once she spoke out about it, and that her writing would be viewed forever through the lens of this stable of emerging activists. She knew this reluctance to label herself as such wouldn't endear her to either Mamie or most of the women in the crowd, but she'd also never heard any of her male peers be called selfish for focusing on their work in isolation, so wouldn't she be as bad as the rest of them if she engaged with it? Isn't that what most men wanted—to flatten women not into individuals with needs and wants and requirements, but into a vague, out-of-focus mass?

Mamie, seemingly having given up on Lane as an ally or even as someone with anything remotely interesting to say, had turned the questions over to the audience, who seemed equally unsure of what to do with her. Partway through a half-hearted question about her favorite restaurant in New York, Lane noticed a familiar presence in the crowd and it felt as if all the oxygen in the room dissipated at once. The man was a few years older than the rest, his long dark hair tucked inside a mustard scarf and charcoal wool coat, his thick brows and deep dimples familiar. He met her eye and she felt instantly winded. After a few seconds, Lane tore her attention from him and forced a smile instead at the young man who had launched into a monologue about the culture of dining in the city, nodding encouragingly until he finished.

"There's one small neighborhood Italian that holds some good memories for me," Lane said softly. "They make the best ragù I've ever tasted."

There were a few murmurs of approval in the audience.

"Where is it?" the original asker of the question prompted.

"Oh, I'm not telling any of you," Lane said. "I'm planning on going there later."

The audience laughed, and Lane locked eyes with the man she'd spotted in the crowd moments earlier. Slowly, he broke into a smile.

AFTER THE EVENT finished and the man had disappeared into the night, and Lane, jittery and unsettled, had signed what felt like four hundred books, the new publicist came over to see her. Mamie had left as soon as the questions were over without saying goodbye, and Lane still felt irritated at the slight. She hadn't even asked Mamie to be her conversation partner (had barely even known who she was) but rather her publicist had decided they'd be a "good match." Why—because they were both women? How original. Pay raises all round.

"Are the questions going to be like that at every event?" Lane asked the publicist, who stared back at her blankly for a moment. Lane wished she could remember the woman's name.

"Well, I think readers always want to hear about the things that inspire you."

The publicist's tone was bordering on snide. *Mabel*, Lane thought. That was it. Mabel had watchful eyes underneath long bangs, and a mouth that barely moved when she talked.

"Those questions weren't about the things that inspire me though, Mabel," Lane said. "She didn't ask me about any of the places I've traveled to, or any of the *many* profiles I've written. Or about the writers or artists whose work I admire. Instead, she seemed hell-bent on giving me intellectual whiplash by jumping from a question about a rock star to my opinion on abortion. Look, if people need to be actively reminded that *The Ringtail* is a novel, not a memoir, then so be it."

Mabel sipped from her paper cup of wine as Lane spoke and,

when she finished, the younger woman's face was still entirely unreadable.

"I'll take a look at the other conversation partners," Mabel said, putting her empty cup down on the signing table. "Congratulations again, Lane, on the sales."

"It felt like Mamie's questions were political," Lane persisted, finding that she was still angry. "And I don't need to speak for anyone apart from myself."

"Wouldn't you say the personal *is* political?" Mabel asked, raising an eyebrow, and now at least Lane could feel the other woman's dislike for her out in the open, where she knew what to do with it.

"That's a very snappy slogan, but I don't see its relevance in the slightest."

Mabel didn't respond for a moment, but then she surprised Lane by leaning close into her, presumably so that nobody else could hear her.

"You're lucky to have the luxury of ignoring what's happening around you if you decide you want access to an abortion, or even birth control," Mabel said softly. "Or, sorry—the characters in your book are lucky. But that's not how it works for most women."

Lane looked past the publicist then and out the window. It was less than 30 degrees outside and snow was just beginning to fall. Suddenly, all she wanted was to be inside the cozy Italian restaurant, the one she'd loved not for the ragù but for the man she was sharing it with, sipping a vodka martini and forgetting that she'd voluntarily exposed herself to any stranger who chose to pick up her book and would now be punished for it for the rest of her career.

"Middle America will be easier for you," Mabel said, almost gently, before she left.

Lane called Esther over and asked her to fire Mabel, effective immediately.

LANE WALKED THROUGH the snow, her camel wool coat wrapped around her. She'd forgotten what it felt like to be this cold. As she got closer to the West Village, her heart raced even as she told herself it was only because she'd been talking about her book and dredging up old memories, that she was inventing an alternate ending. But when she pushed open the door of the restaurant and spotted him at their usual table, Lane stopped lying to herself. She knew exactly what she was walking into, and she'd never stood a chance.

SIXTY-ONE HOURS IS more than enough time to convince yourself you're in love again. It's enough time to hide away from the snow in a hotel room on the eighteenth floor and remember everything you pretended to forget—the way his skin smells like applewood, the way his hand can make you come in five seconds flat, the questions he asks you that no one else thinks to ask. The way he teases you only tenderly, because he knows you didn't grow up in a world where words could be anything but a weapon. Sixty-one hours is more than enough time to forget the destruction you both wreaked.

LANE HAD MET Ezra her second day in New York. He had been holding an Arriflex 16mm film camera and was documenting a pigeon eating the entrails of a dead rat, and Lane, too curious to remember to be shy, had asked him what it was for. He had told her he was making a short film about cosmic insignificance, and his eyes had filled with tears as he spoke, and while this should have been an early warning sign, she found she was too struck by his low voice and his sharp cheekbones to assess the situation clearly.

Over the next three years they had an affair that was so consuming, Lane almost forgot why she'd moved to the city in the first place. She had been a little put out when she found out about his wife, but not as much as she knew she should have been; she believed Ezra when he said his wife was heartless and unloving. The similarities between Ezra's descriptions of his wife, Maddie, and her own mother didn't occur to her until much later. She already understood it was over by then, when she writhed in agony after a swift visit from the only doctor she could find who was willing to help her, and Ezra couldn't quite find the time to visit. It wasn't that he was thoughtless, more that he was weak. And weakness was the one thing she'd learned to fear.

Lane swore she would never be in this position again. She would never again give another human the power to nearly ruin her. She would never again sacrifice her career to support a man. And she would certainly never again love someone so hard she bled for them alone on the bathroom floor of an Avenue A walk-up.

"WHERE DOES SHE think you are?" Lane asked on their final morning together in New York. It was 6:00 a.m., and she was leaving in twenty minutes to catch a flight to Washington.

"Lane," Ezra said, his voice thick with the type of anguish he mostly dealt in. "Why can't you let this be perfect?"

"Please," she said. And she felt him sigh even as he laced his arm around her bare waist and pulled her closer to him. After a moment, she yielded, pressing her face against his chest, blinking to catch his wiry chest hairs between her eyelashes. When she was this close to him, the rest of the world slipped away, and the feeling terrified her. A temporary regression, she told herself. Surely it couldn't hurt if she'd known it was over before it started.

"She thinks I'm editing the film up in Woodstock," he said, his voice quiet.

"Have there been others?" Lane asked, pulling back and fixing her gaze on him.

"Of course not," he said, rubbing his eyes. She could tell he wished they weren't doing this, that she'd just left this morning without making any sort of scene so that he could have lamented his torturous existence for a while and then written a bittersweet, brilliant script about it. Some young actress, someone Lane had met in L.A. maybe, could be paid a hundred thousand dollars to play her in a movie where she would float around in the periphery to represent the path not taken, the missed opportunities, the way life forces a man into a prison of his own making. An ideal in soft focus, always saying more about him than her, even though he'd still expect her to be flattered by it.

"Have you read my book?" she asked then, a question she'd resisted asking since she sat down opposite him at their favorite restaurant three nights earlier.

Ezra shook his head, and she knew he was lying.

"Lane, you're clearly trying to ruin this," he said calmly. "But I want to make sure you know why you're doing it."

Lane frowned.

"You're doing it because you don't know how to be happy," he said. "Because no one ever showed you."

Lane felt as if he'd punched her. She dug her fingernail into her wrist and reminded herself that this was what he always did. He used her secrets in a way that made them both her victims.

This was why she'd never again told another soul about her child-hood in Arizona, not even Charlie, until she'd written this fucking book.

"I'll be your punching bag," he said. "But I'm not going to di-minish what we had by fighting back."

"What we had?" she repeated, even as her eyes stung with tears. She blinked them away, a chasm already opening back up between them. "I'm the most famous writer in the country, and you're washed up at forty. You're lucky I remembered your fucking name."

She threw her clothes into her suitcase, and left him alone in her hotel room.

AFTER NEW YORK, Lane saw ghosts of her past everywhere she looked. In Washington, she saw a preteen who looked exactly like she had in her youth, down to the old-fashioned bow in her hair. In Cincinnati she saw a dog that looked like the only pet her fam-ily ever owned—the old greyhound that had escaped into the night when her mom forgot to close the door. In New Mexico it was a shopkeeper who looked like the teacher's assistant who had grabbed her breasts when they were just forming. In Nevada, she looked out into the audience and finally saw her parents in the back, eyes hollowed as they glowered at her in unison. Her dad was wearing his best brown sports coat, his hair slicked back, and her mom was in her blue dress, eyebrows thin as hairpins. Lane felt the crushing weight of their fury as if she were still just a child, and she knew what they were asking her.

Why did you write those things about us?

And, alone in her hotel room at night, soaked with sweat and unable to sleep, Lane found she couldn't remember.

FIFTEEN

THEN

MAY 1968

It took Gala longer than it should have to realize Gabriel was drowning.

They'd been together for over a year now, and Gala had finally accepted that they were in love. The thing that still surprised her was how primal, how urgent, something as ordinary as being in love could feel when it happened to you. Gala had always felt slightly repulsed by her parents' obsession with each other but now found she understood their compulsion to be intertwined, the way she only felt alive if she was near him. Because how could she be in the same room as Gabriel and not be touching him? What was the point?

At first everything felt like a dream. They whirled around parties in Malibu or jam sessions in the hills where they would steal away to fuck in bathrooms (or sometimes just a dark corner, because who cared who saw them anyway), ending the night skinny-dipping in the ocean or a lilac-hued pool. Money, the thing that had always hung over Gala like an annoying uncle, was no longer an issue, and Gala didn't have to do odd jobs for her friends or parents to make her rent. Instead, she joined Gabriel on Belle Vue's remaining tour dates, watching from her position on top of an amp as ten thousand screaming girls tried to work out what she had that they didn't. She sat in the audience at *The Ed Sullivan Show* as Gabriel stalked around the stage, her heart nearly bursting at the thought that this beautiful creature was hers, and afterward they hit what felt like every club in New York. Of course Gala enjoyed the prestige of it all, the way she too was treated as if she were rock royalty, but most of all she loved spending time with Gabriel. She loved feeling adored, not by the hangers-on, but by him alone.

The problem was, what had started as an extended party, both of them high on success and youth and their blinding love for one another, gradually morphed into something darker. Because the only thing this new, glossier rock star version of Gabriel loved more than Gala was the feeling of a drug hitting his bloodstream. It could be anything—he didn't discriminate. Some days it was just pot; other days he went through two milk bottles filled with Trimar as they lounged around a party for hours, melting into the damp turf of another perfect lawn as the sun rose.

The only drug Gabriel steered well clear of was heroin. Growing up in a grim industrial town, he'd seen a few people lose everything to it, and he swore to his mother that he would never touch it. Until one night in early January, when Gabriel was in London for a few days with the band, and at the house of a Rolling Stone, he thought, *Fuck it*. Later, Gabriel would tell Gala he did it because he missed her, but she wasn't naive enough to believe that. At the time she figured he did it because they were similar—twin flames who couldn't bear to miss out on any fun, which was also why she decided to do it with him on his return.

The first few times they shot up together, Gala felt like she was weightless. But, like all the best things (childhood, French kisses, a steaming bowl of spaghetti from Tana's), she always knew it couldn't last. They were careful not to do it too often, and there were other rules too. They would shoot up only at Gala's, without anyone else around, where they could snake around one another and breathe in the smell of each other's skin as the glow spread through them without anyone else there to ruin it. They did it every few weeks at first, but Gala could sense that Gabriel was having to stop himself from doing it more often, and soon her own trips became less magical, and a little darker. During one of these later trips, their second in a week, when Gala was sprawled across the bed in her underwear, her fingers stroking the sheets as she tried to find some part of Gabriel, a sudden dread cut through her euphoria, and she realized something. Not like an epiphany, but rather the crystallization of something she'd known all along— she needed to find something of her own, otherwise she might lose herself. And she knew that something was writing.

DESPITE LANE'S INSISTENCE, Gala had barely written more than a birthday card since she was a child. For the next three months, however, she wrote furiously. She covered it all—her unorthodox childhood in Hollywood, her life as a sometimes groupie, and the strangely life-affirming encounter she'd had as a teenager with a fading Frank Sinatra at a gas station. The sentences fell out of her, ugly and wrong at first, but soon she discovered how she could revise and rework until they sounded more like her—the voice she spoke in at her most thrilling moments, when the right words would just shoot out of her mouth like she was under a spell—and she could diminish or amplify parts of the story to create a punch line, so that it felt not like stodgy writing but like an anecdote she was telling a friend on the phone, maybe even Lane, and none of it was even nearly perfect, but Gala knew that it was brilliant.

At first, it was almost convenient that Gabriel was so out of it, but then, when she'd almost finished an entire collection of essays, she started to wonder whether she needed to be concerned. The band was staying in L.A. for six months, the longest period of time they'd been in one place in nearly two years, ostensibly writing their second album even if none of them seemed to view it like that. They'd arrived in Los Angeles as awkward kids (not even old enough to drink legally), and they'd transformed overnight into national sex gods with wild hair and a gold record and thousands of girls screaming their names wherever they went, so shouldn't they be allowed to let loose? After being worked like mules while most of their peers were still sitting around in their parents' houses, blowing weed into their family pets' faces? Only, Gala wasn't convinced that what Gabriel was doing was letting loose . . . Most of the time, it didn't look all that fun.

Gabriel wasn't high all the time, but it was worse when he wasn't. When he was sober, or rather, just drinking, he could be found sitting in the dark in his hotel room in his underwear, his skinny chest rising and falling as he chain-smoked and watched old westerns. In these moments, it was hard to coax out the Gabriel that Gala knew, so hard that soon it seemed as if Gabriel was improved by drugs and not devoured by them. And that's when Gala realized that there was a problem.

WHEN GALA BROUGHT up the idea of rehab, there was a moment Gabriel looked relieved. He put up the usual fight, but as she drove them to a "discreet health center" in Malibu, she glanced over and saw he had his eyes closed, face tilted up toward the sun. He looked more peaceful than he had in a long time, and she knew it would be a while before she forgave herself.

"THREE MONTHS," SHE said to him as they sat in the parked car outside the sprawling oceanfront building that looked more like a spa resort than a rehab facility. As it should, at $5,000 a month.

Gabriel nodded. He looked tired, and when he smiled at her, she saw that one of his teeth had chipped, and she hadn't noticed when it had happened.

"I'm sorry," she whispered. "I love you."

He reached into his pocket and pulled out the bag of coke he'd been sporadically dipping a tiny spoon into and snorting through-out the drive. She hadn't been sure if he thought she hadn't no-ticed, or didn't care. Now, as he handed her the bag, she wondered how seriously he was taking this whole thing.

"A memento," she said. "How thoughtful."

He leaned over and pressed his lips to her neck, and despite everything she felt her insides turn to jelly. When he pulled away, he tapped her on the knee.

"You've always handled yourself better than I have," he said ruefully.

Gala shrugged. She sometimes wondered if Gabriel ever thought about how she had been the one to give him his first joint, after his second show at the Troubadour. If he did, it wasn't something he ever brought up, and she pushed the memory from her mind. There were only so many ways she could torture herself over this man, after all.

"One, two, three . . ." she said, and they stared at each other for a moment.

"You first," he said.

"That's not how it works," she said. "One, two, three . . ."

They looked at one another, and Gala took Gabriel's clammy hand in hers.

"I'm scared you won't want me when you're not high," Gala said softly, at the same time Gabriel said, matter-of-factly, "When I get out, we'll get married."

Gala frowned.

"I don't think I want to get married," she said, and even as the words left her mouth, she wished she could be a different kind of person, one who gave the man she loved a flicker of hope for the dark months ahead while he tried to shake a deadly habit she hadn't wanted to notice had spiraled entirely out of hand.

Gabriel swiped his dirty blond hair away from his eyes and grinned at her then, and for just a few seconds it was like the man she first saw onstage at the Troubadour had come back exactly when she needed him.

"You don't know it yet, but you will," he said. "Trust me."

WITH GABRIEL SAFELY in a facility, Gala figured she was faced with two options. One, she could punish herself for having been negligent with Gabriel, for not having seen his sadness earlier, for assuming everyone was like her and doing drugs only for the objectively right reasons (to feel even better than you already did) instead of the wrong ones (to fill a gaping hole). Or two, she could channel her energy into her writing, using the unusual emotions she was feeling to add depth to stories that naturally tended to the frothier side.

Her favorite essay was the carnival one, and she chose to focus on this. She thought it captured her offbeat upbringing perfectly, and the way her parents enthusiastically supported her in any endeavor—how they seemed as excited to meet the woman she would become as she was herself. It was also an excellent showcase for her sense of humor when it turned out she was both wholly unsuited to life as a carnie (all that ugliness) and, more importantly, was in fact almost blindingly talentless. It was a playful nod to her reputation as a groupie, but she knew that the essay itself also disproved its own theory—by the end of the piece, it was clear that there was at least one thing she was good at.

Gala was still a fixture on the Laurel Canyon scene, but she found that she was drinking less because she knew she wanted to wake up to write. By the end of May, the essay was ready. She just didn't know what it was ready for. She knew she could send it to any number of the editors or writers she'd entertained in the past, but she had a feeling they would be primed to look down on her regardless of the quality of her writing. Instead, she did something that surprised even herself. She invited Lane over for dinner.

SIXTEEN

THEN

JUNE 1968

L ane hadn't heard from Gala since the morning after her
Musso and Frank no-show more than a year earlier. The
memory no longer stung in the way it once had, but she
hadn't exactly been seeking out Gala since she'd gotten back from
her book tour either. Instead, she spent almost all of her time with
Charlie, who now seemed to view her as a personal project as well
as a best friend, and dedicated most of his free time to strategiz-
ing her next career move.

Lane had a feeling that, if they had been talking, Gala would
argue that she was just another shiny toy for Charlie—one he
could shape and mold and send out into the world as another ex-
tension of his own brand. And Lane could even occasionally admit to herself that there may have been some truth to this. But
who was she to judge? All she had ever wanted was to prove to the
world how brilliant she was, how worthy of love, so she could
hardly fault someone else for wanting to be a part of it—she was,
after all, now famous even in L.A. And what Gala didn't know

was, since his breakdown at the Formosa Cafe, Lane had felt protective of Charlie. Such a glorious being—so celebrated and accomplished, and yet he felt as sad as she did. There was comfort in their shared loneliness and, for Lane, their closeness couldn't have come at a more prescient time—ever since she'd seen the ghosts of her parents at her book event, she hadn't felt much like being alone.

WHEN GALA PHONED out of the blue and invited her over for dinner, Lane called Charlie to get his read on the situation.

"She's lonely," he said, stretching the word out in a way that stripped it of any compassion. "And bored. And didn't I tell you she'd destroy that poor boy? His publicist told me he barely drank beer before he got to L.A., and now he's so out of it he nearly drowned himself at a party in the hills last month."

Lane twirled the phone cord around her finger. She should have known that it was barely worth talking to Charlie about anything Gala-related. They'd known each other for a while, but had never deemed the other worthy of friendship. If she were being ungenerous, Lane would wager that Charlie had realized Gala had little to offer him in the way of power or reputation, and Gala had found Charlie to be overly concerned with how things looked, and neither of them would be entirely wrong.

"Maybe," she said. "But I'd still like to see what she wants from me."

"Money? It can't be drugs or sex. Or maybe it *is* sex. Did you two ever . . . ?"

Lane shook her head. "She's not my type. And I doubt that I'm hers."

"Money then," Charlie said gleefully. "There, I've saved you precious time and a poorly cooked meal."

Before they hung up, Charlie made one last attempt to dissuade her.

"Be careful," Charlie said. "I wouldn't trust her with my enemy, let alone my best friend."

IF GALA HAD cleaned up in advance of Lane's arrival, it wasn't obvious. Her apartment was even more cluttered than usual, with a strange smell in the air. When Gala went to the kitchen to get a bottle of wine, Lane identified the stench as coming from a vase filled with decaying purple roses. She picked up the vase and walked into the kitchen with it.

"I think these are dead," she said, but the look Gala shot her was so withering that Lane walked back out and placed the vase back where she'd found it.

"Where's Gabriel?" she asked, looking around the room for any proof that they lived there together.

"Rehab," Gala said as she handed Lane a glass. "Naturally I would fall in love with someone who's hell-bent on dying."

Her words were glib, but Lane could sense her pain. She sat down on the sofa and frowned.

"Sorry," she said, and even though there were a hundred other things she wanted to say about life with an addict, she didn't quite trust Gala enough to share any of them.

Gala nodded dully. Now that Lane looked at her properly, there was a general flatness about her—it was as if she'd fallen in love and had emerged on the other side a little less shimmering than she'd once been.

"How are you?" Gala asked.

"I don't think you've ever asked me that," Lane said, narrowing her eyes. "Can you be a little more specific?"

"I meant how are you dealing with your success," Gala said. "The golden child of the literary world. The savior of publishing. And fashion, depending on who you ask."

Lane glanced down at her navy silk two-piece, finely embroidered with a web of silver stars. It was one of the looks chosen for her by the stylist Charlie had hired, but now, noting Gala's jeans and loose oxford shirt, Lane wondered if it was too much.

"Things are different," Lane said, choosing her words carefully. "But also the same."

"Illuminating," Gala said. "Aren't you a writer?"

"I never used to understand why famous people were so intent on insisting they were 'still the same person' they were before they got famous," Lane said slowly. "It seemed like a futile thing for them to say, but now I think I understand. You can have everything you wanted from the world, but somehow you're still that small child waiting on the curb for someone to pick you up from school."

There was a long pause, and Gala for once seemed lost for words.

"Fuck, Lane," Gala said eventually, before she lifted her glass of wine to her mouth. "That's depressing."

"Not for you," Lane said. "Some people are built to be happy."

Gala shrugged. She stood up then and reached for the loose pages she'd stuffed underneath an encyclopedia of clouds.

"I have something to show you," she said.

LANE READ GALA'S story in bed that night and found herself absorbed from the first sentence, which read, *There are a million places to find out you're talentless, but the best has to be at forty feet in the air, with a burly Russian man reaching for your fingertips and your own father yelling at you to arch your back.*

As she read on, Lane could feel both admiration and a complex envy growing inside her. She'd known what a quick mind Gala had, and that she told stories in a way that meant they bubbled and pulsed as if they had a life of their own, but even Lane hadn't realized this would translate to the written word quite so effectively. Gala's sentences were deceptively simple—syrupy observations swiftly followed by a sharp barb in the next breath, and the story itself was the same—funny and propulsive yet undeniably powerful.

When she'd finished, and reread it four more times, Lane put down the story and turned off her night-light. She lay awake, so consumed by Gala's writing that for hours she watched the shadows from the street outside dance across her walls like the acrobats in the story she'd just read. The problem was that Gala was exactly the type of girl Lane would have hated in high school—brilliant but in an effortless, cooler-than-thou way that meant she got to pretend she barely cared at all. Lane had never had that luxury—she'd worked herself to the bone for everything she had. It wasn't that she wasn't naturally gifted, but there were several layers of ego and self-loathing to cut through in order to reach the part that actually meant something. Somehow, she knew that Gala had just decided one day to give writing a go and that this sparklingly self-aware piece was the product.

Lane hadn't exactly been lying when she told Gala that her success hadn't fixed everything, but it wasn't the whole truth either. She couldn't deny the buzz she felt when she saw someone's eyes light up with recognition on the street, or if she was invited to some Hollywood luncheon or awards ceremony to add a certain literary sophistication. And although she would never admit it to anyone, not even Charlie, sometimes—when she felt particularly lonely, or like an impostor—she would stare at the striking portraits Richard Avedon had taken of her to remind herself of who she was and what she'd achieved. Sometimes, she could even convince herself that this woman, the one staring seriously into the lens as she smoked a cigarette in the shabby courtyard of the Chateau Marmont, deserved her unwieldy success and the love of strangers. And to lose it felt inconceivable.

Sometime around dawn, Lane convinced herself that Gala's style—gossipy, colloquial, almost soapy—was nothing like her own much more elevated prose, and that they weren't in competition. In fact, she was so insistent that Gala wasn't a threat that a few hours later, she sent the short story on to her editor at *Vanity Fair*, with a note advising they publish Gala at the earliest opportunity. And would someone who was jealous do that?

SEVENTEEN

NOW

SUMMER 1975

G ala's parents still live in the same bungalow she grew up in, opposite the Magic Castle on Franklin Avenue. The house is dark green with white woodwork, and is unremarkable until Lane is close enough to spot the quirky features dotted around the front yard—a finely carved rabbit hanging upside down from the branches of the oak tree, a dismembered arm rising gruesomely from the soil in the neat flower beds. Little touches to showcase the craftsmanship that thrives inside the double garage studio of Stan and Penny Margolis. Lane pulls out her notepad and quickly jots down the eccentricities in a shorthand legible only to her.

She walks up the porch steps, and, as she eyes the stained glass door, she feels a sudden sense of discomfort at what awaits her on the other side. She wants to blame Gala but she knows that, as always, it's her own hunger that drives her. Just that morning she had received a postcard from her editor, Esther, with the words *WE NEED TO TALK ABOUT THE BOOK* written in giant, looping letters, and Lane had felt the shame down to her bones. *What book?* she'd thought as the words that had once thrilled her now swam precariously in front of her eyes.

Lane reaches out to ring the doorbell. As she waits, Lane wonders if Gala would be looking for her if the situation were reversed, but knows it isn't the same. If Lane were missing, it would be a national news story—two kids without a mother, the literary world without its former darling. Lane would never be able to slip out of her own life like a ghost. Does she envy Gala for that? (Should she write that down?)

The door is flung open by a striking woman in her late fifties with blond hair almost to her waist, wearing a flowing paisley top over a pair of cutoff denim shorts.

Lane opens her mouth to introduce herself, but Penny is already stepping toward her, arms spread wide.

"I know exactly who you are," Penny says into her ear. "It's so good to finally meet you, Lane."

THE HALLWAYS OF Gala's childhood home are a mustard color and lined with old magic memorabilia—Chung Ling Soo and Carter the Great posters; a pair of handcuffs mounted in a frame underneath a signed photograph of Harry Houdini. Lane wants to ask about all of it—the posters, the handcuffs, the cracks in the wall, but soon they are in a room at the rear of the house, this one painted tangerine. Every surface is topped with old-fashioned automatons—a monkey poised to play a cymbal, a large cabinet filled with a mechanized graveyard, ghosts from the past poised to come to life. As if the sheer number of curiosities weren't overwhelming enough, there's a distinctive smell in the room that Lane can't quite place. Something heavy and acidic.

Penny opens the door to the backyard and yells, "Stan?" while gesturing toward an emerald velvet couch. Penny announces that she's going to grab a pot of coffee, before leaving Lane alone with the relics from the past, until a short, sinewy man with glasses and a thick black mustache comes in, kicking off his clogs as he approaches. Lane braces herself for the hug this time, this one even longer than Penny's. He smells of sawdust and oranges.

"Thanks for stopping by," Stan says, and, when the hug finally ends, Lane is horrified to find that his eyes are already filling with tears. Her own father cried often and with little warning (a result of the perpetual five fingers of American whiskey in his favorite coffee mug), and her revulsion feels familiar.

"I'm actually a fan of yours," Stan says. "Your story on the declining impact of jazz clubs was truly heart-wrenching."

Lane smiles carefully. The actual piece she'd written wasn't, in fact, heart-wrenching, but she's learned by now that every reader has their own lens through which they read a story, and they tend to give the artist far too much credit. This was a lesson she'd learned early on, and one she'd tried to share with Gala: As a writer, you rarely needed to tell people how to feel—in fact, the less you told them how to feel, the more inclined they were to fill in the gaps for themselves, and the more brilliant they'd think *you* were as a result. Interviewing people was a similar balancing act, but one that required slightly more improvisation.

Penny walks back into the room then and hands Lane a cup of coffee. Lane takes a sip and sinks back on the velvet couch. Stan sits down on a wicker chair, and Penny perches on his lap, and he kisses the bare skin on her upper arm. The exchange is so unassumingly intimate that Lane averts her eyes even as she feels a pang of envy for what Gala's childhood must have looked like.

"What can we do for you, honey?" Penny asks.

Lane shifts in her seat before answering.

"I wanted to ask you a few questions about Gala."

"For an article?" Stan asks eventually, frowning.

"Not exactly," Lane says, and there is a silence.

"I've been feeling sort of helpless since I found out she was missing," she says. "And I want to do something. And if it *were* a story I was writing, I figure I'd start here."

Lane feels a twist of guilt in her gut. Can they tell that she's lying? Can they see how knotted her soul is, how self-serving she has always been? Do they understand that she needs to know how it ends for Gala mostly so she can prove to herself that she is the opposite of washed up—*dripping* in brilliance and worthiness like people used to believe?

"Oh, honey," Penny says. "You've already done so much for Gala."

"She was very proud of everything you've accomplished," Stan says. "And she's never forgotten the way you encouraged her at the start of her career."

For just a moment, Lane can see Gala, sitting cross-legged on the rug at her parents' feet in a white peasant dress, a lit cigarette hanging out of her mouth. *Liar,* she says to Lane, out the side of her mouth. Lane pinches the inside of her wrist hard, digging her nail in so it leaves a white crescent shape in her pale flesh. The moment the pain signals reach her brain, Gala disappears.

"She helped me too, in her own way," Lane says. Then: "She was a lot more than people think."

Lane adds this for the benefit of Penny and Stan, because who wouldn't want to hear that about their own child? And of course it is true, in ways Lane doesn't necessarily want to think about right now.

"Oh, we know, honey," Penny said. "The thing is, with Gala, it isn't an act—she really doesn't care what people think of her. Or at least, she never used to care."

"Even as a child?" Lane asks, but she can hear her tone is too eager, and she wonders if these people, open even in their grief, will notice and think her emotionally deficient in some way.

"You could never pin her down, even as a child," Stan says. "But this is very unlike her. She'll throw herself out of a plane strapped to the back of someone she just met, but she'll tell you about it first, you know?"

As he talks, Lane can hear how proud he is of Gala. How much love he has for his fearless daughter. She wonders if she'll ever feel ownership of Dahlia and Audrey like this, or whether she'll always feel like they were created entirely by chance.

"And when did you realize she was using drugs?" Lane asks.

The silence is heavy as Penny and Stan exchange a look.

"You'd probably know more about that than us," Stan says, after a long pause. "We've always been close but . . . maybe we should have looked a little harder."

"Nonsense," Penny says, her tone now sharper than before, even with the smile stretched across her face. "It isn't in Gala's nature to lie or keep secrets. Especially not from us."

"So she told you that someone took over her rent," Lane says.

Another pause.

"Probably an admirer," Penny says eventually. "There's never any shortage of those."

Lane can't help but think of the gibes flying around the past few years about Gala's declining desirability.

"If it's okay with you, I'd like to go to Gala's and take a look around to see if I can find anything there that might . . . indicate

where she's gone. I'd just need you to make a call to her landlord
to give me the all clear."

Penny frowns.

"I don't know what you're looking for," she says slowly. "We've
been through it so many times already."

"I know," Lane says. "But perhaps a fresh pair of eyes wouldn't
hurt."

Penny and Stan exchange another look.

"I don't think so, Lane," Penny says. "We still want it to feel
like home when Gala comes back."

Lane is considering her next move when she hears a strange
squeaking sound and, looking down, finds a bluish cat slinking
toward her. That's the smell, she thinks. *Cat litter.* She reaches
down instinctively and touches his silky coat. The cat purrs and
simpers beneath her touch.

"Is this one of hers?"

"Stan's allergic but we couldn't turn them away," Penny says.
"Gala would *kill* us if we got rid of them."

Penny stands then and reaches for Lane's half-drunk mug of
coffee.

"Thanks for your hospitality," Lane says as she reluctantly
stands too. She smiles in Stan's direction, but he is already lost,
seemingly a million miles away.

"Out of interest, who brought Gala's cats over here?" Lane asks
as Penny leads her back down the mustard hallway.

"You know, we've been in such a daze over the past few weeks,
I don't think we ever caught his name," Penny says as they reach
the door, and then she surprises Lane by stepping out onto the
porch after her and pulling the door gently closed behind them.

"There are things a father shouldn't know about his daughter,"
she says quietly, leaning in close to Lane. "And Gala's struggles

were one of them. We never wanted to . . . change her, but maybe we could have tried a little harder to understand her."

After a moment, Lane nods.

Penny closes her eyes briefly as if to gather strength.

"When the police came, they must have heard a little about Gala's . . . reputation, and they made some assumptions about her lifestyle. They barely spent twenty minutes in there, and, as far as I could tell, they spent most of that time rifling through her bedroom. They told me after that it was most probably a *liaison* gone wrong, as if that justified anything, as if they'd just solved the whole mystery. I wanted to tell them that I don't know if that part of Gala even still existed after Gabriel, but I didn't think they deserved to know anything about her. Either way, you know as well as I do that that girl never did one thing in her life she didn't want to, not out of necessity or for any other reason."

"Gala doesn't deserve that," Lane says, and she means it.

"No woman does," Penny says, and she squeezes Lane's shoulder.

"When was the last time you talked to her?"

"It was New Year's Eve," Penny says softly. "That morning."

Lane pauses. She too had last seen Gala on New Year's Eve. An unfortunate coincidence, surely.

"How did she . . . seem?"

"Brighter than she had in a while," Penny says. "She was looking forward to meeting an old friend."

Lane feels her cheeks flush. She glances at Penny, but the other woman seems entirely oblivious to her discomfort.

"Okay," Lane says. "Well . . . thanks again."

She turns to leave, a slow churning sensation in her stomach.

She is halfway across the front yard when Penny calls her name again.

"Lane? The friend of Gala's who brought the cats? He was handsome, well-spoken. And he had a scar above his lip. I remember that much," Penny says. "And, honey, if you find him, give me a call. Maybe he knows something that can help us."

Lane pastes on a smile, but the churning only intensifies.

What the hell was *Charlie* doing at Gala's place?

EIGHTEEN

THEN

AUGUST 1968

Three months and three weeks after Gala dropped Gabriel at rehab, at the end of a cracklingly dry August in which wildfires tore through the hills of Malibu and Topanga, Gala threw a party in Santa Monica. The event, celebrating Gabriel's return to real life *and* the publication of Gala's first essay in *Vanity Fair*, was held at Chez Jay, a small bar on Ocean Avenue within walking distance of the hotel Gala and Gabriel had temporarily moved into after his release.

It was rumored that Marilyn Monroe and JFK used the windowless spot for their secret rendezvous, but, reputation aside, the venue was an otherwise unassuming place. There was a banner on one wall that read CONGRATULATIONS GALA and one on the other wall that read CONGRATULATIONS GABRIEL, and while Lane wasn't sure if resisting heroin for ninety days while under twenty-four-hour supervision was a feat worthy of congratulations just yet, she knew that Gala wouldn't have shared her moment with just anyone.

Lane waded through the crowd. Almost everyone Lane had come across in her three years in Hollywood was there, and as Lane watched Gala, her arm thrown around the shoulders of an unmistakably fleshier Gabriel, she felt a flush of warmth. Gala may still act like she was the same party girl, curating people like curiosities, but she'd also allowed the world to see another, more serious, side of her with her writing. Lane felt proud to have been the one to help her bloom creatively.

Gala spotted Lane across the room then and blew her a kiss so exaggerated that people turned to stare. After a moment, Lane blew a kiss back at her, and Gala caught it hard on her cheek, leaving a pink mark. Then Gala turned back to Gabriel and ran her hand down the side of his face. She leaned in close to him and whispered something in his ear, and Lane watched as he shifted his weight from foot to foot before nodding. Seemingly satisfied, Gala grabbed the arm of a passing blond woman before steering her conspiratorially toward the bar. For a few seconds Gabriel stood alone, blinking under the colorful lights, and Lane saw just how rudderless he was without Gala.

LATER, LANE FOUND Gabriel outside the bar when she went out to take a break from all the people hanging off her as they congratulated her on her success. She appreciated the compliments, but these people were just proving their ignorance when they asked her to do a shot with them at the bar, or a line of coke in the bathroom—her work was only good because she was an observer of people like this. She wasn't one of them.

Gabriel was smoking what looked to be his fourth cigarette, by the collection of simmering butts at his feet. He was leaning against the white stucco, his eyes closed and his head angled up toward a streetlamp.

"Light?" Lane said, waving her cigarette in his direction. Gabriel opened his eyes, and Lane observed as he struggled to place her. After a moment he shrugged and held out his lit cigarette instead. She lit her own off the red cherry.

"Lane Warren," she said as she handed it back. "We met a couple years back at the Troubadour."

"Lane," Gabriel repeated, and then his expression shifted into something not welcoming exactly, but less wary. "You're the one who helped Gala."

Lane felt a flash of irritation. Sending Gala's story to her editor at *Vanity Fair* was probably the least interesting thing about her, but she supposed it was contextual.

"Among other things," she said smoothly. "How are you feeling?"

Gabriel opened his mouth to say something, then closed it again. He shrugged, and Lane wondered if he was going to cry.

"You're a journalist too, right?" he said then, and Lane frowned.

"Again," she said. "Among other things."

"I don't trust journalists," he said simply, his northern accent making the first syllable of *journalists* feel as long as a transatlantic flight.

"You've probably had some bad experiences," Lane said. "Baby music critics scratching around for a story wherever they can."

He smiled wryly.

"We're all scratching around for a story wherever we can," he said. "Don't you think? About our friends. Ourselves."

Lane felt a shiver go down her spine. She was struck by how different he was from the kid she'd met at the Troubadour that night—the attentive outsider with an appealing awareness of his own charm. She employed a classic journalist trick of saying nothing, letting Gabriel expand, but he didn't fall for it. Instead they stood in silence until Lane felt compelled to speak again.

"You probably shouldn't be here," Lane said softly. "It's too soon."

Gabriel looked at her then.

"You're worried about Gala," Gabriel said. "And I'm not going to pretend I've got this all worked out yet, but I love her more than I know what to do with sometimes, so I figure that's a good place to start, right?"

There was a starkness in his eyes that felt painfully familiar to Lane. Her dad had looked at her the same way the day he celebrated a year of sobriety when she was sixteen, after her mother's overdose had shocked him into changing his ways. Even though it was against the rules of AA, Lane had made him a tray of brownies to celebrate his first alcohol-free year, and he blew out the melting pink candles with the ghost of a smile on his face, and they both knew it was still going to get him in the end.

"It's not enough," Lane said, and, after a moment, Gabriel nodded grimly, as if it was confirmation of something he already knew.

"Someone should warn her," he said quietly, before heading back inside.

LANE CONSIDERED LEAVING the party, but the thought of being alone felt almost inconceivable. She pushed through the crowd, searching for Charlie, but the room began to distort around her until each guest transformed into a grotesque caricature of themselves, dripping with greed and excess, and she found herself gripping the back of a booth to keep her balance. When she opened her eyes, she saw the ghosts of her parents sitting at the table beneath her, tight-lipped and grim.

Lane stumbled across the room, and when she finally smelled Charlie's familiar spiced woody scent, she felt the relief crash through her in waves.

"Where the hell have you been?" she said as she fell into his arms. He pulled her in and kissed the top of her head before slowly turning her around to face the man he had been talking to when she approached.

"I was waylaid by this fascinating stranger," Charlie said, before leaning in close to Lane and adding in a whisper, "who is *also* your biggest fan."

The man in question had impressive chestnut hair that fell in waves over a tanned forehead, a simple face with a wide smile and perfect teeth (too many of them?) now being offered in her direction. Gala's neighbor, Scotty Ryan, Lane thought as she stared at him. He was tall and had the build of a swimmer. He looked straightforward. And healthy. He looked so different from her father.

"I wondered when I'd see you again," she said.

Charlie let out a small laugh. "It sounds like you have some catching up to do," he said smugly. "I'll be over by the bar trying to strike up a conversation with that woman dressed like a Victorian ghoul. Spare a thought for me while you're falling in love."

And with that he was gone. Lane stared after him for a moment, but then she thought she saw her mom standing behind the bar, staring at her with cool, loveless eyes. Lane closed her own eyes for a moment, and when she opened them again, Scotty was watching her intently.

"Do you want to get out of here?" he asked.

"Very much so," Lane said, and she let herself be led through the crowd by him. It felt nice, finally, to cede control to someone else.

GALA WATCHED LANE leave with Scotty and felt a faint flush of disapproval. She remembered Lane had asked about him, and she thought she'd made it clear that he wasn't worth pursuing. Scotty was stuck up and, she figured, the worst type of "friend" to women—someone quick to argue for equal rights in theory but entirely negligent in practice. As far as Gala knew, he'd never once included work by a female artist in a show at his gallery, and Gala had the idea that he was a traditionalist at heart—someone who would talk the talk until it came time for him to actually settle down, when he'd change the terms suddenly.

Gabriel nuzzled his head into her neck then, and Gala felt her legs weaken against her will. Since Gabriel had gotten out of rehab, it seemed as though all he had to do was leave her side for longer than five minutes for her to feel unable to breathe. She told herself that it was because she'd nearly lost him, but she also knew it wasn't sustainable, feeling like this. She'd just had her first story printed in one of the country's most respected magazines, for god's sake, she should be feeling on top of the world, not panicking about where her boyfriend had gone for half an hour.

They'd been shacking up in a hotel room that opened out onto the beach for the past three weeks, and Gabriel woke her every morning with the same warm lips pressed to her neck, the same perfect voice sighing her name like a prayer. This morning, however, she'd woken up to find an empty space in bed beside her, and had experienced a true plunging terror for the first time in her twenty-eight years on earth. She'd pulled on a robe and searched the hotel not frantically but tentatively, as if she wanted to delay the inevitable for as long as possible, but, by the time she got back to their room, she was shaking all over. Eventually Gabriel had appeared at the window, topless in jeans that were dripping wet from the ocean, his expression slightly bewildered. Gala pulled him inside and onto the bed, her lips pressed against his skin as she kissed him hungrily. Gabriel took off his jeans, and she ran her hands over his salty skin as the sound of his groans filled the small room. Halfway through, Gala realized that tears were streaming down her cheeks.

Later, she'd pinpoint it as the exact moment she knew she was going to lose him.

NINETEEN

THEN

AUGUST 1968

After they left Gala's party, Scotty drove Lane to the Dresden Room, a restaurant on Vermont, farther east than Lane usually ventured. When they arrived, Lane understood why he'd chosen it. The valet was at pains to swiftly refer to him as Mr. Scotty, and the barman sent over two martinis as soon as they were seated at the best table in the packed, low-lit restaurant. Not long after, a waiter appeared with the veal scaloppine and a chef's salad, the latter of which he presented to Lane with a flourish.

"Were they expecting us?" Lane asked dryly as she looked down at the dish in front of her. She felt irritated at the presumption she would want a salad, not only because of its connotations about her preoccupation with her weight, but because it made her feel like one more in a line of countless women Scotty had rolled out the Dresden routine for. She was about to tell him that she'd forgotten about an imminent deadline, when the waiter reappeared and whisked the plates away.

"Wrong table," he said. "My apologies, Mr. Scotty."

Scotty laughed, clearly genuinely bemused by the exchange, and Lane felt herself soften slightly. She had to admit there was something disarming about Scotty, with his all-American good looks and almost childlike frankness. He had an aura of confidence that didn't seem overblown or faked, which was rare in Hollywood.

"So, Scotty Ryan," she said once they'd ordered (steak for Scotty, veal scaloppine for Lane, because she was making a point). "I know where you live and that you like to read Saul Bellow. What else do I need to know about you?"

"Where should I start?" he asked, leaning back a little.

"Wherever it gets interesting," she said lightly, not intending to trade childhood war stories if she could help it, even though she was well versed at spinning hers, cherry-picking certain details to make it sound as if solitude could yield peace and creativity as well as utter devastation.

"I've learned not to concern myself in the slightest with being interesting," Scotty said, and then he began to tell his story.

SCOTTY GREW UP lower middle-class in Vacaville, a small town about thirty miles west of Sacramento. He was the youngest of three boys, all of whom possessed near-identical wholesome faces paired with just-below-average intelligence and slightly above-average agility. Their parents were by many measures happy, but he'd never seen them so much as hold hands in public. Scotty's pops (John) had a job with the post office, and his mom (Patty) raised the kids with boundless enthusiasm. The three boys were directed into different sports so that they were never in direct competition with one another, and Scotty was pushed toward tennis, because he was the baby and his mom didn't want him to risk injury playing a contact sport.

From a young age, Scotty felt different. He desired things. At first it was a new bike, a TV set, a bigger house with a pool, impulses he learned to keep to himself, until one day in sixth grade when he found himself lying to the other kids at school. He told them he had spent the summer in India (in reality he'd been at their grandmother's house in Bakersfield), and that he was distantly related to James Cagney, who he claimed had taken him to a baseball game and refused to sing the national anthem for political reasons.

Scotty soon found that the lies spilled out of his mouth as seamlessly as the truth, but even with the other kids' awe as fuel, the disparity between his real and fake life soon soured into a heavy resentment. He was disgusted with his ordinary, suburban existence—the stench of mediocrity clinging to everyone he knew. Nobody in his life, not his parents or his teachers, had ever put any pressure on him to excel, so he decided to put it on himself. He knew he was never going to win any academic awards, so instead he threw himself into tennis, training every morning, and then again after school, until he ended up at UCLA on a scholarship, where he realized once again just how wholly unimpressive he was.

"My whole life I wanted to be special, but I just hit roadblock after roadblock," Scotty said, a warmth to his voice, as if he understood the irony of telling Lane all of this while wearing what looked to be a bespoke jacket, over a glistening steak that cost more than most of the restaurant staff's weekly salaries. "And the harder I tried, the more frustrated I felt. So one day, I just gave up trying."

Lane had another sip of her martini and raised an eyebrow. "You gave up striving for excellence?"

Scotty shook his head. "I gave up trying to be anything other than exactly who I am."

He picked up his fork and speared a piece of steak. Lane tried to work out if she was repulsed by this man, this solidly average human who had seemingly more than made peace with it, and was surprised to find that she wasn't. Maybe it was her bleak exchange with Gabriel or the ghosts of her parents following her around, heavy with the skeletons of their own unrealized dreams, but she found she wanted to know more about the man sitting opposite her, enthusiastically throwing chunks of meat into his mouth as if he truly had given up the burden of trying to impress anyone and was all the happier for it.

"And in practice?" Lane asked. "Who are you?"

"That's what I had to find out. First off, I gave up lying. To myself or anyone else. Which meant not lying about the things I liked and disliked. I gave up tennis. I dropped every subject except for art history. I took up pottery and reading, things I'd have never done in high school because I didn't want to be seen as an outcast. And you know what happened?" he asked, a smile spreading across his face. "People were drawn to me. Every girl at UCLA thought I was the most fascinating person they'd ever met. Do you know how many guys walked around with the same copy of *On the Road* that year? Apparently they had a rotation system going. But it didn't work for them like it had for me, because it wasn't authentic. And from there, I just kept going. When I trust my instincts about people, things work out. And when I don't, they don't. That's my superpower; that's what I've built an entire career on. The first artist I took on at the gallery looked like a punt—a photographer from Poland who worked out of the mental asylum he'd lived in since the thirties—and his work was completely against the fashion, self-portraits mostly, severe, very European in their austerity. But I stuck to my guns and now he's the most commercially viable contemporary artist in Europe. People could sense his authenticity just like they can sense mine."

Lane watched Scotty come alive as he spoke about his charmed existence as if it were something he'd earned, and again, she waited for the revulsion to hit. Because what did this person expect from his life, really? Didn't he see how easy his childhood had been, and that the only true roadblock in his life had been his own discontentedness? Or perhaps he did see that, perhaps that was why he was smiling almost apologetically as he told her about his blessed life, while Lane had needed sheer grit and a humiliating dose of luck (if that's what you'd call fielding a fishbowl to the head and a murder-suicide) to get where she was today, regardless of her natural talent.

"How interesting," she said noncommittally, once he seemed to have finished. "Or rather, how uninteresting."

He studied her thoughtfully as he ran his hand through his hair. He had great hair, Lane thought. Presumably another virtue of being true to oneself.

"You've been lied to," he said then, and Lane felt something electric run through her.

"Hasn't everyone?" she asked, trying to keep her tone light.

Scotty seemed to think about it.

"Everyone lies in Hollywood," she said.

"Not me," Scotty said. "All I have in this world is my instincts, and I protect them at all costs."

She cocked her head to one side. "Really? You never lie?"

"Never," he said. And it felt as close to a promise as you could get on a first date in L.A.

"So what are your famous instincts telling you about me?" Lane asked after a moment, and her tone wasn't suggestive so much as curious. She'd realized that since she'd been with Scotty, the ghosts of her parents had disappeared back into the ether, and she wondered if it had to do with how grounded he seemed, as if there were no room for half-truths and regrets, or people from your past coming back to remind you of your moral failures.

"Oh, I knew from the moment we met," Scotty said, a wide smile stretching across his perfect mouth as he leaned back in his chair. "You're my ending."

Despite his brazenness, Lane felt a kick of anticipation in her stomach.

"I bet you say that to all the girls at the Dresden," she said, but she knew he was probably right. Because how could she ever feel unsteady again if she was with someone who was so damn certain about everything?

TWENTY

THEN

SEPTEMBER 1968

For the next six weeks, Scotty barely slept in his own apartment. For some strange reason, instead of staying in his sprawling home at Hacienda Heights, he preferred Lane's one-bedroom rental on Holloway Drive. She sometimes wondered if he liked it so much because it made him feel nostalgic for a time before he owned the most lucrative gallery on the West Coast and could have anything he wanted—the last time he'd had to struggle for anything at all.

While he wasn't shy about physical affection, Scotty seemed equally enamored of Lane's mind. He asked her opinion on current affairs on a daily basis, and really seemed to listen to her answers even when it was clear he disagreed with her. He asked her to read passages of *The Ringtail* to him so that he could hear the words "how they were intended to be read," and when she glanced up at him over the page, his eyes were always filled with some combination of desire and awe. They dined out a couple of nights a week, but mostly they stayed in bed, talking and fucking and reading the newspaper and joking that they were already acting like an old married couple. And it was true that things were moving quickly, as if they were working to some unspoken deadline, trying to discover everything they could about each other before it approached. Lane sometimes worried that the deadline had to do with her age (an ancient thirty-one) and Scotty's desire to have children, but when she asked him if this was the case, he laughed it off, much like he laughed off her general ambivalence toward being a mother.

"My own mother wasn't . . ." she started to say one morning, when he casually referenced their future children yet again, as if it were already a fait accompli. They were lying in bed on a rare rainy afternoon in Los Angeles, and Scotty was reading aloud to her a chapter from the stodgy psychology book that now also lived at her place. (He'd been wading through the same book for as long as Lane had known him, but she was trying not to let this put her off.)

"Your mother wasn't what?" Scotty asked, turning to look at her. He knew that her parents weren't around, but she had never elaborated on this vague fact.

Lane pulled the white bedsheet up over her body and focused on a hairline fracture on the opposite wall.

"I don't know if I want a baby, Scotty," she said quietly.

Scotty didn't say anything, and Lane figured she might as well see it through now.

"My mother was unwell," she said. "And it was my fault."

Scotty reached out and took her hand in his.

"No," he said. "It wasn't."

Lane turned to him, looking for a sign that she had ruined whatever magic existed between them, but she found only steadiness in his brown eyes.

"The parents in *The Ringtail*?" she said. "That wasn't the half of it. My mother didn't . . . love me."

Scotty frowned.

"Of course she loved you," he said. "It's a basic instinct."

"No," Lane said. "It isn't."

Lane watched a small flicker of doubt cross Scotty's beautiful face.

"You know what it sounds like to me?" he said as he stroked a loose piece of hair out of Lane's face. "It sounds like your mom just didn't have the right person holding her up."

Lane thought about this for a moment, wondered if it was true. If anyone could have made Alys a better mother. And even if it wasn't, could Lane tell herself it was true for long enough to turn herself over to this man? She knew that there was a chance that Scotty would view her differently now that he knew the core of her, and the thought made her stomach roil. She realized then just how desperate she was to be the person Scotty already thought she was—someone capable of a normal life.

"You'll see," Scotty said then, as if reading her mind. "You'll feel differently when it's your own baby."

And, as always, he said it with such confidence she almost believed him.

TWENTY-ONE

NOW

SUMMER 1975

It's the end of July, and Lane has missed another deadline for her book.

Her mind moves like molasses in the day but, at night, it comes alive—bursting with unanswered questions as she tries desperately to close the loop of Gala's life. The knowledge that Lane herself may have been the last person to see Gala makes it feel as if she is blocking the story somehow, changing its flow when all she wants to do is take a step back and observe from a distance. Sometimes Lane has the thought that Gala has disappeared just to fuck with her, but other times she understands how unhinged, how egotistical, that sounds.

For the first time since she started the project, Lane finds herself questioning her own motives for writing about her old friend. Up until Gala went missing, Lane had believed she was constructing a nuanced portrait of a woman she thought she knew better than most, but she was also clearly trying to uncover something about her own past, her own relentless pursuit of cruelty.

What was it in Lane's nature that led her to be so consumed with yet another human who would instinctively put their own needs before hers?

And then there's the question of Charlie. However Lane looks at it, she can't figure out what her best friend could have been doing at Gala's apartment. And, if some spectacular twist of events meant he had indeed found himself in the glamorous squalor of apartment 4, Hacienda Heights, why on earth wouldn't he have told her about it. After a week of stewing over every possible explanation, Lane feels no less troubled by Penny's claim. She knows she could just ask Charlie about it outright, but to do so feels like she would be crossing some unspoken line. Over the years they've been friends, Lane and Charlie have propped each other up and challenged each other to be better, but they've never once doubted each other. And she's never, ever lied to him. Despite not discussing the topic of her third novel with a single soul but her editor, Lane had even felt the need to casually mention to Charlie that Gala's footprints had somehow made their way into her book. She had felt strangely nervous about it, but he had only raised a withering eyebrow and said, "I hope it's a big book," presumably in reference to Gala's size 10 feet.

The truth is that Gala is the antithesis of everything Charlie and Lane have bonded over—their reverence for self-determination above all else: how one's own talent and conduct can directly affect one's life, regardless of what vast black hole you've emerged from. Gala, on the other hand, is messy, undisciplined, and gluttonous. She drinks what she wants, ingests what she wants, and says whatever the hell she wants. Occasionally, Lane has wondered if it's also Gala's lack of deference that has allowed Charlie to dismiss her so easily, but she'd never suggest this to him outright. Lane has always felt a little lucky that Charlie chose her that night at Tana's, and it's meant she's never rocked whatever boat it is they are both clinging to for dear life. Her father used to tell her to never look a gift horse in the mouth, and the attention Charlie has bestowed on her has felt something like a gift up to this point. But sometimes, you can't afford not to look.

ONE EVENING, CHARLIE drops by unannounced with a bottle of rich Cabernet Sauvignon he picked up from his friend's vineyard in Napa Valley over the weekend. Lane could usually listen to him talk for hours about the grapes, or about his friend's wife, an aristocratic equestrian champion from Sweden, but tonight she barely listens at all before she finds herself interrupting him, the words collecting at the back of her throat until she's compelled to say them out loud.

"Why didn't you tell me you went to Gala's apartment?" Lane asks, her tone more accusatory than she intends it to be. She has worked herself up so successfully that she wonders now if Charlie views her less as his equal and more as someone in need of his protection—as if he is Lane's own personal wizard, spinning the evil in the world into something beautiful just for her. She remembers the emotional acrobatics required in any exchange with her mother, the soothing tone both she and her father instinctively adopted with her, and the comparison makes her even more furious.

"Is that a question, my dear?" Charlie asks after a pause in which he doesn't quite meet her eye. "Can I get some more details perhaps of when this visit was rumored to have taken place?"

Lane steps closer to him, her fingers laced around the stem of her wineglass. The liquid is syrupy, a deep shade of red, and she knows she won't drink another sip of it.

"It was last month," she says slowly. "And it doesn't sound like something that could have slipped your mind—you liberated her cats apparently."

Charlie frowns and leans against the fridge. Behind him is a picture drawn by Audrey depicting the two girls, Scotty, Lane, the nanny, and Charlie, who always seems to be wearing a fedora in Audrey's five-year-old mind.

"I have no idea what you're talking about," Charlie says. "You know cats make me break out in hives."

Lane frowns.

"Had you seen her recently?"

"You're a writer, Lane, so you'll have to paint more of a picture for me than that. 'Recently' being nearly three years ago, when she hurtled into a party in this very room? Or 'recently' being in the past few weeks, in which case you seem to be accusing me of something I don't quite understand." Charlie smiles dazzlingly at her. "As I'm sure I don't have to remind you, Gala doesn't exactly float my boat in more ways than one."

"So you're saying you haven't seen or heard from Gala this year?" Lane says.

"That is correct, Nancy Drew," he says, mimicking her formal tone. "But the more interesting question is, why would it upset you so much if I had?"

Lane stares at him.

"Because you would have lied to me," she says, but they both know that's not quite it. Charlie raises an eyebrow just as the front door swings open and Scotty stands in the frame, soaked from the rain.

"Welcome home, darling!" Charlie says enthusiastically, much to Scotty's dismay, before he turns to Lane one last time. His voice is smooth and pleasant as he leans in close. "Whatever happened between you and Gala happened without me being there. Don't forget that."

Then he strides over to Scotty and slides the jacket right off his back as if he's a '50s housewife, before hanging it with a flourish on the back of the door, where Lane knows it will drip rainwater onto the floor and create a puddle that someone is bound to slip on unless she mops it up. She watches from the kitchen as he and Scotty then attempt to hold a conversation in that dry, stilted manner they've always had with each other, and she tries to unravel what's just happened.

Because her best friend is charming, and kinder than he'd ever want anyone to know, but he has never been any good at lying to her.

CHARLIE LEAVES BEFORE Scotty and Lane sit down for dinner. In silence, they eat a salad and some wood-fired chicken thighs that Scotty picked up from a Brazilian place, Lane still reeling from her conversation with Charlie. It's only when they're getting ready for bed that she offers up any sort of explanation for her silence, and this rare glimpse into her psyche feels like an act of generosity, as it always does. Lane often thinks that there are hundreds of tiny fractures between her and Scotty, and for the best part of a decade, it has felt as if they're only moments away from connecting to form a chasm that is too magnificent to navigate. As a result, she considers each small explanation she gives Scotty to be a bridge across the void, even though she knows she shouldn't feel as charitable about it as she does.

"Do you trust Charlie?" Lane asks as she unbuttons her shirt. She can feel Scotty stop moving across the room.

"Trust him with what?"

It's an odd response, and Lane frowns at him.

"Trust doesn't have to be absolute," Scotty says. "I can trust someone to pick up my mail while I'm away, for example, but that doesn't mean I'd leave Audrey or Dahlia with them, or trust them with my bank details."

"And what would you trust Charlie with?" Lane asks.

Scotty, who is on his way into the bathroom, turns to look at her properly.

"What's going on, Lane?"

Lane pauses for a moment before shrugging. She should have known Scotty wouldn't understand.

"I think we might have outgrown each other," she says.

Scotty laughs warmly. "Lane, you're thirty-eight years old and a mother of two, aren't you a little beyond outgrowing people? How much growth do you have left to do?"

Lane frowns at him. This is exactly the type of thing she'd predict he'd say, and is exactly the type of thing she'd usually complain about to Charlie—Scotty's fundamental lack of interest in viewing her as anything other than his wife, or the mother of his children, despite his protestations to the contrary. She wants to tell him that she used to be brilliant, but she knows it is a waste of breath.

"Come on," Scotty says, his tone gentler now. "What did he do this time? If it's something you've done that's offended him, don't take it personally. That guy thrives on being offended about something or other."

"I thought you'd jump at the chance to be rid of him," Lane says. "Aren't you always asking why he has to be around so much?"

Scotty considers this as he unzips his trousers, still damp from the rain. "I guess so, but I don't think we want him out of our lives completely."

It strikes her as an odd way to word it, but she lets it slide. She sits on the bed and turns her face up to her husband.

"I think he's lying to me," she says. "About Gala."

"Gala?" Scotty repeats, sounding confused. "Why?"

"I always felt like Charlie didn't want me to be friends with her," Lane says slowly. "As if he thought she would tarnish my reputation or something. And I allowed him to push her away because it was easier for me too, but now I'm wondering if I'm missing something. Why did he care so much?"

Scotty sits next to Lane on the bed and gently puts his hand on her leg.

"I think Charlie is protective of you," he says. "And he's smart about people. He's always known that nothing good can come of being close with Gala. Look at what happened to Gabriel."

Lane feels a wave of irritation at the mention of Gabriel.

"That's completely different," she says.

Scotty sighs then. "Look, Laney. You and Charlie have a closeness that almost everyone I know envies. And if he's lied to you, it's probably to protect you. You know what he's like."

Lane is surprised to find a sliver of comfort in this unlikeliest of places. Scotty is right—she knows Charlie better than she's ever known anyone, and it feels a lot more comfortable to trust him than to doubt him.

"I also don't think Charlie McCloud is the type of enemy you want," Scotty says, laughing. "Why do you think I've kissed up to him for the past seven years?"

Lane laughs a little too, and when she glances over, she sees that Scotty is watching her almost fondly. He puts his hand on her cheek and turns her head toward him. There is a split second where Lane can decide if she wants to kill any chance of intimacy but, to her surprise, she finds she doesn't want to. Instead, she leans in and kisses him, their lips touching gently at first and then, as they ease into each other's familiarity, a little harder. Soon he pulls her onto his lap and their bodies are pressed together for the first time in months, hands touching every inch of flesh as they move wordlessly together. They finish at the same time and then they lie facing each other, noses nearly touching for a while.

"Hey," he says softly.

"Hey," Lane says back.

Hey, Gala says, from the corner of the room.

TWENTY-TWO

THEN

OCTOBER 1968

One Saturday morning, eight weeks after the party at Chez Jay, Gala stood outside Lane's apartment, uninvited and unannounced. When Scotty opened the door, she struck a pose in her silk caftan with the matching headscarf, pretending she was less surprised to see him than he was her. She had thought about Lane often over the past two months, but, as it turned out, keeping Gabriel on the straight and narrow was a fairly consuming pastime, and she hadn't had much time for social engagements. At least now she could confirm that the rumors were true and Lane had been busy too, shacking up with Gala's neighbor—dull, handsome Scotty, who had always refused to flirt, let alone sleep with her.

"Gala," Scotty said. "You're looking . . . expressive, even for you."

"I'm going to take that as the first compliment you've ever paid me." Gala smiled winningly. "May I enter?"

She pushed past Scotty and surveyed Lane's apartment for the first time.

"Ah," she said, noting the stark interior and distinct lack of tchotchkes. "Like a monastery."

Scotty sighed. "Not everyone wants to live in a hovel," he said.

"Yes, I suppose Lane would hate to let on she had any personality," Gala said dryly. "Where is the woman of the hour?"

"She's taking a bath," Scotty said, and before he could stop her, Gala flounced past him and down the small hallway.

"Lane!" she called, peering first into the kitchen, before knocking on the closed bedroom door. "I'm coming in."

She pushed open the door and stepped inside. Lane was wrapped in a towel in the middle of a yellow room, furnished only with a perfectly made bed and a small bamboo bedside table with a half-drunk glass of water on it.

"Jesus, Lane," Gala said. "Would it kill you to hang a picture?"

Lane just stared at her. "What are you doing here?"

"We're going to the beach," Gala said. "Nobody's seen you in months, and I'm breaking you out."

Lane started to protest weakly, but Gala held up a hand.

"No arguments," she said. "You owe me."

Lane frowned. "Do I?"

"I've lost count," Gala replied, shrugging. "But you're coming anyway."

GALA WAITED IN the living room while Lane got dressed. She sat on the couch with her long, tanned legs tucked underneath her while Scotty leaned against the wall, his arms folded across his chest.

"Everything makes sense now," Gala said. Then, mumbling as she lit a cigarette: "Can I look after your place since you're never in it?"

Scotty walked over to the window and opened it. "No, Gala, it doesn't quite work like that."

Gala raised an eyebrow. She could hear the sound of a hair dryer coming from Lane's bedroom.

"Why are you so edgy around me?" she said. "You're not secretly in love with me, are you?"

Scotty surprised her by laughing. "You should be so lucky."

Gala smiled a little. They were finally getting into a rhythm at least. Maybe she'd push it even further, see if she could lure him away from Lane (theoretically, of course; she would *never* do that to Gabriel). Because, the more she thought about it, the more she disliked the idea of Scotty and Lane together. While he'd never said or done anything to prove it, she had a feeling he wasn't quite as cool as he wanted people to believe. She found this was often the case with men who feared her. If Lane saw this through, Gala figured she'd be done with writing within the year.

"Why wouldn't you ever fuck me, Scotty?" she asked next, her eyes wide beneath her wispy bangs.

Scotty hid a smile. "You're not my type, Gala," he said.

Gala exhaled a stream of smoke. "Too charming?"

"Not exactly."

"Too liberated?" she asked.

"Something like that," Scotty said, just as Lane walked into the room. She was wearing a crisp white oxford shirt and a pair of linen pants, with a broad straw hat. She looked between the two of them, Gala spread languidly across the couch, Scotty upright by the open window.

"Everything okay?" she asked.

"You look like a beekeeper," Gala said. "You know we're going to the beach?"

Scotty rolled his eyes as Lane kissed him on the cheek, a little self-consciously.

"Bye, ladies," he said as Lane unlocked the door. "Don't drive too fast."

Gala flounced over to him and kissed him on the other cheek before following Lane outside.

IT WAS A glorious day, and Gala drove surprisingly well as they headed down Wilshire in Gabriel's newest car—a teal Ford Thunderbird convertible. The sun was beating down as they pulled up at the lights by Beverly Glen, and a pickup truck pulled up in the lane next to them. The window rolled down, and a handsome face appeared. He turned down his radio and called Gala's name.

"Ed!" Gala said, visibly delighted. She hissed to Lane, "Ed *Ruscha*, the artist."

Lane smiled at him when he waved.

"Nice car," he said. "Where are you going?"

"The beach!" Gala said. "Virgins only though, sorry."

Ed laughed. "You haven't been a virgin since 1955, Gala."

The lights changed, and Gala blew him a kiss before pulling off with a screech of the tires, cackling as she cut into the lane ahead of the pickup. At the next set of lights, once Ed's truck had turned off, she glanced over at Lane.

"Do you think Ed's cute?" she asked.

"He's attractive," Lane said.

Gala flipped down the sun visor and checked her lipstick.

"Well, unfortunately he's married," she said. "But there's others like him. There's a whole *world* out there."

Lane stared at her. "What's going on with you? You're acting strange."

The light turned green, and Gala pulled away from the junction without answering. In the distance the ocean unfolded before them, twinkling golden in the sun.

GALA HAD PACKED a large box of cherries, a bottle of Coppertone, and a handful of colorful sarongs, which she unfolded on a clear stretch of sand, close enough to the volleyball nets that they could watch, but far enough away that they were unlikely to get hit by a stray ball. It was as if the rest of Hollywood had migrated for a rare beach day too, and all around them beautiful people basked in the warm October sun, the smell of coconut and monoï bright in the air. Gala watched them with the ghost of a smile on her face; she'd almost forgotten how much she loved L.A.

Gala slipped out of her caftan and stretched out in her white bikini, her huge sunglasses obscuring most of her face. She pulled out a small notebook from her straw bag and started to jot down a few sentences describing the scene around them. Lane carefully took off her linen trousers and folded them, leaving her white shirt over her black bathing suit. Her spine was straight as she looked out at the ocean, her eyes occasionally flicking over to Gala.

"Spit it out," Gala said eventually, her eyes not leaving the page of her book.

"What?" Lane asked.

"Whatever it is that's making you even more tightly wound than usual."

Lane cleared her throat. "You don't like Scotty, do you?"

"It's not a question of liking him," Gala said, after a pause. "But I do know him. Or men like him, anyway."

"What does that mean?"

Gala stretched out like a cat and put her book down.

"Oh, you know, men who pretend like they're cool and hip with whatever until they have you, when they want you to be exactly like their mother."

"Scotty isn't like that," Lane said.

"I don't know, Lane," Gala said. "I tend to find that if a man dislikes me, he's usually threatened by what I represent."

"Oh, *that's* what this is about then . . ." Lane said.

Gala raised a questioning eyebrow.

"This is because he wouldn't sleep with you."

Gala laughed. "Is that what he told you? Honey, there are enough men in this city who will sleep with me, I assure you." She shook her head. "It's not about that. Can I ask what it is you see in him?"

Lane thought for a moment. "Scotty's very grounded. He's . . . rooted in his principles."

Gala laughed again before realizing Lane wasn't joking. She turned to look at Lane properly, her expression quizzical.

"That's great and all, but you do realize he's a man, not a vegetable."

Lane didn't smile. "It's different for me than it is you," she said slowly. "I don't have a family, so I can't afford to bet everything on somebody's potential. I'm looking for consistency."

"Consistency," Gala said wryly. "The new foreplay."

Lane smiled weakly.

"What happened to your family?" Gala asked. In *The Ringtail*, both of P's parents had died before she turned seventeen, but Gala had assumed that there was more than a little wish fulfillment tied up in their tragic but conveniently neat demise.

Lane waved her hand, about to brush the question off, but then she stopped herself.

"It was all true," she said. "They were suburban addicts. Incapable of looking after themselves, let alone a child."

"Oof," Gala breathed, propping herself up on her elbows to get a better look at Lane now that she possessed this information. The missing piece to the puzzle that made Lane the way she was.

"Go on," Lane said dryly. "Tell me it's the most interesting thing about me."

Gala didn't laugh, just reached out and touched Lane's shoulder gently.

"I'm sorry," she said. "That must have been awful."

For a moment, Lane looked crushed, but she recovered quickly. "It happens."

She seemed suddenly restless, desperate to be talking about anything but this and Gala felt a sudden pang of tenderness for her friend.

"Can I have a cigarette?" Lane asked, and Gala tossed her gold cigarette case, followed by a pack of matches. Lane lit a cigarette and exhaled before blowing out the match. "Are you writing?"

"What?"

Lane gestured toward Gala's notebook. "Are you writing another story?"

"Oh," Gala said tightly. "Not really. Just little observations."

A young woman with golden curls approached then, standing above Lane in her yellow swimsuit and blocking the sun.

"You're Lane Warren," the woman said excitedly. She was young, barely out of her teens, and she had a sweet gap between her front teeth.

Lane smiled politely. "I am."

"I'm obsessed with *The Ringtail*," the woman said, her words tumbling out. "I actually just quit my job to write my own memoir. My parents met in a cult—the Great Eleven Club? Have you heard of it?"

Lane stared at her over her sunglasses as Gala winced.

"*The Ringtail* isn't a memoir," Lane said, her voice entirely neutral. Gala watched as the younger woman seemed to deflate.

"Oh," she said. "Sure. I just wanted to . . ."

"I understand," Lane said, then smiled. "Thank you for coming over."

"Sure," the woman said again. She frowned slightly, then turned to leave.

"Good luck with the book, honey!" Gala called after her.

Lane picked up a cherry and popped it in her mouth.

"What?" she said when she turned to find Gala staring at her.

"Nothing," Gala said, raising an eyebrow. "I'm just surprised you have any fans left if that's how you treat them."

Lane narrowed her eyes at her. "I don't think it's healthy to idolize anyone."

"Clearly," Gala said.

Lane shrugged.

"Anyway," she said, taking another cherry. "Have you written anything at all lately?"

"I haven't exactly had the time," Gala said.

"How is Gabriel anyway?"

"Lane." Gala's voice was now a warning shot.

"What, so you're allowed to express your opinion, but I'm not?"

"He's trying," Gala said.

"He can try all he wants," Lane said. "But he's not going to change."

"That's a bleak way of looking at the world," Gala said.

"Maybe," Lane said. "But it's the truth."

As she spoke, a volleyball landed in the sand next to them. They both just stared at it as a teenager ran over to collect it.

"Just because your parents couldn't change for you, doesn't mean Gabriel won't for me," Gala said quietly.

There was a long pause, and then Lane let out a long exhale. "I wish that were true," she said.

Gala shrugged and Lane lit another cigarette. The rest of Santa Monica frolicked around them as the two women looked on in thoughtful silence.

TWENTY-THREE

THEN

NEW YEAR'S EVE 1968/69

Scott Douglas Ryan and Lauren "Lane" Warren were married two months later, on New Year's Eve. The ceremony at Los Angeles City Hall was brief but affecting, and the reception was held at Scotty's gallery, a brutalist structure on La Cienega. The most influential people from the world of art, literature, and music were in attendance, and guests flew in from New York, London, and Paris. The bride wore a bronze silk long-sleeved column dress and diamonds from Harry Winston, picked out by her best man, Charlie McCloud, and the groom made a rousing speech about the importance of always trusting your gut, particularly when it came to matters of the heart.

LANE SAT AT a beautifully dressed table facing out into the main exhibition room. The more expensive art had been removed from the stark walls, and the space had been transformed into a chic monochromatic ballroom with bouquets of gardenias hanging

from the steel rafters. Lane was flanked on either side by Scotty
and Charlie, and (as she had no family to invite and his parents
were in poor health) it was just the three of them, plus Scotty's
two brothers, who had driven down from Sacramento with
their impressively interchangeable blond wives and masses of
children.

As Lane pushed her tarte tatin around her plate, she scanned
the glamorous crowd for Gala before spotting her, finally, at a table in the back corner of the room, her arm wrapped protectively
around the back of Gabriel's chair. Lane tried to remember whom
she'd sat them with, but she couldn't quite recall anything other
than they were friends of Charlie's she'd invited to make up numbers on her side of things.

She hadn't wanted to admit to Scotty how few people she really counted as friends, and he'd seemed so taken aback when
she'd suggested only Gala and Charlie alongside a few work con-
tacts, that she'd had to invite twenty or so more people that she
barely knew to make up for it. She didn't want this good-natured
man, who had *childhood* friends and *college* friends and *fraternity*
friends and *family* friends and *work* friends to invite, to think she
was impaired in some way. That she didn't know how to be normal. And it wasn't as if there weren't people out there desperate
to have her at their dinner parties, she had just never had much
use for casual friendships. They struck her as both a distraction
from her writing and inherently flawed—the parts of themselves
people were willing to show were almost always a fabrication, and
never the parts that mattered in any meaningful way. (And Lane
should know; she'd spent her whole life pretending.) So she snuck
Gala onto a list of twenty or so people she'd exchanged a few
pleasantries with at parties over the years and pretended like
they'd all been the best of friends for years. Only, now that she

looked around the room, she couldn't quite remember who she'd claimed was hers, and who was Scotty's.

Gala's wedding gift to Lane and Scotty was Gabriel. Or rather, Belle Vue. They'd been on hiatus while Gabriel was out of action, and Gala seemed to have decided it would be a good idea for them to ease back into life as a band by performing a few songs at the reception. The gallery had the space for it, plus, on the surface of it, who wouldn't want the biggest band in the country ringing in their new era as a married couple?

Both Charlie and Scotty advised against it, but Lane hadn't known how to refuse. She'd understood that Gala was partly making a point after their conversation at the beach, but there was also a shade of desperation about the way she'd suggested it, as if she'd identified this as the solution to whatever it was that had kept her from writing any more since her *Vanity Fair* article, which (while it hadn't set the world alight like Lane's goldfish piece had) had been received generously by people whose opinions mattered. Lane, in return, felt desperately sad for Gala, who seemed hell-bent on throwing everything away for a losing horse. Lane knew only too well what it was like to be eaten alive by someone who was supposed to love you.

"She's fine," Charlie said, following her eyeline to Gala.

"I know," Lane said. But she wasn't so sure.

LATER, THE BAND took to the makeshift stage at the back of the room, and Gabriel took his place behind the mic, a guitar slung around the open neck of his suit. He looked blankly out at the crowd gathered to hear him sing, as if he couldn't quite remember when or why he'd agreed to it. Lane scanned the room for Gala again and eventually found her, sitting at a table of kids whose names or origins Lane couldn't recall if her life depended on it, her eyes locked on Gabriel.

The performance was short and flat. The band sang two of their old songs and one average new one (Lane assumed it was about Gala, from the lengthy descriptions of crooked teeth), and then Gabriel mumbled his congratulations into the mic before leaving the stage. Whatever magnetism the front man of Belle Vue had charmed the world with not even three years ago seemed to have left the building. Gabriel himself seemed to have left the building.

Lane watched as Gala stood up and wrapped her arms around Gabriel. She seemed relieved, kissing him tenderly, and Lane wondered how she couldn't see it. That the thing that had destroyed him was the same thing that made him.

"Jesus," Charlie muttered under his breath beside Lane.

"It was bad, wasn't it," she said quietly. "It wasn't just me."

"It was worse than bad," Charlie said. "It was boring."

Scotty grabbed Lane then and pulled her up with an expansive smile on his face, and they started to dance to "Cloudy" by Simon and Garfunkel. It was their official first dance choice, somewhat disrupted by Gala's gift, but it didn't take the shine off the moment for either of them. Scotty hummed along with the melody into the top of her head, and Lane closed her eyes and wondered if all this love could one day fill the holes left in her by her parents. In this moment, she figured anything was possible.

FROM THE EDGE of the dance floor, Charlie sipped his old-fashioned. As the song faded and Scotty wrapped his arms around his new wife, Charlie felt something pull in the back of his throat, and he understood that he was jealous. Not jealous of Scotty obviously (as much as he adored Lane), and certainly not jealous of Lane (who, on Charlie's own advice, had chosen someone whole-some and successful, but who wasn't exactly the most inspiring creature), and not even jealous necessarily of this wedding (al-though he'd worked hard to make it as chic an affair as possible), but more of the thoughtless abandon of it all. Since this very night two years ago, Charlie hadn't set foot in another gay bar, or any-where remotely perceived to be gay-friendly, again. And he wasn't sure if he ever would. He was terrified of seeing the cop again, the one with the fox eyes, and he knew it wasn't worth the risk. He told himself that not everyone had to be a revolutionary, not everyone had to expose the most vulnerable parts of themselves to exist, but he still felt lonelier than he ever knew possible. He missed Elijah every second of every day, even when he was asleep.

And all of these people here (or rather, most of these people, since Charlie recognized a few of the men from his more adven-turous days) were free to throw their arms around one another as they danced, or rest their heads on one another's shoulders during the speeches—there, even Gala was having a tender mo-ment on the dance floor with her junkie boyfriend, as miserable as they'd both looked all day. All these people just living their own lives without even thinking about any alternative, about how it would feel to hide what felt like the most significant part of your-self from everyone you knew. *They have no idea how lucky they are*, Charlie thought as he watched Lane dance with her new husband. If you thought about it too much, you could hate every single one of them.

WHEN LANE SPOTTED Gala dancing quietly with Gabriel on the edge of the dance floor instead of with the other merry reprobates of Laurel Canyon, Lane realized how long it had been since she'd seen Gala steal any show. Lane watched as Gala and Gabriel swayed to the music instead, both of them sipping on sparkling water, and Lane tried to look for signs of life in Gala, but she couldn't find any.

After a moment, Lane strode across the dance floor and cut in, smiling apologetically at Gabriel.

"Help me touch up my lipstick?" she said to Gala. "The line for the restroom's too long."

"You're not wearing lipstick," Gala said, frowning. "Although, god knows why not."

"Bride's prerogative," Lane said. "Now come help me?"

Gala shrugged and kissed Gabriel on the cheek.

"I won't be long," she said, before she followed Lane across the dance floor.

When they reached Scotty's office, a bright room filled with shiny white space-age furniture, Lane turned to Gala, who was rifling through her purse for some makeup.

"You're scared to leave him alone," Lane said.

"Excuse me?" Gala said, but her hands were shaking slightly as she pulled out her lipstick and applied it in a reflective chrome statue on Scotty's desk to avoid looking at Lane. Once she was done, she wordlessly held it out to Lane.

"Will you do it for me?" Lane asked and, after a loud sigh, Gala started to apply it, her amber eyes narrowed in concentration.

Midway through, Lane opened her mouth to say something and Gala shushed her. When she was finished, Gala appraised her work and nodded.

"Ready?" she said, but Lane hesitated.

"You still haven't written anything," she said eventually.

Gala raised an eyebrow. "How do you know that?"

"I know," Lane said. "Because you can't do anything when you're around someone like Gabriel."

Gala's tone was sharp when she spoke again. "Lane, I know you're used to everyone blowing smoke up your ass but, if I were you, I'd be careful about what I said next."

Gala was right—it had been a while since anyone *had* spoken to Lane like that. She was used to Charlie's fascination, or Scotty's adoration, or the awe of strangers as they came up to her in the street to quote lines from *The Ringtail* back to her, but not the scorching resentment she detected in Gala's voice. Still, Lane knew she couldn't drop it.

"When we met, I asked you what you did and you couldn't give me a straight answer because you've spent years making other people rich and famous," Lane said, the words tumbling out now with a sense of urgency. "But maybe *you're* the thing you were waiting for all along. Have you considered that?"

"Lane," Gala said. "Just give it a rest."

"Prove me wrong and I will."

"Excuse me?"

"Prove he's not holding you back. I'll introduce you to three editors tonight, and you better walk out of my wedding with at least one commission lined up," Lane said, her tone still challenging.

"I don't need to prove anything to you."

"Maybe not," Lane said. "But prove it to yourself then."

"It's your *wedding day*," Gala said, but Lane could tell she was softening. "Don't you have anything better to do?"

"Fortunately for you, no."

Gala sighed wearily, but she still let Lane guide her back into the ballroom, and straight over to a tall man in horn-rimmed glasses, who Lane whispered was an editor at *Esquire*.

"This is Gala Margolis," Lane said. "And she's the most talented writer I know."

Lane watched as Gala stood blinking under the lights for a moment as if she'd forgotten how to be herself, before she finally came to life, pulling her lips back into a dazzling smile so that her charmingly crooked teeth were on full display.

"Mr. Turner," she purred as she leaned forward to kiss him on the cheek. "Can I tell you about the time I met Frank Sinatra at a gas station in Palm Springs?"

LANE STOOD IN the glass entrance of the gallery as the setting sun streamed through the conservatory, and realized that a part of her wished she could walk out of her own wedding and leave this room full of glamorous strangers to celebrate on her behalf. She had left Gala chatting happily with the third editor she'd introduced her to, but their exchange in Scotty's office had drained Lane of much of the optimism she'd felt earlier in the day. The problem was, she'd meant every word she said to Gala—Gabriel was a vampire, and he was going to ruin Gala if she let him. Not because he wanted to, but because he couldn't help himself. And Lane knew better than most what could happen when a woman sacrificed herself for someone else.

Lane spotted Scotty across the room, dancing with one of his nieces, who was standing on his shoes. She smiled as she watched him and, once again, thanked the universe that she'd found a man who seemed wholly incapable of lying about anything.

When the song finished, instead of rejoining the party, Lane slipped away to the restroom, where she locked herself in a cubicle and took a long, quiet moment to herself.

———————

WHEN LANE RETURNED, she spotted Scotty looking for her, his face bewildered as he stood at the edge of the dance floor with a crystal tumbler in his hand. She walked up to him and slid her bare arm around his waist. Scotty bent down and kissed her cheek.

"Where have you been?" he asked in her ear.

"I needed a second," she said.

"Everything okay?" he asked, and she offered him a smile to show him that, now at least, she was exactly where she wanted to be. He frowned a little and took a sip from the glass in his hand. It was filled with an amber liquid and crushed ice.

"You're drinking," Lane said, her tone more curious than barbed.

"It's my wedding day," he said.

"I've never seen you drink liquor before," she said and, while she knew better than to say this part, it was one of the reasons she'd chosen him. He seemed to have the opposite of an addict's disposition—he could pour himself a glass of wine and drink half of it without ever thinking of it again. The first time she'd spotted that half-empty glass of wine still on the kitchen table the following morning, it had felt like a pure tonic swimming through her.

"What's that on your lips?" Scotty asked then, his brow furrowing.

"Lipstick," she said. "It's Gala's."

"You looked prettier without it," he said, handing her a napkin from one of the tables. She fingered the pretty scalloped edge.

"Oh," she said.

They stared at each other, and eventually she handed him back the napkin. She wasn't about to wipe off her lipstick because he was sulking that she'd needed a break for half an hour.

"Have you seen Charlie? He wanted to talk to you about the honeymoon—" she said, but Scotty was already abruptly walking away. She watched as he slapped his brother Glenn on the back before pouring himself some more scotch. He seemed in excellent spirits, particularly when Glenn said something that made him laugh so hard he nearly spat his drink out. And look at this man—Kennedy handsome with a family who loved him, in a beautiful concrete and glass palace of his own making. It was as if nothing had happened, and perhaps it hadn't.

TWENTY-FOUR

NOW

SUMMER 1975

"What do you know," Esther breathes into the phone, her voice serrated. "She lives."

Lane clears her throat. "I haven't been well."

"The migraines," Esther supplies wanly. "My mother swore hers were worse when it was a full moon."

"Is it a full moon now?" Lane asks.

"How the fuck would I know?"

There is a silence, while Lane waits for the question she knows is coming.

"Where's the book, Lane?"

Lane twirls the phone cord around her finger.

"Did you know she was missing?"

"I'd heard something," Esther says vaguely, and then it's as if she understands what Lane is trying to tell her. "It's fiction, Laney. Nobody's expecting you to see into the future."

"It's not just that . . ." Lane starts, then breaks off. She knows Esther won't understand, and how would she say it anyway? That she hasn't been able to write a word since the day she found out Gala was missing? That she feels like her oldest (only?) friend knows more than he's letting on? That, sometimes, in the dead of the night, she thinks that Gala has done this on purpose to punish her?

"Lane. We've both got a lot on the line here . . ." Esther pauses, and Lane knows what's coming next, can almost mouth the words along with her as if she were playing it for laughs and not sitting alone with her back pressed against the kitchen fridge and a lump in her throat. *You've already taken the money.*

It had been a big advance—rumored to be the biggest advance Parker Hessler had ever paid out. If Lane is being brutally honest with herself, she knows that a substantial part of the book's appeal to the publishers is in its link to Gabriel Ford, and Lane's well-established influence within the Laurel Canyon community. And it is because of said absurd advance (clearly more than anyone should have accepted) that the book needs to come out in November, in time for the Christmas rush and sales boost, and while interest in the subject is still high. Missing her slot will skew the publishing house's annual budget, not to mention put Lane in breach of her contract over funds she'd already spent. In short, time is running out.

"I vouched for you," Esther says. "If you can't deliver, you needed to tell me yesterday."

"I know," Lane says tightly. "I can deliver."

And of course Lane doesn't want to wait another year either. After the dismal failure of her sophomore effort, the publisher's excitement about this book has felt like a crucial turning point, and she can't imagine waiting another sixteen months to find out if she is still worthy of the adoration she once amassed. But it's not even just that the sentences won't come anymore, it's that every time she tries to write, she feels a clawing sense of panic that she's doing something very wrong. And though she would never tell another living soul this, often it feels like Gala is in the room with her, waiting to see what she has to show for her betrayal.

"Do you think it's fair?" Lane asks quietly. "To write it now that she's not here?"

There is a long pause and the crackle of a cigarette through the line.

"Don't let anyone get in your head," Esther says wearily. "If you can take it, it was never really theirs."

They hang up, and Lane feels the thrum of dread in her chest intensify.

NORMALLY, LANE WOULD turn to Charlie with her writing woes. They have built her career and celebrity together over the past decade, and it is under his watchful eye that she has been so particular, carefully selecting opportunities that serve their shared creation of "Lane Warren": someone to be both admired and feared in her role as the unofficial scribe of Hollywood. Lane used to think that if she earned enough respect from the people and institutions that mattered, then she might actually turn into this fabricated version of herself, but she figures it's unlikely now. Without writing, she's just another suburban housewife, hiding from herself in a house that's too big, too clean, too opulent, to inspire anything other than ennui. Without writing, she's just like any other woman in the country. Without writing, she's just like her mother.

LANE ASKS AROUND for Ruby Roblex's number, eventually tracking it down from a Liquor Locker employee who once sold Ruby some coke. Lane does nothing with it for a few days until one evening when Scotty is out, and she works up the nerve to call Gala's best friend.

"Any word?" Lane asks, once she's introduced herself.

There is a short silence on the other end of the line.

"You went to see her parents," Ruby says.

"It was a waste of time," Lane says. "They couldn't see anything past their love for her."

"You sound jealous."

Another pause.

"Maybe," Lane says.

"So you do have a heart, or is it a conscience?"

"Ruby," Lane says. "Please."

She bites at the skin around her thumbnail.

"That night she found out you were writing about her?" Ruby says slowly. "It was rough, Lane."

Lane swallows hard.

"What happened between you two?" Ruby asks. "Before you pulled that shit with the book. She was always cagey about you."

"It doesn't really matter," Lane says, then—"I think we were too different. I wanted her to be someone she wasn't."

"A lot of people are different but they don't end up enemies," Ruby says. "And I think it does matter. I think it mattered to her."

There is a muffled crashing sound on the other end of the line, and Lane senses that her time is running out.

"Did she blame me for what happened to Gabriel?" Lane asks, her voice low.

Ruby is quiet for a moment.

"I think she blamed herself," she says. "I never understood why."

Someone shouts Ruby's name in the distance, and she sighs. "I have to go."

"Let me know if you hear anything," Lane says.

"Maybe," Ruby says.

Lane is about to hang up, when Ruby speaks again.

"I wasn't . . . there for her either, before she disappeared," Ruby says. "I tried, but she wasn't always the easiest person to be around, and life got in the way, you know?"

Lane clears her throat, unsure of what Ruby wants from her exactly.

"I'm not great at advice," she says in the end.

Ruby lets out a sharp laugh.

"Well, I don't think you and Gala were as different as you thought," Ruby says. "And I have a feeling you're going to find that out one day."

FOR THE NEXT few weeks, instead of working, or talking to Charlie, or spending time with her family, Lane leaves the house before anyone else is awake to roam the grittier streets of Hollywood, searching for the only person who holds the answer to what will become of them both. And at first glance, it is Gala on every street corner: legs splayed, dirty soles of her feet showing, devouring a bowl of cherries as dark red juice dribbles down her chin. Waiting for Lane to find her.

TWENTY-FIVE

THEN

JUNE 1969

Charlie had existed in a perpetual state of autopilot for a while. While he was out almost every night of the week at various events, he had a chef prepare twice-daily meals for him to optimize both nutritional value and maintenance of his weight, and every Tuesday evening he would take himself to a doctor on Third who would replace any lost fluids and vitamins via an intravenous drip in his arm. As always, he excelled at work, flawlessly executing publicity campaign after campaign with the easy charm he was known for, whether it be producing an industry showcase in the presidential suite at the Beverly Hills Hotel or securing discreet medical intervention for a saccharine all-American country star who overdosed after a show in Peru.

Charlie was self-aware enough to know exactly what he was doing. He had single-handedly manufactured a life of constant pressure, existing in a state of forward motion solely to avoid dealing with the gaping hole in his chest left by someone who was only ever meant to be a fling anyway. It was of cruel fascination to him that something so wholly inappropriate, something that was never built to last, could have left him feeling so obliterated. Every single inch of his beloved home was now a gaping vacuum Elijah had left behind.

One Sunday in June, when news of the Stonewall uprising spread and thousands of people took to the streets of New York City to fight for the rights of people with hearts just like his, Charlie experienced a swell of gratitude and fear and love so strong that he found himself dialing Elijah's old number. Elijah's roommate, Eddie, the one who had enthusiastically fielded all of Charlie's calls two years earlier, answered, and he seemed just as thrilled to inform him that Elijah no longer lived there.

"Do you know where he's gone?" Charlie asked, still burning with hope and fury and the pressing need to tell the only person he'd ever loved how much he meant to him. He would tell him that he was right, that the world was on fire, but that nothing mattered if they had each other, and that—

"He's gone to San Francisco, baby," Eddie said. "To be with someone who knows how to love him."

Charlie hung up the phone and felt like he was going to be sick.

LATER, HE PUT on a baseball cap and a dirty old fleece he occasionally wore when it got chilly in the hills, and he drove himself down to Sunset. There was a bar, the Snug, that he'd heard about and, when he drove past it, Charlie could see a swell of people outside, people who would understand exactly how he was feeling.

Charlie parked a few streets away and joined the line. The group in front of him was so big that he could have slipped in with them, but instead he stopped in front of the man on the door, unsmiling with a thick mustache, who glanced at him quickly.

"Sir, how can I help you?" the man asked, his voice polite but firm.

"I'm . . . looking for somewhere I can have a quiet drink." Charlie heard how uncomfortable he sounded as the man looked him up and down in a way that wasn't unkind, but that wasn't exactly welcoming either. Charlie figured that this was an adaptation from the years of being raided by undercover cops, and he pulled at his sweater and wondered if it would help if he took off his baseball cap. He racked his brain for something to say that might convince this person that he wasn't there to cause trouble, that he actually belonged in here too, but for once he was lost for words.

"We have a private event tonight," the man said eventually. "You might want to find somewhere else down the street."

Charlie stood dumbly for a moment, until it felt like the people behind him walked right through him to reach the door, and then he stumbled away.

For a while afterward, he stood in the shadows across the street, watching as groups of men and young couples walked confidently up to the door and talked their way inside. There seemed to be a secret code, a language everyone was fluent in except for him.

He had never felt so alone.

IT WASN'T LONG before Charlie came up with the idea of hosting Sunday Salons at Lane and Scotty's. The idea was that every Sunday afternoon, Lane would throw a glitzy party at her beautiful new home in the foothills of Laurel Canyon. With Charlie's help, they would create an environment in which the elite of Hollywood's film, music, and literary scenes could drop by and relax, or take copious amounts of drugs, or act in generally debauched ways without fear, because every guest was vetted and preapproved by Charlie himself.

The house, with its creamy open-plan interior and sprawling outside entertaining space, lent itself perfectly to the occasion, and once Charlie added a few signature touches (poolside cabanas like they had at the Beverly Hills Hotel and enough foliage to rival the Garden of Eden), the space felt like a paradise.

Scotty had seemed less than thrilled by the idea of hosting a weekly party, but he couldn't really say no when Charlie presented it as a shrewd business move—something else to help build the mystique around them both as a couple, but particularly Lane, whose entire career depended on her reputation, when you thought about it. She was, after all, one of the only women writing in this particular milieu, and while she still felt like an outsider most of the time, hosting parties like this would secure her position as the most influential writer in Hollywood.

Of course, Charlie knew that the parties were as much for him as they were for Lane. Through them, he had secured a role for himself as the unofficial patron of the glitzier side of Laurel Canyon, and his days were soon stacked with calls and invitations from people desperate to score an invite to the next salon. Every Sunday morning when he was running around the Los Angeles Flower Market downtown or sampling hors d'oeuvres prepared by the sushi chef at Kawafuku, Charlie would breathe a sigh of relief that on the loneliest day of the week (when most people had lunch with their families or drove to the coast or spent a lazy day reading the Sunday papers with their partner), he had something not only to distract but to consume him.

Sometimes, while they were choosing which records to play or inventing a new cocktail, he would look at Lane and feel the closest thing to security that he'd ever known. She would never leave him, not really. They were too alike in that way, both looking for adoration but far too scared to ever accept it.

TWENTY-SIX

THEN

JULY 1969

Gala's second article was published seven months after Lane's wedding, in the August issue of *Esquire* magazine. It had taken her a while to follow up with the editors Lane had introduced her to, but the editor with the horn-rimmed glasses had not only remembered her but formally commissioned the piece she'd pitched to him at the gallery. In the weeks that followed, Gala nearly killed herself drafting and re-drafting her account of the moment she asked Frank Sinatra for life advice, honing each sentence until the final line of the piece (the only words he'd uttered to her during their encounter) read like a perfect punch line.

Gala had come across Frank at the gas station in Palm Springs in 1960, when he was at the height of his frustrations with his record label, Capitol. Gala, aged nineteen, had just escaped a rotten weekend trip with the married man she was seeing, and she was feeling uncharacteristically unsure of herself and the choices she'd made. She was a Sinatra fan in the way that everyone her age was—he was a Californian institution, but you couldn't quite remember why (like the burgers at Bob's Big Boy in Burbank, or the counter at Schwab's), and she found herself pouring her heart out to him underneath the relentless Palm Springs sun.

She told him about the famous actor she'd been fucking and about how she'd packed all her very best outfits for their weekend trip but he'd refused to leave the house for fear of being spotted by someone who knew his wife, so she'd had to sulk in the pool for two days straight until her skin turned green with chlorine, and then this morning the wife had shown up unannounced and Gala had had to climb into the closet while the actor convinced his wife to go to breakfast with him, and how she was too young and too beautiful to be locked in a goddamned closet, because life was meant to be *fun* even though everyone else seemed hell-bent on forgetting that the second they hit thirty, but that *Frank* seemed to have it all figured out in the fun department, although she was sorry to hear it hadn't worked out with Ava Gardner, or his first wife, and she hoped he'd never stop trying to get it right, if that's what he wanted. He'd listened patiently, his eyes locked on her, and when she finally stopped talking, she waited for him to say something. Everyone she knew who had either worked with him or met him had described how he had this unwavering ability to see through whatever facade you tried to present to the rest of the world, and how one observation from him could set you spiraling in a new direction, into a new *dimension*. And after spending over an hour in a dark closet, breathing in another (lesser, Gala thought) woman's musty dresses, Gala found she was holding her breath as she waited for this familiar stranger to tell her the thing that could change her life forever.

"Baby," Frank Sinatra had said, his famous blue eyes dancing with gentle amusement. "Have you ever thought maybe you talk too much?"

THE ARTICLE WAS received just as well as her first, if not better, and soon Gala's phone was ringing each week with commissions from editors at publications ranging from *New York* magazine to *Cosmopolitan*. She wrote more and more, and more again, until she had a piece published in almost every magazine. She felt proud of what she'd achieved, but a lot of that was a childish sense of glee that she'd shown people who'd dismissed her as a talentless dolt just how wrong they were. Still, she didn't know if she felt the way about writing that someone like Lane did. It wasn't the beginning and end of everything for her, it was just one more wild experience she would never regret. And some things were more precious to her than her career—despite being begged by nearly every editor in the country (and being offered more money than she'd made in the past five years), Gala flat out refused to write about Gabriel. Maybe she would one day, if he ever regained whatever it was he'd lost, but right now he still seemed too fragile, like if she pulled hard enough at one thread, he might unravel entirely.

LANE HADN'T SPOKEN to Gala since her wedding. Or perhaps Gala hadn't spoken to Lane. And despite being the only person in the world who seemed to care about Gala's writing career, Lane had a feeling she was still annoyed about their conversation about Gabriel. Lane knew they were at a fundamental impasse on the subject—she would never apologize for telling Gala the truth.

She'd partly assumed that Gala would just appear at one of her parties, until she realized how carefully Charlie vetted the guest list; how much consideration went into honoring the golden ratio of beauty and power so that you might find an up-and-coming starlet from John Huston's latest movie challenging an erudite scholar of Plato to a race in the pool. Lane knew then that Charlie would never deem Gala worthy of an invite, however many articles she may have published. So one week, Lane took matters into her own hands and called Gala to invite her to the following Sunday Salon. And, because it was the third Sunday of the month, this one had a theme.

"Celestial wonderland," Lane said. "Don't ask me, Charlie's idea."

"I never would have guessed," Gala said. Then: "Is Gabriel invited?"

Lane thought carefully before she responded. "If you think that's a good idea."

In the end, Gala came alone, making her way up Sunset dressed in a short white negligee with hand-painted gold wings resting on her shoulder blades. She had a halo of bronze wire and glitter on her cheeks, and every time a car honked at her, she'd execute a flamboyant twirl to show off her otherworldly beauty.

FOR THE FIRST two hours of the party, Lane hovered around the door, waiting for Gala's arrival. She hadn't told either Scotty or Charlie about the invite, and she didn't want Gala's initial impression to be one of humiliation (not that rejection seemed to leave the same mark on Gala as it did on other people). The house was already filled with dozens of guests, most of whom had pushed the ostentatious theme to its limits in creations of baroque excess.

As it happened, Lane was in the bathroom when Gala arrived, but Scotty had answered the door and his good manners had prevailed. He was leading Gala across the room when Lane intercepted them. Gala looked even more *Gala* than usual, a full head above most of the women in the room, covered in glitter and what appeared to be gold-dipped feathers on her back.

"You came," Lane said, smiling at Gala.

"I thought you said there was a theme," Gala said, putting her head to one side as she assessed Lane curiously. Lane was wearing a loose cream silk suit and gold-wire glasses, and next to Gala she felt suddenly like a bad sport.

"Lane always looks like an angel to me," Scotty said, slinging his arm around her shoulders. Lane tried not to stiffen at his unsolicited touch. Scotty had grown up in a world where affection wasn't rationed, and, even after a year together, Lane found she was never quite prepared for it.

"Oh yes," Gala said. "We all know Lane is perfect."

Lane smiled at her husband then. "Scotty, could you check on the pool temperature? Charlie will murder us both if it's a degree below eighty-two."

Scotty gave an amiable military-style salute and then wandered off.

"I always thought Scotty would make a good soldier," Gala said, raising an eyebrow as they watched him retreat. "He has the disposition."

Lane let the comment slide. She knew it wasn't a compliment. "What can I get you to drink?"

For the first time, Gala looked almost sheepish. "Coke?"

"You're not drinking?" Lane asked.

"Well, it's a school night and I'm on deadline," Gala said.

Lane smiled as she walked over to the fridge, feeling pleased
that she might have had something to do with this shift in priori-
ties in Gala, even if Gala hadn't directly thanked her for anything yet.

Gala followed, taking in the scene unfolding around her—the
cigarette smoke spiraling ever higher, the beautiful people draped
over furniture as they exchanged asides like they were in an eternal battle to care the least, the rich tones of a legendary folk
singer sitting cross-legged on the lawn and serenading guests
outside—as if she'd seen all of it a thousand times before. And,
Lane realized, she probably had.

"This house is really something. Is that book money or art
money?"

"I don't think you're supposed to ask that."

Lane crouched down to open the drawer at the bottom of the
fridge. She was hidden behind the fridge door, sifting through the
cans of root beer and club soda to find one of Scotty's Cokes,
when someone approached Gala.

"Gala Margolis?" the voice said. "I'm a huge fan of your writing. Your piece where you lived like a retiree in Ojai killed me."

"Oh, thank you!" Gala said, sounding genuinely thrilled at the
compliment. From her crouched position, Lane smiled too.

"Honestly, it's so rare to possess both tenderness and wit," the
disembodied voice said conspiratorially. "Unlike *some* women,
who write like they've got a stick up their ass and one down their
throat for good measure. It's probably how she stays so thin, if you
know what I mean."

Lane closed the fridge door abruptly and stood up to find Doris King, a screenwriter who had just been nominated for an Os-
car, standing in front of her. Gala was wincing slightly, as if

hoping Lane somehow hadn't heard, but Lane could tell part of her was relishing it too.

"Lane," Doris said, looking anywhere but at Lane directly. "What a beautiful, beautiful party."

"Thank you, Doris," Lane replied coolly. "Have you caught any of the canapés? Enough cocktail sticks to skewer even the most uptight of asses."

Gala let out a snort, and Doris looked as if she'd just been sentenced to death by firing squad.

"Anyway, I'm sure you two have plenty to talk about," Lane said. "And I need to find my husband."

Lane's cheeks were burning as she walked away, but instead of Scotty, it was Charlie that Lane searched for, brushing off the dozens of guests trying to catch a few minutes with her as she made her way outside. She found him reclined on a lounge chair in his favorite cabana, the one that looked out over the entire party, where he was smoking a cigarette next to a younger man wearing a white Speedo and covered in gold body paint. Charlie took one look at Lane and poked the man with his foot.

"Sid, darling," Charlie said to him, a smile on his lips. "Would you mind excusing yourself so I can have a moment with my dear friend? We have grown-up business to discuss."

Sid walked out of the cabana, hips swaying, before he dived gracefully into the pool, barely creating a ripple in the glittering turquoise water. Lane lay down next to Charlie on the pink-and-mint-striped lounge chair.

"Do you think I'm funny?" Lane asked, and Charlie turned toward her, his Ionian blue eyes just inches away from hers.

"Of course," he said. "Would we be friends if you weren't?"

Lane shrugged.

"Am I charming?" she asked, her voice quieter now.

"Some people are so brilliant they don't need to be charming," he said. "Charm is for people who are trying to convince you of something, most often themselves."

Lane snuggled into Charlie's armpit.

"There's no one in the world like you, Lane. I swear on Sid's glistening abs."

Lane let out a small laugh.

"Love you," she said.

"Love you too," he said, and he kissed the top of her head again.

Lane and Charlie watched the party from the cabana as the Los Angeles sky darkened to a deep navy, and, as if by magic, the tiki torches were lit. They spent the rest of the night blithely skewering the costumes, careers, and relationships of their guests as if they were the king and queen of Hollywood. And, for a moment, that's exactly what they were.

TWENTY-SEVEN

THEN

AUGUST 1969

Lane learned she was pregnant the day after Sharon Tate and her unborn child were slain, along with four others, in an unfathomable night of violence that stopped the city in its tracks. Nobody would learn who committed the ritualistic murders until three months later. Instead, on that sticky August afternoon, it just felt to Lane like something formless was descending on the city, on their circle of friends—a sinister shadow cast across their existence. As Lane and Scotty sat in their perfect house, eyes trained on the TV screen, Scotty's hand resting lightly on her small bump, Lane felt a sense of dread that they had willingly chosen to bring new life into such a cruel world.

What had she done?

LANE HAD BEEN self-reliant since her father's death when she was seventeen. She had felt so lonely in that house in Arizona, so entirely at the mercy of these two adults whose flights and furies she didn't understand, that she decided to never again depend on anyone else. Since then, her life had been a series of calculated choices—move to New York to capitalize on your fluke success, leave New York when you become too jaded, move to Los Angeles to write the novel that will change your life, marry the man who promises to keep you safe and who is so gloriously straightforward that you'll never have to guess what he's thinking.

What she didn't account for, even after all his hints, was just how badly Scotty wanted a baby. And it wasn't as if having sex with her new husband was some hardship for her—she loved the feeling of Scotty's warm skin, the sweat that dripped from his temples that she could stick her tongue out to catch—but she didn't realize it would all happen so soon. She was older than most first-time mothers, but still, when the doctor told her she was pregnant two months after she stopped taking her pill, she found that she wasn't surprised. In her thirty-two years, Lane found she got the things she didn't want just as often as the things she did.

Scotty was thrilled. Or, no, thrilled wasn't enough. He was almost delirious, as if the news of his virility had validated his natural sense of optimism—his view that the world was a benign place in which good things happened to good people. And perhaps they did, for men like Scotty, Lane thought as the doctor listened closely before telling her there were two heartbeats beating inside her. But at what cost to her?

THE FEELING OF dread that set in the night of the Tate-LaBianca murders never truly left. Lane tried to work on her second novel, but all she could think about was how her own contentedness was once again out of her control, and perhaps always would be. The

Sunday Salons were paused indefinitely by October, and Lane knew she would never again be able to take herself back to New York for a weekend, or to Paris, or even for a pistachio ice cream at Villa Mia, without first having to justify it to someone. Her life now would be expected to be in service to these two beings she'd never met, and whose existence she hadn't truly thought through, not really. Not in the way she should have, at least. Scotty could reassure her all he wanted that he would be a true gem about it—bathing the twins if she needed a break and even changing their diapers, but Lane knew how it would play out. Scotty would win praise and adoration for every tiny thing he did, while Lane would be accused of neglect if she didn't do them.

Lane knew what the novel was about (a young mother who, after the death of her husband, begins to suffer from violent delusions she doesn't want to suppress), she just couldn't remember why she had wanted to write it. As the months passed and Lane found she could barely write a word, it started to feel more and more like a sick joke. She began to resent Scotty, who was going about his normal life with, if anything, extra vigor and charm. He had turned the gallery into the most exciting hub for emerging artists outside of New York, and was constantly at dinners with fascinating people from this world: painters who started out as street artists in Madrid, collectors who had rumored links to emerging drug cartels in Colombia, Rubenesque models who were almost as famous as the old white men who immortalized them.

And Lane was at home, too large and cumbersome, too messy, to leave the house. She felt the indignities of pregnancy like a plague: the swelling, the gas, the nausea that swept through her each afternoon, the way her body became something other people (women!) were allowed to comment on in the street. Lane thought often of her own mother who, toward the end, was found mostly in the local bars or the bedroom of seemingly anyone in town who would have her, and Lane wondered now if she had been trying to reassert control over some part of herself. And the thought that she could now see this crack of light in her mother's otherwise intractable psyche frightened Lane more than anything else.

TWENTY-EIGHT

NOW

SUMMER 1975

Life in Laurel Canyon has moved on without Gala, like a train sucking an animal under its wheels. The summer is almost over but the community still swells, sweet music filtering out of the jewel-colored houses lining the hills or from the deck of the Canyon Country Store. Nobody has even mentioned Gala in weeks, and Lane has all but given up on her search until one Sunday in August when, during a rigorous family outing to Disneyland of all places, she chances across a ghost from Gala's past.

They've only been at the park for two hours, and Lane is already exhausted by the level of enthusiasm expected of her not from the girls (who are so enthused themselves they wouldn't notice if she were comatose) but from Scotty, who keeps stealing glances at her as if to make sure she's engaging appropriately in the day's merriment. In order to seek refuge from both his relentless enthusiasm and the inhumane Anaheim heat, Lane has taken

Audrey into the penny arcade while, outside, Scotty waits in line with Dahlia for popcorn.

Scotty has been showing an unnerving level of interest in Lane since she opened up to him about Charlie, as if he's finally located a void in her life that needs to be filled. As if, up until now, he's been an understudy in his own marriage, finally called upon for the role of a lifetime. He comes home from the gallery for lunch most days and, on the weekend, has taken to organizing increasingly exhausting activities for the whole family, as if enough of these outings might distract Lane from her growing disconnect from her life.

In the arcade, Audrey stops abruptly in front of Esmeralda, a machine featuring an animatronic fortune teller with long black hair, electric-blue eyeliner, and a colorful silk headscarf (and who, to Lane's eye, resembles only Gala), and begs Lane for twenty-five cents to play. Lane roots around in her jean pocket and, as Esmeralda whirs into action, spots a familiar figure about twenty feet away—Aiden, the guitarist of Belle Vue. He's wearing black jeans and a heavy leather jacket, an incongruous presence among the towering swirls of cotton candy and Minnie Mouse paraphernalia. And Lane, who doesn't believe in fate or providence, thinks it must be a sign.

Esmeralda is still whirring away, and Audrey is rapt, her nose pressed against the glass cabinet as Lane crouches down next to her.

"Audrey," she says. "I've just seen someone I know—can we come back to Esmeralda later?"

Audrey turns to her, cheeks pink. "No," she says. "I haven't got my fortune yet."

Lane feels a rush of frustration. "This is important to Mommy," she says, even though she hates when Scotty does this—refers to her in the third person as if her identity has simply been sliced neatly in two instead of shattered into millions of pieces she will always be searching for but never fully retrieve.

Lane watches as Aiden walks toward the arcade exit with a freckled child. She's about to lose him to the crowd streaming toward Sleeping Beauty's castle. Lane grimaces, weighing her options.

"Audrey," Lane says, talking slowly to make sure her daughter understands exactly what she's saying to her. "Once you have your fortune, I need you to go find Dahlia and Daddy in the line for popcorn, okay? Can you see them?"

Lane points through the exit to where Scotty and Dahlia are near the front of the line. Audrey nods, still transfixed by the machine, and, after only a short pause, Lane turns and walks out of the arcade, pushing through the crowd until she reaches the worn leather jacket, the mane of wild hair.

"Aiden," Lane says, grabbing him by the shoulder. "Lane Warren."

Aiden turns, frowning at her from behind his sunglasses. In recent years, Belle Vue has become the type of famous no child dreams of being—notorious as opposed to revered, and Aiden's expression is appropriately wary, his mouth set in a grim line.

"I know who you are," he says levelly, and Lane feels a glint of satisfaction that she is still known by people like this, that even in a kids' theme park on a suffocating August day, the most famous person here knows exactly who she is.

"You're Gala's friend," he says then, and Lane's smile drops.

"Do you want an autograph?" Aiden's son asks, squinting up at her in the sun.

"That's what I wanted to speak to you about," Lane says to

Aiden, ignoring him. "Did you speak to Gala much after . . . Gabriel?"

Aiden glances down. "This isn't really the place," he says, and Lane can hear that his accent has mellowed over the years, lilting and dipping in all the wrong places for either his home or adopted country.

"Could we meet sometime then?" Lane asks quickly.

Aiden is about to answer, when Scotty marches over, the girls in tow. Audrey, clutching her fortune, won't meet Lane's eye, but Scotty looks furious, his jaw tightly clenched. When he reaches them, he grabs Lane's arm.

"Where did you go?" he says to Lane, his voice low and simmering.

"I'm right here," Lane says calmly.

Scotty just stares at her. "Audrey was alone in the middle of the arcade, lost."

"She wasn't lost. I told her to find you," Lane says. "And she clearly did."

Scotty opens his mouth and closes it again, as if there aren't enough words in the world to convey the depth of his frustration with her.

"Hey, man," Aiden says then, nodding at Scotty.

Scotty ignores him. "You could have just walked her over to me," he says, his voice low and strained. "She's *five*."

Lane feels a swell of anger because this isn't about Audrey's age. This is about how, despite it having been Scotty who pushed for a child in the first place, it is Lane who isn't allowed ten minutes without one of the girls pulling at her hand or shirt, demanding something.

"Scotty," she says, her own voice low and sharp. "I need two minutes."

Scotty shakes his head, but the girls are already pulling away, drawn to a jaunty melody floating toward them.

"It's the parade!" Audrey says, tugging at her dad's hand. "You promised!"

Scotty looks at Lane pleadingly.

"Two minutes," Lane repeats. "I'll find you."

Scotty exhales and turns his back on her. Lane watches her family disappear into the crowd, then turns back to Aiden, who is now looking at her curiously.

"Gala?" Lane says, tired now. "Have you heard from her?"

"Look, I don't know what you're after exactly," Aiden says. "I had to close that chapter a while ago, along with some others. It got a little heavy, you know?"

"She's disappeared," Lane says flatly.

"Shit," Aiden says, looking away. "Look, I know what everyone thought, but I never had a problem with her."

"If memory serves, that isn't what you said at the time. Publicly," Lane says.

Aiden's cheeks flush again, and Lane figures he's about to break. They always do, once you find the right tactic. And it turns out that, like so many famous men, the tactic that works on Aiden is shaming. (Someone, a writer who is now dead, once told Lane that the worst thing that could happen to a man was for his dreams to come true.)

"She tried to talk to me," he says. "Once. But it was years ago. I was still . . ."

He breaks off and glances at his son, before mouthing the word *using* over his head.

"We all figured she could handle the shit people were saying about her, but she . . . cared more than people thought," he says, and Lane is about to press him further when the kid steps in between them, his freckled forehead puckered.

"We're going on the Jungle Cruise now," he announces, his voice clear and resolute. Aiden smiles then, a slow and grateful grin.

"The kid's not wrong," he says, and then his eyes narrow slightly. "You know . . . come to think of it, I don't remember *you* having much to say at the time either, about Gala. Hiding out in your castle, away from the blood and guts of it all."

It takes Lane only a second to rearrange her face, but it's already too late.

Aiden smirks as he slings his arm around the boy's shoulders. "See you around, Lane Warren."

LATER, IN THE car home, when they're sitting in a heavy line of traffic on the I-5, and the girls are asleep in the back, Scotty finally looks at Lane. He's barely said a word to her all afternoon, and the girls had sensed the shift too, becoming unpredictable in their efforts to alleviate the tension. Lane isn't sure what's worse—watching them gripe and pinch each other all day, or watching them contort themselves to please their parents. Either way, the day was ruined, and everyone knows it's Lane's fault.

"It was five minutes, Scotty, give me a break," Lane says, before he can say anything.

He shakes his head, his knuckles white on the steering wheel.

"It was work," she says next, because Lane knows that Scotty will at least try to understand this.

"Work," Scotty repeats.

"Sure," Lane says. "I've been asked to interview Belle Vue for *Rolling Stone.*"

Unsure, Scotty shoots another look at her before flicking his eyes back on the road ahead. A gap has opened up, so he crawls forward.

"Hasn't everything already been said?" he says, and Lane shrugs.

"There's always more to every story," Lane says. "Once you start digging."

"I don't know about that," he says.

Another gap opens up. Scotty is a beat behind, but eventually the car lurches forward. Lane's eyes instinctively flick to the rear-view mirror to check that the girls are still asleep, that they haven't woken up with a start that will send the rest of the journey further south, but their eyes are still blessedly closed.

"Lane," Scotty says. "Do I need to be worried about you?"

Lane turns to him, her face neutral.

"In what way?"

He frowns, the brake lights from the car in front casting a red glow over his handsome face.

"Today, with Audrey . . ." he says quietly. "That wasn't . . . acceptable. You know that, right?"

"We were at Disneyland, for god's sake," Lane says. "And nothing happened."

Scotty just stares at her.

"It's like something's missing," he says. "In your brain."

Lane feels a hot thrill of shame run through her.

"I know it was . . . tough when they were babies, but I thought it would be different by now," Scotty says, and his tone isn't vindictive. Instead, he sounds like he's trying to understand, which makes it infinitely worse.

"And maybe you tried to tell me, and maybe I didn't listen, but I just thought . . . I thought somehow you could find a way to become the mother they need. But, five years in, you're still . . ." Scotty breaks off, either struggling or unwilling to find the word that would land the final blow. In the rearview mirror, the girls are fast asleep, their chests rising and falling. When Lane looks back, her husband's cheeks are wet with tears.

"Me," Lane says quietly. "I'm still me."

THAT NIGHT, THE nightmares start.

TWENTY-NINE

THEN

OCTOBER 1969

Gabriel was, Gala tentatively thought, improving every day. Only now that they were finally emerging from the woods could she see just how rough the past year since Gabriel had gotten out of rehab had been on them both. Even his hair had grown back in after he buzzed it, and when she kissed him, it sometimes felt like he was her Gabriel again, not this impostor who they both knew had only been pretending for her benefit. Sobriety had made it seem as if everything inside Gabriel—his thoughts, his fears, even his veins—were sitting too close to the surface, like his tender skin was no longer able to provide the protection he needed. It hurt Gala to look at him sometimes because she could see how hard he was trying. Every so often, the thought crossed Gala's mind that Gabriel was too gentle for this world, and it terrified her.

While it wasn't in Gala's nature to change for anyone, she also occasionally found herself wondering what impact her success might have on Gabriel. Before rehab, he had been the one with the sense of purpose, with strangers clambering for even a minute of his time, not to mention entire teams of people whose livelihoods depended on him. He was the one whose blessed existence they would excitedly dissect as they shared a midnight spliff on the hammock in their backyard, sticky legs entwined, temples touching. And now it was Gala who came home late most days, curling up beside Gabriel in bed as she told him about a new opportunity that had come her way. He seemed genuinely happy for her, and she didn't think Gabriel's ego would be bruised so easily, but you could never be entirely sure what was going on under the surface of any man, particularly one who'd once had the world at his fingertips.

So when he told Gala in early October that Belle Vue would start tentatively recording their second album at a studio in Hollywood, mostly songs that Gabriel had written on lazy afternoons on the wicker couch next to Gala as sunlight dappled their skin, she felt a flush of relief. She had never learned to diminish herself to protect a man's pride, and she wasn't about to start now.

THE NIGHT GABRIEL pulled his fourth consecutive all-nighter at the studio, Gala felt as if the world were collapsing around her. The sharp October sun was already rising as he struggled out of his jeans and climbed into bed beside her. He draped a warm arm over her, and she wanted to turn to face him, but she was scared of what she might find. Anything that might explain how someone who didn't even drink coffee anymore could stay up until 6:00 a.m. in a windowless studio with bandmates who were almost certainly doing cocaine at the very least. She wanted to trust him, and could never resort to becoming one of those women who checked their husband's phone logs or Diners Club card bills, but she still felt a rash of doubt prickling under her skin.

"Missed you," he said, just before he gently bit the back of her shoulder with his sharp teeth.

Gala instinctively moved closer so that her back was pressed against the warm skin of his stomach. Gabriel reached his arm around her then and turned her to face him, their noses touching in the golden sliver of sunlight. His violet eyes seemed clear and lucid, softening as they locked onto hers, and she felt weak with relief when she saw that he was sober. He smiled a little and stroked a piece of her hair behind her ear.

"Love you," she said softly, her eyes closing again.

THIRTY

THEN

MARCH 1970

The day Lane went into labor started like any other day. Over a bowl of cereal, Lane read a short piece about a former Vietnam nurse turned anti-war activist, and wondered if there was a wider story out there, only to be reminded of her current situation when one of the babies headbutted her sharply in the bladder. She was already scheduled for an early induction in a week's time, but her water broke hours later while she was making herself a tuna salad sandwich for lunch (she had reverted to the unfashionable foods of her childhood partway through her second trimester).

At first, she tried pretending it wasn't happening. She found that the liquid gushing down her thighs could be ignored as long as she was submerged in water herself. So she sat in the bath for over three hours, trying to focus on her book before the pain reached a critical mass and she finally called Scotty at work.

Scotty was pale as a ghost when he arrived at the house minutes later (practically in a cloud of dust, like a cartoon), but his manner was relentlessly upbeat—he told joke after joke as he drove Lane to Cedars of Lebanon Hospital, while Lane retreated further and further into herself.

The thrashing, throbbing pain in her stomach felt personal. Because why had nobody warned her? And how could something that was natural feel so incredibly violent? It suddenly made no sense that the female body hadn't evolved in a way that made giving birth more effortless, more dignified. Lane's maternal grandmother had died during childbirth, and Lane thought now that perhaps this was the issue—perhaps her mother was never meant to survive to pass on whatever defective gene it was that made this entire experience so unbearable for the women in their family. Lane watched her adopted city out the window, the jacaranda trees that were already blooming, and felt as if she would never feel like herself again.

By the time they reached the hospital, Lane was slipping in and out of consciousness, which she assumed was her brain's only way of handling the pain, until she noticed the growing bloodstain between her thighs. Scotty, who she now realized was crying, grabbed the first doctor he saw. "You need to do something," he said, and even through her haze Lane could hear how frightened he was. Was he scared he was going to lose her? Or was she already just a vessel for these two new humans who were trying to claw their way into the world however they could? Either way, the doctor took one look at her and ordered her onto a stretcher and into surgery, where they injected her with something that made the world a sparkling, effervescent green and then a dull black.

LATER, LANE THOUGHT she must have dreamed she was her mother. Because suddenly it made perfect sense that Alys hadn't survived childbirth, not psychologically at least. How could you, when you knew that you were the reason your own mother was no longer here?

WHEN LANE WOKE up, she was in a different, smaller room. As the world came into focus, she saw that Scotty was holding something wrapped in a blue blanket while peering into another bassinet, his eyes shining with tears. Watching them for a moment, entirely oblivious to her, Lane wondered if she too had died giving life. And perhaps she had already done what she needed to do. She had created a family of three who would survive without her.

THIRTY-ONE

NOW

SUMMER 1975

Lane's nightmares always start the same way.

It is a crisp fall morning in a suburb just outside of Phoenix, and Lane is woken up by the sound of her parents fighting. She can't make out the exact accusations, but she can hear the unnatural pitch of her mother's voice and the sound of her father crying. At fourteen, this has been the soundtrack to Lane's childhood, and she dresses calmly before heading down to the kitchen to make herself a tuna salad sandwich for lunch. When she closes the fridge, she finds her dad standing in his gray bathrobe, his eyes already bloodshot. He reaches out a freckled hand to Lane, but she steps around him to grab a bar of chocolate from the drawer next to the oven. His sadness already repels her, just as it does her mother.

"She isn't herself," he says, and in Lane's dream, her father's voice is never quite right, but it's close enough.

"Okay," Lane says as she zips up her bag and slings it over her shoulder. She wonders if it's true that it will rain later, because right now the sky is beautiful and clear—the perfect fall morning. In the Enid Blyton books she still reads, they call it *autumn*, and she thinks there is something so wistful about this word, unlike *fall*, which is almost embarrassingly pedestrian. (It is only later that she will come to appreciate such simplicity in language and make it a trademark of her own writing.)

"Do you still know where she hides them?" her dad asks, and there is an urgency to his voice now. Lane pretends she doesn't know what he's talking about.

"I'm going to be late," she says over her shoulder as she leaves. He doesn't tell her to have a good day or offer to drive her to school. There is no space for anyone but her mother in this house.

The school part of the dream is always slightly different. Sometimes, at lunch, Lane eats her sandwich alone outside on a red bench, and sometimes she eats it in the jarring cafeteria opposite the kid whose dad is in the county jail. They never talk, just eat in silent comradery as the politics of high school unfold all around them without ever touching them.

When school is over, Lane begins to walk home. Then, when she reaches the playground on Maple, she remembers a library book she knows will be in that day. Lane may never have a new bike or a radio in her house, but she is always the first kid in her class to have read any book. So instead of continuing down Maple to her house, she takes a left on Church Street and wanders down to the public library.

This is the worst part of the dream for Lane, worse even than when her dad asked her where the pills were and she didn't tell him they were in the bottom drawer of her mother's vanity in the silk pouch that used to contain Lane's milk teeth, and even worse than when she finds her mother an hour later for the last time. No, this is the part where Lane always tries to change course, screaming at her younger self not to take the left on Church Street, but to continue straight home instead. But, every time, Lane makes the same mistake, over and over again, and the worst part is, she knows it.

SOMETIMES, WHEN SHE wakes up, Lane reaches an arm out to touch Scotty, just so she knows she's here. And it always takes a moment for the final image of her mother to clear, the one of her on the bathroom floor, beautiful black hair trapped underneath her, and even longer for her to forget the agony in her father's voice as he screams at Lane that he warned her, that it's her fault, but eventually it all fades, and Lane is left to go through the motions of her day, knowing it's just a matter of time before she is back in that bedroom in Arizona, putting on her old gingham dress to the sound of her parents fighting.

THIRTY-TWO

THEN

AUGUST 1970

The twins were freakishly quiet at five months old. Everyone told Lane how grateful she should be about this, but volume had never been her problem. She barely noticed a difference if they were screaming or gurgling, or making cooing baby noises as she mechanically changed their diapers. No, their sound frequency wasn't the issue. It was the way they instinctively looked at her for everything—food, comfort, pain relief—like she was some sort of magical being with all the answers. *That* was the problem. What was she supposed to do with that?

Lane often wondered if she'd have handled everything better had there not been two babies. Everything just felt so unwieldy— her still-engorged belly, straining under even Scotty's largest shirts, the double stroller people exclaimed over every time she left the house, even just to grab a newspaper from the newsstand down on Sunset. The excess of soiled diapers and empty formula packets and ruined shirts in piles around the house. The way Scotty looked at her as if she was missing some crucial thing that would have made this entire experience enjoyable, his disappointment in who she'd turned out to be palpable during even the most innocuous interaction between them. *I know,* she wanted to tell him as she mopped up yet more vomit from her shoulder. *I know, I know, I know, I know.*

IT WAS NEVER a question of loving them. It was that her love for them was so irrevocably tied to the knowledge that she would let them down that she couldn't begin to untangle the love from the loss. She felt overwhelmed, nauseated almost, every time she looked at them, as if she were being flooded with something she wasn't equipped to handle. And it terrified her, because she didn't know how to learn.

IN EARLY SEPTEMBER, Scotty asked one of his assistants to babysit the twins while he took Lane to his favorite new restaurant in Beverly Hills. The dinner was ostensibly for her birthday, although it was a week early, as he'd be in Buenos Aires over her actual birthday, meeting a dealer who seemingly had the net worth of an entire European country to spend on building his art collection.

Lane had been privately dreading the dinner for days, but when they arrived and she spotted Charlie waiting at the table, Lane realized just how little Scotty wanted to be alone with her too. She tried to work out when they'd stopped trusting each other, but the past year was too tangled to unpick. They were still very much submerged in whatever haze parenthood had thrust upon them, but she knew it was more than that too. As she

watched Charlie and Scotty greet each other warmly, she understood that this was convenient for both of the men in her life—
Charlie had stopped by only a couple of times since she'd had the
babies, and, each time, he couldn't have left faster, as if he was
desperate to escape the corporeal realities of her newly airless life.
He seemed mildly disturbed anytime either of the babies made a
noise, and the most recent time he had left after twenty-two minutes, leaving half a cup of still-warm coffee behind. She figured
this dinner was a perfect opportunity for him to alleviate some of
his guilt while also seeing her only at her glittering best, without
the twins around to distract her attention. Even if that meant
hanging out with Scotty too.

"Lane darling," Charlie said, standing up and kissing each of
her cheeks. "Happy almost birthday."

"Charlie," Lane said coolly as she took her seat. "Have you
been out of town?"

Charlie and Scotty exchanged a look that Lane understood
instantly. *See?* Scotty was saying. *See what I have to contend with?*

"Just inexcusably busy, Laney," Charlie said as he picked up
the menu. "Dirty martini?"

Lane shrugged and looked down at the tablecloth. There was
a smudge of something maroon on it. A cherry smear? Raspberry
coulis? Another woman's blood?

"How's work, Charlie?" Scotty asked, his voice loud and con-
fident. Lane winced at the effort he was making, and how false it
all felt already.

"Charlie doesn't like to talk about his work socially," she said
slowly. "It's one of his many, many rules."

"Only with you," Charlie said lightly. "Because we have so
much other stuff to talk about. Scotty and I, however . . ."

He laughed a little as Lane considered this. He was cozying up to her, showing where his allegiances still lay, and even though she knew exactly what he was doing, she softened ever so slightly.

"Come on . . . artist wrangler to artist wrangler, what's the biggest scandal you've covered up this year?" Scotty persisted, and Lane watched as Charlie worked to disguise his distaste at the line of questioning. Did Scotty really think he was about to tell him something that could end his own career, as well as that of someone he was paid to protect? What was it with self-satisfied straight men that made them feel deserving of everything? Normally Lane would have jumped in and smoothed the moment over, but she figured she would let this one play out. She wasn't going to let either of them off the hook tonight.

"Well," Charlie said carefully. "This isn't one of mine, but I've heard that a certain Mancunian sex god is using again."

Lane looked at him sharply. "Gabriel?"

Charlie nodded.

"Interesting," Scotty said, sounding anything but as he opened the menu and scanned the appetizers, even though he ate here at least twice a week and surely had the whole thing memorized. "I can't imagine Gala did much to encourage his sobriety."

"What does that mean?" Lane asked.

Scotty seemed to hear something in her voice and adopted an infinitely more irritating tone of placation. "I just mean . . . she's never going to retire from . . . you know. The lifestyle. This is just a phase, like everything else with her."

Lane stared at him questioningly.

"The free love, groupie thing . . . the murals . . . now the writing . . . this current pretense at domesticity with Gabriel . . . I just mean that Gala's a wanter. She's always looking for the next shiny thing."

"And what exactly is the opposite of a wanter?" Lane asked.

Scotty opened his mouth to answer, but he must have sensed something dangerous in Lane's tone, because he closed it again. Lane calmly closed her menu. She had never understood exactly what Scotty's issue was with Gala, but now she could see it only once it was too late for her. Gala had been right that day at the beach—Scotty didn't like her because she was a woman who didn't give a shit what anyone thought of her. And Lane's progressive, bleeding-heart liberal husband who said all the right things was worried she was contagious.

"You like to pretend that you have nothing to do with the kid in Vacaville, making up lies to impress his friends, but you want things too, don't you, Scotty?" Lane asked slowly. "You wanted to run the most successful gallery in Los Angeles. You wanted to marry me and have babies. You wanted me to come to this absurd non-birthday birthday dinner to make you feel better about leaving tomorrow. None of this just fell into your lap, so does that make you a wanter too? Or is it only women who should be satisfied with what they have? Am I a wanter, Scotty?"

Charlie cleared his throat and looked around the room before signaling to a waiter that they were ready to order drinks. He'd stifled a laugh at the birthday dinner part of Lane's speech, but he clearly wasn't drunk enough for the rest of the exchange.

"Wanting comes from unhappiness," Scotty said, smiling gently across the table at Lane. "She's unfulfilled in her life. Why would you be unfulfilled? You have everything you've ever wanted."

"Everything I've ever wanted," Lane repeated as the waiter approached their table. Charlie glanced at Lane sympathetically as she stared back down at her menu.

"Well," Charlie said brightly. "I'll tell you exactly what I want right now . . . a dirty martini, please, sir."

"Seconded," Scotty said with relief.

"And keep them coming," Lane said flatly.

LANE MADE IT through dinner, but only because Charlie and Scotty did the heavy lifting in the conversation. It was strange to witness how little these two men, the most significant in her life, had in common. They cycled hastily through conversation topics to find any common ground at all: baseball (Scotty no, Charlie yes), old western movies (Scotty yes, Charlie no), French movies (Scotty no, Charlie yes), Russian literature (Scotty yes, Charlie no), sushi (Scotty no, Charlie yes) before they discovered they'd both been to Chicago and quite liked it. Watching them both make an effort to drag this fact out for nearly an hour put Lane in a marginally better mood than when she'd arrived (or maybe it was the three martinis), so when Charlie suggested that Scotty be the one to relieve the babysitter so that he and Lane could get a nightcap, Lane didn't instantly reject the idea.

"I don't think Lane would . . ." Scotty said doubtfully as he handed the valet his ticket.

"You don't think I would what?" Lane said, pulling her coat tighter around her. "I'm a deeply unfulfilled woman, remember? And I want to get a drink with my friend on my non-birthday."

Charlie laughed and took hold of Lane's arm. Scotty looked between the two of them, aware that he'd made some error of judgment in arranging this dinner, but also that his wife seemed the most animated, the most like herself, she'd been in the past year. And even if it was at his expense tonight, he felt a vague sense of relief at that. When the valet pulled up in his car, he tipped him a dollar and kissed Lane goodbye, telling Charlie to make sure she got home safely. Lane laughed loudly at this, and

Scotty was aware he had already been cast as the villain of the night, he just couldn't quite remember why.

CHARLIE CHOSE THE Polo Lounge at the Beverly Hills Hotel for their nightcap, which they both knew wouldn't just be one drink. They were three martinis deep, and the banana leaf wallpaper had started to drastically warp as Lane ranted about Scotty and motherhood and her writer's block, until she remembered that she was angry at Charlie too.

"You," she said, squinting at him and jabbing a finger in his chest. He looked down at it, bemused, then back up at her face.

"You," she started again. "You abandoned me. Because I got boring. Because I'm no longer Lane Warren, famous writer, and instead I'm this other thing that is incrementally eating me alive until I'm just like every other woman in this country. Do you know how many strangers now feel the need to patronize me with unsolicited advice every single day and I just have to smile and thank them and pretend like it's the most fascinating thing I've ever heard? Because this is now the defining thing about me, Charlie. This is how I'll be judged. And you can't handle that either."

"Darling, it's not forever," Charlie said gently, once she'd finished. "They'll be at school in a few years."

"Well, I doubt you'll be around to see it," Lane said. "If the past year is anything to go by."

"Lane," Charlie said. "You haven't exactly been available lately either. If it wasn't for the parties, I think you'd have dropped off the face of the earth the moment you met Scotty."

"You introduced me to him," Lane shot back. "Don't forget that."

Charlie was about to whip something back, but then it was as if the air was drawn out of him and he crumpled beside her.

"I've been a little . . . lost without you," Charlie said quietly.

"Oh," Lane said, putting her head to one side. Their friendship had always had an instinctive quality to it that meant, while they frequently sought refuge in one another, they rarely opened up in any meaningful way. Lane had always assumed it was because they were both only children and allergic to vulnerability, but perhaps she just hadn't been asking the right questions.

"I haven't had the easiest time," Charlie said then. "There was this guy . . ."

"The same one?" she asked.

"Yeah," Charlie said, and a fleeting something crossed his face, making him look younger than his years.

"He wanted me to be more . . . available, but I couldn't," he said. "I still can't. He didn't seem to care that there are risks involved . . ."

Charlie's voice cracked slightly and he drifted off.

"Like your job?" Lane asked.

"Not only that. I don't want to expose my family," Charlie said, his voice firm again. "My parents have already done more than any parents should have to do."

"In what way?" Lane asked.

"By still loving me," Charlie said.

"Oh, Charlie," Lane said sadly. "You're actually pretty easy to love."

WHEN LANE FOUND out that Charlie hadn't stepped foot inside a gay bar for three and a half years, she insisted he take her to one then and there. For their real nightcap.

"I'm not going home until you take me," she said. "So you can explain that one to Scotty."

"We might not get in anywhere," Charlie said. "It's late. And, Lane? It's not just . . . fun. It could get raided."

"I'd welcome a night in jail," Lane said, her hands on her hips as she waited for Charlie. "And you won't get into trouble if I'm there."

She grabbed his lightweight trench from the back of his seat and pressed it into his arms.

"Come on," she said. "We're going."

Charlie groaned but he left some money on the bar and slid off his stool.

For reasons he couldn't quite explain, he took her to the Snug, the club that had turned him away the summer earlier. There was less of a line this time, and a different man working the door. By the time they reached the front, Charlie had worked himself up so much rehearsing different ways of saying he had a right to be there, that he found his heart was beating hard in his chest. The man on the door took a quick look at him and then raised an eyebrow in Lane's direction.

"She's okay," Charlie said, finding his voice. "She's my friend."

EVERY MONDAY NIGHT after that, Lane and Charlie would go to a gay bar. And while Charlie knew that it wasn't the same as showing up at a protest or being part of an uprising, it was still a small act of resistance that made his heart grow a little in his chest each time he walked inside the door.

THIRTY-THREE

THEN

SEPTEMBER 1970

Unlike most things in her career, Gala's monthly Hollywood column for *Vogue* came about quite by chance. She'd been studying the array of glistening meats and salads behind the counter at Canters Deli, waiting to pay for a pastrami on rye, when she felt someone's eyes drilling into the back of her head. She turned around to find a smallish man squinting up at her, a paper take-out menu clutched in his hand.

"Gala Margolis," he said. "I'm a fan. But you must hear that a lot these days."

Gala smiled winningly at him. "Not from enough men, unfortunately."

He cocked his head to one side. "They must be threatened by you."

"Funny, that's what my mom's always said," she replied, and by then she'd reached the cashier, so she handed over her change before turning back to the man.

"What's your name?" she asked. "Just so we're even."

"Harold Carter," he said, and the name was vaguely familiar to Gala.

"You're a writer?" she asked.

"Publisher," he said. "I'm managing director of Condé Nast."

"Of course," Gala said smoothly, embarrassed she hadn't placed him sooner. Half of the publications she wrote for were owned by Condé, and therefore managed by this person. Lane would have known that from the moment she saw him, if she'd been in Gala's shoes. (Gala felt a sting of guilt when she thought about Lane—she'd been so busy with work and Gabriel that she hadn't managed to stop by since she'd had the babies, although she had sent over a bottle of champagne.)

"You've never written for *Vogue*," Harold said curiously.

"I've never been asked," she said. "My essays are a little more risqué than their usual fare."

"I don't know," he said. "I'd say that's the illusion of your writing—the overall impression may be risqué, but the actual content is fairly chaste. It's the push and pull that makes your work so fascinating. And you so alluring."

Gala stared at him, unsure of how to feel at having been called chaste, but Harold had already moved on.

"How would you feel about lunch?" he asked.

Gala glanced at the sandwich being prepared behind the glass counter.

"Now?" she said.

"Why not?"

GALA SAT IN the brown leather booth opposite Harold, who, over the past ninety minutes, had told her exactly how much revenue had increased since he took over at Condé, the menu of his second

wedding in Sicily (down to each canapé), and how much he'd
spent building a pool on the roof of his Manhattan town house,
and the whole time he had a blob of egg salad on his mustache
that wouldn't budge, despite his tongue darting out to meet it every
so often.

"You're dating someone famous," he said at one point. "Remind me."

Gala smiled coyly and slurped the end of her iced tea, the ice
rattling loudly.

"I've dated a few famous people," she said. "Get me drunk one
day and I'll tell you some stories."

He nodded and leaned forward, his gaze now almost las-
civious.

"Well, I have a proposition for you," he said next. "If you'll humor me."

Gala felt her heart sink. She should have anticipated that this
was where this was all leading—the compliments about her writing, the stories designed to impress her. She should have expected
that someone like this would never take her seriously without a
heavy caveat in the form of a hand job under the table at Canters.

"Mr. Carter," she said. "I have to tell you, I'm not really . . .
looking for anything right now."

"You're not?" he asked, surprised.

"I can't sleep with you," she clarified, before adding (because
it cost her nothing and she didn't want to *humiliate* the man),
"right now, anyway."

Harold's cheeks turned a dramatic shade of pink.

"No," he said. "No, no. No. Not that."

"Oh," Gala said, breaking into a relieved smile.

"Didn't I just tell you about my wedding?" he asked, squinting
at her. "The wild boar arancini?"

"Sure," Gala said. "But that doesn't stop most men."

Harold laughed a little, but his cheeks were still pink.

"Well, the more I think about it, the more obvious it seems," he said.

"Sorry—what seems?"

"A column," he said. "A diary, more. Your observations about the world around you."

When Gala still looked perplexed, Harold added, "This world."

"Canters Deli?" she asked uncertainly.

"Hollywood," he said. "You grew up here, right? Everyone wants to know what really happens in L.A. You'll be our girl on the inside."

Gala thought about it for a moment. Writing a column about her life in L.A. would mean turning the lens on not only her circle of friends, but also herself. And not just on Gala of the past, as she was used to doing, but Gala of the present. Would she find anything she didn't like? She pushed the obvious issue of Gabriel out of her mind and smiled winningly.

"Send me an offer and I'll consider it," she said. "Could I change identifying details if I needed?"

"You could make the whole thing up for all I care," Harold said with a shrug. "As long as it's possible that it could have happened, what's the difference?"

Gala nodded, warming to the idea even more. She wouldn't make everything up, but if she wanted to lean into the mythology of Hollywood, it sounded like it wouldn't be too much of an issue. She'd done more with less.

WITHIN WEEKS, GALA had the monthly column booked and her presence in the world of *Vogue* announced by a giant billboard on

Sunset. She loved her new role as the town crier of Hollywood, and the added sense of purpose it gave her. Every party she went to now felt like a secret assignment, and she often found herself writing into the early hours of the morning when she got home, desperate to crystallize sentences that had been rattling around her mind for hours. *Everyone knows [redacted] has slept with over half of the men in Hollywood, but we all have to pretend she's a virgin because she has a backyard that looks over Warren Beatty's pool.* Or, *Party tip #3: Always say no when a man asks if you've tried a particular drug. Much like with oral sex, they're more likely to service you if they think they're your first.* (This one didn't quite make it to print, but it did make her editor call her up cackling.)

Soon after, a collection of her essays was rushed out by a small but prolific publisher. It was titled *Inhalation*, and, after excellent sales, Gala's position as ingenue of the L.A. literary scene was established.

Gabriel was almost as tickled by her newfound fame as she was, and would tell strangers passing under the billboard about Gala's job at the most prestigious women's magazine in the country. They occasionally walked up from their apartment just to see it, before stopping in at Barney's Beanery for a bowl of chili and a side of onion rings. It was over this exact meal that Gabriel told Gala he was going on tour with Belle Vue in the spring, and Gala felt the greasy meat turn to cement in her stomach.

"You couldn't have told me this over a juice," she mumbled as she wiped at her mouth with a napkin.

"We both knew this would eventually happen," Gabriel said, reaching out and touching her cheek with his hand. "It's a good thing—we're getting back to normal. And it's sixteen weeks. Not six months, not two years. I'll be back by autumn."

"Fall," she corrected grumpily, even though *autumn* was a

much nicer word for a season that hardly existed in L.A. anyway. But why did he have to do this at Barney's of all places? People were staring at them.

"And are you sure it's a good idea?" she asked, her tone more judgmental than she'd intended it to be. "It just feels a little soon."

"I'm not just sober in L.A., or sober when I'm with you," Gabriel said. "I'm sober period. And I need you to trust me."

He looked so desperate to believe himself that Gala instantly pasted on a smile and kissed the palm of his hand.

"Of course I trust you," she said as a heavy dread laced through her veins. She knew Belle Vue's label was keen to capitalize on the runaway success of the band's first album, but couldn't they just stay a little closer to home until everyone was sure that Gabriel's fledgling sobriety was going to stick?

And if Gabriel was so certain he'd be okay, why had his hands been shaking when he told her?

THIRTY-FOUR

THEN

NOVEMBER 1970

Every Saturday morning, Lane would take the double stroller and walk to the Farmers Market on the corner of Third and Fairfax. Once there, she would stop off at Magee's, where she would order the roast beef on a French roll with a side of jus, and she would manage about a quarter of it before her stomach inevitably began to roil. Then she would head over to the pony ring, which would be filled with divorced dads on their day of custody, and she would convince herself that she and Scotty were somehow superior to these sad sacks because they at least managed to live under the same roof as their children.

One Saturday in late November, Lane looked up from her sandwich to find Gala standing over her, watching her curiously. It had been over a year since the celestial wonderland Sunday Salon, where they'd last spoken, and Lane felt a vague resentment that Gala hadn't made any effort to get in touch with her, even if she understood it. In New York, she too had written off her friends when they got married and had babies.

"Hi, Lane," Gala said carefully, as if talking to someone who was incapacitated. "Are you doing okay?"

Lane shrugged. She was pretty tired, yes, and she was wearing navy blue overalls that had seen so much action recently they never truly felt clean, and a red baseball cap of Scotty's that she'd grabbed as she was walking out the door, but she didn't think any of that merited Gala looking at her like she'd just escaped from the state hospital.

"'Okay' feels accurate," she said mildly, but Gala continued to squint at her. "Quit looking at me like I'm deranged, Gala."

"And how are these precious angels?" Gala asked, peering now inside the double stroller. Lane hadn't had Gala down as a baby person, but her face softened into a genuine smile as she reached out and gently touched one of the babies' cheeks. Whichever one was strapped in on the left today, Lane couldn't quite recall. Scotty was always patiently telling her to be consistent with their placement in the stroller, but for reasons that were out of reach to her, she could feel herself resisting every time she prepped them to leave the house.

"Hey, sweetie," Gala cooed. "You going to be as smart as your mama?"

She straightened up and squinted at Lane.

"How is it?" she asked.

"A little greasy," Lane said, glancing at her French dip, but Gala wasn't letting her off the hook. She waited for Lane to say more.

"It's okay," Lane said, after a long pause.

"Just okay?" Gala asked. "Not transformative? Not earth-shatteringly magical? Not better than having sex with Jim Morrison after two tabs of LSD?"

"I don't know, Gala," Lane said wearily.

Gala looked at her carefully and then seemed to make a decision. She pulled out the chair opposite Lane and sat down.

"Tell me about it," Gala said.

"I don't know how," Lane said, after a moment. And it was true. She didn't know how to put into words how ashamed she felt that she didn't understand any of it. At all.

"You look so glamorous," she said instead. And she wasn't lying—Gala looked almost inconceivably prepossessing in a white peasant blouse and jeans, her Pre-Raphaelite beauty more apparent than ever in this least auspicious of circumstances, surrounded as they were by tourists devouring pizza slices and root beer floats. Gala just shrugged as if, for once, the compliment didn't interest her.

"You feel like your identity is in tatters," she said instead, leaning forward. "You feel so lonely you don't know how you're even getting through the day."

Lane looked up at her sharply.

"It's okay, Lane," Gala said. "I don't think you're a monster."

"Sometimes . . ." Lane started, her voice quiet as she finally put the frantic, twisting shapes in her mind into words. "Sometimes I think about what my life would be like if I'd never met Scotty, had never done any of this. I should know better than anyone that motherhood isn't the default; it's not like we're all born to do this. What if . . . I was never meant to be a mother?"

Lane said the next part only in her mind. *What if nobody ever taught me how to love?* And then she started to cry.

Gala watched her for a moment, her expression unreadable. "I don't know," she said. "I think the fact you're worrying about this is probably a good sign. And if not, fuck it, you're rich—there's always boarding school, right?"

Lane smiled even as the strange tears continued to run down her cheeks. She'd felt so numb lately she'd forgotten how to cry.

"You're coping, Lane," Gala said then. "Look at you—you're doing it."

"I don't know if I'd call this coping." Lane gestured at her face.

"Coping is a scale, not a binary," Gala said. "You just need time to remember what it is you love about your life. And that will come back, I promise."

Lane looked down at the stroller and wondered if the twins were too cold without a blanket. They were almost always too something. When she glanced up, Gala was still watching her.

"Have you ever heard of the uglies?" Gala asked. "Also, are you eating that?"

Gala pointed to the sandwich in front of Lane. Lane pushed the plate toward her in response and watched as Gala dipped it into the jus before taking a large bite. When she finally swallowed, she started talking again.

"The uglies are what you have right now."

"Cute name," Lane said dryly.

"No need to get offended—although that is a key feature of the uglies," Gala said thoughtfully. "It just means that life has knocked you around a little, and your heart has become a little harder. It won't last forever, but right now, the world looks a little uglier than it once did."

Lane felt a surprising lump form in the back of her throat as she listened. Recently, it had felt as if something inside her chest (something she might say was her heart if she were someone else, someone more prone to sentimentality) had calcified, and to let so much as a crack of light inside would risk shattering the entire thing.

"Everyone with any sense gets them at some point," Gala said. "But they always pass."

Lane nodded and distracted herself with a loose thread on the girls' stroller until she trusted herself to speak again without crying.

"How's Gabriel doing?" Lane asked.

"Fine," Gala said slowly. "Great, even. He's going on tour in the spring, and I think it will be good for him to get back out there."

Lane raised an eyebrow but said nothing, and Gala sighed.

"You were wrong, you know," Gala said. "People can change. Addicts don't always die addicted. Maybe it's in his nature, but it doesn't mean he can't fight against it for the rest of his life."

Lane nodded and for once avoided saying what she believed. She cleared her throat and looked down at the smear of old seagull shit on the table.

"I hope so," she said.

"He's asked me to join him on tour," Gala said, watching a kid snatch a yo-yo from his younger brother when his mom wasn't looking.

Lane's head snapped up.

"That's a terrible idea," she said. "You're not his mother."

"I don't think he'd want his mother on tour with him," Gala said, and her voice had the defensive edge it always had when she was talking about Gabriel. "Unlike some couples, we actually like being around each other."

Lane ignored the barb, presumably intended to distract her.

"It's a terrible idea," she said again. "You've achieved too much to go back to being a groupie."

"Believe it or not, I never minded being a groupie," Gala said. "It was only other people who cared. I was actually very content being a square-mile celebrity with zero ambition."

"Hmm, that must be easy to say now you have a weekly *Vogue* column and a billboard on Sunset," Lane said archly. "But I know how hard you've worked to get here."

Gala broke into a winning smile. "Well, we can't all be 'the singular voice of trash Hollywood' unfortunately."

"All right, let's talk when you've written something longer than three thousand words," Lane said, rolling her eyes.

"I would never debase myself like that," Gala said airily. "Too establishment. Too male. Too Lane Warren."

Sparring with Gala made her feel almost human again, but Lane still felt a rush of relief that Gala wasn't planning on moving into her sphere anytime soon. It was something she thought about more often than she'd like to admit as she was writing—what a novel from the irreverent and charming mind of Gala Margolis would even look like. Lane didn't know how she'd cope if she lost that part of herself too, even if it was to the closest thing she'd ever had to a female friend.

THIRTY-FIVE

NOW

FALL 1975

Ever since Lane left Audrey in the Disneyland penny arcade, Scotty has been watching her in a way that makes her feel like the world is closing in on her (in a way that makes her chest feel thick with something familiar), and the nightmares are so frequent she often has two, three in one night. Lane has never felt less in the mood for a Sunday Salon than she does now, but at least stepping into hosting duties feels almost like a second skin; Lane no longer feels the need to be witty or charming or fulfill anyone's expectations of her for the party to be deemed a success. Or perhaps she just no longer cares. Instead, she steps out from the shadows in the same cream suit she always wears and watches as the same people arrive with the same jokes and air-kisses, only to drink the same drinks and dance to the same music before taking the same people home as they do every week. As the afternoon unfolds in a display of blinding predictability, Lane has the sensation that she might set fire to it all if she ever has to do this again.

Lane has been avoiding Charlie as much as she can without creating unnecessary drama, or *grist* for the Laurel Canyon rumor mill, as her mother would have put it. (*Why* is she thinking about her mother right now?) Instead, she imagines Gala is next to her, and how bored she'd also be by these people, grotesque and spoiled as they fall over themselves to make the cruelest joke or tell the same story about the time they went on a mescaline run with Hunter S. Thompson.

No fun, Gala would say from Lane's side, looking at the young starlet who is only there to seal the deal on a part she wants.

No heart, she'd say, looking at Dimitri as he tells a vicious story about an ex-lover of his.

"*No* plus-ones," Charlie says loudly, cutting across Lane's hallucination. "This isn't a wedding in Poughkeepsie, for god's sake."

Lane steps toward the commotion, where a man with a pencil mustache is standing in Charlie's line of fire, looking dazed. His friend, a beautiful Italian model, is already backing away from him in mortification.

"I'm sorry," Charlie says. "But this won't do."

The man touches Charlie lightly on the shoulder, as if checking to see whether he is joking, but Lane knows Charlie never jokes about matters of etiquette. "Come on, we're friends, aren't we?"

Charlie smiles at him. (*Coldly*, Gala points out. *Like a reptile.*)

"This is nothing against you," he says calmly. "But we have rules."

"Charlie," Lane says, stepping into the fold. "It's fine."

Charlie frowns at her, but she doesn't back down.

"It's fine," she repeats firmly.

"Hostess's choice," he says eventually, but he doesn't ask whether the man wants a drink or point him in the direction of the coat check. Instead, he links his arm through Lane's and tries to guide her away, but Lane doesn't budge.

"I'm Lane," she says to the stranger.

"Davide," he says, his cheeks still mottled with humiliation.

"Davide," Lane repeats. "Welcome to Laurel Canyon."

Davide nods graciously, and the crowd around them starts to disperse.

"Do you live around here?" Lane asks, and when he shakes his head, she asks, "How do you know Charlie?"

"From the Magic Castle," Davide says. "I work there."

"Oh, how interesting," Lane says. "I've never met a magician. Will you show me a trick?"

Davide hesitates for only a second before he reaches inside his pocket and pulls out a deck of cards. Lane watches as he fans out the deck face up and gestures for her to choose a card. She points to the queen of spades.

"Do you know the Margolises?" Lane asks as he expertly shuffles the cards. "They run a prop shop over on Franklin."

"Lane," Charlie says from behind her, sounding exasperated. "This is a party."

"I do sleight of hand," Davide sniffs. "I don't work with props."

Lane pauses. "Maybe you know their daughter Gala?"

Davide shakes his head, and then holds up the card at the top of the deck. It's the queen of hearts.

"That wasn't my card," she says, but Davide just smiles and places it back on top of the deck, face down.

"I know your husband though," Davide says. "Scotty."

He taps the deck again and gestures for her to turn the top card over herself this time. Lane reaches out and flips it. It has transformed into the queen of spades. She claps a little and Davide smiles.

"It's funny," Lane says as she hands him back the card. "I'm always asking both Scotty *and* Charlie to take me to the Magic Castle. I didn't know either of them had ever been."

"They haven't been in a while," Davide says, looking pointedly at Charlie. "In *fact*, the last time I saw either of them, a woman was throwing a martini over them."

Lane frowns.

"Who was the girl, Charlie?" she asks, turning to him.

When Charlie doesn't answer, his handsome face strangely still, Davide answers for him. "Beautiful, tall woman. Black hair, sad eyes."

"That's Gala," Lane says.

Davide shrugs and lights a cigarette. Lane slowly turns to Charlie, his hand now holding on to her forearm tightly.

"Charlie?" Lane asks. "What's he talking about?"

Charlie ignores her.

"Davide," he says calmly. "Why don't you head on outside? There must be *one* young woman in Hollywood you haven't already terrorized."

Davide's jaw tightens even more, but he says nothing as Charlie finally succeeds at steering Lane away.

"What's going on?" Lane says quietly, her voice strained as they make their way through the crowd toward the champagne fountain (the theme is, rather unimaginatively, the jazz age).

"Not now, Lane," Charlie says, and, for the first time in their friendship, she sees that he is tired of her. Charlie is as tired of her as her husband is and, long before that, as her parents were of her. And even though she knows this, can feel it in her bones like a curse that will never leave her, she still can't drop it. He extracts a glass and takes a sip of champagne.

"Have you seen Dimitri's latest paramour? I don't know who her surgeon is, but he needs his license revoked."

"Charlie McCloud, I swear I will scream this fucking house down if you don't stop lying to me," Lane says through gritted teeth. "When did you see her?"

Charlie meets her eye, and they both know she won't do it. Lane Warren is a lot of things, but out of control isn't one of them.

"It was sometime last year, Lane. Long before she disappeared."

"What did you do to her?"

Charlie looks tired suddenly. "I didn't *do* anything. She was out of her mind on something. You know how Gala could get."

You know how Gala could get. Lane turns the words over in her mind. Everyone had wanted Gala around when she was beautiful and magnetic, but it's as if they'd always understood that just around the corner lay an abyss she would inevitably disappear into, only nobody thought to mention it to Gala herself. Lane wonders if she'd known it too, if that's why she had been compelled to help her, but that's not quite right. There was something in it for her too. Sometimes Lane wonders if she and Gala were the only two people in L.A. who had ever been honest with each other.

"Why didn't you tell me?" she asks Charlie quietly.

"We're all allowed our secrets," he says. "Even you."

"Meaning?"

"Meaning I'm asking you to please drop the entire thing, for your own sanity," Charlie says.

"Excuse me?"

"Darling, you know how much I adore you, but your recent behavior is . . . worrying," Charlie says quietly.

"Worrying," Lane repeats.

"Creeping around Gala's apartment, going to her parents' house. Leaving Audrey alone in the middle of Disneyland. Accusing me of god knows what and lying about your book to everyone," Charlie says, almost breathlessly now. "I could ask what's missing in your life that you're so willing to risk everything for her, but I wouldn't do that to you."

"What do you mean lying about my book?" Lane asks slowly, her eyes flashing.

"Everyone knows who you're writing about," he says. "And nobody's said anything out of respect for you, but people are talking, and none of us can understand why you're so fixated on this woman. Something's off, and we're getting . . . a little concerned, Lane."

For just a moment, Lane feels as if she's falling. And the feeling is strangely familiar.

"Why doesn't anyone else care what's happened to her?" she asks. "This shouldn't even be about me."

"Oh, Laney," Charlie says, laughing a little. "It's always about you."

Lane understands now that Charlie is shaping a new reality around her and she is powerless to stop it.

She hurls her glass to the ground and watches as it shatters into thousands of jagged shards.

SCOTTY IS SITTING on a lounger by the pool when Lane finds him. The party is pulsing around them both, but she sees now that he is barely aware of it, oblivious to the couple practically fucking in the shallow end or the artist who has climbed up their pine tree purely so he can launch cones at people's heads.

"Scotty?" she asks, and she knows from his expression that he has not only heard about Davide but had perhaps witnessed it for himself. "What happened with Gala at the Magic Castle?"

"Davide is a drunk and a provocateur," he says, after a long pause. "Why listen to anything he says?"

"Please don't lie to me," Lane says slowly. "Charlie told me."

Scotty stops, his face flickering.

"Okay," he says. "Okay."

He takes Lane's arm and pulls her closer to him.

"Charlie and I were having a drink at the Castle, and Gala was there. She could barely stand, and she made an awful scene, so she was asked to leave. That was all that happened."

"Why didn't you tell me?"

"Because we wanted to protect you," Scotty says wearily. "Why else do you think?"

Lane feels a rush of panic.

"Protect me from what?" she asks, her tone sharp.

Scotty glances at her quickly.

"We were worried about you, Lane," Scotty says, after a moment. "We *are* worried about you. You haven't always been the most stable in the past, and we want to make sure that we're always in the best position to support you. And that means making sure that nobody is going to derail you, but particularly not someone as . . . unpredictable as Gala. We knew it would only upset you to see how bad things had gotten for her."

"I'm not crazy," Lane says, her voice louder than she intended. "I don't need to be managed. And you're not trying to protect me, you're trying to control me. Why were you even together without me?"

"Oh, Lane," Scotty says, and he reaches out and puts his arm around her. A few people are looking over, and he smiles reassuringly to let them know everything is okay, that he's in control of the situation and his hysterical wife.

"We just know things can get difficult for you sometimes . . ."

"Difficult," she repeats. A difficult woman. A Difficult Woman.

As her husband pulls her close to him, Lane feels a slippery, urgent need to escape. Is this how Gala felt at the end too?

"We need to consider the girls," Scotty says quietly so that only she can hear. And it is this that finally sends her over the edge.

"Get off of me," she says, her voice low and dangerous, but Scotty doesn't listen.

"I'm just trying to help you," he says into her hair, his grip tightening around her shoulders.

"Get the *fuck* off of me," Lane says again, and she shoves Scotty so hard he stumbles backward, nearly falling over. The crowd falls eerily silent, all eyes now trained on Lane. And as she scans the faces of the people she has welcomed into her home year after year, she understands that *this* is what they have wanted from her all along. While she has been proving she is worthy of their love, they've been waiting for her to shatter. Lane looks over to the house and catches Charlie's eye. He is standing by the window, calmly shaking his head, willing her to stop jeopardizing everything they've built together. And that's when Lane realizes just how alone she truly is. And she thinks of Gala.

THIRTY-SIX

THEN

MAY 1971

A few weeks before he was due to leave on tour, Gabriel had a change of heart about going alone. He asked Gala to join for the duration, had almost begged her in the end, but, however tempting it was to follow her lover around the country, Gala knew that Lane was right—the one thing that could tank their relationship faster than the drugs would be if Gabriel began to feel like he had to stay close to Gala in order to survive. She wasn't sure either of them would last very long under that type of duress, so instead, as a compromise, she agreed to travel with the band to the California dates at the start of the tour. As an added buffer, she suggested that Gabriel invite along someone else he trusted for the rest of it—perhaps the mysterious healer he'd been visiting for a few months and who seemed to have had a calming effect on him.

The first show was at the San Diego Sports Arena, and Belle Vue was performing to a crowd of over ten thousand restless fans desperate for their favorite band to return to the stage after an unreasonably long hiatus. As Gala left Gabriel to huddle with his bandmates in anticipation of the show, she thought she seemed more nervous than any of them.

Gabriel had asked Gala to watch from the side of the stage, and she stood there in her brown suede dress and platform boots, braiding and unbraiding the same few strands of her hair as she waited. The crowd was already hyped up, stamping their feet and chanting, and the energy in the stadium wasn't so much contagious as virulent. As the band's stage time approached, various younger women joined Gala in the wings, bouncing on their toes with excitement as they checked each other's lipstick and eyeliner for imperfections. Even without looking at them, Gala could feel the gazes of these young girls who knew she had once been one of them.

"So you and Gabriel are, like, the real deal," one girl said to her eventually as the crowd noise ramped up below. She had used liquid eyeliner to paint exaggerated eyelashes under her eyes and had short, apostrophe-shaped eyebrows that gave her the effect of looking permanently awestruck.

"You're like a super groupie," another girl added. She was even younger, cute rather than beautiful, with blond hair that grazed her waist and pale freckles across the bridge of her nose. Gala was about to correct her, but then she stopped. She hadn't lied to Lane—she really wasn't ashamed of anything she'd done, so why not give these young girls some hope for the future, something to aspire to while they were working their shifts at the local movie theater or gas station.

"Sure," Gala said generously. "I guess you could say that."

"What's the sex like?" another girl asked loudly. Gala thought about answering, then just smiled coyly instead. To think that, at thirty, she was already ten, even twelve years older than some of these girls! She'd never thought that she'd be anything other than one of these bright young things, itching to devour everything in life before her time was up, but now she could see that the other side wasn't too bad either.

"Have you girls heard about the actor Ray Donaldson? Let me tell you a story about his cock," Gala said conspiratorially, and the girls screamed with delight.

AS SHE WATCHED the band take the stage, Gala felt like she might actually be sick. She knew how important this first show was not just for Gabriel but for both of them—even one negative review or comment could ruin it all, toppling the fragile foundation they had rebuilt for themselves over the years. And even though she'd never admit it to him, it hadn't been easy for her to stand so close to someone so delicate either, someone who often felt more like a threadbare moth she needed to protect than a partner. Someone who held her heart in the palm of a hand that was also reaching for a peace they both knew he might never find.

As she watched Gabriel strut up and down the stage, howling into the microphone like he'd never left, Gala felt a sickly sweet relief take over. Even knowing Gabriel as well as she did, it was hard to tell if he had actually returned to this former version of himself or if he was just doing a damn good impression of it, but, as Gala looked at the euphoric hysteria of the crowd, she figured it probably didn't matter. All that mattered was that he could accept the adoration of millions at the same time as knowing it meant nothing at all.

———

AFTER THE SHOW, Gala walked into Gabriel's dressing room to find him sitting topless at the feet of a gray-haired man who was wearing an elaborately embroidered white tunic. Both men's heads were bowed, and the older man was wafting a stick of burning wood around Gabriel's shoulders. There were two women, girls really, sitting on the floor next to Gabriel in white dresses, and they both had the same oddly glazed, beatific look on their faces as they chanted something quietly. Gala felt sick for a moment, like she'd walked into something she shouldn't have, because why was Gabriel here in the thrall of these strangers when he should have been looking for her?

"Oh," Gala said. "Sorry."

Gabriel's head snapped up then, and his face broke into a grin. He jumped up and strode over to her before picking her up and nuzzling his sweaty face in her neck. He seemed normal, Gala thought with relief. Not high, not low, but exactly where he should be after performing in front of thousands of screaming fans for the first time in years.

"That's Billy, my healer," Gabriel said, gesturing behind him to the man who was now staring at her. "And these are his friends, Zadie and Sky."

The two women smiled at Gala, but Billy still wore an odd expression on his face as he watched their reunion. His eyes were the cool blue of ice on a swimming pool, and Gala felt a strange chill as they roved over her. *Fuck Billy*, Gala thought as she turned back to Gabriel.

"You're salty," she said, licking his exposed collarbone exaggeratedly.

"You're perfect," he said, smiling down at her with his shining violet eyes.

———

A COUPLE OF days later, when Gala was having a bath with Gabriel in another hotel room in another city, she brought up the scene she'd walked in on after the San Diego show. She was combing conditioner through her hair, and Gabriel was watching her like she was the most magnificent creature in the world, so now seemed as good a time as any to bring up the thing that had been bothering her since it happened.

"What's Billy's deal?" she asked casually.

"His deal?"

"Come on," Gala said. "The white outfits, the two sacrificial lambs, the kissing of his feet."

Gabriel smiled a little as she spoke.

"Are you jealous?" he asked. "Because you know that your massive feet are the only ones I would ever actually kiss."

Gala splashed some water at him.

"Fuck you, I'm being serious," she said. "Look, it just seemed a little . . . off to me, but I'm trying to understand, and I'm asking you to explain it to me."

Gabriel nodded and wrapped his fingers around her ankle under the water. He seemed to be debating how much he should share with her, and she wanted to tell him that she wanted all of it. All of him.

"I was raised Catholic," he started slowly. "And while I never bought into all the devil stuff, I did like the idea that there was something bigger than any of us at play. Like we're not just stumbling around with no purpose until the day we're lucky or unlucky enough to kick it, you know? And after I met you, and after you helped me get sober, that thing I was missing felt even more critical . . ."

Gabriel smiled ruefully at her, and Gala felt her heart ache for him.

"I know this has been rough for you, maybe even worse than it's been for me in some ways, and I can't tell you how many times I've known I should let you go. But something stops me every time and I think *that's* what I believe in. That's the faith I've been looking for. And Billy, with all his weird shit and rituals that make me feel like a fucking fool half the time, is just someone who reminds me of that on a daily basis, when you're not around. Does that make any sense?"

Gala thought about it, then she took Gabriel's hand and squeezed it. She wanted to understand, but there was still something about the way Billy had assessed her so starkly, so unflinchingly, that told her it wasn't a good idea. That people who were searchers, like Gabriel, were the most vulnerable of all. Because what was the point in freaking out about the meaning of life all the time? Why not try to have as wild a ride as you could without wasting your time constantly ruminating over the *why* of everything? For Gala, *that* was the path to insanity. *That* was the devil at work. *That* was the opposite of faith.

"Can't you just believe in me instead?" she asked instead. "In us?"

Gabriel studied her for a moment.

"Of course," he said. "Anything for you."

Then he leaned forward and kissed her on the nose.

"On that note . . . Will you marry me, Gala girl?"

AFTER CELEBRATING THEIR engagement all night in their hotel room, Gabriel sent Billy home and asked Gala again to stay with him on tour. And, to her own surprise if not his, Gala found herself declining again.

Lane had been partly right. While Gala had loved watching

Gabriel onstage and hamming it up for the younger girls, and she certainly had no regrets about the heady days (and nights) she had spent following beautiful men around the country in her teens and twenties, it no longer felt right for her to be there. It was infinitely more satisfying to be somebody rather than somebody's plus-one.

THIRTY-SEVEN

THEN

JUNE 1971

Gala was never quite sure whether the *Rolling Stone* feature came about because of her writing or her reputation, or a combination of the two. The concept of the shoot was the new Hollywood literati, and Gala was included in a list of five up-and-coming writers from the L.A. scene (the rest of whom were men) whom *Rolling Stone* was calling the saviors of Los Angeles culture. Lane was notably absent from the lineup, but Gala assumed this was because she was a little older and already firmly established in her career. On the day of the shoot, it crossed Gala's mind that three of the men were actually older than Lane, and one was on his third bestseller, but she didn't dwell on it for too long. All that mattered was that she got to spend a day dancing and pouting in front of one of the most lauded photographers in the country, with a wardrobe and makeup team just for her.

When asked if she had any ideas for the shoot, Gala had suggested a concept that had come to her in the middle of the night.

To symbolize how she was shaking up the publishing industry, Gala, wearing something suitably flamboyant, would strut through the middle of a corporate office (the grayer and less inspiring the better) leaving a trail of ordinary-looking men staring after her, visibly scandalized. The creative director had adored the idea, and Gala had spent the day flouncing around in glitter, chain mail, and feathers, before joining the other men on a bench under the Hollywood sign for their group shot. As she gripped a bottle of champagne and pouted under the dying sun, she realized now that all the men whose career changes she'd encouraged, whose art she'd inspired, whose egos she'd built up had simply been a dress rehearsal for her own success. Lane was right—she shouldn't have to modify or doubt herself for anyone.

BY THE TIME she sat down at Ben Frank's for the interview with a journalist who didn't look a day over seventeen (Pete or Bobby or some equally wholesome name), Gala was amped up and hyper, and a little drunk as she devoured a grilled cheese between chain-smoking cigarettes and drinking the champagne she'd smuggled in with her.

"Okay, this next round is a quick-fire one . . . I'm going to say a name, and you say the first word that comes into your mind," Pete or Bobby said, grinning at her.

Gala leaned forward and nodded.

"Jim Morrison."

Gala frowned for a moment. "Lost."

"Jack Nicholson."

"Naughty."

"Roy Donaldson."

"Sorry—" Gala said, frowning as she caught on to what was happening. "What exactly does this have to do with my writing?"

"Oh," he said. "We thought it would be funny to revisit a few moments from your past. Add some background color—you know?"

Gala took another swig of champagne to buy herself some time. She didn't want to come across as uptight or ashamed of anything, but she also didn't want her moment in the spotlight to be overshadowed by the specters of men she'd fucked, even in the interest of "background color." She pulled out a napkin from the dispenser and rummaged in her bag until she found an eyeliner. She wrote down a couple of dozen names, then handed the napkin over to the journalist.

"I'm not interested in any games, but feel free to ask any of these men for a quote about me."

The journalist read through the list and whistled through his teeth.

"All right," he said, tucking the napkin into his pocket. "Now—tell me about how you got your writing break . . ."

Gala thought for a moment about how she might encapsulate her essence in a way that would both immortalize herself in the pages of the most iconic magazine of the decade, and make it clear she was serious about her writing, however silly and effortless it seemed to everyone else.

"I spent years turning men into gods, but it turned out I was the star I'd been waiting for all along," she said, almost dreamily. She imagined seeing the words in print, blown up next to a photo of her stomping through the office as she left a trail of gray-faced men in her wake, but when she glanced at the journalist, she could tell that this wasn't exactly what he had been after. He nodded, but didn't move his pen from its position poised inches above his notepad. She was boring him, she realized. He was about to wrap the entire thing up because he thought she, *Gala*, took herself too seriously, and was no fun at all.

Gala lit another cigarette before breaking into her signature crooked smile.

"Or maybe it was glitter, grit, and blow jobs."

The journalist grinned and wrote the line down immediately.

LANE KNEW HER second book wasn't good enough, but she felt like she was stuck in an elevator that was hurtling toward the ground with no emergency brake. She felt the effort of every single sentence, as if she were having to gut herself just to get each word to match up with the one before. She knew the book worked only in the most basic sense—each sentence was identifiable as such, and there was a beginning, a middle, and an end to her story of a young mother in Reseda who'd developed homicidal tendencies after the car accident that left her husband dead, but that was about as good as it got. She didn't let anyone read her working draft as she was writing, not because she was precious about it, but because she couldn't bear to have anyone tell her how subpar it truly was.

At fourteen months, the twins were a little less blob-like than they had been (even Charlie commented on their cuteness whenever he dropped around to check in on her), but each stage seemed to bring with it a new sense of doom for Lane. She could now no longer leave them unattended for fear of their trying to kill themselves, or each other, generally by reaching for any object that could wreak the optimum damage, or by sticking their chubby baby fingers into electrical outlets. They seemed to instinctively know what they needed from her at any given moment, so why didn't she have the first clue of how to give it to them? And how did everyone else (women of inferior intelligence, if she was being honest) seem to find it all so easy?

Scotty had become something of an enigma to Lane. It was as if he was afraid that the darkness that had taken hold of her was contagious. He didn't get home from work until after midnight most nights, and he was always out of bed before she opened her eyes in the morning. On the surface, he helped out with the twins—changing diapers, bathing them in the morning if it was clear Lane had neglected to do so the night before, even occasionally getting up in the night to comfort them while Lane squeezed her eyes shut beside him. But the straightforward man Lane had chosen to marry seemed lost, and the thought that she had been the one to rub off on him instead of the other way around made her feel a clinging sense of shame on top of everything else.

ONE NIGHT, DURING one of her Monday outings with Charlie, he broached the subject of her marriage for the first time. He had been acting strangely since he picked her up, his eyes not really meeting hers and his finger flicking through radio stations like he was trying to land on the perfect soundtrack, as if it was of the utmost significance what song they listened to at this exact moment in time.

Charlie pulled up on a side street of Sunset and turned off his engine. Lane reached for her door, but he put a hand on her knee to stop her. She turned to him, not surprised exactly but with a strange feeling of dread that something was about to change.

"Lane," he said carefully. "How's Scotty?"

"He's okay," she answered levelly. "Busy with work."

Charlie nodded.

"You know a friend of mine works at the Dresden, and she said that Scotty's there most nights."

"Yes," Lane said. "He entertains clients there."

"Have you ever asked him about the demographic of these clients?" Charlie asked softly, and the burgeoning pit in Lane's stomach expanded into her chest.

"Charlie," Lane said quietly. "Stop."

Charlie turned to face her, and his expression was so pitying it made Lane feel sick.

"I don't know how not to tell you," he said, and she could feel a strangled fury rising inside her. She wasn't someone to be pitied. She wasn't some pushover who could be made to look like a fool, like her father.

"I'd be careful what you say next," Lane said, her voice uncharacteristically icy. Then she opened the car door and stepped out into the crisp summer night, the air thick with the smell of eucalyptus. She slammed the door behind her and started to walk.

After a moment, Charlie joined her, slipping his arm into hers and commenting on the unseasonable coolness of the night.

They never spoke of Scotty's nights at the Dresden again.

A COUPLE OF nights later, when Scotty came home late stinking of whiskey, Lane recalled their first date. As she watched him stumble around the bedroom in the moonlight, his foot stuck in his trousers, she felt a thrum of anger for the ways he'd mis-sold himself to her too. Yes, she may have pretended to be more lovable than she was, but he had acted like she *fascinated* him as a human when all the while he was planning to snuff out her light at the earliest opportunity. As her blistering fury grew, Lane understood that anger was an infinitely more straightforward emotion than any of the others she'd been navigating since the birth of the twins, and therefore was dangerously addictive.

"Where were you tonight?" she asked, and Scotty froze in his position above their bed. He was naked, his arms folded across his chest.

"The Dresden," he said, slurring his words only slightly. "With clients. Go back to sleep, Lane. It's late."

"Clients," she repeated. "Collectors? Dealers? Men? Women?"

"A mix," he said, his voice sharp angles. "Look, why don't I bring you one time? Maybe you'll even find someone there who interests you, because god knows I don't anymore."

"I thought interesting was passé," she said. "I thought you wanted authenticity. The only non-liar in Hollywood, remember?"

Scotty frowned down at her, his profile illuminated by the light of the moon shining through the curtains.

"What?" he said, more than a note of irritation in his voice now.

"That's what you told me on our first date. You're the only non-liar in Hollywood," Lane said slowly. "But at least you were telling the truth about one thing—you really are the most mediocre person I've ever met."

She turned over and closed her eyes, tears pricking the backs of her eyelids.

The next morning, she mailed her rotten manuscript to Esther, along with a piece of paper that read only *NO NOTES*.

THIRTY-EIGHT

THEN

AUGUST 1971

Not long after Lane sent off her book, she told Charlie that, after an eighteen-month hiatus, she was ready to reinstate the Sunday Salons. Both Scotty and Charlie seemed surprised, but she was characteristically bullish about it once she'd made up her mind. Gala had been right—she needed to rediscover the parts of herself she'd lost. And if she was bound to the house for a while longer, why not bring the party to her?

The theme they'd chosen for the first party back was icons, and Lane, remembering how much of a killjoy she'd felt at the celestial party, had spent hours reconstructing James Dean's iconic look from *Rebel Without a Cause*, complete with slicked-back hair. The living room was transformed into a Parisian night club, with a rotating glitter ball and dark red bistro tables, and Charlie had flown over an underground DJ from Philadelphia who was pioneering a type of music called disco.

Lane felt strangely nervous as the guests began to arrive, filtering in amid a haze of perfume and air-kisses, wearing extravagant costumes ranging from Marie Antoinette to four different versions of John Lennon through the years. Lane hadn't seen many of their old friends in over a year and was somehow both relieved and deflated to find them almost entirely unchanged, as arch and restless as ever. For the first time, Lane found herself wondering whether they were all as unhappy as each other, but she pushed the thought out of her mind, reminding herself that the presence of all these talented and worthy people meant her own star hadn't fallen as far as it sometimes felt after her enforced break.

Lane and Scotty avoided each other carefully, having barely spoken about anything other than the kids since their fight about the Dresden. For Lane, there was something soothingly familiar about it all—she knew exactly what to expect with frigidity; it was warmth that unnerved her. And tonight, Lane found she was far too busy fielding compliments from people on her triumphant return to the scene to even notice Scotty's presence. She felt faintly ridiculous in her costume, but she could tell it endeared her to the people who assumed she was too uptight to get stuck into any theme.

A little after 9:00 p.m., the door swung open, and Lane noticed a small ripple of laughter run through the people closest to it. Lane moved to get a better view of who was causing such a stir. Through the shoulders of other guests, Lane saw Gala standing in the doorframe, wearing a cream silk suit and gold glasses, her hair tucked into a dark blond shoulder-length wig. She held a copy of *The Ringtail* in one hand, and a placard that read DEATH TO FEMINISTS! in the other. The guests around her were laughing loudly now and searching for Lane, itching to see what she would make of it.

"Lane," Gala shouted gleefully across the room. "Do you see? I'm you!"

Lane forced a laugh and waved, even as she felt a thick heat climb up her neck to reach her cheeks.

"Almost!" she said. "Almost."

LANE KNEW THAT Gala hadn't meant to humiliate her, but she still felt like the butt of the joke. She'd never quite learned how to handle being mocked and, ironically, Gala was the only person she had ever let push her buttons, perhaps because it had never felt cruel. Only this felt slightly different—this felt like a joke at Lane's expense. Lane would now have to spend the majority of the night laughing off comments about Gala's costume to prove she didn't take herself too seriously, and it would no longer be remembered as the party that heralded Lane's return to the top of the Hollywood hierarchy (after a year in which she had sometimes felt irrevocably lost even to herself), but just another showcase for Gala's infamous sense of humor and penchant for risk.

Like many things of late, it felt as if Gala had stolen the moon from under Lane's fingertips.

CHARLIE APPROACHED LANE cautiously, handing her a glass of red wine. She rarely drank at her own parties, but he seemed to know that she would welcome it tonight. She took a large, grateful gulp.

"It was cheap," Charlie said to her as they watched Gala performing for a crowd of guests who wouldn't have given two shits about her before her *Vogue* column and billboard on Sunset, or the *Rolling Stone* spread where she was practically naked, draped across the laps of the four other writers, grinning smugly as if she hadn't realized *she* was the punch line while her male peers looked on, fully clothed and refined. "Glitter, Grit and Blow Jobs" had been the subheading of the trashy piece, and this was what Gala had attributed her success to—not natural talent, not hard work or sacrifice, and certainly not Lane's guidance. Didn't Gala realize how low it was to debase herself in that way? How damaging it was not only for her, but even for someone like Lane, who had established her entire career and stellar reputation *despite* being a woman? Not to mention the younger generation coming up who would look at the *Rolling Stone* spread and think that big tits and trashy sound bites were all it took to become a famous writer. Looking at Gala now, Lane realized that some things weren't teachable—there was a difference between being infamous and famous, and Lane was starting to wonder if she had wasted her time on someone who was only interested in the former and didn't deserve the latter.

"Did you invite her?" Lane asked Charlie.

"Unfortunately," Charlie said, having the grace to wince. "I thought she'd add a certain flair to our grand return."

"Well," Lane said. "She's certainly done that."

Gala caught Lane's eye then and lifted her glass of champagne in Lane's direction. The DJ had gone on a break, and an old soul song played gently from the speakers in his absence.

"I want to toast the woman of the hour," Gala said loudly, clearly already drunk. "I'll always rib her a little, but truly, this woman is an icon in my eyes. A writer, a wife, and now a mother. She's who I want to be when I grow up."

Lane was perfectly still for a moment. Had Gala intentionally emphasized the words *wife* and *mother* to the point of derision? Was she actually trying to belittle Lane in her own home by

reminding everyone of Lane's new, inescapably unglamorous re-
sponsibilities? But no, Gala looked genuinely admiring as she
waited for Lane to say something, her glass still raised. The room
was preternaturally quiet, the rotating lights of the glitter ball
bouncing off her guests' familiar faces as they waited expectantly
for Lane's response. Lane pulled herself up and tucked a stray
piece of heavily waxed hair behind her ear.

"Oh, honey," she said, channeling Gala with everything she
had. "A couple less blow jobs and maybe you'd have stood a
chance."

There was a moment of silence, then the guests erupted into
surprised and gleeful laughter, a few people even whooping and
stomping their feet. It was unlike Lane to even speak in front of
this many people, let alone swear or be cruel, and her guests ate
it up like she'd just performed a gravity-defying feat. Lane smiled
as she absorbed the adoration she knew would be as short-lived
as any other high, and her steely gray eyes stayed locked on Gala's
the whole time.

GALA HAD, ADMITTEDLY, been a little drunk when she came up
with the idea to dress up as Lane. And, if she was being honest,
she'd also been a little drunk when she turned up at the party.
The truth was that Gala was aware that, in her excitement over
the *Rolling Stone* shoot, she'd neglected to mention Lane's role in
kick-starting her writing career, and she figured that choosing
Lane as her "icon" might help soften the blow. She hadn't considered the idea that Lane would find it anything other than
flattering—if anyone had dressed up as *Gala*, she wouldn't have
left their side all night.

It wasn't so much what Lane had actually said at the party that bothered Gala, so much as the fact that Lane had been the one to say it. Everyone knew Lane as calm and self-restrained, someone who preferred to reveal her scathing observations only in the form of her beloved written word. The other guests had been positively gleeful, adoring the fact that she'd laid into Gala so publicly, and the interest wasn't going to die down anytime soon. And it wasn't exactly what Gala needed right now, considering she hadn't heard from Gabriel in over two weeks.

He'd called her once he'd read the piece, and she could tell he was trying to disguise the fact that she'd embarrassed him. He would never dream of trying to change her, or suggest that he had ownership of her body in any way, but for the first time Gala realized that just because he wouldn't do it, didn't mean he didn't want to. She'd tried to explain how the feature would raise her profile, meaning more commissions, more sales, more *money*, and Gabriel had told her that she never needed to write another word if money was what was driving her. This had infuriated Gala, and they'd had their first real argument, with Gala sticking stubbornly to her guns. Privately, she didn't love the way either the article or the shoot had turned out (she both looked and sounded a little more flippant than she'd intended), but she would rather die than admit that to anyone, even Gabriel. At the end of the call, he flatly told her that he loved her, and that Belle Vue's tour had been extended for another six months, until the end of February. This time, he didn't ask her to join him.

So, having been humiliated by Lane in front of nearly everyone she knew, and sold out by *Rolling Stone*, and abandoned by Gabriel, it made complete sense to Gala that she would do what she did when she had a spare couple of lines at the end of her October *Vogue* column. In a thinly veiled blind item, Gala obliterated Lane's new novel.

This serial-suit-wearing, Laurel Canyon–dwelling author has a new novel coming out next year that everyone is already talking about for the wrong reasons. A word of advice from one Hollywood scribe to another—maybe if you actually learned to like yourself, it might feel less like a capital punishment to read. Or maybe another L.A. darling needs to show you how it's done . . .

AN EDITOR FRIEND of Lane's called to tell her about Gala's comments before the magazine hit the stands.

"Just a courtesy," he said, his voice strained. "Everyone knows to take Gala with a heavy pinch of salt. Plus, by the time the book comes out, everyone will have forgotten about this anyway."

Lane cleared her throat and tried to ignore the sting of Gala's words. Aside from anything else, she hated that Gala had dragged her into this, particularly because she had no other option than to laugh it off. If she admitted that she cared, then this man, this editor whom she relied on for work, would relegate Lane to the same ranks as Gala. She would just be one more hysterical woman he had to either manage or avoid.

"Thanks for letting me know," she said. "But I don't think anyone reads Gala's column for her intellect."

The editor laughed, relieved that Lane wasn't going to cause a stink about it. "I suppose they don't, no."

Lane said goodbye and hung up the phone. She felt cold with fury as she dug her fingernail into the tender part of her wrist. She could laugh off Gala's comments as the rantings of a jealous rival, but, deep down, she wondered if she was right. Hadn't she known the book wasn't good enough when she sent it to her editor? The thought that people were already talking about her, laughing at her, made her want to crawl out of her own skin. She thought of what kind of novel Gala would have written in her place, and she knew that, however flawed or vacuous it may be, it would never be described as a punishment to read. And the idea that one day she might try made Lane feel sick.

THIRTY-NINE

NOW

FALL 1975

Lane has been asked to sit on the panel at the opening event of a literary festival in downtown Los Angeles. The subject of the discussion is a loose "identity in California," and when she arrives at the venue, an old art deco movie theater, she discovers that she will be in discussion with two male authors she's never met. One wrote a book about a group of rich kids on Catalina Island, and the other about a group of rich kids in San Francisco, and Lane is entirely unenthused at the prospect of debating identity with two men barely out of their twenties. The feeling is only compounded when she spots Scotty in the front row with the twins. He hadn't mentioned he was coming and, on the surface, it is a sweet gesture, but Lane knows her husband has only brought the girls as an insurance policy. Since their fight at the last Sunday Salon, it's as if he has been waiting for her to snap again, like her mother before her.

The conversation is stilted at first, but soon the writers get to know each other's styles, the ebb and flow of their ideas, and

Lane is almost relaxed when the moderator (a male journalist in his twenties) asks her what she thinks is gained from being a woman writer. Lane frowns at him.

"I don't think I understand the question," she says.

He laughs a little, as if she's being deliberately obtuse. "All right, all right. Let me reframe that for you. I don't think we can talk about identity while ignoring the gender question. What would be different about your novels if they were written by a man? What would be gained, what would be lost?"

Lane sits for a moment under the bright lights, her mind strangely blank. In the front row, Scotty is helping Audrey untangle the hair of her favorite doll, and Dahlia is picking at some dried gum on the sole of her Mary Jane. Lane knows the answer she should give (that not only is there fundamentally no difference, but that the question is moot—they couldn't have been written by "a man" because they were written by Lane), and it is an answer that would usually roll off her tongue instinctively, but for some reason, today, the words die at the back of her throat.

"Ummm," Lane says, and suddenly she is no longer here, but in the living room of Gala's apartment nine years earlier, telling Gala that she doesn't think women should have to rip open their souls to be worthy of consumption, and now she understands that while she was right about that, she was also naive, because isn't that what everyone wants from her, wanted from Gala? Didn't they want to see the price they paid for keeping up with the men around them?

"I don't . . ." There is a tightness in her chest, and Lane finds she can't utter another word. Her cheeks flush, and the crowd is uncomfortably silent, but there is also something else—a muted delight at this rare lack of composure. She can feel all eyes on her as her own fill with tears. Then, Lane spots a glimpse of shiny black hair in the crowd, a flash of white fur, and for a perfect moment, everything makes sense again. Because why *wouldn't* Gala be here in this moment, watching Lane flounder onstage, struggling to provide an answer she once could have rattled off in her sleep? Before she knows what she's doing, Lane is standing up to get a better look, her chair clattering behind her.

"Ms. Warren?" the moderator asks, his face etched with confusion.

"Excuse me," she mumbles, and now she is making her way offstage and running down the aisle, searching for the figure in the crowd.

Scotty stands up. "Lane!" he calls, but she streaks past him too, pushing through the standing members of the audience until she finds the woman she has been looking for. She grabs her by the shoulders and spins her around, only to be faced with a complete stranger, an older woman who stares at her in shock as the entire auditorium watches, unsettled by this strange display from a writer known for her sense of decorum, her unwavering respect for order and control.

"I'm sorry," Lane says. "I thought . . ."

She feels a sturdy hand on her arm and turns to find Scotty and the girls, watching her carefully as if she is a wild animal who might bolt. As if she is anyone other than Lane Warren, destined to make her way back onstage to apologize for the interruption before smoothly continuing with her answer, that no, it makes zero difference that she is a woman writing about women. That it is a coincidence, and that her next novel will be about a young soldier coming home from war only to get lost in the Alaskan wilderness he used to call home. Because isn't that what everything has been for all along? This insatiable desire for not only respect, but the specific type of respect that rewards her for not letting her womanhood get in the way? But Lane is so tired of doing the same dance, over and over again. She's so tired of everything.

She breaks away from Scotty's ever-tightening grip and runs toward the exit.

LANE RUNS AND runs and runs, farther than she has in years. Downtown is grimy and still, and the sun has dipped behind the anonymous gray buildings, making Lane feel as if she could be in any city in the world. Her lungs are burning, and she has a sharp stitch in her side that reminds her of being a kid—how has she moved through her adult life so slowly, so deliberately that she had forgotten side stitches even existed?—and there is a satisfaction in the way her body is coated with a heavy sweat that seeps through the silk of her suit.

After a while, over a mile at least, Lane finally stops running as she reaches a small, near-empty diner. She pushes open the door and slumps in a booth before ordering a hot dog and cheese fries with a strawberry milkshake. Still breathing heavily with exertion, she eats every last scrap and then uses her greasy fingers to scrape up the excess cheese still caked to the paper-lined basket. She finishes off with the milkshake, the thick, creamy texture nearly bringing tears to her eyes.

"More," she says to the waitress when she comes back over. "More, please."

FORTY

THEN

MARCH 1972

Lane's second novel, dubiously titled *The Unraveling*, was both a critical and commercial flop. It felt like people wanted to hate it, perhaps after the runaway success of *The Ringtail*, but knowing the vitriol was rooted in envy didn't make Lane feel any better. If anything, it felt all the more personal. A prominent literary critic and writer (and, perhaps crucially, founding member of the newly launched Women's Action Alliance in New York) panned it in *The New York Times*, likening Lane's account of a homicidal woman driven mad to a "bawdy" hotel lobby mural that thought it was a Rembrandt. The most cutting line of all suggested that an anvil would have had more subtlety than some of Lane's imagery on motherhood.

Scotty came home early from work on the day the review ran, and they had a fraught dinner with the girls, during which even the twins were freakishly well-behaved, as if even at two years old they already understood the gravity of the situation. After they'd finished eating, Scotty put the girls to bed while Lane washed up the remnants of the salmon and potatoes they'd eaten.

"Laney," Scotty said, walking back into the kitchen just as Lane dropped another plate into the sink with a clatter. "It isn't the end of the world . . ."

"'Warren displays zero sign of empathy, humor, or even connection to the world around her. Much like the gratuitous mutilated bodies in the motel, the entire endeavor was dead on arrival,'" Lane recited, her voice hollow. "It certainly feels like the end of the world to me. Are you saying I'm being irrational?"

"Laney," Scotty said. "Come on."

Lane turned around slowly.

"Why are you drinking?" she asked, scowling at the glass of whiskey she now saw he was gripping. "Why are you always drinking now?"

"I never said I didn't drink," Scotty said, defensiveness creeping into his voice.

"It's embarrassing," she said. "How much you need it."

Scotty stood up and walked over to the sink. He poured the rest of his glass down the sink, and then did the same with the entire bottle of whiskey on the counter. Lane watched the liquid run out, but she didn't feel satisfied.

"Did you know it was trash?" she asked. "When you read it."

Scotty shook his head. "I didn't know."

Lane shook her head. She didn't believe him. Whatever else you wanted to say about Scotty, he'd always had good instincts about art.

"Do you remember our first date?" Scotty asked, as if he were reading her mind. "I told you that if you trusted your gut, everything would work out. Did you trust your gut with this book?"

"Of course I did," Lane said scathingly. *Not even close*, she thought.

"Then I have no doubt it will find its audience. And maybe it won't be among your peers, who clearly have an ax to grind, but somewhere out there the right people are going to find it and they're going to cherish it."

Lane watched her husband talk, his handsome face filled with effort as he desperately searched for the right words to comfort her, and she felt a new level of revulsion for him.

"You did say that," Lane said coldly. "But you said a lot of things that night. And I'm not sure how many of them still hold up."

"Don't do this," Scotty said, his voice a warning shot. "I'm trying to be nice. Despite the fact that . . ."

He broke off and walked over to the fridge.

"Despite what?" she asked.

He shook his head.

"Say it," Lane commanded, and Scotty turned around wearily.

"Despite the fact that the deadly boring husband shares a lot of characteristics with me, before he's cleaved neatly in two by an oil tanker," he said quietly. "It's a little humiliating, Lane."

"It's hardly *my* fault that you relate to the character who thinks limericks are high art," she said witheringly, even as her cheeks grew hot. (Was it true? How had she missed it?)

Scotty just stared at her in response.

"Maybe this is the problem," Lane continued. "Maybe I've wasted so much time with you, such a deeply uninspiring person that you don't even *attempt* to hide it, that I've forgotten how to be brilliant. I've forgotten how to do the one thing I was good at. And maybe that's what you wanted from me. You wanted someone you could trap and stifle until I became as unremarkable as you are."

If Scotty had fought back in some way, Lane might have forgiven him. Instead he stared back at her with eyes that seemed to be glistening with tears, and the thought that he might be the one to cry made her so furious she stood up and grabbed the copy of her book from the bookshelf behind her before hurling it at Scotty's head with all her might. He ducked just in time, and it hit the cream wall behind him, leaving a dark mark on the paint. There was a noise from above, and that was when Lane noticed Audrey and Dahlia blinking at the top of the stairs in their pajamas. They started to wail in unison, and, after a stunned few seconds, Scotty regained his composure.

"Leave," Scotty commanded, his voice an unrecognizable bark. Lane felt a thrill at the fury she'd finally evoked in this unflappable man.

"Fuck you," she said, and Scotty took a step toward her, his cheeks burning.

"Leave," he said again, his voice more controlled now. "Get out of this house."

Lane felt a grim satisfaction as she grabbed her bag and walked out the front door without a second glance at everything she was leaving behind.

IN HER RUSH to escape, Lane had left her car keys in the house, so her only real option was to march the mile down to the Chateau Marmont in the relentless rain. As she walked, head down, headlights swinging over her and fury still roiling through her, acquaintances stuck their heads out of their windows and called out to ask if she was okay. Nobody walked in L.A., but particularly not in the rain. Lane ignored them and carried on walking.

When she arrived at the hotel lobby, Lane was soaked through.

She held her chin high as she requested a bungalow with a private pool, even as water puddled at her feet. Once she was in her room, she stripped and wrapped herself in a bathrobe before picking up the phone, dialing 0 to make a long-distance call. The nonplussed operator made the connection quickly, and Esther answered after her trademark two and a half rings.

"Why didn't you tell me?" Lane asked immediately.

"You said no notes," Esther said, after a short pause. "Anyway, I liked it."

"How?" Lane asked, because already her book felt tainted by the opinions of strangers, like a starfish that had been left out to rot in the sun.

"Look, Lane, it's not going to be the best or last book you'll ever write, so just try not to get too caught up in it. Bad reviews are a rite of passage, and if anything, it's just a testament to your success. They wouldn't tear you down if they hadn't built you up."

"I should be flattered," Lane said slowly. "I should ignore the fact that every review has pointed out the fact that I'm a woman, and yet, somehow, both women and men seem to revile me equally."

"That's true equality, darling," Esther said drolly.

Lane let out a short, bitter laugh.

"Where are you calling me from?" Esther asked.

"Chateau Marmont," Lane said. "Scotty asked me to leave."

"The man has impeccable timing," Esther said.

Lane traced her fingertip along the faded wall. Someone had carved the initials G + I into the paint.

"Lane, while I have you . . . I've been meaning to pick your brain about something," Esther said. "Or someone, rather."

"Who?"

"Your friend Gala Margolis."

Lane dug her fingernail into the paint, adding a line to the *I* so that it turned into an *L*. G + L. Gala and Lane.

"What about her?"

"I'm flying her out to New York on Friday," Esther said. "But I wanted your read on her before I make anything official."

"Official," Lane repeated. "You're planning to publish an essay collection?"

"Not essays," Esther said. "We've been talking about a novel."

Lane swallowed hard as a strange, hot sensation rose inside her.

"Gala's writing a novel?"

"We're talking about it," Esther said. "I thought you were close."

"We're close," Lane said slowly. "Or as close as anyone can be to someone like Gala."

"Meaning . . . ?"

Lane knew she had only seconds to figure out what she wanted to say, but she didn't quite know . . .

"Just that she's a little temperamental," Lane said after a short pause. "Unpredictable."

"Is that a West Coast euphemism for something?" Esther asked impatiently.

Lane paused.

"Lane, I trust you to give me an honest opinion on this."

Lane wrapped the phone cord so tightly around her finger that it went puce.

"Gala has always been a party girl—that's obviously part of her shtick—but I don't know. I've heard that she and Gabriel are getting into some . . . heavier stuff since he's been back from tour," Lane said, after a moment. "I've heard it's getting a little dark . . ."

"A lot of writers do drugs," Esther said, then paused. "Do you think she wouldn't be able to deliver because of it?"

There was a silence and Lane felt a jolt of panic. Her stark room at the Chateau, moments earlier so comforting in its anonymity, suddenly felt like it was spinning, and she was transported back to when she was a little kid on a swing carousel at the local carnival, legs dangling thirty feet in the air as her dad waved from below and she cried desperately to get off, all the while knowing nobody could hear her. Her entire life had felt like this recently, as if the world were swirling away from her on an axis, and all she could do was stay as still as possible and stare very hard at one spot, trying not to lose herself in the process. But as Esther waited for Lane to speak, Lane had the sudden and distinct thought that maybe the time for staying still had passed. Maybe now all she could do was act, in order to salvage whatever parts of herself were still left.

"Heroin, Esther," Lane said, and she told herself that she wasn't lying exactly—she was just repeating what she knew to be true about Gabriel at one point at least, and knowing what she knew about addicts, he'd eventually drag Gala down with him one way or another. It was really also Lane's reputation on the line if she were to vouch for Gala's reliability. Surely it was preferable to give Esther as much information as possible so that she could reach her own conclusion, outside of anything Lane might or might not believe.

Esther made a noncommittal sound on the other end of the phone, and Lane felt a burst of anger. Why couldn't Gala find any other editor in the country? Why did it have to be her editor? Lane thought of the adjectives used to pan her novel—*humorless, weighty, stodgy*—and she knew that Gala's writing would never be described as any of these things. Gala's writing was effortless.

Gala herself was effervescent. Why had Lane ever thought Gala was deserving of her help? Everything Gala had ever wanted had been handed to her already, and all Lane had done was feed the beast.

Lane cleared her throat.

"I also don't exactly know how to say this, but I've heard that Gabriel helps her a lot with her writing," Lane found herself saying next. "And I'm talking significantly here. He's a great story-teller, if you think about it, and I think he's always been there to . . . you know, collaborate with her. And the more far gone he gets, the less comprehensible her writing gets. That's just . . . that's just what I've heard. I think it's risky, Esther."

Lane could hear Esther lighting a cigarette over two thousand miles away.

"Thanks, Lane," Esther said finally. "I appreciate your candor."

"I'm sorry I didn't have better feedback," Lane said.

"And I'm sorry you're today's shark meat," Esther said. "But I can promise you it won't last forever."

They hung up a few minutes later, then Lane flung open the doors and stepped back outside into the rain. She carefully undid her robe and dived naked into her private swimming pool. Under the black palm trees, Lane screamed underwater for as long as her lungs allowed it, all the while telling herself that she'd done the only thing she could to save them all.

WHEN ESTHER CANCELED Gala's meeting twenty-four hours before she was supposed to fly to New York with Gabriel, Gala considered going ahead with the trip and demanding to know what had changed. All Esther would say was that she'd asked a trusted friend for a reference, and she was no longer convinced that their ethics aligned. And while Gala didn't know exactly what that meant, she had a feeling Lane Warren would if she asked her.

"Did Lane have something to do with this?" she asked, and she heard Esther exhale smoke from her office in New York that Gala would now never see.

"Whatever happened between the two of you has nothing to do with me," Esther said. "But I'll give you a word of advice, Gala. In my opinion, Lane isn't an enemy you want."

Gala hung up, her blood firing in her veins.

"Let's go and firebomb their offices," Gala said later. She was pacing around her bedroom furiously, indignance rolling off her in waves. "Or Lane's house."

Gabriel was sitting on the foot of the bed, watching Gala like one might an unpredictable lioness. It was only his second week back from tour, and he hadn't expected to have to navigate a homicidal fiancée on top of everything else, but he counted to three in his head, repeated his personal mantra, and tried to defuse the situation without provoking further ire.

"I get it," he said carefully. "But all they've done is expose themselves as being unworthy of any part of you, and isn't that a gift too, in a way? That clarity?"

Gala was very grateful that Gabriel had discovered Transcendental Meditation on tour, but there was a time and a place for everything, and this wasn't exactly the moment for him to flaunt his spiritual awakening. She'd forgotten that it was always like this after a prolonged absence—the two of them trying to remember the ways they used to fit together until they felt like home again.

"What a lucky girl I am to be living with John Lennon," she said, and Gabriel, noting the disdain in her tone even if he didn't fully understand it (Lennon was *god*), tried a different approach.

"There'll be another offer, another deal. I know it doesn't feel like it, but this is Esther's loss," Gabriel said, and Gala finally stopped pacing. She swiveled to face him, her eyes flashing.

"I know," she said haughtily. "Do you think I actually care? I fucking hate New York anyway."

But Gabriel knew Gala better than to take her at face value, and he stood up off the bed and lifted her into his arms, until she buried her face in his shoulder.

"Come on, Gala girl," he said gently. "You'll always be my star."

FORTY-ONE

THEN

MARCH 1972

That night, Gala and Gabriel skipped the red-eye they had booked to JFK. Instead, Gala dressed in a sheer white minidress wrapped in swaths of organza and her highest platform boots, and she put on enough gold eye makeup to rival all the drag queens in New York. Gabriel wore a pair of black jeans with one of Gala's lace-up peasant blouses and his favorite suede jacket slung over his shoulder. Gala drank a glass of wine at the house, and then they drove up Laurel Canyon to the party of an acquaintance who lived in a small wooden bungalow on Lookout Mountain.

On the way up the winding road, a Belle Vue song came on the radio, and Gabriel changed the station before landing on an old blues tune that seemed to delight him. As he sang huskily along with it, Gala glanced at Gabriel's profile and thought again how lucky she had been to find him.

THE PARTY WAS in full swing when they arrived, and the air was thick with the pungent smell of hash—the unofficial scent of Laurel Canyon. Bodies were packed into the heaving cabin, and Gala could pick out dozens of people they'd both known for years but who represented markedly different things for each of them. For Gala, growing up in L.A. had always felt like a thrilling joy-ride, but for Gabriel, it must have seemed as if darkness had been closing in since the moment he arrived in this strange city. Gala reached over and squeezed Gabriel's hand.

"Are you going to be okay?" she asked, and he smiled back reassuringly.

"I survived tour," he said. "I can survive anything."

Gala squeezed his hand and chose to believe him.

They danced for a while, Gabriel murmuring the lyrics into Gala's ear, and then someone turned the music off and handed Gabriel a set of bongos, which he played good-naturedly while a woman with a far inferior voice sang a melancholy rendition of Belle Vue's biggest hit, "Talk Nothing to Me." When someone offered him a mirrored tray filled with neat slivers of cocaine mid-song, Gabriel's eyes met Gala's blankly, as if he couldn't remember how he was supposed to respond. Gala put her body in between Gabriel and the drugs, and whispered to him that they could leave the moment he wanted. He just beat harder on the drums, jaw clenched and sweat dripping down his temples.

AFTER SHE WENT to find him a glass of water, Gala lost Gabriel for what felt like hours. He had told her he'd join her in the kitchen when he finished playing, but she waited for a while, her hand wrapped around a warm mug of water, and he never showed. As she pushed her way back through the crowd, searching for his familiar smile, a strangled panic coursed through her veins. When she couldn't find him, she threw open the back doors of the house, but all she saw was a bunch of teenagers jumping the fence into the yard, shouting obscenities when they realized they'd been spotted. She left them to it and turned back inside to continue her search as a feeling of dread seeped deeper into her bones.

Later, she'd understand that only around twenty minutes had passed before she found Gabriel in the bathroom, but by that point it didn't matter. By then, the only measure of time that made any sense was before and after.

There were half a dozen bodies crammed into the tiny tiled bathroom, and it was so clammy that the sole window was steamed over with condensation. The room smelled like bodily fluids and something else cloying that stung her nostrils. Gala's panicked eyes scanned over the slumped reprobates until she found Gabriel collapsed against the bathtub, his eyes half-closed as whatever he'd taken licked through his bloodstream, his body strange and slack. When Gala let out a moan, more like an animal than a human, his violet eyes briefly met hers, but it was like he couldn't see her at all.

Gala felt the fiercest terror claw at her heart, and she stumbled out of the room.

FORTY-TWO

THEN

MARCH 1972

Gala was halfway down Lookout when she heard the voice calling her name. For just a moment, she wondered if it could be Gabriel, somehow already out of his stupor and wanting to apologize for blowing up both their lives while she had been waiting for him by a stranger's fridge. It wasn't Gabriel following her, though, but Scotty Ryan. He hurried down the hill to meet her, and when he got closer, he looked genuinely concerned, like a fucking Boy Scout.

"Are you all right?" he asked, putting his hand on her forearm. "Here, take my jacket."

Gala allowed him to drape his sports jacket over her shoulders as she leaned against a wall and cursed this entire fucking day.

"Why are you being nice?" she asked. "I hate it."

Scotty smiled at her, but Gala knew she couldn't allow herself to collapse now, not in front of anyone who looked down on her as much as Scotty had always seemed to. She clenched her hands into fists in an attempt to stop them from shaking. How had she been so stupid as to trust someone who hadn't even trusted himself?

"What are you even doing at a party like this, Scotty?" Gala asked wearily.

"Would you believe me if I said I was looking for drugs?" Scotty said.

"I imagine you didn't have to look far," Gala said, unable to keep the bitterness out of her tone.

"I don't know," he said ruefully. "Apparently I look like a narc."

Gala let out a crooked laugh, despite herself.

"Just ask me next time," she said, and then she remembered Gabriel's face in the flickering light of the bathroom and wondered if she might vomit all over Scotty's designer shoes.

"Is Lane here?" she asked grimly.

A flash of torment crossed his face and Gala paused.

"Oh," she said. "I guess we've both been fucked tonight."

"Gabriel?" he asked, but she just closed her eyes.

"I'm sorry," he said, but he didn't sound satisfied or smug, or like he was about to run back to Lane at any moment to tell her what a mess Gala's life had become.

Scotty stood next to her then and leaned back, his face tilted toward the sky. The stars unfolded above them, the moon a glowing orb to anchor them. For a moment, they were shoulder to shoulder, both silent under the weight of their own battles.

"An artist once told me that you can only ever see one side of the moon from earth," Scotty said. "Whether you're in Rome or Sydney, it's always the same side."

"Oh," said Gala, who wasn't of a particularly philosophical nature at the best of times.

"Isn't that strange? Its presence is so familiar, but there's this whole other side of it that nobody will ever see. How can we ever really appreciate it, knowing that?"

Gala shrugged. "I don't think the moon could care less if we appreciate it or not. The moon's just doing what it's made to do and we're the ones making up stories."

As she spoke, Gala's eyes filled with tears. She wondered now if she'd been so obsessed with changing Gabriel that she hadn't stopped to think about whether he was actually capable of it, even for her.

"Do you think we can ever love all of someone?" she asked. "Or just the parts they want us to know?"

"I'd settle for knowing anything about Lane at this point," Scotty said grimly.

There was something in the simple way he said it that made Gala turn to look at him, and then suddenly they were kissing, and, even though they both understood it wasn't about the other person at all, their hands still moved with a feverish inevitability as they clawed first at each other's clothes and then their own. Gala angled herself against the wall so that Scotty could enter her, and when she thought briefly of Gabriel's beautiful body twitching against the porcelain, she grabbed a handful of Scotty's hair and pulled it hard until he moaned into her ear. The wall was scraping Gala's back, but the pain felt necessary, distracting, and Gala clamped her legs tighter and tighter until she felt Scotty move inside her. As he finished, he murmured something over and over. It took her a moment to figure out what he was saying, and once she did, she felt a surge of devastation for them both. He'd been saying, "I'm sorry, I'm sorry, I'm so sorry."

SCOTTY AND GALA were still adjusting their clothes when they heard the explosion. Gala's heart jolted in her chest, and she turned back toward the house, ignoring Scotty shouting at her to stop. As she got closer, she could smell it—the scent of burning wood and melting flesh and animal fear. She could hear the screams of panic as she pushed through the fleeing crowd, making her way toward the burning house. She was about to step over the threshold inside, black smoke billowing out the door and windows, when someone grabbed her from behind and restrained her.

"It's okay," Scotty murmured into her ear. "Everything's going to be okay."

Gala let out a wail as she felt her knees buckle. Scotty supported her and let her scream as she waited for the answer to a question she'd never have to ask. Her heart had gone black, and the world was suddenly too heavy to bear.

FORTY-THREE

THEN

APRIL 1972

After a short investigation, it was concluded that the old gas radiator in the bathroom may have been leaking for months, possibly even years, and that all it would have taken was a flick of a lighter in the wrong place for the entire room to go up in flames. The windows of the house were blown out instantly, and the entire back of the bungalow was obliterated into ash. The public was told that Gabriel and his five companions would have died instantly, but Gala didn't believe that was possible. Surely it would have taken longer than a few seconds to extinguish a life so precious?

THE FUNERAL WAS in Manchester, and Gala flew over for it with Gabriel's three former bandmates. The service was Catholic and, even through her Valium-and-quaalude-induced haze, all Gala could think about was how much Gabriel would have hated it. All that talk of obedience and service, of the *solace* to be found in God, and those awful hymns. Would he even remember any of these people, with their pallid gray skin and sad navy suits? Where were the fans who had known and adored him? And where was the part about leaving behind his pain to be reborn as a monarch butterfly or a mockingbird? Where was the life, the color, the music?

When Gala introduced herself to Gabriel's mother, a small woman with blond curly hair and hundreds of tiny lines tugging at her mouth, the woman barely registered her. She allowed Gala to hug her and then accepted her condolences with a stoicism that bordered on sociopathic. When Gala tried to tell her how much Gabriel had meant to her, her voice breaking under the futility of her own words and how little justice they actually did to the man they had both lost, his mother simply asked whether Gala had brought a jacket as it was looking set to storm.

Gala left without going to the wake. No wonder Gabriel couldn't wait to get away from this place.

ON THE FLIGHT back to Los Angeles, one of the band members, Aiden, let slip that Gabriel had been using since before the band went on tour. The healer Gala had sent home, Billy, had been hired to help Gabriel stay clean on the road.

"He tried," Aiden said quietly. "He thought he could stop again."

"I don't want to talk about it," Gala said, and she turned away from him. When she opened the window shade next to her, the entire world around her was black.

FORTY-FOUR

THEN

JUNE 1972

Lane had moved home as soon as she heard about Gabriel's death. Suddenly the shabby allure of the Chateau just seemed bleak rather than glamorous; the relative peace lonely instead of blissful. When Lane got back to the house in Hollywood, she and Scotty didn't talk about their fight or any of the things she'd said, instead settling back into a rhythm that was cordial, if not exactly tender. It was as if the stark realization that life could change in an instant was enough to make them reaffirm their commitment to each other, however tentatively at first.

For her part, Lane tried to be kinder, softer, with her family, and Scotty, perhaps noticing the effort, went out for fewer dinners, and the ones he did attend were noticeably shorter and less boozy than before. Perhaps chastened by the three nights he spent without Lane, he suggested they hire a nanny to help Lane with the load of childcare so that she could focus on her work. Lane accepted the offer, and, once the intimidatingly capable Rose started, Lane found she was able to ease herself back into journalism—a domain in which the stakes felt infinitely lower than writing another novel, and the gratification of cracking a narrative faster. Her biggest assignment was for *Time* magazine, which flew her to Cambodia in late October to cover a story of the injured soldiers who had fled across the border from Vietnam but who were now experiencing the destabilizing impact of the war on their safe haven. After she returned home and submitted the copy, Lane's editor assured her that he would be submitting the story for the Pulitzer Prize. "Without being sentimental, you make the political unavoidably personal," he told her, and, after thanking him, she tried not to wince when she remembered her heated response to a woman who once posed a similar idea at her first book reading in New York.

IN THE WEEKS following Gabriel's death, Lane had thought about going to see Gala nearly every day. She just never quite made it. She told herself instead that Gala would undoubtedly be surrounded by her closest friends and family, and that fielding a visit from someone she rarely saw anymore would be more effort than help. Particularly someone who had warned her of the danger of this very thing happening.

But as the weeks passed, and the three-month anniversary of the accident approached, Lane knew she was hiding from something too. She knew that things had gotten a little . . . *complicated* between her and Gala before the fire, but she wondered if this might put everything into perspective. And, who knows, maybe this tragedy could be the thing that grounded and matured Gala's writing, as well as her public persona.

One night, over dinner at La Scala with Scotty and Charlie (the unlikely duo who had seemingly decided their mutual affection for Lane was enough to warrant dinner together every now and then), Lane finally voiced her thoughts out loud.

"Have I been a coward?" Lane asked. "I told myself she wouldn't want to see me, but is that even true?"

Scotty looked up helplessly from his food, and Lane thought again how useless her husband was when faced with the messiness of real life. He had built himself a glass and concrete kingdom where every join was visible and every angle perfect, and he didn't understand why the rest of the world couldn't be that way too.

Charlie put down his cutlery and frowned as he thought about the question. Lane always found him to be very considered in matters of etiquette, perhaps due to his having grown up wealthy. However specific the scenario, it was as if Charlie had a range of formulas in his mind to determine the best course of action. Lane usually appreciated her friend's certainty, even if it meant life felt a little like a board game, as if there were a specific set of targets to hit in order to have *done the right thing* before you could move forward.

"You sent flowers, didn't you?" he mused, and Lane nodded. "So now you wait to hear from her. The ball is in Gala's court, and she knows she can reach out if she wants to. You don't want to badger her, after all."

"That makes sense to me," Scotty said, nodding. "She probably has a lot of friends around her, checking in. More wine, Charlie?"

As her husband reached out to enthusiastically top up Charlie's glass, Lane imagined a tennis ball flying from her house to Gala's apartment, landing on the parquet floor, and rolling under the couch or somewhere else Gala wouldn't know to look for it. So that's how it worked—Lane had sent flowers, so now her conscience was clear. The only problem was, Charlie's formula didn't quite encapsulate everything that had happened between them over the years, and only Lane knew it.

A WEEK LATER, Lane made the short trip to Gala's apartment, stopping at the market to pick up a small cactus in a terra-cotta pot along the way. She told herself she'd show her face, perhaps stay for a coffee, and she'd have a clearer idea of whether Gala wanted her in her life. As she stood on the doorstep, Lane was surprised to find how nervous she felt.

When Gala opened the door, Lane had to try not to recoil. The other woman looked awful—pale and too thin, her hair a tangled knot over the stained men's work shirt she was wearing. Unsure of what to do, Lane presented the cactus.

"People overwater cacti," she said. "They only need it every few weeks, and even then not much at all, and only at the base."

When she finished talking, Gala only stared back at her in dazed confusion. Lane had thought the present was vaguely symbolic with a small purple flower blooming from the prickled orb, but she realized now that all she'd given Gala was something else to keep alive besides herself.

The house smelled sour, like unclean sheets. There were bowls and glasses left out with clumps of mold climbing the sides and cigarette butts floating inside. When Gala slumped back down on the sofa without saying a word, Lane lingered, a deep pit forming in her stomach. After a moment, she started picking up the dirty dishes, walking them through to the kitchen, where she filled the sink with warm, soapy water. Once everything was clean, she took a rag from the cupboard under the sink and wiped every surface until the cloth was black with grease and dust. Next, she emptied the ashtrays into the festering trash bag, which she left resting outside the front of the apartment. When she came back inside, Gala was smoking a cigarette and staring at the black TV screen.

Lane took a seat opposite her, and Gala swiveled her eyes onto Lane without moving, like a lizard.

"I should have come sooner," Lane said. "I'm sorry."

Gala didn't react. She looked almost catatonic.

"What are you taking?" Lane asked gently.

Gala shrugged and rubbed her eyes.

"Is it okay if I sit here with you for a while?" Lane asked.

Gala looked down at her bare feet, which were curled underneath her. The soles were black, her toenails long and curved. Lane took her lack of denial as permission, and pulled out a book she had been asked to blurb from her bag. Lane opened it and tried to read, only she could feel Gala's eyes on her, and it made it nearly impossible to concentrate. Instead, she let her eyes scan the words, and every so often she'd turn a page. When she got to the third chapter without having taken in a single word, she noticed that the sky outside was already beginning to darken. It was dusk.

"I can come back tomorrow?" she asked, as she placed the book down and stood to leave. She touched Gala's shoulder as she passed her, but Gala still didn't move. Then, as Lane put her hand on the door to open it, Gala finally said something.

"I'm sorry, I didn't catch that . . ." Lane said.

Gala didn't turn around, but she spoke again, her voice louder this time.

"We were supposed to be in New York," Gala said. "The night he died. We were supposed to be flying to New York. But you already knew that."

Lane gripped the cool metal door handle to steady her balance. She felt like she was going to be sick.

FORTY-FIVE

NOW

FALL 1975

The rumors of Lane's meltdown at the literary festival range from detailed descriptions of an onstage breakdown to eyewitness accounts of her streaking naked through the crowd. Whispers ripple through the Canyon for weeks, and Lane knows that one phone call to Charlie could put a stop to it all, but she can't quite bring herself to make it.

Ruby Roblex calls Lane one morning to ask her what happened, and Lane doesn't know how to answer her. All she can say is that she could have sworn she saw Gala, only for her to disappear into thin air.

"It sounds like you need a vacation from yourself," Ruby says, and she can't hide the smirk in her tone. "Have you got any weed?"

"I'm fine," Lane says. And it's all she finds herself saying these days. *I'm fine, I'm fine, I'm fine, I'M FINE.*

SINCE LANE ARRIVED home from the diner and refused to discuss what had happened, Scotty has been increasingly reluctant to leave her alone in the house. His working hours are shorter than ever, and Lane knows he's instructed Rose to keep an eye on her when he's not around, even when the girls are at school. Every time she does anything (makes a coffee, throws out dead flowers, takes a breath), Rose is hovering nearby, nervously asking if Lane needs her help, as if her presence alone will stop Lane from cracking.

IN THE EXPANSE of free time Lane now has on her hands, she has taken to reading through Gala's old work. It starts when she finds the first story she'd ever read of Gala's, the one about her attempt to join the circus, and as she reads, she again experiences the familiar mix of envy and awe that these beautiful, fizzing words could just tumble out of anyone, as unpolished and raw as her writing was back then. Next, Lane reads Gala's collection *Inhalation*, and, as she makes her way through the tales of abandoned ballet classes and absurd encounters with serial killers and life-changing records, something strange begins to happen. Lane feels as if Gala is next to her, telling her to cut the bullshit in the way only she could. In the way Lane finds she misses more than she could have imagined. And since Lane has spent her whole adult life trying to be someone nobody wants anyway, she figures she might as well just fuck it all.

LANE WAKES UP one morning in mid-September from a hazy dream about her day at the beach with Gala. It's already slipping out of reach, but as she remembers their drive down to the coast in the Thunderbird, Gala's hair whipping in the breeze, her tanned hand drumming lightly on the wheel, Lane finds herself smiling for the first time in weeks.

Lane waits until Rose is cleaning the kitchen after breakfast to suggest a day out to the girls. The twins, unused to this sort of impulsivity from their mother, react with a combination of delight and suspicion that Lane pretends not to notice as she shepherds them outside and into the car. The beach bags are already in the trunk, and as she starts the engine, Lane waves goodbye to Rose, who is staring open-mouthed by the front door.

"Be back for dinner!" Lane calls brightly, but she has no idea if the younger woman hears her, and, frankly, she doesn't care.

The girls chat away in the back of the car, and Gala's ghost sits up front with Lane.

I guess I'm going to have to break myself out this time, Lane says to Gala.

The ghost of Gala grins. *I don't want to say I told you so,* she says. *But you told me so.*

ON A WHIM, Lane takes the girls to the churro stand first, buying them one each to make sure their blood sugar levels don't drop before they even reach the water.

"But, Mommy," Audrey says, staring up at her. "The sugar . . ."

To hell with the sugar, Gala says, and Lane smiles and hands over the money.

They sit on a bench that looks out onto the beach, and Lane devours her churro along with the girls, only surrendering it when Audrey drops half of hers onto the ground and looks like she's about to cry. The girls are quiet in a reverential way that suggests they don't want to do anything that might disturb the magic of the day, and Lane wants to tell them that they don't have to hold their breath, that days like this don't have to be rare, but she's not sure if it's true.

Once they've found a relatively quiet area, Lane lays down the jewel-toned towels she bought and sets up a large parasol for the girls to sit under, along with some of their dolls and a bucket and spade. She sits on a separate towel and picks up her book, but, when she still feels two pairs of eyes tracking her every move, she places it back down.

"Shall we swim?" she says, gesturing toward the ocean, the sea-foam that almost reaches their feet every time the waves crash hard enough.

Dahlia and Audrey exchange a glance.

"But, Mommy," Dahlia says carefully. "The waves."

Lane remembers now that the few times they've taken the girls to the beach in the past, she and Scotty have always made a point of explaining how the ocean needs to be respected, how the waves are dangerous and can sweep small people out to sea, never to be seen again. Why are they teaching their children to be afraid of everything? Lane can't quite remember anymore.

"To hell with the waves," Lane says, and then she stands up and holds out a hand for each of the girls before heading toward the churning water.

FORTY-SIX

THEN

AUGUST 1972

Gala had discovered early on that grief wasn't a continuum at all. No, grief was relentless waves of thick black tar clawing at her feet, her stomach, her heart. Some days she woke up and felt well enough to venture outside; other days just the faintest smell of eucalyptus in the morning air would make her heart splinter in her chest, and she would slam every window shut and lock herself in her bathroom.

Despite having met Gabriel half a dozen times, her beloved parents mentioned him by name only once, when they visited a few weeks after his death. They had seemed gutted by the state of both Gala's apartment and Gala herself, who, despite heavy sedation, was sobbing into one of Gabriel's old tour T-shirts. They were so out of their depth that Gala had instinctively wanted to protect them from the cruelties of the world that she knew now would inevitably find them too. They weren't a family accustomed to dealing with grief or bleakness—they had taught her from a young age that there was so much magic in the world, why dwell on the parts you couldn't control? It wasn't their fault that Gala had fallen in love with a man who had needed her in ways she hadn't understood.

Her Hollywood friends seemed either unable or unwilling to bear the force of her grief. They had come by at the beginning, always in groups, and once they saw the empty pill bottles left carelessly around the place and noticed Gabriel's battered tour suitcase still unpacked next to her bed, their eyes would invariably light up as though they couldn't wait to leave to dissect everything they'd seen. Then, soon, it was as if they just . . . forgot she was there altogether. She noticed that, when she did run into people she'd once known, they treated her as if the sadness she held was contagious or, much worse, as if their own grief was comparable to her own. And that was the strangest part about mourning someone beloved by so many—in death even more than life it felt as if Gabriel didn't belong to her so much as he belonged to the world.

Lane had come by only once.

ONE MORNING IN early August, Gala opened the latest issue of *Vogue* to a page that featured a photo of a glamorous redhead, and the heading "Diary of an Avenue A Muse." The writer had been one of Warhol's girls, and she was now dating a British rock star— this one a solo artist with flowing hair and platform boots. She described herself as a Bowery fashion rat, but she seemed to spend most of her time at her boyfriend's compound in Morocco, or his villa in Florence. And yet, somehow she was also finding the time to write a monthly diary column for *Vogue*, drawing back the curtain on New York's vibrant club scene. The accompanying photo showed her posing in a chain mail minidress in the middle of the *Vogue* offices, while dozens of mortals looked on admiringly. It was a clear rip-off of Gala's *Rolling Stone* shoot.

Gala's own *Vogue* column had disappeared months earlier, when she had sent over a raw and abstract meditation on grief, and her editor had called to tell her that he wasn't certain it was quite right "tonally" for the column. Readers had an expectation, and this wasn't exactly in keeping with it. Now, if she wanted to write a *eulogy* for Gabriel, that was completely different. They could give her an entire spread. Gala had icily responded that what she actually wanted was out of her contract, and that was the end of the matter.

She hadn't written about Gabriel when he was alive, and she wasn't about to start now that he was gone.

AT FIRST, GALA ignored the rumors that the less discreet of her acquaintances would tell her about if she ran into them at the grocery store (or, more likely, the Liquor Locker) when she was buying supplies for the week ahead (there were so many weeks, somehow they just kept coming). But then the stories started to appear in tabloids and magazines (some she'd written for not a year earlier!), and people she'd once counted as dear friends began avoiding her on the street.

None of the publications wanted to be the first to commit to overtly blaming her for Gabriel's death—it was all catty blinds and anonymous sources stating that certain people believed Gala to have been a bad influence on Gabriel. But soon it felt like open season, and people from her past came crawling out of the woodwork to denounce her as being careless at best, destructive at worst. Photographers waited outside her apartment and called her names, and her former friends were stalked at restaurants and asked for comments. There were rumors of petitions circulated in Northern California and fan protests in the Midwest, all calling for justice for Gabriel. Then the final blow, a statement from Gabriel's devastated family, who denounced Gala as the reason he left home in the first place, casting her as the depraved L.A. woman who lured him into a doomed life of drugs and sex.

Through tears, Gala had called Aiden, Gabriel's former bandmate, and asked him to meet her somewhere private to talk. She could barely leave the house if she wanted to now, so brutal were the whispers and stares from people she had once believed were her friends. She'd known L.A. could be cruel, but she couldn't believe that, even after everything she'd given it, it would turn on her too.

Aiden pulled in a favor and they met at the bar at the Troubadour one morning before it opened. He didn't want to be seen in public until the dust had settled either, so they sat at the bar in which she'd met Gabriel almost seven years earlier, and Gala listened as Aiden, head in his hands, lamented the loss not of her fiancé or even his bandmate, but of his career.

"No one wants Belle Vue without Gabriel," he complained, while Gala poured herself another shot of scotch. She wondered if she would flatter him, tell him what he wanted to hear in the hopes that he might help her in return. But Gala's days of catering to the egos of the men around her had passed. She had reached capacity.

"No," she agreed. "Gabriel *was* Belle Vue."

She wondered later if it was this bluntness that meant he refused to help her set the record straight when she asked.

"I don't expect an official statement," Gala said. "But maybe you could just . . . explain that it's not how they're saying? That we weren't bad for each other. That he . . . loved me."

Gala's eyes filled with tears as she spoke. She hadn't cried much since Gabriel's death—most of the time she felt too empty for that.

Aiden looked uncomfortable as he rubbed his stubble with the back of his hand.

"I don't know, Gala," he said wearily. "We've been advised not to say anything. Publicly."

"Well," Gala said. "It seems like everyone else in Laurel Canyon is saying something, so why can't you?"

When he didn't respond, she glared at him. She was drunk now, the room spinning and the ground pulling her under like a wave. Some voice in her head told her to leave before it was too late, but she knew if she stood up now she would be woozy and messy, and would most likely have to grab onto something to steady herself.

"Do you think Gabriel would have wanted people to be saying these things about me?" she asked quietly, and she hated him so much for making her say his name.

"I don't know," Aiden said again. Then his eyes met hers, and he looked as lost as she felt when he spoke next: "Everything changed when he met you."

Gala had instantly felt hot with horror—because wasn't it true? Hadn't Gabriel been little more than a teenager when she met him, and Gala, at twenty-six, an adult? And hadn't she been the one who handed him his first joint after his show at the Troubadour? She felt herself yielding to this new version of their story, and for the first time in her life, self-revulsion came so easily to her it was as if it had been hiding out just under the surface all

along. So she went to the bathroom and took a few more Nembu-
tals and quietly accepted it as her punishment. If she hadn't been
so preoccupied with her career, with herself, perhaps she could
have saved Gabriel. Everyone else seemed to believe it was her
fault, so why shouldn't she?

FORTY-SEVEN

THEN

OCTOBER 1972

Every weekday morning for as long as he could remember, Charlie had made his way from his home on Appian Way down Laurel Canyon to the National office on Hollywood. And, as he drove under the clear sky and elegant palm trees, he would remind himself how lucky he was to be doing the thing he loved, in the greatest city in the world. Los Angeles had always been his home, and he loved everything about it. He loved his job, and the office with the magnificent view from Koreatown to the coast, and most of all he loved the way those around him would yield to his version of events even in the presence of blinding evidence to the contrary. This awe had always come easily to him, but recently it had felt like he was instructing himself to be grateful, to appreciate all he had managed to salvage, as if he had never really deserved it in the first place.

ONE MORNING IN early October, he was called in for a meeting with the founder and president of National, a man who was in the office so rarely that much of the senior staff had never actually met him. Charlie had a lot of respect for Johnny Fraser and considered him a friend, but they both knew that, in all the ways that counted, it was Charlie who was in charge: He was the one the A&Rs came to for advice when their talentless artists decided they wanted to write their own songs, and he was the one who was called in to settle the petty skirmishes that arose within the label itself. His office (and salary) reflected his status, but still he wanted more, and so he had put his head down and worked harder than even the hungriest kid in the mail room, believing that one day Johnny would officially offer him the job that would make him the most powerful man in the music industry.

As Charlie took a seat, he noticed the newest addition to Johnny's office—a marble Buddha in the middle of his desk—and wondered which ashram Johnny's fourth wife had dragged him to most recently.

"Drink?" Johnny asked, and Charlie shook his head. A drink to Johnny generally meant something suspiciously homemade-tasting, like kombucha, but, to his surprise, Johnny walked over to his bar and poured himself a vodka tonic. Charlie had never known the older man to drink in the middle of the day, but he watched as Johnny took a sip before walking behind his desk to sit down on his cowhide chair. He paused for a moment, then: "Denny Amor."

Charlie relaxed a little and leaned forward in the chair. Despite Johnny's quirks, Charlie had always found him strangely easy to deal with, in that straight male way. He had a habit of throwing stuff (pens, a bagel, a signed golf ball once) at his staff's heads in meetings if he disagreed with them, but he tended to be softer in private, and particularly with his favorites like Charlie.

"What about him?" Charlie asked.

"He's found himself in a situation . . ."

"Go on," Charlie said, leaning forward with a thrill. National had set Den Amor up to be the latest teen idol, complete with the requisite dimples and blindingly white teeth and his dating of August Meyer, an up-and-coming actress also seemingly destined for stardom.

Johnny looked uncharacteristically unsure, and, for the first time, Charlie thought Johnny was getting too old for this. His sixtieth birthday party had been a good eight years earlier, in a cavernous strip club in the depths of suburban Las Vegas, and he hadn't slowed down since.

"Denny's got himself tangled up with someone, a boy, really, in New York, and August is threatening to go public with it."

Charlie tried not to smile as he absorbed the information.

"No problem," he said smoothly. "Give me half an hour with August and all will be resolved."

The thing about Charlie's job was that everyone wanted something. And he was a master at identifying what people desired, sometimes before they even knew it themselves. So he would sit down with August and figure out what she wanted. And then he'd give it to her.

Johnny nodded, but he still looked troubled.

"The thing is, Charlie," he said. "This isn't a good look for the reputation of National, among everything else."

There was a pause, then Charlie nodded.

"Of course not," he said. "Trust me, I'll handle it."

Johnny was still frowning, and Charlie felt a sinking in his chest now. He'd never seen the older man look so physically uncomfortable.

"Johnny, whatever it is, just say it."

Johnny exhaled. Finally, he met Charlie's eye.

"The rumors . . . have been . . . getting louder . . ."

Charlie shifted his position slightly.

"The rumors," he repeated.

Johnny grimaced. "Your lifestyle."

"Well, let me assure you that my *lifestyle* has been consistent since you've known me, and I've never let it affect my work."

Johnny nodded again, but avoided Charlie's now fierce gaze. He was holding a pen, and he clicked the cap off and on, off and on.

"You know I like and respect you," Johnny said. "And I've always wanted it to be you who takes over when the time's right."

"But."

"But," Johnny said, and now he looked almost gray. "Some people might say that being the man at the top is a job for a family man. And I don't know, there's something to be said for stability. Marrying Elle was the best decision I ever made."

Charlie just stared at him. Elle was forty-two years Johnny's junior and most often found dancing on tables on the Sunset Strip.

"I thought you called me in to talk about Den Amor," Charlie said quietly, but Johnny just looked back at him helplessly.

"Johnny, I've given everything I have to this company for fifteen years," Charlie said next, his voice low and thick. "I don't think me being married would have made me work any harder for you. Quite the opposite, probably."

"Maybe not, Charlie," Johnny said wearily. "I'm just saying, it might be a little easier if you could just play along, in many ways."

Charlie met his eye. "Easier for who?"

"Everyone," Johnny said. "You. Me. Our investors, the board."

That's what this was about. The group of shadowy men who met once a quarter, presumably to compare watches and egos and vacation homes and who didn't have the first idea what was happening outside of the sprawling glass meeting room on the ninth floor and who didn't seem to care. Until now.

"Just think about it," Johnny said. "We have time."

Charlie stood up stiffly.

"Is that all?"

Johnny looked up at him wistfully.

"You're the wizard of spin," he said. "Can't you put a gloss on things?"

Charlie felt his heart break as he walked out of the room. *Elijah*, he thought. *Elijah, Elijah, Elijah.*

When he got back to his own office, he called Lane. While he was waiting for her to answer, a wave of something like grief crashed so violently inside him that he found he could no longer breathe in the same way he had for thirty-four years.

"Lane." He gulped when she answered the phone. "Help me."

FORTY-EIGHT

THEN

DECEMBER 1972

It had been six months since Lane last saw Gala. Lane justi-fied it by telling herself that, in keeping well away, she was only doing what Gala wanted. If Gala had wanted to see Lane, or anyone really, she knew where to find them, but instead she had retreated into her own darkness, and Lane knew better than to force her hand. Still, every time she heard a new rumor about Gala's descent, she wondered if the cactus she'd given her was still alive.

Occasionally, as she was putting the girls to bed, or attending a fancy dinner with Charlie, or fucking her husband, Lane won-dered if she needed to feel guilty about Gabriel's death. She knew that Gala and Gabriel may not have been at that exact party on that exact night had she not lied to Esther, but surely you couldn't look at life like that, could you? You couldn't fixate on the paths you didn't choose or the infinitesimal decisions that may or may not have ended up changing the trajectory of your life. Life couldn't be unpicked like that—it wasn't a cheap quilt.

And how far back would you even go before you discovered where the buck stopped? By the same logic, wouldn't this be Gabriel's fault, not for being an addict exactly, but for never having been strong enough to set Gala free? Or Gala's—for the hubris of having believed she could save him? Or had it all begun the night Gala swooped in and ambushed Gabriel when he was in the middle of a conversation with Lane at the Troubadour? Lane had always known that it would end badly, and she'd tried to warn Gala, but perhaps she hadn't been clear enough. And that, Lane could admit, was her fault, but she still wasn't going to kill herself for feeling guilty over someone else's death. That was a direct path to insanity.

SOMEHOW, CHARLIE CONVINCED Lane that a respectful amount of time had elapsed since the fire to reinstate the Sunday Salons in time for Christmas, but Lane still nearly canceled the party four times. She felt uneasy about celebrating so publicly after the tragedy, but the moment she saw Charlie back in her living room, bellowing orders like he was choreographing the New York City Ballet, she'd understood how badly he'd needed it to restore his faith in the only thing he'd ever believed in—the order of the L.A. hierarchy.

After his disastrous meeting with the president of National, Charlie was the lowest he'd been since Lane had met him, lower even than when he'd split with Elijah for good. He was still going to work, despite knowing it couldn't end how he'd always believed it would, and while Lane had tried her hardest to lift him up with expensive dinners and weekends spent trawling his favorite antiques market, there was a darkness about him that frightened her.

Privately, Lane herself wasn't doing much better. After the flop of *The Unraveling*, she'd found herself filled with a scathing sense of self-loathing that had never quite subsided. Charlie assured her over and over again that in Hollywood, unlike New York or London, perception (rather than output) was king. If she created the illusion of still being on top, people would never think to question it. And he turned out to be right—either in an act of mercy or naivety, most of the guests who came to the Christmas party seemed to have already scrubbed Lane's failure from their memories. While she knew she should feel grateful, it made Lane feel strangely disappointed, because if the quality of her work didn't matter to these people, then what did? The fact that she had a glitzy house in Hollywood and threw parties that catered to their every carnal need? Or did they revere her for the simple fact that she was best friends with Charlie, or (even more disturbingly) because she was married to Scotty?

As Lane scanned the familiar faces in her living room, she had the sinking awareness that, while she was surrounded by the most successful actors and baby rock stars and thinkers of her generation, there was also not one single thing any of these people could say that would interest her in the slightest. She'd once heard the adage that if you were the most intelligent person in the room, then you were in the wrong room, and Lane felt it to be truer now than ever. She was trapped in a shimmering purgatory entirely of her own design.

The party had started like any other party, only with more tinsel, worse music, and a heavy scent of cloves in the air. It was raining, so everyone was packed inside the living room, the French doors fogging up, and Scotty had spent longer than ever putting the twins to bed, even though he knew as well as Lane did that one or both of them would end up in the arms of an inebriated guest by midnight. Charlie was hanging around the DJ, instructing him on exactly which Christmas songs were fun and campy and which were just tacky, and Lane was trapped in a truly abominable conversation about religion with Scotty's unscrupulous friend Dimitri, and Eva, a young music exec who always slipped into a German accent when she was high.

"God is for people who have no money," Dimitri said, in the authoritative way he had that grated on Lane. "Only poor people believe in God."

"An absurd thing to say," Eva said. "Back me up, Lane."

But Lane was distracted. Because, just a few feet away from where they stood, the front door had been flung open, and Gala Margolis was standing in the doorway in a white dress drenched with rain, wringing the water from her hair. Lane felt a rush of something complicated—relief laced with dread at seeing her old friend, after everything that had been said about her in the months since Gabriel's death. None of the other guests made a move to greet Gala, everyone just froze as if waiting to be told how to act—was Gala an old friend who deserved their sympathy? Or the woman who destroyed a fragile man they had all once adored and adopted as their own? As always, Lane found herself searching for Charlie's steady presence in the crowd, but all she found was Scotty, who was standing at the bottom of the stairs, looking as astonished as Lane felt.

"Aren't you going to invite me in?" Gala asked, her eyes locked on Lane's. There was another ripple as the guests also turned to look at Lane, who froze. After a few seconds, Lane stepped forward and wrapped her arms around Gala, hoping nobody else could tell that Gala remained stiff as a cadaver beneath her touch.

AS LANE LED Gala through to the French 75 bar, she allowed herself to believe that Gala had come to the party because she wanted to see her. She even felt a flutter of excitement at the thought that Gala might apologize for what she'd said the last time they saw each other, and that Lane might even say sorry too, for having been right about Gabriel.

"Are you okay?" Lane asked Gala quietly once they reached the bar. She could feel that all eyes were on them and wondered if Gala could too.

"I'm alive," Gala said, but her affect was odd, her eyes glazed. She looked anywhere but at Lane. While Gala had never been perfectly groomed exactly, there was something downright slovenly about her now, as if she were unraveling at the seams. Her hair was matted and long, her dress stained, and she smelled odd—strangely sweet, like an overripe nectarine. As Gala searched the room, Lane could see that her movements were slower than usual, languid even, and with a sinking feeling, Lane recognized all the hallmarks of heavy barbiturate use, her own mother's favorite brand of low too. A feeling of dread crept back in as Lane considered what she might say next. Only, before Lane could get so much as another word out, Charlie appeared and firmly took her arm. He looked Gala up and down, his expression unreadable.

"Gala," he said calmly. "What a surprise."

Gala laughed darkly, and Lane felt even more confused. She wished Charlie would leave them alone.

"Lane," Charlie said. "Could you excuse us for a moment?"

"Excuse *you*?" Lane repeated, aware she sounded like a half-wit.

"Could you give me and Gala a moment together, alone, darling," Charlie said, and Lane frowned at the unfamiliar firmness of his tone.

She turned back to Gala for her confirmation, but Gala wouldn't engage with her, her eyes unfocused as she searched the room, perhaps noticing the ravenous eyes memorizing every last detail.

"What can I do?" Lane asked quietly, but Gala ignored her question.

A friend of Lane and Charlie's came over then, Kate, a British stylist in head-to-toe sequins who could barely contain the curiosity dripping out of each pore as she kissed a stiff Gala on each cheek.

"Darling," she said, assessing Gala as if she were sizing up a calf at the county fair. "It's been too long. How are you *coping*?"

Gala stared at her as if she didn't understand the question, and Lane had a sudden desire to take her old friend by the arm and lead her far away from here, away from the people who pretended to be her friend but who viewed her vulnerability only as currency.

"We all assumed you knew Gabriel was using again," Kate said, her voice treacly. "What a cruel, cruel thing."

For just a moment, Gala's eyes met Lane's, and they both stared at each other helplessly. Then the mask descended once more and Gala looked away.

"Why don't you go grab another cocktail, sweetie," Charlie said to Kate. "This is the first time all night I've seen you without one."

He gave her a push in the direction of the bar and looked once more at Lane.

"Lane," he said, his voice strangely urgent now. "Please. A moment."

But Lane was still watching Gala.

"Let me help you," Charlie said gently to Gala then, and somehow she allowed him to guide her past Lane, through the crowd, and outside into the rain, which was coming down harder than it ever did in L.A. Lane watched through the window as Gala and

Charlie argued, Gala's white dress clinging to her frame like a rag as she gestured at him.

"What are they fighting about?" Lane heard a famous record producer say to his neighbor.

"God knows," the woman replied. "But she looks terrible."

"Such a shame," the man said, with the least amount of warmth possible. "She was a lot of fun for a while."

"I liked her writing too," the woman said. "In a guilty-thrill kind of way."

"I never read her writing," he replied vaguely. "But I heard she was a great fuck."

Lane felt a chill run through her.

FORTY-NINE

THEN

DECEMBER 1972

Charlie led Gala toward his car. The weather was fucking biblical, and his new Pucci jacket was ruined, but all he could think about was getting Gala as far away as possible from Lane.

Charlie had known for a while that things were shaky between Lane and Scotty, but Lane had made it clear that she didn't want to discuss it, and Charlie knew how important it was for her that they kept up appearances at least. It was the thing he had recognized in her from the start, the way she hid parts of herself from even those closest to her so seamlessly that he was never sure she was even aware of it. He more than understood her desire for control in such a turbulent, strange world, because he felt exactly the same. And it was this desire that meant, when Scotty had come to him after the fire, turning up on his doorstep at 4:00 a.m. like a sheepish ex-lover, Charlie had instantly understood the magnitude of the situation. A media furor was about to hit their community, and if Scotty's affair were revealed, not only would it spell the end of Lane's marriage, but it would destroy the mythology they'd created around her. Lane's appeal was in her superiority, her detachment from the depressing reality of familial life, and to get dragged into a cheap tabloid scandal would be almost unbearable for her, particularly on the heels of her disastrous second novel.

As horrified as he was to hear what had happened, Charlie would do anything to protect Lane from something he knew would shatter her in more ways than one, so he had invited Scotty in the night of the fire, and he'd listened to him talk about loneliness, and how cold Lane could be, and how he'd known for a while she wasn't happy, and, in the end, Charlie had agreed to help him.

CHARLIE OPENED THE passenger door for Gala before circling around to the driver's seat, and she let out a bitter laugh.

"Always the gentleman," she said as she flopped into the seat.

"Gala," Charlie said, once he was inside. "You said you wouldn't do this."

"What, I can't show up to see my dear old friends?" she said. "I thought they'd be a little more pleased to see me."

"Don't bullshit me," Charlie said wearily.

Gala slumped sulkily in her seat. She was soaked through, and it would take days to dry out the upholstery, Charlie thought.

"Are we going somewhere?"

"You're going home," Charlie said, and he started the engine. He thought she might object, but Gala just pressed her face against the window, her eyelashes fluttering against the condensation.

CHARLIE WALKED INTO Gala's apartment as though he were walking into an abattoir.

"What's the smell, Gala?" he asked, his face pinched.

"Fuck you, Charlie," Gala said as she headed straight for the kitchenette. She opened a bottle of white wine and poured herself a glass. She took a long sip before holding it up in Charlie's direction. He shook his head, looking vaguely disgusted.

"Why do you feel the need to act so superior all the time?" she asked, her fingers now safely wrapped around the stem of the glass. "We're not that different. You just bury your sadness like a scared little squirrel, while I don't give a shit who knows I'm broken."

If Gala's words affected Charlie, he didn't show it. Everything was coming out somewhat slower than she intended, but she didn't care. She'd never felt intimidated by men like Charlie and Scotty before, and she wasn't about to start now.

She walked over to the couch, but he remained standing by the front door. *Fine*, she thought as she pulled off her soaking dress and sat down in her underwear.

"What do you want, Gala?" Charlie asked simply. Which was the exact question he'd asked her when he turned up at her apartment two days after the fire. Only that time, she'd told him to go fuck himself—how dare he walk into her home, acting as if she were about to demand some booby prize for her entire future going up in flames? Briefly, she considered doing the same again, but she knew it would be self-destructive at this point.

The issue was her rent. When she was young, Gala had mostly relied on the generosity of friends and lovers to help her out financially, but those arrangements had ended when she met Gabriel. Once they were together, Gabriel had insisted on covering her rent and bills, and he paid for almost everything they did together too, leaving Gala to spend her writing income on whatever she wanted (platform boots, French cigarettes, towering plants she

insisted on naming after dead presidents). This arrangement obviously ended when Gabriel died, and, since there was nothing
official to tie them together, not even a fucking ring, his fortune
had ended up over in Manchester, where his dour mother was
presumably spending it on synthetic housedresses and rescue
animals.

"Gala . . . ?" Charlie prompted. "What do you want?"

Gala lit a cigarette and exhaled before answering the question.
What did she want? She wanted Gabriel back. She wanted her
career back. She wanted to piece back together the fragments of
a life she once thought was hers to keep.

"Money," she said flatly.

IN THE PAST, Charlie had always found Gala's directness repellent. He had learned to fear people who didn't have any secrets,
and Gala was a self-proclaimed open book (the worst kind). Even
now, her vulnerability was so close to the surface he felt like he
could reach out and touch it, and he felt a strange envy for this
woman who had never thought to lie about anything.

"How much?" he asked, after a pause.

"I'm a month late on my rent," Gala said. "And I barely have
money for groceries."

Charlie nodded. It was strange hearing her talk about anything as pedestrian as groceries. Could Gala cook? What did
someone like her even eat?

"Girl Scout cookies," she said, as if reading his mind. "I can't
even afford a box of Girl Scout cookies."

Charlie cracked a smile.

"Leave it to me," Charlie said, and he turned toward the door.
Then he turned back.

"How exactly," he said, "has this happened?"

Gala shot him a look from the couch. She was practically na-ked, her bare legs stretched out on the coffee table.

"Meaning?"

"Meaning you had a fine thing going. Why can't you start writ-ing again?"

Gala let out a dry laugh.

"My brand is flirty and frothy. You think anyone wants me like this?"

Charlie frowned. Couldn't she just pretend? Wasn't that what they were all doing anyway?

"That wasn't all you were," he said.

"No," she agreed. "But I was happy."

She didn't look at him, and Charlie told himself to leave, but something stopped him again.

"Have you considered rehab?" he asked, after a short silence.

"Whatever do you mean, Charlie?" Gala drawled, her head tilted back, eyes now tracking his. "You can be so puritanical sometimes."

"We can find you someplace," he said curtly. "The payment will be arranged."

Now Gala sat up and stubbed her cigarette out. She turned around to look at him, and for just a moment it was as if the old Gala was back in the room, eyes blazing.

"I would rather die than give Scotty Ryan the satisfaction of putting me in a bughouse," she said, each word clear as a Decem-ber morning in L.A.

Charlie smiled at her then, and she almost smiled back.

"Bye, Gala," he said, and he let himself out.

As he walked back to his car, Charlie realized he felt sorry for Gala. It may have taken her longer than it should have to realize that the world wasn't a kind place, but he didn't enjoy seeing any-one in pain. He knew there was almost zero chance that she would tell the world she'd been fucking Scotty at the exact mo-ment Gabriel was killed, but he figured it wasn't worth the risk—if he'd learned anything in his line of work, it was that people could do crazy things when their backs were against the wall.

Plus, it wouldn't hurt for Scotty to have lost something for his betrayal. Men like that thought they could get away with any-thing.

FIFTY

THEN

DECEMBER 1972

Neither Charlie nor Gala came back to the Christmas party, but, after they left, all anyone wanted to talk about was Gala. Whether she'd actually been the person to turn Gabriel onto heroin and whether she would ever write again, or if the rumors were true and it was *Gabriel* who had written her best work. Lane felt sick when she finally understood that she was part of it all—this salivating mass of people who had built Gala up only to ruin her.

At around 10:00 p.m., Scotty finally reappeared, but by this point Lane was already restless and irritable as she cut the music and asked everyone to leave. For the first time, the Sunday Salon ended prematurely, and the guests were suitably miffed as they filtered out in their glitter and sequins, half-drunk champagne glasses still in hand.

AFTER THE LAST guest had left, Scotty poured himself a glass of scotch and Lane a club soda, and she followed him wordlessly outside into the backyard. The rain had finally let up, and the air was fresh as Scotty lit Lane's cigarette before his own, like he always used to do.

They sat together in silence for a while, the pool glowing at their feet as cigarette smoke spiraled toward the stars, each one clear and crisp in the black sky.

"Everything okay, Laney?" Scotty asked, his voice strangely soft. Lane glanced at him and could tell he was in a rare introspective mood. Lane shrugged and took another drag of her cigarette.

"I don't know if I can do it anymore," she said eventually. "The parties."

Scotty glanced at her then. "Not even for Charlie? These were always more for him than you."

Lane frowned. Since when did Scotty care about protecting Charlie?

"I haven't written a word in nearly a year," she said. "And the worst part is that none of those people in our house tonight even care, so long as we keep hosting parties and shoving champagne down their throats."

Scotty looked at her tenderly. "You put too much pressure on yourself."

"A second failure isn't an option," Lane said.

Scotty didn't speak for a while, and Lane felt herself close up again. But then Scotty surprised her by leaning toward her, his eyes burning with an intensity she rarely saw from him.

"Write something that matters," he said. "Write something with guts and a beating heart. Write something that only you, Lane Warren, could write, and leave other people to argue over what it's about."

"But *The Ringtail* . . ." Lane said. "People liked it because they

could relate to it. Everyone comes of age, everyone feels lonely . . .
It was universal."

"To hell with *The Ringtail* and to hell with universal," he said.
"You just write the thing that feels the most urgent to you,
right now."

Lane thought about this for a moment. She didn't know
whether he meant their marriage, or the two children dreaming above them, but it wasn't either of these things that came
to her mind first. It was Gala, turning up at Lane's house in a
rain-drenched dress and desperately fighting to stay alive, despite
everything. After a moment, Lane reached over and took Scotty's
hand. They sat side by side on their deck chairs as the crickets
hummed, and she tried not to notice how tightly he held her
hand, and how grateful he seemed that she had momentarily
reached out across the chasm she still knew would eat them alive
in the end.

THE MORNING AFTER Gala's appearance at her Christmas
party, Lane made the short walk to her office, and sat down
with a fresh sheet of paper in her typewriter. She felt a little
uncomfortable about committing to paper any of the rhythmic
sentences that were swirling through her mind, but she told herself that it was a *good* thing she was doing. Lane, more than anyone, knew that Gala didn't exactly deserve the vitriol that was
being thrown her way, and felt responsible for part of it. Or guilty.
Guilty was the word. And if Gala was going to be mythologized
in Hollywood lore, at least let Lane tell it how it really was—how
she'd been naive about Gabriel but never destructive, how she
was both a talented writer and a flawed human, and how layered

she'd turned out to be underneath the white fur coat and bawdy jokes.

It was surely the least Lane could do, to tell Gala's story as it deserved to be told. And if it also solved the problem of Lane's writer's block, that was just the cherry on top. What harm could it do, really?

Dirty nails and soles of her feet.

Glass thrown at man's head. Shards of glass in the rug.

Always eating, dropping things, dripping, making a mess.

Fingers stained from cherries.

A rare creature—a Hollywood native.

Does she think of you when you're not there? Does she think of anyone?

A reluctant romantic.

Believes she's going to die young. An L.A. curse?

Lane's first notes on Gala were disjointed and scrappy, disparate observations with no fluidity, but soon the words came freely, falling onto the page so effortlessly it was as if Lane had been writing Gala's story for years in her mind.

As she sketched Gala's childhood on Franklin Avenue and her teenage years at Hollywood High (snippets she'd picked up from Gala over the years but would have to fact-check eventually), Lane found herself questioning her own motives for writing until the questions felt too significant to avoid. So, she started including them in her work. Some days it was as if she was trying frantically to convince the imagined reader—Gala perhaps?—that her intentions were selfless. That she just wanted to share the woman she had known with the rest of the world, to make sure that she was remembered in the way she deserved, as opposed to the way she was now, after life's tragedies had rendered her little more than a punch line. Other days Lane knew that there was also anger driving her fingertips—that the reason they flew so furiously across the typewriter was that she felt betrayed by Gala, who had accepted Lane's help and friendship only to prove herself unworthy of either. Somehow, Lane knew that this dichotomy was the key to the entire thing, and she found that all she wanted to do was write, write, write her way to an answer.

Occasionally, Lane wondered whether writing about Gabriel was a step too far, but the more rational part of her brain assured her that it was critical that she tell the whole story. And, while Lane wished it were different (had tried her hardest to make it so), you couldn't talk about Gala without Gabriel.

After three months of writing in a fever dream, Lane sent Esther the first few chapters. She called back instantly.

"Perfect," she says. "We'll sell it to the world on the Gabriel angle, but we both know it's a Trojan horse. It's the *perfect* synergy of your fiction and your journalism—raw and sophisticated but with a delicious sting in its tail, because the subject you're really interrogating here isn't Gala, but yourself. I fucking love it."

Her words gave Lane pause for a moment because, if what she was saying was true, then was Lane as guilty of using Gala as the worthless men she let into her life? A vessel through which Lane could manifest her own creativity and gain a better understanding of herself, her past? An objectively fascinating question, and one Lane delved into in her next chapter as a way of proving to herself that this wasn't a vanity project, that she was serious about being honest. Past, present, future—Lane refused to hide from any of it.

When Esther offered her an advance of $50,000 for the book, Lane didn't even need to think about her answer.

Why would she, when this was the thing that could save them both?

FIFTY-ONE

THEN

OCTOBER 1973

The night before Gala's parents' fortieth wedding anniversary, she was lying on a bench in the Hollywood Memorial Park cemetery with a guy she barely knew, snorting speed off the back of her hand. She hadn't realized she'd brought the party up, hadn't realized she'd said anything at all, until he turned to her and smiled a grimy-toothed smile that made her shudder even in her altered state.

"I'll come with you," he said. "Parents dig me."

Gala closed her eyes and pretended she was anywhere but here.

IN THE EIGHTEEN months since Gabriel's death, Gala's drug use had escalated significantly. These days, 300 milligrams of Nembutal was her baseline, and anything else (marijuana, LSD, cocaine, mescaline, quaaludes, PCP—everything but heroin) was a welcome, if not particularly rare, bonus. Gala told herself that she could stop whenever she wanted, she just didn't ever seem to want to enough.

She had tried to get clean over the summer, when her best friend from high school, Ruby, had moved back to the city and wanted to help, but the withdrawal from the barbiturates in particular was brutal. Obviously, Gala had known that anything that made her feel that good must have a steep decline on the other side, but she hadn't realized quite how dark things would get without them. She hadn't realized that, instead of Ruby's concerned face surrounded by her halo of pink hair, it would be Gabriel she saw standing above her, but that his once-beautiful face would now be covered in raw, blistered skin flapping to reveal shards of rotten bone. She hadn't known that her body would convulse and rack and that at points she would barely remember her own name, let alone what she had to live for. If that was sobriety, she didn't want it.

So she gave up giving up and succumbed once more to the security of the pills, and whatever else she could find to make the colors of the city she once loved a little brighter again.

GALA'S PARENTS HAD given her six months' advance notice on the party, delivered in the form of an official invitation on a thick purple card, at least seven phone calls, and an in-person visit from Penny a week earlier. They were desperate for her to be there, and if Gala was feeling cruel, she'd say it was because her absence from such a significant occasion not only would signal a public shattering of their illusion of the perfect family, but would make it impossible for them to ignore her pain any longer. It would be a gigantic HELP ME sign planted in their front yard that they would finally have to acknowledge. And that, Gala figured, just wouldn't do.

Gala had tried to reach out to her parents over the past year, only to be outmaneuvered over and over again by their stifling expectations of her. A few months earlier, she had told her mom about the uglies for the first time, but it was as if Penny couldn't hear her. She could only see Gala as the seventeen-year-old she had once been: glossy-lipped and shameless, leaving a string of lovestruck men in her wake as she shimmied her way around Hollywood High, taking not only what was hers but what was everyone else's too. And didn't her parents realize that Gala wished she were still that girl too? She wished she hadn't been hardened by life, by losing the man she loved, by wasting her ability to even think straight, let alone write anything vaguely coherent. She would give anything to turn back time to when she was still adored and charming, but that wasn't an option. Sometimes it felt like she had nothing left to give that anyone wanted.

THE PARTY WAS held in the Parlour of Prestidigitation at the Magic Castle, and Gala slipped in half an hour late to find her parents sitting together onstage on a love seat, hands clasped and faces glowing with delight as they watched their long-standing clients perform a variety show just for them. Gala, who had promised herself she wouldn't be entirely out of it for the event (just faded enough to take the edge off), found that she felt not joy for the parents who had raised her but resentment, as they kissed and beamed at each other like they were the only two people in the world. If they hadn't set this precedent that love was the only answer, the singular route to happiness, perhaps Gala wouldn't be where she was today.

Gala had hoped to slip out before the end of the show, but she found she was soon transfixed by the spectacle onstage—the perfectly rehearsed movements and leading music, the expectant faces of the performers as they worked for their applause. As she watched, a few tears trickled down Gala's cheeks. Everyone was so desperate to be loved.

Afterward, the group gathered at the bar for a champagne and beer reception. Gala stood alone, watching as her glowing parents made the rounds at the party before finally reaching her.

"You came," Stan said, beaming as he kissed Gala sloppily on the cheek.

"Congratulations," Gala said, forcing a smile as Penny wrapped her arm around her daughter, pulling her close.

"We're so happy you're here," she said into Gala's ear, and she smelled like lavender, just like she had since Gala was a kid. "And that you're okay."

I'm so sad, Gala thought. *I'm so sad and I don't know how not to be.*

"I wouldn't miss it for the world," Gala said.

"Isn't it wonderful?" Stan said, looking around the room at the evidence of their happy life. "Celebrating magic like this."

"It is," Gala said, knowing he wasn't referring to the illusionists onstage or the magician behind the bar. Gala forced a smile and was about to tell them to go work the room, when, to Gala's dismay, Penny's face turned uncharacteristically somber and she took both of Gala's hands in hers.

"One day you'll find someone else," Penny said. "And it will be built to last."

It was only then, with a twist in her chest, that Gala realized that the only thing worse than her own parents having been oblivious to Gala's pain was their having seen it all along.

———

ON HER WAY out, Gala spotted Scotty Ryan and Charlie Mc-
Cloud sitting at one of the green close-up magic tables. They were
drinking whiskey, and there was something about the smug,
oblivious expression on Scotty's face that made Gala's heart ex-
plode with fury for everything that she had lost, while his life
remained exactly the same. She grabbed a drink from a woman
sitting at the bar and marched over to the table. The magician
looked up at her with a glint in his eye over a fanned deck of
cards, but his face soon fell when he understood she wasn't here
to admire his sleight of hand. Even this stranger could tell she was
defective. Gala's resolve hardened, and she tapped Scotty on the
shoulder before throwing the drink over his perfect golden face.
He blinked at her for a few seconds, and then she felt the arms of
a security man wrap around her, dragging her away. As the cool
October air hit her, Gala felt not glee, but a strange sadness for
her former paramour. For just a moment, they had met each other's eyes, and she had seen that he was broken too.

FIFTY-TWO

NOW

FALL 1975

The wave that almost kills Dahlia comes out of nowhere. The girls are knee-deep in the water, and Lane is reaching for Audrey's sun hat, which has blown off and is floating nearby. The wave, unusual for Santa Monica, closer to the waves that would delight surfers up the coast in Malibu, approaches silently and folds Dahlia into its midst like she is nothing more than a paper airplane.

As Lane watches her disappear, she feels a fear like nothing she's ever experienced before. For a moment it feels as if it's Lane herself under the waves, the black water filling her own lungs and dragging her into its roily core. Her terror is visceral, almost unbearable, but all she can do is grab hold of Audrey and scream and scream until half a dozen men rush past her, enthusiastically diving under the surface of the water as if they are hunting for a lost pair of sunglasses and not her daughter.

It is a middle-aged man who finds her, her body too floppy in his arms, and he rushes her to shore, but the water is waist-high and it seems like he's wading through it in slow motion. *HURRY*

UP, Lane screams, but she isn't sure if she says it out loud or if it's inside her head—if she's had to retreat inside herself like she'd also done in the hospital when the twins were ripping their way into the world the only way they knew how.

Lane follows, gripping a silent Audrey, and watches helplessly as the lifeguard takes Dahlia and pumps her small chest on the sand a few times before breathing into her mouth. Has he done this before? He looks no older than seventeen—a child himself, and he is sweating, his face pale and contorted when he comes up for air as if he's in the midst of a panic attack. (Will that affect his oxygen? Is he about to hyperventilate?) After a few moments in which time stands still, Dahlia hacks up a lungful of water and the lifeguard rolls her onto her side. Lane rushes to her, tears running silently down her cheeks as she kisses every part of her daughter's cold, salty face. It's only when Dahlia finally lets out a beautiful, anguished wail herself that Lane thinks to search for Gala's ghost in the crowd gathered around them.

Once Dahlia is calmer, sitting up and blinking in the bright sunlight as if she has no idea how she ended up there, strangers rush to tell Lane that it wasn't her fault, that they had been watching and it was a freak twist of the ocean—just one of those things. But Lane knows they are wrong. The feeling she's had from the moment she discovered she was pregnant, the feeling that had curdled and settled so deep inside her that she has felt like it's in her blood, has finally come to the surface.

Much like her mother, Lane is a danger to everyone she loves the most.

THAT NIGHT, SCOTTY can barely look at her.

"What were you thinking?" he asks, over and over again. But

quietly, when the girls aren't around, and this small act of mercy makes Lane feel worse than anything as she shakes her head, unable to answer the question.

Neither of them can sleep that night, both taking turns to check on their sleeping babies. The final time Lane goes in, when the dawn light is already starting to creep underneath the heavy pink curtains, Lane thinks she sees Gala sitting cross-legged in the middle of the floor. And, to Lane's horror, she is laughing.

FIFTY-THREE

THEN

SEPTEMBER 1974

A brilliant idea had come to Gala a few months earlier, in the midst of a July heat wave, and she'd found herself writing again for the first time since Gabriel died. She was mostly loaded when she wrote (because she was always at least a little loaded these days, and if Hemingway and Thompson could do it, why couldn't she?), but it was like the world around her was becoming a little clearer by the day. She hadn't realized she was writing a memoir at first, had thought she was writing another short story, but soon she realized that this was the book she'd been destined to write all along. She would tell the story of her life all the way from her unorthodox childhood to her social exile in the city she thought would always be her home.

So far, she had only six chapters and a messy outline, but she was writing most hours of the day, the words falling onto the page like they had when she'd first started writing. Her friend Ruby had unofficially moved in with Gala with her five cats (needy, slinking creatures that watched Gala while she slept and were somehow stealing her heart), and as Gala wrote at the kitchen table with at least one cat on her lap and her friend cackling along with the TV, she started to feel a little more like her old self.

One Thursday night, over a bottle of wine and two grams of cocaine, Ruby suggested Gala try to sell the book before she wrote too much more of it.

"Before I waste my time, you mean," Gala said wryly.

"Kind of," Ruby said, in the way only an old friend can.

"Do you think anyone will want it?"

"How the hell would I know?" Ruby said, smiling as she dipped her pink head to do another line. "But better to find out sooner than later, right?"

It wasn't exactly a vote of confidence, but it was enough to spur Gala to action. The following morning, when Ruby was at work, Gala dug through her vanity to find the card she was looking for, then called Esther Mazer at her office in New York to pitch her memoir.

"OH."

It wasn't exactly the response Gala had been after. She twirled the phone cord around her index finger and tried again. "We'll sell it as a novel, but it's more a memoir. It's drugs and fucking and death and palm trees."

"I understand the concept, Gala," Esther said, in that strange way she had. "I'm just trying to think if I could make it work."

There was a long pause, then: "You'd be writing about Gabriel?"

Gala cleared her throat. "Not exactly. The emotions and . . . ashes, but he wouldn't be recognizable as . . . himself."

"Right," Esther said, then there was another long pause.

"Is that a no then?" Gala asked.

"I don't think I can help you with this," Esther said slowly. "For a variety of reasons."

"Can you give me one?"

"Well, firstly, I think you lack the killer instinct necessary for this type of writing," Esther said.

Gala felt a tugging in her chest.

"I can give you anything but Gabriel," Gala said quietly. "Anything."

"I understand," Esther said.

"And secondly?"

Esther paused, and the line crackled slightly.

"Secondly, there is already a somewhat similar book on our roster."

Gala almost laughed. "A similar book? Another memoir from an infamous L.A. muse turned public enemy?"

There was another long pause in which Esther didn't laugh. Gala felt a strange, hot feeling wash over her, and afterward she would wonder whether she knew what was coming.

"No, Gala," Esther said. "Another book about you."

WHEN RUBY CAME home that night, Gala was already deep in a Nembutal haze. She could hear herself slurring as she recounted her conversation with Esther to Ruby, who listened with growing fury.

"I always knew there was something warped about Lane Warren," Ruby said finally, her pink mouth twisting in disgust. "I don't care how much people love her, that woman is *damaged*."

Gala thought back to what she did with Scotty the night Gabriel died, and wished she could tell Ruby the whole truth. But she found that she could no longer find any words at all. The shame had returned and settled somewhere deep inside her.

OF ALL THE things Gala had endured over the past two years— all the thousands of ways people she had once trusted had let her down—the thought that her story was no longer hers felt the cruelest. At first, she wondered whether she could just write harder and faster, if perhaps she could get her side of the story out first, before Lane had a chance to release hers. Only Gala knew that she would never write about Gabriel, and that Lane would have no such qualms writing about a man she had instantly dismissed as destined to die. And even through her fury and grief, Gala knew that if this was the killer instinct she lacked, she didn't want it.

AS THE DAYS turned into weeks turned into months, Gala found it harder and harder to breathe. Ruby was dating someone new, some drug dealer deep in the Valley, and she was spending most of her time over the hill. She still came back to visit Gala, but Gala could tell even her patience was wearing thin. Gala no longer did the drugs that were deemed sociable (the type designed to make you think sharper and talk faster and feel more alive); instead she found herself drawn only to downers—the magic blend of chemicals that could blunt the sharp edges of the world. Sometimes she wondered whether she was trying to slow everything down to get closer to wherever Gabriel was now, but she tried not to think too much about anything these days.

The problem was that, without writing, Gala found she was unable to find a reason to get into bed at night, let alone out of it.

So she spent most of her time on the couch in the living room, medicated to the point of sedation, and anytime a memory came to her (Gabriel strumming his guitar in the dappled sunlight or stroking her hair off her face as she drifted off in his arms), she took another pill until the world felt safe again.

FIFTY-FOUR

THEN

NEW YEAR'S EVE 1974/75

In her note to Lane, Gala suggested a New Year's Eve lunch at a dim sum restaurant in Chinatown. It wasn't one of the fashionable spots, so they were unlikely to bump into anyone else—she didn't want to give Lane the satisfaction of being able to talk about her with any more authority than she seemed to think she had. Gala had seen her former friends for exactly what they were now—heartless vampires who would turn on you at the first opportunity. She didn't know how she hadn't noticed it sooner.

The issue wasn't getting Lane to agree to meet her (Gala had long ago realized that Lane was obsessed with her and had been from the day they met) but getting herself to a point where she was able to deliver her thoughts clearly enough to persuade Lane to stop what she was doing. So, on the morning of the lunch, as planned, Gala took 150 milligrams of Nembutal, which she would supplement with 10 milligrams of Valium and a small glass of wine just before the meeting time. She had tried the combination a few times in advance and knew she could still construct a cutting insult through it, could still fool Lane into thinking she'd gotten the wrong girl or at least the wrong story. Part of her wished she could unleash fury and chaos into Lane's life by telling her everything—about her and Scotty, and the secrets they'd all kept since—but Gala knew she would never do that to Gabriel, could barely think about that night without wanting to die.

Gala dressed in a denim dress and suede boots, and she washed and blow-dried her hair so that it fell down her back in loose waves. Her cheeks were flushed, her lips fleshy with just a coat of clear gloss. She looked almost like she had before her life had changed in an instant. But even Gala knew it was all lies. Smoke and mirrors like the tricks her parents sold out of their house on Franklin Avenue.

AS GALA DROVE herself to Chinatown, she found her hands were shaking, so she took another Valium to take the edge off. When she arrived at the restaurant she sat outside in the car and poured a small pile of coke onto the back of her hand. She had probably overdone it with that last Valium, and she needed something to bring her back to life. A small line would be just the thing.

Gala entered the restaurant, and, as the red and gold furnishings shimmered and warped around her, she took a moment to steady herself. Then she saw Lane already waiting at a table in the back of the room, and, for just a moment, Gala felt untouchable, like she was floating across the room to meet her destiny. Before she met Lane, Gala had been in love with the world, and Lane's only solution had been to steal that from her in every way she knew how. Now Gala wanted to destroy the other woman with each perfect half-truth that flew out of her mouth. She wanted Lane to understand the devastation she'd caused.

Gala pulled out the chair opposite Lane and sat down, placing her gold cigarette case and lighter on the table in front of her. Lane had already ordered a club soda and some shrimp dumplings, but it didn't look like she'd touched either. She looked almost gray with nerves and, as Gala motioned for the waiter, she felt a surge of something unfamiliar. Power, perhaps.

"A glass of Chardonnay," Gala said. "Soda and ice on the side."

The waiter nodded and handed her a menu. Gala placed it down on the table between them, and met Lane's eyes for the first time. How had she not noticed how cool, how snaky they were when they first met, all those years ago? She should have known that this woman wasn't a friend, or someone to be trusted. She opened her case and lit a cigarette, her eyes never leaving Lane's the entire time.

LANE FELT SOMETHING clamp across her chest. She didn't know what she'd been hoping for, but she could already tell that Gala was strung out, her skin ghoulish and damp. When she ordered a drink (wine at noon on a Tuesday?) her words came out unnaturally fast, while her eyes were heavy-lidded, each blink a fraction too long. There were bruises on her legs, and her dress hung off her unfamiliarly skinny frame. It was clear to Lane that Gala hadn't emerged from her grief like a butterfly, but had embedded herself within its gnarled walls instead. (The moment Lane thought of that line, she felt a mortifying rush of adrenaline. She hoped she wouldn't forget it.)

AS LANE WATCHED, Gala picked up a quivering dumpling with her chopsticks and popped it into her mouth whole. She wasn't hungry, but it felt like a concession to admit that to Lane. And she wasn't prepared to concede anything today.

"You know," Gala said casually, once she'd finished chewing. "I used to think you hated women, but I think actually you just hate yourself."

"That's not true," Lane said quietly.

"Which one?"

"Either," Lane said as Gala lit another cigarette and inhaled deeply.

"I know about the book," Gala said, once she'd expelled a perfect ribbon of smoke in Lane's direction. "Funny how you were always warning me that Gabriel was going to be the one to ruin me."

Lane's cheeks were already flushing pink as she spoke, her voice strangled: "And didn't he in the end? This is what they do, Gala. They make you feel like it's anyone's fault but their own."

Even through the blend of chemicals dulling her nerves, Gala felt a kick of fury. She wondered whether it would be obvious if she reached into her bag and took another pill. Maybe she should start lacing her cigarettes in the future.

"Is he in it?" she asked.

"Gala . . ."

For a moment, Gala couldn't speak.

"Look, it's not what you think," Lane said, her voice more level. "The book isn't about Gabriel, and it isn't even about you, not really. It's about L.A., and the last decade, and what it means to be a woman, and a writer, and it's about—"

"Perfect," Gala said, cutting her off. "It sounds like it's about anything other than yourself. We'd hate for you to have to look too hard at any of the things you've done."

"That's the thing," Lane said. "It is about me too. Will you just read it before you make a judgment?"

Gala stared at her incredulously. "Will I just read it? Before I make a judgment? You don't think I deserve the right to tell my own story?"

"I'm happy to take your input into consideration," Lane said stiffly. "But that's not exactly how this works."

Gala let out a bark of laughter then, black and mirthless as she jabbed her cigarette in Lane's direction.

"Say it," she said. "Say what you mean for once. There's no Charlie here to jump in, no Scotty here to protect you, no type-writer for you to hide behind. Say exactly what you want to say, and don't hold back."

"I just think . . ." Lane started carefully. "You're not exactly in a position to tell your own story right now."

"Because?"

Lane didn't answer, instead tracing the back of the menu gently with her finger. Gala reached out and snatched it away. This was so typical of Lane, to execute the dirty work and then hide behind her timidity, playing the eternal victim. Gala wouldn't care so much if Lane would just own the darkness inside her instead of denying its existence, as if women weren't supposed to want and rage and kill too. As if Lane could actually afford to observe and record dispassionately, like an archaeologist, because she was somehow above the petty skirmishes involved in being a woman.

"Because . . . ?" Gala said again, her voice serrated.

"Because you're a junkie and a punch line," Lane finally exploded. "Is that what you want to hear?"

In a strange way, Gala did feel almost satisfied. She smiled slightly and leaned forward over the table.

"You talk about what it means to be a woman as if you've invented feminism, but you have no idea. You have no idea what it actually means to support and love and nurture any relationship with another human, let alone a woman. You don't know what it takes to push back against the idea that there's only ever enough space for one of us at the top, and to not constantly belittle everyone else by insisting you've made it there *despite* being a woman not because of it. And what are you going to teach your daughters? That life is another test they have to ace? That it isn't going to be messy and brutal and devastating, however perfect or obedient they are, and that they won't wish they were dead one week and thank the fucking stars and moon that they were ever born the next? Lane, you have spent your entire life watching other people live, and that's why you will never be great. Not because you're a woman, but because you're a ghost."

Lane's face crumpled and, for just a moment, Gala thought she could see the child Lane must have been once, frightened and alone.

"But I'm just a junkie and a punch line," Gala said. "What the fuck do I know."

She stood and walked out of the restaurant, the trace of a smile on her face for the first time in a while.

FIFTY-FIVE

THEN

NEW YEAR'S EVE 1974/75

Gala left Lane at the restaurant and drove fast to a New Year's party downtown that Ruby had told her about. In a vast abandoned warehouse, it was on the grittier end of places Gala had chosen to lose herself recently, and she felt the shift in energy the moment she walked inside. There were no decorations, no pretense at celebrating anything at all, but it was the kind of party where Gala knew she would find whatever she needed to forget the past year (or five) had ever happened. While it had felt good at the time laying into Lane like that, she felt strangely numb now, and she wondered whether she would ever feel anything but empty again.

Gala half-heartedly looked for Ruby, who she knew wasn't likely to come after her boyfriend had landed her in the hospital with a shattered cheekbone a few weeks earlier. Not only did it look like Gala was stuck with the cats for a while longer, but she could feel her oldest (and only) friend slipping through her fingertips and knew she didn't have any fire left inside her to stop it.

Gala said hi to a few people she vaguely recognized, trading a couple of her Nembutal for a tab of acid with a woman who also went to Hollywood High. Gala put the tab under her tongue and settled alone on a threadbare sofa with a pack of cigarettes and the remainder of her pills in her hand. As reality slowly started to warp, shadows coming to life and colors fizzing around her, she started to feel a little better.

Perhaps Gabriel had been right when he'd been searching for anything to believe in, in a world filled with such hardness. As she closed her eyes and succumbed to another ferocious rush, Gala wished she could tell him how much she missed him. And just then, in the blinding canvas of her mind, Gala saw Gabriel's smile unfurl, beautiful and infinite, and she felt his presence fill her up with the kind of joy she'd forgotten existed.

But then, as always, reality began to seep back in, and Gala was plunged into a cruel darkness. Even with her eyes shut she could feel the malevolent presence of the users and drunks swirling around her before soon even they fell away, leaving her to reckon with her shattering loneliness in an empty warehouse at the turn of another year. She swallowed a Nembutal, then a couple more, and finally allowed herself to surrender to the churning darkness that had been clawing at her feet since the moment she lost Gabriel.

It wasn't that Gala wanted to disappear exactly. But sometimes life had its own plans, and who was she to fight back?

FIFTY-SIX

NOW

WINTER 1975

After the incident at the beach, the ghost of Gala doesn't leave Lane's side. Every morning Lane wakes up and wonders whether today will be different, but, as she walks numbly around the grocery store or struggles through another dinner with Scotty, Gala is there, watching her. The insides of Lane's wrists are marked with scars from her own nails, and she wears long sleeves even to bed. Even she understands the irony that she is simultaneously unable to find Gala and unable to escape her for even a second.

There are so many rumors about her now, but, for the first time in her life, she doesn't care. She doesn't care if the whole of Hollywood thinks she's crazy, or washed up, or no fun. She realizes now that none of them ever knew her, not really. They just wanted to be near her because they thought her glory might rub off on them, and now they're scared her deficiencies will do the same. Even Charlie knows to keep away, frightened as he is of her now that she no longer trusts him.

Lane avoids being alone with the girls, calling Scotty or Rose in to do even the simplest of tasks, and she finds that she can barely talk, barely think, when she's in their presence, so consumed is she by fear. Because she knows now that Gala was right. Lane isn't capable of anything true. Maybe her mother had seen this when Lane was born; maybe that's why she had been so alone in the world. She tells herself that if she never writes again, it is a fitting punishment for someone who's destroyed anyone she's ever loved.

LANE HAS BECOME so used to seeing the ghost of Gala, carefully navigating her way around her old friend in a way that won't allow Scotty the satisfaction of packing her off to a psych ward, that she almost walks straight through Penny Margolis at the grocery store one afternoon in November. Penny is frozen in front of a display of Canadian maple syrup as a sticky, fragrant puddle forms around her worn sandals. Lane watches for a moment, trusting that the other woman is real only when an irritated employee of the store rushes over with a mop, all but shoving a dazed Penny to one side. Penny stares helplessly down at the young woman cleaning up the shattered glass around her syrup-covered feet, and Lane steps tentatively toward her.

"Mrs. Margolis," she says, and she holds out her arm for Penny to take.

Once they're away from the mess, Lane offers Penny a tissue from her handbag, which the older woman takes and dabs between her toes. When she looks up, her eyes are glinting with tears.

"It's okay," Lane says, even as she feels an inexplicable lump form at the back of her throat too.

———

LANE AND PENNY sit opposite each other at Canters, each with a mug of black coffee. Penny has recovered enough to devour a cream cheese and lox bagel in a way that reminds Lane of Gala.

"I figure you'd have been in touch if you found anything," Penny says, without looking at Lane, as she pops the final caper into her mouth.

"I'm sorry," Lane says.

Penny nods.

"I've been killing myself going back over everything, trying to figure out what I missed. What I could have done differently."

"And?" Lane asks.

"And I think when you're a woman, and particularly a mother, the world needs you to feel like you're failing. Because you're easier to control that way," Penny says. "But I did enough, and Gala is exactly who she is, for better or worse."

Lane nods. The way Scotty is with her now, so reassured by her smallness, makes her think Penny is probably right. Women are easier to control when they are crumbling from the inside out. She wonders whether this is what Gala knew all along, what she was fighting against when she clung doggedly to her self-belief, refusing to feel ashamed of herself until the wave became too strong, even for her.

"Was Gala always a writer?" Lane asks, and she realizes that she isn't asking for her book. She's asking because she wants to know. Next to Penny, the ghost of Gala raises an eyebrow.

Penny's eyelids flutter closed for a moment, and she smiles at a memory only she can see. When she opens them, she is still smiling.

"She used to write every day when she was a kid and never needed anyone to read it, let alone praise it. But she just got caught up in that cycle, you know."

They sit in silence for a while, and Lane wonders whether, of all the things she has done to Gala, teaching her to care might have been the worst of all.

"We're giving Gala's apartment up next week," Penny says eventually. "The paid year is up, and we can't afford to pay her rent when she's not here."

"That makes sense," Lane says carefully.

"So, if you still want to have a look through it, now would be a good time." Penny exhales heavily. "Maybe there's something we missed in there, who knows."

"I don't know if she'd want that," Lane says. "I wasn't a good friend to her in the end."

Penny smiles sadly at Lane across the table.

"Honey, whatever you two went through, you did it together. It looks to me like you've punished yourself enough for it. And Gala wasn't exactly a pushover, was she?"

"Not exactly," Lane says, with a small smile.

And, for just a moment, Lane thinks she sees Gala crack a smile too.

PENNY DRIVES LANE to Gala's place in her beaten-up Ford Pinto, the harmonies of Fleetwood Mac's "Rhiannon" playing from the radio as they pull up outside. The landlord is less exasperating than the first time Lane met him, perhaps due to Penny's presence, and he doesn't argue when she asks to be left alone in Gala's place for a while. Penny declines to come inside, choosing to wait in her car despite Lane's repeated assurances that she can make her own way home.

Gala's apartment is exactly how it looked through the window. Exactly how Lane expected to find it. Rotting, with the scent of acrid cat piss heavy in the air. Lane picks up the copy of *The Unraveling* from the coffee table and leafs through it. Every few pages, Gala has underlined a sentence in pencil and scrawled a note in the margin. Often it is critical (*Cowardly* she writes next to a description of a dead body Lane knows she didn't fully commit to), other times begrudgingly appreciative. Lane almost smiles as she slides the book into her bag to take home.

Next, Lane walks into Gala's bedroom. Always a mess, it is now closer to a hovel—clothes strewn across every surface and stained bedsheets marked with burns. A rancid smell emanates from an ashtray filled with dozens of stubbed-out cigarettes, some still with a smudge of Gala's lipstick on the filter.

Lane looks through the drawers of the dressing table next to Gala's bed, but all she finds are empty pill bottles and dried-out beauty products. Everything else in the room seems to be on display, thrown across the floor, when Lane notices something in the lower half of Gala's large wardrobe, the doors of which are flung open. There are four cardboard boxes of papers almost hidden by the clothes hanging from the rail—swaths of sequin and mesh fabric grazing what must be every piece of correspondence Gala has ever touched.

Lane begins to search through the documents closest to the top of each pile, looking for anything that might hint at her last known location or state of mind. Lots of it is useless (invoices and unpaid utility bills) and some of it would be gold on any other day (frantic notes from politicians and artists and one Oscar-winning director), but nothing is particularly illuminating until, partway down the third pile, Lane finds a sheet of paper with the heading *Hacienda Heights*. She pulls it out and scans the details—it's a receipt of payment for Gala's rent, a year up front, just like Ruby said.

Lane's eyes move quickly down the page until she catches the name that makes her heart drop. At the bottom, under payer, are the bank details of Scott Douglas Ryan.

LANE LETS HERSELF back into the car, and she can feel Penny's expectant gaze land on her.

"I'm sorry," Lane says, staring straight out of the windshield. "I didn't find anything."

In the rearview mirror, Gala stares at her curiously.

FIFTY-SEVEN

NOW

WINTER 1975

Lane waits for Scotty to return home from work with Gala's invoice in her hand. Rose has put the kids to bed early, and Lane has told her that she won't be required this evening. Whatever is about to unfold between Lane and Scotty needs no witnesses.

When she hears the key in the lock, Lane stands up stiffly. Scotty walks through the door, and his tentative smile slides off his face when he sees her expression.

"Are the girls all right?" he asks, a note of panic in his voice. He walks toward Lane, and she holds the invoice out to him—a barrier between them. She can tell the exact moment he clocks what has happened—the precise millisecond their life together officially crumbles.

"Lane," Scotty says, and he pulls out a chair at the dining table to sit on. He slumps down, and the expression on his face is both so devastated and so familiar that Lane doesn't know how she never noticed it before.

"Were you fucking her?"

Scotty shakes his head miserably.

"Was she selling you drugs?"

"Drugs?" Scotty repeats wearily. "Of course not."

"So could you please enlighten me as to why you were funding the life of someone you claim to want nothing to do with, without telling me?"

Lane sits down opposite Scotty, leaning forward, her eyes searing into his.

"Lane," he says. "The girls are asleep."

She hadn't realized she was shouting.

"I was there," he says eventually. "The night of the fire."

Lane is about to correct him, when she sees the look on his face.

"You were always . . ." Scotty starts but Lane cuts him off.

"This isn't about me," she says sharply, and, for the first time, he listens to her.

"I'd heard about this party, so I thought, to hell with it. If you could just walk away from our family home, why couldn't I leave for a few hours too?"

Lane fights a primal wave of shame at the thought of Dahlia and Audrey asleep in their beds alone while she was at a hotel less than a mile away and Scotty was doing god knows what in the Hollywood Hills. Was this what other parents did too, or were they just defective?

"You went with Charlie?" Lane asks, trying to piece together her friend's connection to this.

"No," he says. "Charlie came . . . after."

Another part of her heart hardens.

"I saw Gala at the party, and she was upset. I didn't know it at the time, but my guess is she'd found out Gabriel was using again.

And we—look, Lane, this isn't going to be easy to say, but I know it's got to be worse to hear. The way I want to put it is that we were both looking for something, and we tried to find it in each other, but it was never about that. We were just both broken, and lonely, and sad and—" Scotty breaks off, as if he can hear his own words and knows how absurd they sound.

"So you were fucking," Lane says, and he has the audacity to wince at the word, as if she's offended him.

"Not fucking continuously," he says. "But . . . once, yes."

"Thanks for clearing that up," Lane says, and now of course she can't shake the image of Scotty and Gala together, his hands clenched around her waist, her face buried in his golden neck. She thinks of the men her mom used to bring home when her dad was away, furtive shadows she'd see using the bathroom at night, figures climbing into cars and driving off with no headlights, and digs her sharp nail into the softest part of her wrist.

"And Charlie?"

Scotty has been watching her closely, and he seems to sense a change. He reaches a hand out across the table, palm up, and looks at her tenderly. Lane stares blankly at his still hand until he is forced to withdraw it.

"After the fire, once we knew what had happened, I went to see Charlie," he says, a note of resignation in his voice now.

"For what exactly? His cleanup services?"

"His advice, Lane," Scotty says. "He knows you better than anyone. Even me."

"And did you *pay* him for this betrayal?"

Scotty shakes his head.

"Charlie has his own reasons for doing what he did," he says. "But for my part, I didn't want to let this one ugly mistake ruin the rest of our lives. Charlie worked out a deal, which ended in

January when I wired Gala the final payment. And that was it. I don't know where she is, or what she did with it."

Lane shakes her head because Scotty is wrong. Their entire marriage has been the ugly mistake.

"You acted like I was crazy," she says.

"I tried to do the right thing," Scotty says.

"No," Lane says. "You didn't."

Lane feels a crushing disappointment, despite everything she knows. She thinks of the Scotty who sat opposite her at the Dresden that first night, the one who promised her a future filled with stability and quiet hope, and so many other things, but never this.

"I meant every word I said when we met," Scotty says, as if he's reading her mind. "And I could have done it if you'd ever wanted me to."

Lane wonders whether this is true. If, on some level, she never wanted him to live up to his promises that first night because then she would have had to too, and that would have made her not someone to be revered and admired but someone ordinary. Someone to be forgotten, like her parents. Lane closes her eyes, and when she opens them, Scotty is still there, but the thousands of tiny chasms between them have finally joined up to create that magnificent crater, and there's something beautiful about it all, as they both finally understand the magnitude of what they've done to one another.

BEFORE SHE LEAVES, Lane lets herself into the twins' bedroom and sits on the foot of Audrey's tiny bed to watch them sleep—little chests rising and falling almost in unison, as if they're still inside her belly, curling around each other like cats. She thinks of the ways she and Scotty have already let these scrappy, hopeful girls down, and she feels a deep ache for them.

LATER, WHEN LANE is alone in her room at the Chateau, she calls Charlie for the first time since their final doomed party, two months earlier. It's 3:00 a.m., but he answers, his familiar voice thick with sleep.

"Why did you do it?" she asks, and then she listens to him breathing for a while.

"I was the one who introduced you to Scotty," he says eventually. "I felt responsible."

"Barely," she says.

Charlie pauses, reassesses. "I knew how much you'd been through already."

"Bullshit."

Keep spinning, Charlie.

"You never liked me being friends with her," she says.

"I never understood what you saw in her," he corrects her. "There's a difference."

"You helped my husband pay her off. And then you lied about it to my face."

"I brokered a mutually beneficial deal between them. To protect you."

"You've forgotten how to exist," Lane says wearily, but she knows that's not quite right. She tries again: "You've forgotten how to love."

Charlie clears his throat.

"Darling, I'm not sure we ever knew," he says.

FIFTY-EIGHT

NOW

WINTER 1975

That night, alone in her hotel room, Lane dreams of her mother. It's not the usual dream, the one that starts with the crisp fall morning and the floating sound of her parents fighting, but a different one. This time, her mother is sitting at the kitchen table, dressed in her favorite blue dress with the holes climbing the hem, frowning as she writes something. Lane watches from the doorway as her mother shifts position slightly to reveal a card. Today is Lane's fourteenth birthday, and Lane's mother is trying. She stares out the window at the morning sun that is still finding its feet, and then she writes a couple more lines in her precise script. Once she's sealed the envelope and hidden it under the fruit bowl, she walks dreamily outside to hang the wash, and Lane watches her movements closely for clues. She figures that her mother might well be high on something, but at least she isn't hopeless or hysterical today.

Lane creeps over to the table and carefully opens the envelope to find a homemade card with a beautiful illustration of a ringtail on the front, and her mother's initials underneath—AW. Lane has never seen her draw anything, and she traces her finger across the pencil lines, careful not to smudge anything. Then she opens the card and tries to read it, but the words begin to distort, dipping and switching places so quickly she can't place a single sentence. In the dream she knows her mother will leave her soon, knows this is the last birthday card she will write for her.

When Lane wakes up in her hotel room, her mother is still with her, sitting in the chair in the corner of the room. Her face is partly obscured by a thick blanket of hair, but her expression is calm as she watches Lane. There is a lightness about her that feels both impossible and strangely familiar, and Lane finds that, somehow, this is even harder to bear than the shame. Lane blinks furiously, trying to dispel the apparition, but somehow her mother is still there, refusing to leave her side, as if she's keeping vigil.

And, in the dead of the night, Lane finally knows what she needs to do.

FIFTY-NINE

NOW

WINTER 1975

Lane's mother lives in a small co-op just outside of Berkeley, not dead but something infinitely worse—reborn as if she deserves it.

After the overdose, after the worst day of Lane's life, Alys Warren had been committed to the Arizona State Mental Hospital on the grounds of narcotic addiction and hysteria. Lane had never visited, had been too furious and too wrecked, had stayed instead with her devastated father as he quietly drank himself to death, his organs finally giving up for good on August 12, 1953.

After three years, Lane learned that her mother had been saved by a group of Christian Scientists who spent their days casting around local hospitals and rehab centers for their next cause. Alys had reached out to Lane on her release, but by this point Lane was eighteen and no longer interested in the woman who hadn't loved her enough to survive, not in the way she needed her to anyway. So her mother had left the state she was raised in and never looked back, choosing instead to live among her saviors in a quiet, U-shaped compound in Northern California. Today will be twenty-three years since Lane last saw her, to the month.

Lane parks her car outside the terraced house and walks slowly up the four steps leading to the front door—rubber-duck yellow with a tacky stained glass window. The door opens before she's even reached the top step, and suddenly her mom is there in a pair of overalls, her long black hair pulled into a thick braid. She is older, of course, her forehead creased, and her angles more acute than Lane remembers, but her presence is otherwise undiminished. She looms as large today as she has in Lane's memory, and the smile she flashes Lane is somehow both searching and knowing. Lane's body tenses up at the sight of her.

"Lauren," Alys says. In her letters (hundreds of them sent over the years), she talks about the books she's read, or the white-crowned sparrow in the backyard that brings her a daily dose of joy. She never mentions Lane's childhood or her own madness, just little things that only remind Lane of what could have been.

"It's Lane," Lane says, and her mother nods her benign concession to this small act of control. Lane wonders whether her mother is going to pretend to be this serene the entire time, as if Lane doesn't remember her plunging a knife into her own thigh at the kitchen table.

Lane wordlessly follows her inside and through to the kitchen, which is green tiled and spotless. On the fridge are dozens of sketches—all pencil, monochromatic portraits of people Lane will never meet. But right in the center is a color sketch of Lane at eleven or twelve, stuck in place with an Arizona magnet. The sight of it makes Lane feel disoriented, as if her entire existence can be contained to this single geographical location. As if she had only ever existed in Arizona, which, for Alys, she supposes she had. Lane looks out the window at a small backyard lined with vibrant flower beds and wonders whether she can get through the next half hour without ever really looking at her mother.

"Vegetables," Alys says. "I grew the biggest gourd in Berkeley in '73."

As Lane turns back, she notes that her mother is smiling like she's in on the joke, which, Lane thinks, she's not allowed to be.

Alys gestures to the small bistro table set up by the window, and Lane takes a seat on one of the foldout chairs. On the table is a lit beeswax candle and a plate of uneven cookies. The rim of the plate reads *Home Sweet Home*, the words flanked on either side by an illustration of a hen in an apron. Lane stares at it in bewilderment, and, when she looks up, Alys is swiping briskly at her cheeks. Lane wasn't expecting this, has no memories of her mother crying, and the panic that rises in her feels deep-rooted and frantic.

"You look the same," Alys says after a moment.

"That's funny. You're unrecognizable," Lane says.

Another long silence. Then Alys gestures toward the cookies. "Take one. They're lemon shortbread."

"You bake now," Lane says.

"Life is a series of negotiations," Alys says, again with the same self-effacing smile. "And, in one of my more successful deals, I swapped the downers for flour and sugar."

"And what exactly did our lord savior swap in for? Me?"

Her mother frowns, and Lane feels satisfied to have broken through the veneer even just slightly. Because of all the things her mother could have become, boring and suburban is the hardest to bear. How dare she learn to bake only once Lane wasn't there to lick the spoon. How dare she fix a drawing of Lane to the fridge when Lane had never once seen her own face line the walls of her childhood home. How dare her mother find any peace without her. Lane wonders now whether there's any truth in the story she's told herself all these years: that it's taken her so long to come here because she knew her mother would only let her down again. Lane thinks now that this account is just neater, the arc more forgiving than the other version of the same story: that it's taken her so long to come because she was furious at her mother. Because she still is.

"You have daughters," Alys says carefully, as if aware now that Lane's teeth are sharp.

"Twins," Lane says.

"I always thought I wanted two girls."

Lane grits her teeth.

"Audrey and Dahlia" is all she says.

"Can you tell me about them?"

"Maybe some other time," Lane says flatly. Then: "They need me down to their bones."

There is a silence while Alys watches Lane closely.

"Do you like being a mother?" Alys asks curiously. (What right does she have to be curious about anything, but least of all this?)

"Of course," Lane replies sharply. "What an odd thing to ask."

"Not really," Alys says, but there is a slight, barely perceptible edge to her tone now too. *Finally*, Lane thinks. *I know you.*

Lane stands and walks over to the counter. Behind a pile of letters is a photograph of Alys with a group of women around the same age, sitting around a fire pit.

"You camp?" Lane asks, and her mother shrugs.

"When forced."

Again, a slight edge to her reply. Lane opens the fridge next. Each shelf is perfectly organized, each Tupperware perfectly labeled, and Lane, remembering the relentless tuna salad sandwiches of her childhood, wishes she hadn't looked. She shuts the door and turns back to her mother, still unable to entirely meet her eye.

"You know I've read your books," Alys says. "I couldn't . . . Well, *The Ringtail* was . . . it was . . . uncomfortable for me, but I understand why you wrote it. But *The Unraveling*? I thought it was just a—a masterpiece on female fury. It's the kind of book that I wish had been around when I was younger, when I was—"

As she breaks off, Lane thinks about the nights she'd have to drag her own mother inside because she'd passed out on the porch, and how she'd wanted to pinch her and beg her and scream at her to love her enough to stop. She thinks of the last time she saw her, ashen on the bathroom floor, piss clinging to her, and she wonders whether everything she's done, all the praise and clout she's chased, is to make up for the fact that these words will never mean what they should coming out of her own mother's mouth.

"I know you think you know me, but you don't," Lane says. "You haven't known me as an adult. A writer. A mother. Even if you've read everything I've ever written or any interview I've ever given, you still wouldn't know the first thing about who I really am."

"I know that," Alys says. "I know."

"What do you want then?" Lane asks. "Why did you keep writing to me?"

There is a stretch of silence between them.

"Do you want me to forgive you?" Lane asks.

Alys shakes her head. "No. I don't expect you to forgive me."

"Then you wanted to know that I turned out okay," Lane says. "So you can forgive yourself."

Alys doesn't say anything, just reaches out and touches Lane lightly on the hand. Lane jerks it away instantly and drops it down by her side. Her fury is slowly dissipating, and she feels terrified to find out what's underneath it.

"Everyone I've ever loved has left me," Lane says, her voice smaller than she can bear.

Her mother nods, then looks down at her tanned hands, which are clasped on the table.

"I wanted you to remember me," Alys says.

"What?"

"That's why I wrote the letters."

"How could I forget you?" Lane asks.

"Not just the end," Alys says. "Or the bad times. I wanted you to remember who I was in the moments in between."

Lane looks away, but she can still feel her mother's eyes heavy on her.

"It's selfish," Alys says.

"Since when did you care about selfish?"

Lane remembers sitting on the stairs outside her bedroom at 4:00 a.m., waiting for her mom to come home, and she feels the same longing in the back of her throat. She turns back to the fridge and traces her finger over the drawing of herself—brows furrowed, eyes serious, even back then.

"Do you have any regrets?" she asks.

"Too many to count."

Lane nods. This, at least, is familiar territory.

"You probably wouldn't have made it," she says.

"Made it?" Alys repeats.

"In New York."

Alys looks at her questioningly.

"You were going to be an illustrator," Lane says slowly. "Carl Erickson wrote you a letter."

"Oh," Alys says, as if she hasn't thought of it in a long time. Then a strange fondness crosses over her face, as if she's just stumbled across a lost childhood friend.

"You wouldn't have made it," Lane repeats.

"Probably not," Alys concedes, but she's still smiling a little.

Lane frowns.

"My regrets are mostly missed connections," Alys says then. "You."

Lane doesn't say anything, and Alys meets her eye.

"I don't exactly know how to explain this, but I always felt like I was watching my own life from the outside. Like I could see everything I had, but I could never reach out and touch it. Does that make any sense? I could never hold it."

Lane feels a thick swelling in the back of her throat as her mother talks.

"Alys," she says, her voice quiet. "Am I like you?"

Alys looks away.

"I don't know," she says softly.

Lane's breathing is shallow, audible as her eyes fill with sharp tears.

"No, Lane," Alys says then. "You're not like me."

There is a silence, and Lane closes her eyes for a moment.

"You never taught me how to love," Lane says, but her voice has lost any of its charge. She is simply stating a fact.

"No," Alys agrees. "Possibly not."

She reaches out and touches Lane's arm. Tears are now running down her cheeks. "But I can teach you to grow one hell of a gourd if you're interested."

There is a pause, and then Lane smiles slightly, and, for the first time in a while, she allows herself to think of the woman she buried over two decades earlier. Because before Alys was A Difficult Woman, she had been a kid who wished she had a mother, and a teenager who felt hopeful when it rained, and a young woman who'd dreamed of being an artist in New York. Lane thinks of Gala too, who once wrote just for the love of it, and of Charlie, who spent his whole life creating magic for the people around him to hide his own heart. But mostly, Lane thinks of her own daughters, and how she still has to stroke between their eyebrows to get them to sleep, and she knows she would trade her own soul if it would protect them from loneliness. She thinks now that even if Alys is lying, and Lane is just like her, she will fight against it every single day she is alive, just like her mother has fought against herself every day since she left Lane behind.

Lane finally meets her mother's eyes. Gray and narrow, just like her own.

"I remember," Lane says softly. "I remember you."

SIXTY

NOW

SPRING 1976

Lane's new home in Topanga is preternaturally serene. Instead of the faded glamour of the Hollywood house, with its haunted history and damp patches on every ceiling, everything in the new place is bleached—driftwood floorboards, gauzy sheer curtains moving gracefully in the wind. She writes most mornings in a converted barn in the backyard—a duck-egg-blue shack with a desk, a chair, and a panoramic view of the magnificent, dusty vista. It is almost eerily quiet, but after living in a house that was often filled with strangers and ghosts but no peace, she feels almost blindingly grateful.

The last time Esther called was at the start of the year, and Lane told her she wouldn't be finishing the book about Gala. She has promised to pay back the advance over the next year, and Esther seemed disappointed but not entirely surprised. And so the glorious, expansive book about Gala (and everything else) has been tucked away with all the other ghost novels that will never be finished, and, once again, Lane is a gun for hire, writing as much as she can about the things that set her alight and some that don't, until the next great idea strikes. But this time, she'll make certain that it's her own.

She's been here for six weeks and has yet to see a single soul on foot on the canyon, let alone speak to anyone, until an older man in a cowboy hat knocks on her door. He introduces himself as Derf and tells her he lives down the street. He claims to be here to welcome Lane to the neighborhood, but it seems he also wants to know everything about her situation—or, more specifically, how a woman who is turning forty can afford to live alone in a rambling ranch house like this one. He doesn't recognize her name (he hasn't read a book since fifth grade, he tells her enthusiastically when she mentions she's a writer), but when she admits that she's recently moved over from Hollywood, his face lights up.

"Well, you've come to the right place. This is the hidden Laurel Canyon," he says, and she feels herself wince.

"I hope not," Lane says lightly.

ON THE LAST Friday in April, Lane wakes up with an unbearable case of nerves. Today, for the first time since she moved out of the Laurel Canyon house, the girls are coming to stay with her for the night. She and Scotty have been working up to this for the past six weeks, and while the girls have loved visiting her at the ranch, Lane knows there is a difference between spending the afternoon exploring the local wildlife and spending a night away from the only home they've ever known. And even though she's terrified they will reject her, Lane has been adamant that they still try. Since her conversation with Alys, Lane has been trying to grab hold of her life like this, to reach out and touch everything she can.

Lane spends half an hour choosing what to wear, and then she tidies the girls' already immaculate room (a room she's decorated just like their one at home), before she paces the kitchen, racking her brain for what she might have forgotten. While she understands that it doesn't matter if the orange juice is the *exact* same brand they're used to, the idea that they might not want to come back makes her heart feel like it might shatter.

Eventually, when the pressure becomes too much, and she finds herself longing for the comfort of a familiar voice, Lane sits down at the kitchen table and picks up the phone.

"LANE," CHARLIE SAYS. His tone is as smooth as ever, but he doesn't yet know how he feels hearing from her after six months of silence. He isn't entirely proud of how he handled the situation between Gala and Scotty, but he's only human, and doesn't loving someone mean telling yourself the best story about their intentions? Hasn't he earned that grace at least from her?

"I'm calling to ask you something . . ." Lane says, before breaking off.

"Go on," Charlie says, and something in him softens. Ten years of friendship and he's never heard her sound this uncertain.

"The girls are coming to stay tonight," she says.

"That's nice . . ." he says.

"Yeah."

He hears her take a deep breath. Then—

"Do you think any of it was worth it?"

Charlie pauses. Because of who he is, because of who Lane is, he knows exactly what she's asking. He just doesn't know if he can answer her truthfully.

"For a moment, you were the best," he says softly instead.

"We were the best," she says, and he can hear the hint of a smile in her voice.

There is another silence, and he can picture Lane sitting on the floor with her back to the wall, the phone cord wrapped tight around her hand. Only he's imagining her in the house at the bottom of Laurel Canyon, not her new place, which he only knows about from someone he works with who is a friend of Scotty's nanny. He has been relegated to picking up scraps of information about Lane from the office intern. He feels another beat of resentment at how it all played out, and for what exactly?

"Can I ask you a question now?" he asks slowly.

"Sure."

"Why couldn't you let Gala go?"

"Because she was my friend," Lane says, after a moment. But that wasn't the whole truth and they both knew it.

"Not all friendships are meant to last forever."

"Like ours?" she asks, and Charlie lets out a heavy exhale.

"I know you don't believe me, but I lied to protect you."

"And yourself," she says. "Because you didn't want me to leave you. You were scared to be alone."

"Maybe," he says softly.

"When you last spoke to her—" She stops for a moment. "When she asked for more money from Scotty, did she say what she was going to do with it?"

"I don't know," Charlie says, after a moment. Then: "No. She asked me about the money, and then if I would feed her cats for a while. That was it. But . . . Lane, there were voices in the background."

"Voices like she was at a party?"

"No, voices like she was at a station, or an airport," he says. "She could be anywhere now."

Lane doesn't say anything, and he imagines her nodding.

"Thanks, Charlie," she says. "Listen, I should go. The girls will be here soon. We're going to . . . make meatballs."

Charlie waits for her to say something else, for her to give him some piece of life-affirming advice, but she doesn't say anything at all. And, as he feels something shift deep inside him, he real-izes that, for the first time, he doesn't need her to. He wasn't lying when he said there are some friendships that aren't built to last forever. Some friendships, like his and Lane's perhaps, are built to serve a purpose—to propel one or both of the people forward in some significant way, out of some specific type of stickiness that still clings to them from their past. And so maybe it's okay, the possibility of losing Lane, as long as he ends up someplace different from where he started. He has to, to make any of it worthwhile.

"Lane, if you were asking earlier if it's worth the cost, I don't know," he says. "I really don't."

"All those missed connections," Lane says.

"Exactly," Charlie says, trying to clear the lump that has ap-peared in his throat.

There is another silence.

"Thanks, Charlie," Lane says. "I appreciate it."

"Love you, Laney," he says.

"Love you, Charlie."

And, as Charlie hangs up the phone, he knows that his life is about to change. All this time, it's been easier to focus on Lane—the lore of their friendship, the glorious parties—than on the fact that he has spent his entire adult life hiding from himself. He's been running, spinning, *lying*, for so long that, somewhere along the way, he stopped dreaming too. He thinks now that maybe he'll head up to San Francisco next. He could track Elijah down and tell him how much he's missed him, or perhaps he could start over someplace completely new, building a life in a different state with someone he hasn't even met yet. Whatever he decides, he knows that something beautiful is just around the corner, because he, Charlie McCloud, won't allow it not to be. He is the wizard of spin, after all, and it's finally time to rewrite the story of his own life.

SIXTY-ONE

NOW

SPRING 1976

In the morning, Scotty comes to pick up the girls, who are still asleep. Instead of pretending the night went perfectly to Scotty, Lane admits they had trouble adjusting, and that it might be worth letting them sleep a little longer if he wants a moment's peace today.

The night had started well, with raw mince sticking to the girls' small hands and making them shriek with laughter, followed by a viewing of their favorite, *The Mary Tyler Moore Show*. Then the girls had scuttled off to bed with surprising goodwill, and Lane almost caught herself thinking she'd cracked this mothering thing. And that was when it started: a sharp, unremitting wailing coming from the bedroom. She realized quickly her mistake—in trying to replicate their room at home, all she'd done is remind them of where they weren't. But, instead of berating herself, Lane thought of something Gala had said to her. Perhaps, much like life, motherhood isn't a test she has to ace, but instead is something she can work at every day. So, instead of giving up and calling Scotty for backup, Lane warmed some milk on the stove and let the girls eat sour candy from the secret drawer, and then eventually they all climbed into her bed, where they stayed until the morning, the sunlight casting a gentle orange glow over their earnest faces as they finally slept. And as she lay between them, two sets of milky sweet breath tickling her skin, Lane felt something spread through her bones like warm honey—she may not have known exactly how it had happened, but her new, fledgling existence felt strangely familiar and, perhaps more surprisingly, something like sweet relief.

While they wait for the twins to rise, Lane asks Scotty about work, and his new girlfriend, Fiona, a songwriter who recently moved to L.A. Lane can tell he doesn't fully trust that this isn't a trap, that she's not about to turn around and berate him for moving on, but Lane knows now that there's no rush to stitch the fissure between them—they will be in each other's lives forever, constantly trying and failing to be the best exes, the best parents, the best partners they can be to each other, and they will get it wrong far more often than they ever get it right.

WHILE DAHLIA AND Audrey get ready in their bedroom, the occasional giggle escaping from behind the closed door, Scotty remembers something he left in his car. When he returns with a shoebox filled with some of Lane's belongings, she is unsure of what to say.

"Just some things you might need," he says awkwardly. Inside the box, there is a gray T-shirt, a balled-up pair of black socks, her old (broken) hairbrush, and the small blue box her wedding ring came in. When she spots the box, Lane wonders whether he's trying to get a rise out of her, but when she notices how untethered he looks, she thinks probably not.

"Thanks, Scotty," she says, and she's about to put the lid back on, when she catches a flash of something gold hidden underneath a silk scarf. She reaches inside and pulls out Gala's cigarette case. She had picked it up when Gala left it at the Chinese restaurant, and had taken this unexpected talisman of their friendship home with her. She feels a tightness in the back of her throat as she holds it in her hand now.

"Apparently, this once belonged to Marilyn Monroe," she eventually tells Scotty, who makes a vaguely impressed noise even though Lane knows he doesn't believe it either.

"Do you ever hear the rumors that she's alive?" she asks.

Scotty frowns, shrugs. "Yeah, but those rumors always go around when someone beloved dies. The most desperate of elegies. What was in it for her to disappear?"

Lane thinks about how Gala had put it the night they met, when they were alone in someone else's cloakroom on Wonderland Avenue, but of course she finds she can't recall her exact words. She didn't know then that there would be a finite number of sentences between them before they each combusted in their own ways.

"She was washed up," Lane says. "Imagine that—thirty-six and already washed up. Maybe she just . . . ran out of other options."

Scotty runs his hand through his hair.

"I don't know. It always seemed like she only knew how to be one way—she only knew how to be herself. I don't know if she'd know how to leave that behind, even if she wanted to." Perhaps noticing her frown, Scotty shrugs and acquiesces. "Where do you think she is?"

"I don't know," Lane says slowly, even as it dawns on her. She turns the metal case over in her hand and wonders whether it could be true.

"I guess it would explain the engraving," Scotty says kindly, as if he doesn't want to spoil her fun. When she looks confused, he gently lifts her hand up to show her the underside of the cigarette case.

Engraved on the back, in the faintest of lettering, are two letters: MM.

SIXTY-TWO

NOW

SPRING 1976

Lane's first stop in Paris is, of course, Café de Flore in Saint-Germain, more famous for its glittering history of celebrity and literary patrons than it is for its food. Lane figures it's as good a place as any to start looking for Gala.

The shabby red leather booths remind her of L.A., but the service is distinctly European, the waiters palpably unimpressed with Lane's lack of a handle on the French language. When she shows them two photographs of Gala—one of her vivacious and glamorous at Tana's a few years back, the other more recent and rough around the edges—they show no recognition and even less interest as they dismiss her with a wave of the hand.

Over the next few days, Lane visits every tourist spot she can think of as her despair steadily grows. She ventures out of Saint-Germain and roams the crooked streets of Montmartre and the Latin Quarter, showing the photographs of Gala to anyone who will suffer through her clumsy French long enough. And every night she returns to her hotel room with the smell of the city clinging to her, and she calls Ruby to report nothing except that she might have made a big mistake in coming here.

"Find the person having the most fun in Paris," Ruby always says. "And Gala won't be far."

On her fifth day in Paris, just when she is starting to feel like a terrible human for abandoning her kids with their (more than capable) father and the nanny, Lane lands upon the good luck she needs. She has returned to Café de Flore for an early dinner and is picking at an omelet and a glass of Cabernet Sauvignon when the young couple at the table next to her strike up a conversation in English.

"American?" The woman, elfin with Jean Seberg hair and a short black dress under a gold waistcoat, has an animated smile on her face.

"How could you tell?" Lane asks dryly, and they both laugh.

"New York or Los Angeles?" the man asks, as if these are the only two options. He has a bleached shaved head and is wearing a silver jumpsuit.

"Los Angeles," she says, thinking that perhaps New York might have endeared her to them more. Lane has already found that the farther you get from Los Angeles, the less powerful its grip. She wonders whether one day in the future, when the girls are off to college, she too might leave it behind. She had only ever meant to spend one year there, writing her book.

"And it's your first time in Paris?" The woman again. Lane nods. "Where have you been? Who have you met?"

Lane swallows a mouthful of omelet while she can.

"I haven't really . . ." she starts, then pulls the dog-eared photos of Gala out from her bag. "I'm looking for someone."

The woman looks at the photos before shrugging and handing them over to her companion, who also shows no signs of recognition.

He passes them back to Lane, and she slots them into her bag, not so much disappointed as resigned.

"You haven't been out yet?" the man says, his beautiful face puckering into a frown. "Come with us tonight."

"That's very kind," Lane says. "But I need to leave soon—I need to get home. I have . . . kids in L.A."

The couple ignore this, and the woman waves her fingers in the air as if to dispel the words, heavy as they are with the threat of suburban obligation that would have once made Lane itch too.

"*Non, non,*" she says. "Tonight. Now. We will take you out."

Lane swallows another forkful of salty omelet and considers her offer. The alternative is a ten-minute walk back to her hotel room, followed by a few hours of trying frantically to fall asleep, either aided by another glass of wine or not.

"I don't need to change?" she asks, gesturing at her white shirt, jeans, and ballet flats. The man shakes his head firmly.

"You are with us," he says. "You could come in a bathrobe."

THEY ARE CALLED Andre and Anais, and they aren't a couple, but best friends. The club they take her to is called Le Sept, and they walk straight to the front of the line snaking around the exterior before being shuttled inside, nobody batting an eyelid. The scene puts Los Angeles to shame—mirror balls catching on sequins and acid tabs, and androgynous faces shining with the wonder of being alive in this exact, perfect moment. Lane knows that this is exactly the sort of place Gala would once have made her home, except Gala isn't the twenty-four-year-old she met anymore, the one with glitter on her cheekbones lounging on the bar at the Troubadour, clutching Gabriel's face in one hand and a cigarette in the other.

Anais and Andre sidle up to a glamorous group sitting at a table, and they hand Lane a flute of champagne while gesturing for her to take a seat in the booth beside them. Lane awkwardly lingers on the fringes of the group until she realizes that the more champagne they drink, the less they remember she doesn't speak French. After a lot of aimless nodding, she tells them she needs the bathroom before slipping off into the crowd.

Lane circles the bar a few times and wonders whether anyone would even understand her if she were to show them a photo of Gala with the music so loud and the lights strobing and so much pleasure to be found in every corner. And that's exactly when she spots her. There, leaning over the bar in her white fur coat, is Gala.

As the disco lights shift, Lane sees that her hair is different— an artificial shade of red instead of glossy black, but it still is unequivocally, irrevocably Gala. There is her trademark swagger, her Pre-Raphaelite beauty in a sea of overstyled wannabes. Lane watches her for what feels like a lifetime before Gala spots her. Their eyes lock, but Gala doesn't show any signs of recognition other than a slight raise of one eyebrow. Lane wills herself to walk toward her, but she finds that she's still waiting for something— some sign that Gala doesn't blame her for any of it, for all of it, and that she would be able to welcome Lane without recrimination or bitterness. Instead, Gala signs a check, slips her white fur coat over her shoulders, and walks out of the bar.

Lane watches her leave, a thick ache in her chest. Perhaps just knowing Gala made it out of L.A. alive is enough.

LANE IS WALKING toward the exit of the club when she feels a firm tap on her shoulder. She turns to find the barman looking at her expectantly. She has a sudden fear that Anais and Andre have left without paying for their table, and that she's about to be lumped with a 4,000 franc check, when he presses something into her hand. She doesn't quite catch what he says but, glancing down, she finds a cocktail coaster in her palm with familiar, messy writing scrawled across it:

Square du Vert-Galant, tomorrow 10am.

Lane thanks the barman, and when he doesn't leave, she hands him some loose change as a tip. Then she tucks the cocktail mat into the side pocket of her purse, next to Gala's cigarette case, and she walks back outside into the cool Paris night.

SIXTY-THREE

NOW

SPRING 1976

At first, Lane isn't sure she is going to show. She'd arrived early at Square du Vert-Galant, a small, well-manicured triangular park located on the western tip of the Île de la Cité, and has looked everywhere for signs of Gala, but she was looking in the wrong place. Instead of waiting for Lane on one of the many benches lining the lush green space, Gala is sitting cross-legged on the edge of the island, a small paved incline all that separates her from the murky waters of the Seine. The sun is already warming up and Lane is dressed wrong, already perspiring under her thick coat by the time she approaches Gala from behind. *Like a ghost*, Lane thinks, when Gala starts slightly.

"Hello," Gala says, a calm resignation on her face as she studies Lane.

Lane holds the cigarette case out to Gala.

"I wanted to return this to you," Lane says. "I hear Marilyn Monroe once touched it."

Her voice is wobbly, uneven, and she wonders if she should be embarrassed about it but decides not to be. Gala takes the case and holds it in her hand.

"She didn't just touch it," Gala says haughtily. "She owned it."

"Have you seen her yet?" Lane asks, but Gala is still studying the case. When she looks up, she seems confused.

"Who?"

"Marilyn," Lane says. "Didn't she retire here?"

Gala stares at her witheringly in response. "So you've finally lost it. People thought I was the deranged one, but I always knew it was you. Marilyn Monroe is dead, Lane."

Lane feels her cheeks heat up but knows there's no point in arguing something she never believed in the first place.

"Can I sit down?" Lane asked, gesturing at the wall next to Gala.

Gala shrugs but she shifts her purse toward her to make space. Lane stares at it as she sits down—Gala's purse is a pale pink ostrich skin, and Lane wants to ask how she can afford it but doesn't.

The river glitters below as, next to them, three teenage boys clown around, pretending to push each other over the edge. They're clearly all so desperate to be touched, to be noticed, that watching them makes Lane feel a little sad suddenly.

"I'm thirty-six today," Gala says then, surprising Lane. "I guess the fortune teller was wrong."

She smiles ruefully.

"Why didn't you tell anyone you were okay?" Lane says softly. "Your parents. Ruby. Me."

Gala frowns as she transfers five skinny cigarettes over from a slim French-branded pack into her gold case, holding one back between her long fingers.

"I had the uglies," she replies, after a pause. "And you know how that goes."

Lane nods and waits for Gala to say more.

"By the end, it felt like I'd locked myself in a room at a party even I didn't want to be at anymore. And the same song was always on loop, but I couldn't figure out how to change the record," Gala says, making sure the tips of the cigarettes line up before she closes the case. "I figured I could either stay at the party and fulfill everyone's expectations of me, or I could get the fuck out of L.A."

"And now?"

"Luckily, it transpires that the uglies simply don't exist in Paris," Gala laughs as she roots around in her bag before pulling out a lighter. "Or maybe there are just fewer ghosts here."

There is a glint of something in Gala's voice that reminds Lane of the young woman she first saw hurling a glass at a stranger's head at a party in Wonderland Avenue—some sense of mischief or playfulness, as if she hasn't yet been flattened by the world. It makes Lane feel nostalgic and a little sad, because the parts of herself Gala has rediscovered inevitably highlight all the ways they've both changed too. All the things they've learned that they'll never be able to forget.

"Nobody knows me here," Gala says then, once she's lit her cigarette. "They barely even know who Gabriel was. It feels like how it used to in the beginning in L.A.—I get to wake up in the morning and decide who I want to be."

"And who are you?" Lane asks curiously. "What have you told them?"

Gala smiles for the first time since they met, a playful smile that sends Lane flying back in time.

"I'm a gold rush heiress," she says. "Waiting for my inheritance to come through. Everyone's been falling over themselves to accommodate me, naturally. I spent two glorious weeks in the Ritz before they realized I had no way of paying the bill."

Lane laughs at the preposterous predictability of it all. It is reassuring, in a way, that Gala still has the ability to shock, and that Lane still has the capacity to be shocked, even if it isn't exactly the happy ending she would have written for Gala. "And where will you go when you get found out?"

Gala raises an eyebrow. "Europe isn't exactly small. And then there's South America, Australia, Japan. I met some Russians in Versailles and I think they'd probably adopt me, if I let them."

Lane is still smiling but is about to ask if there is any sort of backup plan—insurance perhaps for when things go south— when Gala lets out a dramatic sigh.

"You worry too much," Gala says. "Has anyone ever told you that?"

They both watch as a boat passes with a group of tourists gathered on the top deck, despite the wind. A man holding on to his straw fedora waves with his free hand and, after a moment, Gala waves back.

"Will you write again?" Lane asks.

Gala thinks about the question as she stubs out her cigarette.

"I never cared about it as much as you did," Gala says. "But I want to feel things again."

Her eyes land on Lane's when she says this.

"Are you still . . . ?"

Lane shakes her head. "I told Esther it wasn't going to work out."

Gala nods, then Lane makes herself do the thing she's been avoiding for the past four years.

"I'm sorry about what I told Esther before Gabriel died," she says, her eyes tracking Gala for any signs of recognition. She finds that she is holding her breath as she waits, as if Gala's response might dictate whether she too will be able to forgive herself for what she did. "It was my fault."

Gala bites her lip and a shadow crosses her face at the memory. Then, just as quickly, the darkness clears and she smiles a little from underneath her new red hair, which has fallen across her eyes. There is something about her that makes Lane feel both sad and envious at the same time. Because, as Lane watches Gala light another skinny French cigarette from Marilyn Monroe's case, she realizes that instead of letting the brutal knowledge that life can change in an instant make her harder, Gala seems to have chosen something else. She seems to have allowed it to make her softer, more malleable. As if she is reading her mind, Gala's face lights up, and she exhales a plume of smoke in Lane's direction before speaking again—

"Darling," Gala says, her voice husky and familiar. "I've been thinking of trying the circus again."

And then she breaks into a wide smile, at once knowing and shimmering, and Lane knows now that if she was expecting an apology for what happened between Gala and Scotty, she isn't going to get one. Instead, Lane thinks of the myriad paths ahead for them both, all the wild and awful and contradictory choices they are yet to make, all the ways their hearts might break if they only let them, all the rippling waves of joy they might cling to despite knowing that darkness will always fall again. And maybe the possibility of it all is the thing that makes everything worth it, in the end.

ONCE GALA IS certain that Lane has left, under the promise of a final breakfast together at Les Deux Magots the next morning (*vastly* superior to Café de Flore—if only Lane had thought to venture across the street, she might have found Gala a week ago), Gala pulls a small embroidered journal out of her purse. She takes one last look at the world around her, the way the golden sun ripples on the Seine below, and she starts to write.

She's been working on her novel since her arrival in Paris—the story of a jaded party girl who left her life in Los Angeles without so much as a goodbye to all the "friends" dooming her to fail (because even though wanting and expecting weren't exactly the same thing, they had the same effect on a person) and who tracked a dead Hollywood idol all the way to Paris. It has familiar faces and new ones, and love songs and rock anthems, and betrayal and loyalty and broken hearts, and Gala has no idea where it's going to end, but all that matters is she wants to find out.

In the end, it hadn't been as hard to leave Hollywood as she'd thought. After the party in the downtown warehouse—after she had woken curled up on the hard shoulder of the freeway, clothes ripped and headlights swooping, with no memory of how she got there, and with only the vague sensation that some force had intervened to stop her life from ending, some force that she couldn't keep ignoring, some force that was telling her that she didn't need to *die*, she just needed to disappear—the plan had fallen into place in less than a week.

A hurriedly packed bag. A final request for Charlie. Then, watching out of a plane window as the city that had shaped her fell away, the lights that seemed so bright when you were under them soon fading to nothing, just like everything else if you let it. She had climbed to the top of the world, but the champagne had turned out to be poison, the people nothing more than common vultures.

As Gala writes about the boys horsing around by the Seine,

and the old friend who'd followed her to Paris just to return a cigarette case she'd picked up in a thrift store in Reseda a thousand moons ago, a small smile plays on her lips. She isn't sure exactly when the Hollywood idol will pop up in the story, but she knows it must be soon—even Paris has its own ghosts. And if Gala has learned one thing from her old friend Lane, it is to never, *ever* show your hand too early.

ACKNOWLEDGMENTS

Thank you to the women who chose to pursue lives of creativity at a time when it was considered selfish to do so.

Thank you to Jen Monroe—I'm so lucky to work with you. You have unbelievable instincts, and while you never try to temper the women I write, you do make them more human. Your trust makes me braver.

David Forrer, my agent and friend. I'm grateful for your warmth and guidance every day—thank you for being such a calm, wise, and all-round delightful presence in my life.

Thank you to Katharine Myers for your creativity and support, and to Candice Coote, Craig Burke, Jeanne-Marie Hudson, Chelsea Pascoe, Claire Zion, Jin Yu, Elise Tecco, and the rest of the team at Berkley. Thank you for your belief in me, and for getting so many wonderful books into the hands of readers. Your enthusiasm and passion are truly inspiring.

Ryan Wilson at Anonymous Content—thank you for your generosity and boundless knowledge, and for sending me the best email of 2024. It's always a pleasure working with you. And Osnat Handelsman-Keren, Emilia Clarke, and Talia Kleinhendler—thank you for your warmth and brilliance. I would trust you with anything.

Thank you to Alexis Hurley, and the team at Inkwell. I appreciate everything you do for my books around the world, and to Anna Carmichael at Abner Stein.

Thank you to Colleen Reinhart and Jordan Jacob for creating a cover that so beautifully captures the heart of this story—this is my favorite one yet.

Alaina Christensen and Angelina Krahn—thank you for your insightful edits and for saving me from my own bad habits and "Britishisms." One day I'll learn how to spell *dryly*, I promise!

To team RBC for changing my life and introducing my books to so many new readers. What a wonderful and kind community you have built, and what an honor it is to be a small part of it.

To the readers who have reached out to me over the years—hearing from you will always be the most magical part of publishing a book.

To the writers I've met either in real life or online and can now call friends. I'm relentlessly inspired by all of you.

Thank you to every bookseller and librarian out in the world—I appreciate your dedication and passion for stories, writers, and readers every day.

Thank you to the Read with Jenna and Book of the Month teams, and to all the podcasters and creators who use their platforms to celebrate books and bookish things! What a wonderful world.

This book wouldn't exist without the help of Pat Warner, who was a true Hollywood legend. Thank you for the stories and the lunches on Sunset, and every email answered in record time. We miss you.

Thank you to my wonderful, inspiring, and supportive friends for everything. (I'm so grateful to have too many to mention, and more than I deserve!) To Lola—for being my original reader and co-conspirator, and my better half. Twenty-five years and counting! Jazz—I'm not sure a more thoughtful or supportive friend than you exists in the world. Tilda—for being my true Victorian soulmate; I'm so happy we found one another. And Athina—for being the most calm, funny, and empathetic prince—I don't know what I'd do without you!

To Ayla and Lydia—thank you for looking after our sweet girl right when we needed you the most.

Mum(my) + Dad(dy)—thank you for instilling in me a love and respect for this era, and for making it come to life throughout our childhood. D—thank you for making our lives magic; we're all so proud of everything you've achieved. M—thank you for being a forever source of love and strength, and for always (gently) guiding us toward our passions and kindness.

Sophie—I love you madly, and I can't wait to hear what you think of this book in five years. Thank you for being the best big sister the universe (our parents) could have given me. Dan, thank you for all the advice and support, and thank you both for my favorite pal, Jesse.

James, thank you for being the most understanding, kind, and loving human to exist. I don't know if it was good luck or something else that led me to you, but I'm so grateful every day.

And finally, thank you to Joni—you are my whole heart and my whole world.